T0196302

Nimrod

Nimrod

THE MIGHTY HUNTER

In the beginning – again

(2400 B.C.)

Book One

James R. Brady

NIMROD
THE MIGHTY HUNTER

iUniverse books may be ordered through booksellers or by contacting:

iUniverse
1663 Liberty Drive
Bloomington, IN 47403
www.iuniverse.com
1-800-Authors (1-800-288-4677)

ISBN: 978-1-4917-8707-6 (sc)
ISBN: 978-1-4917-8706-9 (e)

Library of Congress Control Number: 2016900786

Print information available on the last page.

iUniverse rev. date: 01/15/2019

(And) Jesus wept

John 11:35

Contents

Chapter One

In The Beginning, Again /(2400 BC)

The land is rocky, the weather cool. It is springtime at the base of the Ararat Mountains. In the distance above the eye-line of the average person is a boat seemingly stuck in the lower crags of a mountain: Noah's Ark. A stream of movement is seen that is akin to ants scurrying from a source of food back to their home. This temporary home is a group of thousands upon thousands of tents in a semi-circle in a natural amphitheater built by God at the base of the mountain. At the head of the amphitheater there is a man-made altar of rock expertly formed, behind which is a large tent with two muscular guards at the entrance. These guards have the appearance of battle-tested veterans with thick black arm and leg hair, black beards and curly black hair that falls on the shoulders. They are armed each with a spear that touches the ground and rises up level with their head.

Children band together, running, yelling and chasing each other in a never-ending game of tag. Older young men tease and flirt, jostling for position around the young women, like young sheep learning to butt heads before they have horns. Even older men practice the art of war with mock swordfights, dagger thrusts and shield-protection moves, as their same age of women watch with appreciative oohs and ahs and giggles. Lots of giggles.

Nimrod can be seen in a mock sword battle with two opponents, sweat pouring from all their faces. Little scrapes and wounds can be found on each combatant and this, combined with the fierce grunts and groans attests to the energy being sucked out of the men for the battle. Nimrod manages to knock one opponent to his knees and with his sword at the other man's neck; the conquered man drops his sword and

1

thrusts both arms in the air. Nimrod turns to then subdue his second opponent after several more minutes of intense struggle. Down goes his second foe and a boisterous cheer erupts from his fellow warriors and the on-looking crowd. Nimrod drops to his knees and embraces both opponents and they embrace him back. "Fenchristo and Rayas, there are no greater warriors with the sword in all the land, much less uglier brothers! Thank you for letting me win!"

Another boisterous cheer erupts with much laughing and the three help each other to their feet and over to some rocks where they sit and are offered cups of drink and fruit to eat by young, giggling girls.

Semiramis stands by silently as Nimrod is giggled over by a mob of younger women. She is not about to become a part of the mob. Serenely she waits. After the giggling and cheering dies down Nimrod comes to her side. Neither of them speak and yet the bond they have is like a forged-steel cage surrounding them. There is no need for hand-holding or physical demonstration between them: they know, even if others do not, they belong to each other. Heart. Soul. No matter what. The respect they feel for each other. The love. This far outweighs any sexual desires they may have. And they do, mighty ones. Concern for the well-being of the other, concerns that seem lost on part of the earth's population, have guided their actions. Lost then. Seemingly evaporated today. This example is not lost on those who followed their lives. Example speaks louder than words. Then. Now.

Behind the large, guarded tent at the top of a craggy knoll is a sheer cliff wall descending several hundred feet, a natural rearguard protection. Men, by ones and twos, enter and exit the tent in obvious preparation for a major event. Men of wisdom. Men of experience. Men of war.

All through the tent sites are small fires hovered over by mothers with babies in their arms and their daughters and toddlers. Lots of toddlers. Livestock can be heard from a distance where shepherds have built temporary enclosures side-by-side to their neighbors and back-to-back with others. Safety in numbers. Fresh food for the family. Fresh sacrifices for the altars.

As the sun prepares to set and blanket the temporary assembly with evening, the people end their trips to the Ark, like ants that shorten their lines to the food source and finally disappear into their temporary homes. Evening fires grow brighter, games and flirting and jockeying for position in the race of life slacken with each family gathering for their evening meal at their family's main tent. There are so many fledgling families and so many fledgling fledglings. Fathers and mothers and their not-so-little groups of ten to fifty children gather to eat and report on the activities of the day. Those who are coming are here. They speak of tomorrow, of the leaders and the prophet who will begin the yearly conference. They guess as to what will be the theme of their talks.

In a small hut hundreds of miles from this gathering, a well-muscled lean man washes his hands and feet, offering a ritualized prayer every so often. He washes his head and shoulders, his stomach and arms, his well-defined abs, each time reciting his prayer. At each step his wife hands him a clean cloth to dry himself, holding back her tears. This assignment is different. She just knows it. Their children peek at their mom and dad with quizzical looks. Tabansi has often prepared himself like this, but the looks on their parent's faces—is different this time. Special. Serious. He dresses himself slowly with a loin cloth, with two bands on each leg and each arm. He inserts a six-inch-long knife under each arm band and eight-to-ten inch knives on his legs-knives for battle. For killing.

The sun has set and he continues his preparation. His wife withdraws and busies herself with their many children, putting them to bed, her face a stone-cold place with all the blood drained out. Oddly sad. Resolute.

Tabansi goes to each of his children and kisses them goodnight. Goodbye. He kisses his wife and stares at her eyes and then disappears into the night. Soon he is lost from all sight of his home as he continues his gentle run. No food or water is with him, just his loincloth and his knives. And he runs. All night he runs, leaving the fertile flatland of his home far behind. The gently rising hill country greets him with the gently rising Sun. And still he runs. He has spent his entire life running for his king. Fighting for his king. Now, perhaps dying for his king.

He has timed this part of his run to be in daylight so he can see the wild animals that live in the foothills of the mountains. Lions. Wolves. And snakes, oh no. Once he hits the taller peaks and crags he will be safer, from at least the snakes. Along with the safety of vision comes the danger of snakes. They will be everywhere. His nimble steps, lithe body and hundreds of runs help him choose his path with the fewest encounters. Not void.

As the sun comes up on the tens of thousands gathered to hear their leaders speak, breakfast fires dot the tent city. The changing of the guard takes place for those protecting the livestock. The wolves and mountain lions are still hungry, due to the efforts of the shepherds. Runners can be seen jogging in a definite pattern through the campsites, stopping briefly and writing, then jogging to the next tent. Census-takers. Today there will be no games, no teasing and flirting, no games of war. Today they listen to a prophet's voice. As the fires are doused, each family sits in the entrance of their tent with the youngest inside; mom is nearby. The father and older children put down their rugs and face the altar in a subdued murmur. They are worshipful, yet still youthful and anxious for the speaker to begin, and end.

Tabansi can be seen with sweat glistening from all parts of his body in the pleasant warmth of the day, his breathing steady. Small drops of blood can be seen dripping from a knife on his left arm and a knife on his right arm. Behind him can be found many snakes with their throats slit and their bodies drying in the sun like cracked leather. His motion to his arm and down to an unsuspecting victim is smooth, immensely quick. Merciful. Practiced. The terrain increases in slope, and yet he glides up the foothills effortlessly even after sixteen hours of relentless running.

The prophet's tent flap opens with a sharp movement by the two guards. Out steps Cush, grandson to Noah, Ham, son of Noah, and several leaders. Then Noah. Cush is a perplexed looking man as though even small decisions cause him much reflection. A well-built man, he does not look like a man of war. Ham, Cush's father, is a hairy, stocky man with piercing eyes that dart to and fro. He is very much a man of war, of cunning. Not a man to be crossed.

Noah has lived for three hundred years. He is a patient man and has needed to be, with a son like Ham. Having been mocked and jeered by family, friends and all who needed a good laugh because of his Ark, his age lines are deep. Deep, as the pool of black in his eyes. Deep with love, with compassion for his offspring gathered before him that now number in the many tens of thousands. They but represent the many millions refilling the earth.

Noah and his three sons and their wives enter the Ark with a handful of children. Even in his old age Noah has fathered another fifty-two sons and daughters. In turn each of them marry around the age of twenty years old, and those twenty-six couples have an average of fifty children, with each of his own three children averaging forty-six children each, who in turn average fifty-three children per couple and so on. In five generations, one hundred years, life has continued in peace, for the most part. Now over fifteen million people populate the earth. This is the Middle East, as we call it.

The modern mind boggles at the thought of a couple, a woman, bearing fifty children.

Yet, when you figure the average lifespan is three hundred and twenty years, it is not so hard to comprehend. What else was there to do? Add to that the purity of the race, the blood, is such that brothers and sisters, male and female cousins, could marry with no thought of disease, disfigurement or retarded children due to inbreeding, for the most part.

Noah looks out upon the gathering, a portion of his posterity, and proudly smiles upon them. All present had risen to their feet for reverence of the man who communes with God, a man who has been obedient to the wishes of their Creator, and they smile back. Smiling. Weeping. Loving their patriarch. Noah raises his hands and motions for the great assembly to be seated. All have risen save his son Ham, who has busied himself straightening the hem of his garment and then quickly rises as all others sit. Noah is not a foolish man. Perhaps his patience could be confused with weakness when it comes to his son Ham. After all, what parent stops hoping a child will change a hardened heart if the parent but continues to be patient? All know that father Adam had been patient and yet his son Cain slew his son Able. Cain the murderer. The Master Mahan. Now the right-hand man of Lucifer. Noah's mind turns to the many thousands assembled to hear the voice of their leader, his voice.

These are his children who have desired to better their lives, those who have waited on the Lord, those who have traveled such great distances to hear their prophet's voice.

Nimrod is present. Young, eager to please his father Cush, his great-grandfather Noah and now eager to take his place someday among the leaders seated around Noah.

He is rather eager to please, especially a distant cousin, Semiramis, who sits in the mouth of her father's tent, helping her mother with her young brothers and sisters just a few tents away from Nimrod. Nimrod would occasionally catch a glimpse of Semiramis coyly sneaking a glance in his direction. His lips are turned up at the ends in a controlled smile, knowing she is his. But what could he offer her: a flock of his father's sheep and a tent? Perhaps his great grandfather could give him some insight as to his future. After all, he is a prophet of God, and prophets, well, they do foretell the future. Right? Never mind, it would be a waste.

Nimrod had tried to speak with his father Cush about how to prepare for the future, but his father is a nervous man. "I don't know what you want from life, Nimrod; your older brothers are shepherds and your sisters have married shepherds."

"But there are those who have traveled to cities and became merchants. They were leaders in their cities. You yourself are a leader. Should I move to a city and ...?"

"Move to a city? For what purpose, Nimrod? What would you do there, aside from a job that you could not do here? Believe me, cities are nothing but problems!"

"I don't know, Father. Raising sheep is not very exciting."

"Exciting? What makes you think life is to be exciting? Is there not enough excitement trying to feed a family, to defend a family from the elements, from danger of wild animals, from thieves?"

Nimrod began to weaken in his resolve for an answer to life's questions. "I don't know, Father. Grandfather Ham is called a king by his people. He trains warriors ..."

"Do not talk to me about my father! He also has many wives, even more concubines, and lives off the taxes he causes his people to pay him. That is not the life for honest men!"

I, Nimrod, stopped asking my father for advice. I am a shepherd's son. Semiramis is the daughter of a shepherd. Much like sheep, we follow our leaders. When does it stop? Should it stop?

Noah's voice interrupted Nimrod's thoughts. "Life is good. Yet, life is not good. It is a struggle. Life is a time to prepare to meet our Maker, to return and report what we have done with this precious gift of life. It matters not the length of our stay on earth, a few seconds, a few years or four hundred years! It has been rumored that infants who die shortly after birth have somehow sinned, or that their parents have sinned. In truth, neither is true. We are here to gain a body – all who are born, you and me, have accomplished that. We are here to work out our salvation. Those who die very young have a special place in our Heavenly Father's kingdom, as they were so valiant in their pre-mortal life that He knew they had no need to spend many years on the earth proving their worth. What does that say about you and me?

You and I are here to honor our Father's name and keep it holy. We are here to be our brother's keeper, to help those in need. It is not our place to judge another's need or his or her worthiness to receive our help. That is God's responsibility. Blessed are they that give and do not remember. Blessed are they that receive and do not forget.

We are here to tame our body's wants, needs and desires. Our daughters, our wives are the closest things to being a God that can be found on earth. Let me repeat, our daughters, our wives are the closest things to being a God that can be found on earth. Not fathers, not sons. Women. How dare any of you treat them with disrespect or treat them like second-class citizens! How dare you! Some of you want sons so badly that you ignore your daughters because they cannot work as hard or as long as sons. Shame on you. God will remember you, and you will have to sit before Him and explain yourself to Him.

Our women give up their bodies to the demands of childbirth. They love unconditionally those children given to them by our Maker. Women, therefore, are man's equal in every way and more. Our God has given men the Holy Priesthood to help equalize our place on earth with women. It is us men who are running to keep up with them. The priesthood is the power and authority to act in the name of God, administrative power. Womanhood is the power and authority to give life. This is holy and divine power.

So it is then that man and woman are married forever and ever. Not until death: what good is that? God did not create second-class people. He created each and every one of us in His image. No one is born without the spirit to know right from wrong. No one." Men are men. Women are women. Each is born with the Spirit of Christ."

Tabansi is in the fight of his life with a pack of wolves. As he quickly searches for a piece of high ground, a black-and-white fanged opponent steadily approaches from his right side. Snarling, saliva dripping from his lean, hungry frame, the wolf launches its self-aiming body for Tabansi's throat. With a lightning fast movement Tabansi draws his longer blade from his left thigh scabbard. With his astute ability to time the attack, he plunges the knife into the wolf's heart from the left side, behind the left front leg. Having hit the heart, blood squirts strongly on Tabansi as the wolf passes chest high, dead before he hits the ground. The next opponent sneaks in low, fast and behind Tabansi. Tabansi spins, slashing the reddish-brown wolf across the nose, removing half of his black nostril as the wolf retreats, howling in pain. The two remaining pack members beat a controlled, grudging retreat. Tabansi continues his unrelenting run up the foothills towards a daunting sheer-wall cliff.

Nimrod is trying to comprehend his great-grandfather's sober messages of life. Women are man's equal? Wow, really? Someone should tell the men!! There are a lot of men that do not comprehend that simple principle, Nimrod thought.

"Still wondering if I am your equal?" Semiramis's voice startled Nimrod. She stood in the mouth of his tent with her shiny black hair flowing over her shoulders and breasts, a smirk of a smile on her pouting lips. Eyes of black, ablaze with a keen understanding that Nimrod was hers. "Stew?" she asked as she handed him a dish of her mom's mutton stew. She turned and left as quickly as she had appeared.

"I would like to have my son Ham say a few words regarding city life and morals." Noah sits down as Ham reluctantly walks forward to the altar area. He places his hands on the altar and quickly withdraws them, standing with his hands clasped behind him. He stares at the assemblage before him, obviously unaccustomed to public speaking about morals.

"City life is not for everyone. Most of you are used to small villages with maybe ten to twenty families. In my city of Anat there are thousands of families. Most of these people are nice enough, but there are always those that I call my ten percent. Now ten percent of twenty families is two. Two families that may cause others grief. Ten percent of one thousand is one hundred, two thousand is two hundred, three thousand – three hundred and so on. If something comes up missing in my city, I can count on one or two of those three hundred for being responsible for causing grief. Seems people feel that in large groups they can't be seen or found doing wrong. Kind 'a like a snowflake in a storm. It is said that in an avalanche no snowflake feels responsible. So it is in a large city. No one wants to be responsible – for anything that goes wrong. People in a large group sometimes want to get lost. They don't want to stand out. Most don't wish to hurt others; they just want to be left alone. Some want to be left alone from responsibility of family life. Some from religion. Some from honesty.

Then, there's the group who want to prey on others. What better place than in a city of thousands? These people look for new faces, faces not used to keeping watch over everything they own, even family members. Many of you have never heard another person lie to you, never had someone purposefully deceive you or purposefully use you for their selfish purposes. You have never experienced someone hurting you just because it just makes them feel good.

Another group wants to make a name for themselves. Not perhaps evil people or mean – just very focused on what they want. They, too, will use you. Others simply want to make a living, grow something, raise some animals to sell, make pottery or other useful things – merchants. If you are careful, know what you want to do and stay focused – you can be successful. Do not think because you are a good person, because you believe in God and go to church, that all will work out. It won't. You will be among the first to fail. To quit. To die.

I am in charge of an army. For many years we didn't have an army in Anat. We didn't need an army. But after a while you see the bad people hiring other men to protect them, to inflict harm on others, and there is no one to protect the little guy, the innocent people. Then, there are those in other places that see people prospering and they want what those prosperous people have. Only they don't want to work for it, they just want it – now. For free."

Slowly Nimrod felt himself drawn to the challenge of succeeding in a city. An army has need of soldiers, he thought, and of leaders. Nimrod started to see his future was not in herding sheep but in working with people. His chest heaved with the pulses of his heavy breathing, which seemed to be telling him that this is what he should do – what he must do. But how will Semiramis feel? That girl, that woman, will not be happy. She has wanted to get married for years, and he has been putting her off out of frustration of no future. And my dad. He will be upset as well, especially after he told me not to go to a city. He hates big cities, even though he runs one, but for Nimrod to go against his advice is a slap in his priesthood and patriarchal face. It just seems unfair to have to even worry about what others think. It's my life, Nimrod thought, not theirs. Is what others think of any importance to my happiness?

At that moment with Nimrod lost in his thoughts, he notices a figure standing near him. He jumps slightly, feeling guilty about his thoughts, as he realizes Semiramis must have been there listening to his thoughts. "Nimrod", she asked, "will you take me with you?" She is as intuitive as his own mother. There never would be any way to lie to her. With her dark eyes staring gently into his soul he attempts to change the conversation.

"Semiramis, your eyes …"

"Save it, Nimrod," she said forcefully but with no anger.

Nimrod pauses as he stood up and approaches her, now standing a few inches from her. Being this close to the only woman he'd ever loved

9

blurs his thought processes. He could smell the faint odor of the flowers she has placed in her hair and her feminine body odor. Someone could pluck out his eyes and put hot rods of iron in each of his ears and he would be able to tell it was her.

As he looks at her she slaps his face gently. "Why not?" she asks with tears forming in her eyes. "You have promised me several times that we would be wed soon, soon Nimrod." The silent pause is deafening. He could hear his grandfather Ham still speaking but the words are unintelligible. Hot blood races through his eyes and ears.

"I love you Semiramis. I've always loved you." Her tears increase. "I have nothing to offer you. I must have something to offer you to feel like a man. I cannot live the life of a shepherd. I am going to make a name for myself – and for you. Please let me do this. Please." Pounding blood is now blurring his hearing. "In two years if I have not accomplished what I hope to do, I, I will return for you and (pause) raise sheep."

"And children, she added, "lots and lots of children." She speaks softly as she moves closer to him, touching her garment against his. Nimrod gently gasps in a breath. "If you have not returned for me by the end of two years, I will no longer wait for you." She kisses him on the cheek, spins around and quietly walks away.

Nimrod closes his eyes and in a forceful release of air says, "What in the world am I doing?" His heart pounds fiercely. "Where will I go?" He knew where he would not go. Not to his grandfather's and not to his father's city. He would not be an underling to a relative or a priesthood holder, nor to someone slow and deliberate-as though years were fast enough to make quick decisions. But where? Nimrod recognizes that Grandfather Ham had stopped speaking and his great uncle Japheth had risen to speak.

"I know nothing about city life. I do know that happiness is found from within, from one's choice of a mate, from one's choice of a life devoted to God like Father Noah. Greatness will find you. Greatness is like the mustard seed. It starts small and it takes nourishment and patience. Then, one day you have a huge, magnificent tree with the spice of life.

"My tree sits next to a babbling stream that fills the tree's silence with vibrant life." The speaker's magnificent babbling to magnificent silence.

As his great uncle babbled on magnificently, Nimrod became lost in his thoughts. His great grandfather Noah had counseled him to start things small and strong rather than big and weak. This was in response to Nimrod's question about purchasing a large herd of sheep so that he could be more prosperous more quickly. Nimrod remembered his feelings at the time that small and strong would take forever. And yet, Nimrod reasoned, there is strength in numbers, right? In war, in wives and in concubines. Strike the wives and concubines. Semiramis would take his small and strong and pound it into dust. Strength in numbers? Who could he get to go with him? His mind ran back pictures of his mock battles. Few were his equal, none were better, many seemed willing but were inexperienced. His Grandfather Ham told him once, "Why hire someone who knows less than you, who is less of a man than you?"

Semiramis appears and speaks, "Zag, Jared, Lugal, and brothers Fenchristo and Rayas …"

Nimrod responds, "Yes, but will …"

"Yes, they will go. I already told, I mean, asked them." And she turned and leaves.

The five men stand awkwardly outside his tent.

Jared asks, "Okay if we come in?"

Nimrod nods weakly as the men file in.

"Semi told us we had to go, or our girlfriends would find other men to marry," Lugal offered.

"Sad. I sad," said Zag.

"We'll leave tomorrow after Father Noah gives his final talk," comments Nimrod.

"Good," Rayas said. "Where are we going?" All stand and stare at Nimrod. Nimrod shakes his head side-to-side.

"Well, "Rayas smiles, "this shouldn't take long." The men all exit.

Now on higher ground, Tabansi cleans the minor wounds and gashes from the wolves. He hears them howling, regrouping. Where is the rope? He looks up the vertical wall of rock. Night is not far off; he cannot start a fire for fear it might be seen from on top the cliff. He cannot stay here or the noise of the ravenous wolves might attract attention, and he cannot kill all the wolves. What is my family doing, he mused? He knows his wife will be in her last preparations for the evening meal. His four oldest sons will be tending their flocks and his oldest daughters tending the youngest children. In his youth he had never pictured himself as the head of a large family. How did the children get to be so loving, so hard-working? He never sat them down and lectured them about work or love. They had only worked side by side with him in building their modest home each time his king required his family to move. Even his daughters had fed the flocks and tended them during the day. Nights were strictly for the boys and him. That is, when he was not on assignment for his king.

Tabansi moves as high as possible in the rocks and is preparing himself for the upcoming battle with the wolves when he hears a strange whistling kind of friction sound well to his right. The last rays of light revealed a rope as thick as his arm seemingly suspended from the heavens. Just before the sound, at the top of the cliff three husky figures could be seen quietly hauling something very heavy. They tie it around a large boulder and with much effort they then throw the huge mass of rope over the cliff. They are sure someone would hear the whistling sound. No one does. They retreat into the growing darkness of night.

As Tabansi reaches the rope the growling wolves reach him. The wolves' leaps turn into angry and frustrated fits of snarls and growls as they frantically jump from all fours and then on their hind legs to reach Tabansi. His feet were bleeding and dripping onto the faces of the wolves further exciting their blood lust – but to no avail. Tabansi is now sixty feet above the wolves, resting on a small ledge on the side of the cliff. He tends his wounds the best he could and rested. The rest of his climb would have to come in the early light of day. The wolves retreat and rest as well. In their minds what went up must also come down and they are nothing if not patient. Hungry. Of one mind. Patient.

Creatures of all kinds lurked in a city. What would Nimrod find as he traveled in search of his identity? Was there a city that even needed his talents in warfare? Would men seek to rob him? Kill him? Would they see him as a threat to their ambitions? The one thing he was sure of as he laid his head down for the night was that Semiramis would be waiting for him. He had no need of finding another woman to keep him company in life or even for one night.

Nimrod thought back many years into his childhood when he would offend his dad. The punishment came quickly and forcefully. Many times he would pick himself up with a swollen eye, a bruised cheek or a bloody lip. Nimrod just seemed to have a knack for making his dad mad. After things quieted down, his mom would come visit him or send one of his older sisters to do so. With a moist cloth and herbs they would tend to his wounds. Nimrod wasn't sure, but he thought this had something to do with the warm feelings he had for women, and the cold place in his heart he had for men he fought in battle.

His dad had mellowed in his later years. It had been twenty or so years since his dad had struck him. Nimrod remembered the last confrontation they had. Nimrod had said something defiant to his dad, and Cush leapt up and crossed the distance between them with remarkable speed. With his fist cocked and blood in his eye, Cush was set to hit his son when Nimrod calmly stood still, hands at his side and said, "Go ahead, Father, hit me. That's how you've always solved your problems, by hitting me. So go ahead." Cush was taken back and stood there with his fist poised in midair to deliver its blow. Cush stepped back and left the room. Never again did he attempt to strike his son. But the damage had been done. "My dad treated me like that, and I didn't turn out so bad, right?"

Nimrod lay in the corner of the tent facing the entrance, a sword at his side, thinking of how he would explain his decision tomorrow to his dad, to his mom. And now he was responsible for these other five men too! Why did they trust him so much? Or did they fear Semiramis more?!

During his fitful sleep that night, Nimrod dreamed his recurrent dream of riding a horse at the head of a large marching army of men. On his head was a golden hat with black cloth covering the top of his head. The men had just come from a battle with blood still on their clothing, some with bloody bandages on their heads, others with bandages on their arms or legs – all jubilant with the thrill of victory. As they marched, they passed the tent of Father Noah, who had a strangely sad countenance: happy that Nimrod's army had defeated an enemy and sad that many had died on both sides. Cush and Grandfather Ham looked jealous, even envious of Nimrod's success.

His dream would then switch to contests of skill with many weapons as Semiramis and other women looked on, cheering him. Nimrod's accuracy with the bow and arrow and sling shot was uncanny, as time after time he found the bull's eye. It was a marvelous dream!

Nimrod would lay there thinking of the other men too. Zag would use brute force to defeat all comers with the spear. He could throw the spear farther than any man and with greater accuracy. No one wanted to fight him in hand-to-hand combat, as he bested two and three men at a time. Zag spoke very little, and when he did he would use very few words.

Jared's strength was with the throwing of knives. From ten to twenty feet he was able to stick a knife in another man's throat, heart, or eyeball with extreme accuracy.

Lugal, young son of Ham, was a constant companion of Nimrod and his friend, Jared. His stocky build, like his father, served him well in hand-to-hand combat. Fighting in close combat with shield and sword would be his strength. Although many years younger than Nimrod, Lugal was loyal to and was loved by Nimrod. Troubling to Nimrod was he could never place Lugal in future scenes of combat in his dreams or thoughts, like now.

Tabansi fights back the pain of his wounded feet and a festering snake bite above the leggings on his right leg. He cuts the wound open several times and tries to suck the venom out, but with little success. He could feel the effects of the bite slowly moving through his body. If he could just keep moving he hopes in time to run the venom through his system. He would have to use mainly his arms to climb to the top of the cliff.

What would he do on the return trip after securing the package he'd been sent to obtain? By all that is holy to him, he would not fail his master. To Tabansi he had knelt, swearing allegiance to death and that was that.

As dawn approaches, Father Noah is in his tent praying, praying for the people who had made this yearly visit to hear him speak, to visit the Ark, to take home his messages of hope for the new year and share them with the people back home who had not been able to make the trek. His faithful wife, Naiama, busies herself with breakfast preparations for the two of them. All their children are now caring for families of their own: not just Ham, Japheth and Shem, but all those who followed, after the destruction and the receding of the Flood. Naima would take her place behind her husband, the only woman behind the altar. She had been asked many times by other women if she felt unappreciated or not her husband's equal as she simply tended the family and her husband's needs. Following the thoughts her husband had expounded, she would say "no" to those who asked if she thought that she should hold the priesthood too. "I hold the priesthood whenever I want!" She followed that humor with the serious thought, "My husband cannot do what I do. I have been entrusted with the closest thing to being a God. I am able to conceive life, bringing the next generation to this earth, teaching them, nurturing them and preparing them for their turn as parents. My husband holds the priesthood and speaks for God. Would you require that I do that too? Where is the equality in that?"

Tabansi is climbing the rope with great difficulty. His right leg has swollen to twice its normal size and he has applied a crude tourniquet to his leg near his upper thigh. Both feet have claw marks on them and with the exertion of climbing, they had again started to ooze blood. What drives a person to complete a task well beyond the normal levels of endurance physically or mentally? Only others with that level of task-completion orientation would understand. He had given his word and nothing else mattered. Allegiance.

Father Noah commences his closing thoughts as Tabansi reaches the top of the cliff. Life is slowly ebbing from his body as he crawls to the large tent. He rests for a few moments before quietly slitting open the tent so he could crawl inside. Once in he finds a place where he can remain and watch the front entrance to Father Noah's tent. He readies his knives by sitting two of them in front of him.

"There is much turmoil in the world today: men and women refusing to marry, refusing to honor God for His marvelous creations. There is talk that all on earth came by chance, that there is no plan for man. Nonsense! Each of us comes here for a purpose and it is our job to find out what that purpose is. It may be as simple as being the best father or mother you can be, or the best son or daughter possible. We know that we came from our Heavenly home willingly and we will return there at the end of our days. What we do here will determine our place forever in Heavenly Father's Kingdom. There are those who suppose that living a righteous life, finding and following our Lord's will, is boring, lazy even. They protest that we are like sheep, blindly following our Shepherd. Easy? Easy to find the will of God as it pertains to us? Easy to not get caught up in making money, in not whoring it up, in being virtuous? Easy? If it were easy then there should be millions in attendance today, not just tens of thousands.

If it is easy then there should be no need of armies as my son Ham spoke of. There certainly would be no need of worshipping idols! The hardest thing in the world is to worship the true and living God and follow His commandments. I prophecy that there will come a day when infants will be sacrificed from the womb by the millions, a day when evil will be touted as good, that millions and millions more will be sacrificed at the altar of war, at the altar of greed and hate. And that in the meridian of time God will send a Savior, even His own Son, to pay for the sins of mankind. And that Son will be slaughtered because of His message of peace and love: murdered for preaching love. That's easy?

We are only a few hundred years from the Flood and already we see the powerful influence of Satan once again on our fellow men and women. While we should be concerned for our fellow man, we are only responsible for ourselves. We must help the needy, the downtrodden, even the sinners. God has told us to forgive all men of their trespasses and then, and only then, will He forgive us ours.

We should judge who we associate with. But we must not judge another's eternal fate. Love your neighbor as yourself, do good unto them that purposefully hurt you and pray for your enemies. That does not mean we follow them, but it means that we lead them. We are to be the example, and if they choose not to follow us, so be it. Each of us shall be judged according to our works. To think otherwise is foolish.

You have chosen well to be here today. I see such a bright future for you, your spouses, and your children, if you obey the will of Him who sent us here, he who set up this wonderful plan of salvation, of repentance and forgiveness. As you go from here, know that God loves you. He is rooting for you, cheering for your success, and He sheds tears over us when we fail. Remember that success is getting up one more time than you are knocked down. If you have sinned, know that He will forgive you as often as you repent. He that is without sin, let him be the first to condemn another. That counts all of us out, doesn't it?

I love you, my sons and daughters. I now want to share with you the sacred clothing, the original birthright of Father Adam and Mother Eve." Noah starts for the tent but is intercepted by Ham, who quickly gets up and motions to Lugal and his servant Logan to come to him. Father Noah whispers something to them and then Ham and Noah return to their seats while Lugal and Logan go inside the tent. The two guards let them in and close the tent flap behind them.

Tabansi sees the two men enter, go to a corner of the tent and uncover a twine-tied package. As the two men turn to leave, Tabansi is standing in front of them with a knife in each hand. Startled, Lugal and Logan stop and stare at Tabansi as his hands quickly comes up and simultaneously flicks the knives at them, each knife piercing the throat of the victim. The two men fall to the floor unable to utter a sound. They both die while Tabansi grabs the package and straps it to his back.

With great difficulty he exits the tent through the slit he made earlier. He grabs the rope and makes his way to the rocky floor below. He hears the whistling sound of the rope falling to the ground behind him followed by the screams of Ham finding his dead son.

Tabansi falls down on his face from the weakness in his legs, his strength sapped. As he lays there gasping for air and the strength to get up and run, he senses the presence of animals. He looks up and is surrounded by the patient pack of drooling, snarling wolves.

Ham stands up and crosses to the tent to see what is keeping the two men. After a few moments a fearsome cry pierces the air, and the thousands present have goose bumps go up their spines, as they stand and stare to see what has happened. The guards hold back the tent flap and out steps Ham carrying the body of his dead son Lugal, with the knife still stuck in his throat. Ham screams again and collapses to the ground. The guards quickly take Lugal back into the tent while the grieving Ham continues his primal screams.

Noah is overcome with emotion and is steadied by his other two sons, Japheth and Shem. At first his expression is of horror, and then a puzzling, quizzical look spreads across his face as he views Ham. Nimrod had risen too to see what had happened. He now understands why Lugal did not appear in subsequent scenes in his dreams.

Tabansi sits surrounded by wolves and expecting to be savagely attacked and killed. He has pulled his last two knives from their scabbards and is prepared to take a few wolves with him as his last earthly act. Suddenly the wolves sniff the air, stop their threatening growls and lay down with their head in their paws, just staring at Tabansi. He gets to his feet and painfully limps away. As he leaves he sees a trail of blood behind him. The wolves, as though hypnotized, stay in their prayerful-looking pose. Tabansi staggers away, having no idea what just happened. He looks time and time again back at the wolves that have now risen to all fours and just stare after him.

Noah stands to address the congregation and it is obvious he is struggling with his emotions. "Why?" is all he can utter. One guard exits the tent and whispers to Noah that the "package" is nowhere to be found. "Father Noah", the guard continues, "there is a slit in the back wall facing the cliff, and at the bottom of the cliff there appears to be a pile of what looks like rope. There is blood on the floor of the tent, on the slit and on the ground near the edge of the cliff. I believe one man did this. If it is a pile of rope, he had help from someone up here.

It looks as though the rope had been tied around a boulder at the rear of the tent. But how did it get undone and thrown down to the base of the cliff? Also, there is a large pack of wolves down there. How did this man survive the snakes and that pack of wolves? That's some man, Father Noah."

"A military man?"

"Yes sir, a military man. With the barren ground below, he would have had a long trip to get here."

"A runner?"

"Yes, a runner with great knife skills."

"Thank you, my son."

"Father Noah, I feel so responsible … I, I should've …" The guard breaks down in tears.

"This is not your fault." The guard goes back to his place at the tent. Naiama and several women go inside to prepare Lugal's and Logan's bodies for burial.

"Here, in this sacred gathering place, in sight of the Ark, in the sight of God, the world has intruded on our spiritual gathering. Someone went to great lengths, great planning, to steal the birthright given by our first earthly father and mother. The garments are not worth great sums of money; they're only animal hides made for Adam and Eve when they left the Garden of Eden. I want to say something regarding Adam and Eve. They were not asked to leave the Garden due to sexual misconduct as some suppose. This is absolutely untrue. God told them not to partake of the fruit of the tree of knowledge. They ate of something God told them not to partake, something that was not for their bodies at that time. They disobeyed God by eating that fruit and that, and only that, was their sin. Now, someone has stolen the garments, the skins Adam and Eve wore to clothe their nakedness after departing the Garden of Eden and ending up alone in the world. How important then is it, for you and me, not to eat what God has forbidden? Not do what God has asked us to not do? If this whole earthly experience was triggered by a piece of fruit, what does that say about God expects of us? Obedience is greater than sacrifice. We must be obedient. Knowing why may come quickly or at a later date."

The person who stole some animal skins took a part of the history of mankind, not exactly a giant step-up financially. Why? Why would someone do this? More importantly, why would they kill two innocent and decent human beings, children of our Father in Heaven? God help the men who did this! I know my son Ham will not be so forgiving when he has the men before him. And that begs the question, should Ham, should I and you, forgive the one that killed Lugal and Logan?"

Ham, face contorted, stands and screams, "Never!" His body is quivering as he enters Noah's tent. "Never!" There is a lengthy pause. "Some people," continues Noah, "would take this occasion to curse God. How could He let this happen to such wonderful God-loving men?" Nimrod listens intently. "Why not let this happen to some idol-worshipping adulterers or to some sinful offspring of the human race? Why not kill someone who disrespects God and daily utters vile, hate-filled speeches in order to convince others that God does not even exist, or if He does exist, He simply does not care for you or me?"

As hard as it is to comprehend, God does not always favor believers, or just handsome men or beautiful women. And God cannot take His vengeance on a man simply because he is about to commit a crime. If He did, He would cease to be God. Only His buddies would be good enough to be protected, like the men Ham spoke of who hired others to protect them while hurting the weak. Only God's favorite few would He stop from even being tempted. Is that the God we want to worship? Of course not."

Life would become a competition to gain God's favor. Instead, men and women are allowed to exercise their agency. Agency, which separates us from the animal kingdom, is what stops God from stopping you or me, or the killers of Lugal and Logan. If God stops all evil in the world, how would He judge us when it was He who took our agency from us?"

This lack of agency was Lucifer's plan in our pre-mortal life. Lucifer declared that he would make sure not one soul would be lost. He would guarantee every spirit who came to this earth would succeed in being obedient. Every one! And what did Lucifer want in return for all his efforts? He wanted God to give him all the credit – all the power, all the glory was to be his. He wanted God to give up His role as the Supreme Being-- just give it up-- to Lucifer."

This plan was rejected. Lucifer was so offended that he went out and spoke against God, against agency, and convinced one-third of the hosts of heaven to follow him. God then banned them all from heaven, from ever being able to come to earth and possess a body. Their eternal progress was blocked by their own actions. Obedience. Notice that they had their agency. God did not stop them from using it. They also received the punishment affixed for their transgressions."

Whether or not we ever find who stole and murdered this day, God has found them. They used their agency, and God will affix the punishment. For there to be a crime, it needs be there is a victim. No one is taken before their time. Each of us is appointed a time to return home. Just like we had a time appointed to be born, we cannot alter that either. No one can thwart the purposes of God."

Now please gather together in your families, and fast and pray for Lugal's and Logan's families to find comfort and the ability to forgive. Forgiveness may not come today or tomorrow, but it must come if we are to find peace. Turn it over to God." Noah then turns and enters his tent as the guards open the flap for him.

In the side of the mountain below the Ark can be seen a small, hollowed-out cave that several men are preparing for the arrival of the bodies of Lugal and Logan. Large boulders have been gathered and rest near the cave. The bodies of Lugal and Logan are borne on litters of branches held on the shoulders of family men and fellow warriors. All along the path below the Ark are small alters with the remains of half-eaten sheep and other sacrificial animals that individual families have made to the Eternal Father, offered up asking God to help their family, or one member of a family, with special needs. These needs might include a sick child, a wayward family member, or a need to understand how to deal with a spiritual problem, a hateful neighbor, and so on. Animal sacrifices made to an unseen God, by most in the name of an unseen Savior, who would someday be sacrificed himself on behalf of all mankind. Only the purest, finest animal in the family's entire herd would do. This was not a time to rid the flock of a crippled animal: only the best would do. Some have called this sacrifice, this showing of one's sincerity, a bribe-- Christ's sacrifice -- a bribe?

"God asks that we offer up a sacrifice and we do so. Today it is a broken heart and a contrite spirit. If He asks us to forgive those who do harm to us and we do, is this a bribe? Is this a chip we put in a pile to later redeem when it suits us? And God has to honor this because …? 'Look God, I did this sacrifice, this offering, this forgiveness thing and so now I am calling in my stack of chips. I want my dying son to live, so do it. I want my neighbor dead, so do it. You OWE me!'"

Many of the sacrifices along the path have been eaten. Wolves, bears and lions do not turn up their noses to a free, warm meal, oh no. Sacrifice or not. Among the litter bearers are found Nimrod, Zag, Jared, Fenchristo and Rayas. Tears can be seen on the faces of some.

Heartfelt pain at their loss and a resolute determination to find and kill those responsible for this loss of life can be seen in the steely-eyed focus of eyes blurred by love. Forgiveness would have to come another day.

Ham, his wife and their multitude of children, follow closely behind the litter of Lugal and are surrounded themselves by Ham's military leaders who feel personally wronged by Lugal's murder. Each has their hand on their sword that hangs from their waistline as though someone might jump up on the path and try to do further harm to Ham's family. To be killed in battle was an acceptable death. To be murdered by a coward was not an acceptable death. And that is what made Lugal's death personal. Each family in the procession was led by the father with his sword in his hand. The mother and children follow. The father is the leader. The mother and children following have nothing to do with male chauvinism; the father is expected to keep the way safe of animals that might wish to do his family harm.

Tearful sounds filled the valley as the rhythmic chant filled the air as well. "Praise to a man who communed with his God." A thought that crossed many a mind in the procession was, "Is the killer among us?" No one had left the conference that anyone had noticed, so …?

A snake with an obvious death-wish slithers across the path in front of Ham's family, and before Ham could raise his sword, the snake is hacked to death by a dozen swords of bodyguards with such fury that it seems to signal the entire animal kingdom that now is not a time for trespassing, or forgiveness.

We see Nimrod's face white with emotions changing from sadness to hate, from grief to cold-bloody resolve, from understanding the pain of death, as Father Noah had mentioned, to despising God. Nimrod mumbles to himself, "You had no right to leave my friend, my brother, undefended. You could have chosen others to die so the murderer could still have been condemned. My friend. Why not kill me? You are a mindless, thoughtless God to have allowed this. Thoughtless. Bungler."

It was though life immediately left Nimrod's body. He stumbled and fell as the procession moved on without him. Even breathing was suddenly painful, his strength was gone, and lifting his arms was a chore. He sat by the path with his head bowed forward in his lap. Countless families passed by him and he heard their cries of grief and their chanting. All was a blur as two men reached down and pulled him up and carried him toward the cave. Zag. Jared.

Gasping at every step, Tabansi has found the most incredible thing. As he nears each and every snake, every animal of every kind, in his path, they lie down prostrate on the ground. Where he had to kill every snake on the way to the cliff, they are now offering him free passage through their domain. Why? In his entire life he'd never experienced such a marvelous thing. He spies a small cave in the hill where he decides to stop and rest. The color of his leg, the size of it and the pain therein scream at him to rest. Still days from home he welcomes this chance to rest. As Tabansi approaches the cave he could hear the warning rumblings of a large lion from within the cave. He draws one knife from its scabbard in preparation for the impending attack. The thought came to him first of the wolves and then the snakes. What is happening? Do the animals sense he is dying and are allowing him safe passage? If so why? Are the animals gearing up for him as the guest at a feast?

Predator animals, like predator humans, always seem to sense weakness in a foe and go in for the kill. Always. That's why appeasement never works with humans or animals. As he gasps again with pain and stumbles closer to the cave, the menacing snarls and rumblings stop. Anticipating a charge at any moment by the beast, sweat is now trickling from all his pores like a torrential rain, not so much from fear, but from the pain. The constant throbbing from his leg and feet has grown to the sound and force of a hammer striking an anvil.

It starts to rain and the longer he waits for the lion to charge, the heavier the downpour becomes, until he can no longer see the opening of the cave. Claw marks on both bleeding feet, a swollen, infected-with-snake-venom right leg, scrapes and bruises galore all over his body from climbing the cliff up and down, and now blinded by rain, he feels like his neighbor's half-dead dog, Lucky.

Lightning pierces the gloomy sky, and there in the mouth of the cave stands the lioness. Tabansi's heart skips a lifetime of beats as he sees the size of the lioness. To his dumbfounded utter amazement, the lioness lowers her head and almost apologetically passes by him, hugging the wall of the hill as though she did not want to even touch him. She is followed by her two cubs in like manner: a lioness with cubs leaving the confines of a secure cave in a rainstorm, for him? Lucky. Woof woof.

His head dizzy now from the loss of blood, Tabansi enters the cave. In the corner, by the light of another strike of lightning, he sees a stack of wood and kindling. With two provided stones he strikes sparks, lighting the fire and promptly falls asleep. It was still raining when Tabansi awakes, but now the cave is very warm, like his home. The home he had lately thought he would never again see. He crawls to the stack of wood and back to the fire, blows on the embers and starts a fire once again. Who has placed the wood here: someone who hunts this area, or a runner like himself?

His leg actually begins to feel somewhat better and some of the swelling is subsiding. He slits the wound open again and squeezes some of the puss out with his hands, watching some of it squirt across the fire. The agony is exhilarating, as he knows he has a good chance of seeing his family again. It is while Tabansi is in this painful state of euphoria that a dark, stocky figure fills the cave entrance. Tabansi reaches for his knife when he hears a familiar voice, "I am not here to harm you, Tabansi."

"My king, I am sorry ..."

"That does not matter, my most trusted servant."

"How did you find me, your majesty?"

"When you did not show at the appointed place two days ago, I feared something terrible had happened to you. I mean, it had to be terrible to keep you from making your appointed time. I then tracked back the path I knew you would have taken and saw the fire."

Tabansi fumbles with the strap that holds the package to his back, the strength in his fingers now gone. The figure bends over and finishes untying the package. "You have done well, my faithful servant."

"My family ..."

"...will be taken care of as I promised, from this day until each child is on his or her own. Your wife as well."

"Thank you, but I am feeling better. I just want you to tell them that I will be along in a few days. Thank you, my king. The strangest things happened on my return with the package." Tabansi then related the happenings with the wolves, then the snakes and finally with the lioness and her cubs. "I do not understand. It was like someone cast a spell over all these animals and they dared not injure me."

"Ah, so the stories are true, and unfortunately for you, you are feeling better." The man picks up Tabansi's black horn-handled knife and plunges it into Tabansi's heart. "Forgive me, my friend. It would have happened this way, regardless of the snake bite. I can have no witnesses." The figure leans forward over Tabansi's body to see and hear if Tabansi is truly dead. Satisfied that he is, the figure exits the cave. Over the next several hours, he places large boulders in the mouth of the newly created tomb to seal up the body. As he finishes he is covered with mud over his entire body and clothing. He picks up the package, protecting it from the rain, and makes his way to his horse. As he mounts, a bolt of lightning fills the sky with unbelievable noise and trembling, splitting the darkness for a second, and we behold the face of Ham.

Chapter Two

Weeks have passed since the death of Lugal and Tabansi and life has seemingly gone on. Mariana, Tabansi's widow, sits in the kitchen of her home trying to prepare dinner. Her two eldest daughters watch over her and exchange pained glances for their mourning mother. Her preparation for the dinner meal is to sit and stare with her hands in a raised position, as though she is about to do something, but the something never gets done. Several of the younger boys rush in laughing and playing tag. The two older girls try to shush them and herd them once again outside. "Oh yeah," says the youngest boy, "There's a man outside who wants to talk to Mom." As the boys exit the house the two daughters see the man sitting on horseback with fifteen other men armed with swords and spears a few paces behind him.

"May I speak with your mother, please?" says Ham.

"Mother has not been feeling well, my Lord Ham", says Ava, the eldest daughter, "since, since my father ..."

"I know my dear, but perhaps what I have to tell her will help cheer her up. I promise not to take much of her time."

Mariana appears at the door very shaky and unsteady on her feet. "Please excuse my daughters, your Grace." The girls go to her and support her. "They mean well." The girls guide her back in the home and sit her down again in her chair in the kitchen.

Ham dismounts and follows them in. "I promised Tabansi, as I have all my elite warriors, that should anything happen I would take care of his family. I know money can never replace your loss. I lost a son just about the same time and can sympathize with your loss, your pain." He moves around the kitchen looking at the humble manner in which they live. "I want to encourage you to have faith and courage in the face of this adversity--courage that I'm sure Tabansi taught to your children--to not allow his death to limit you or your children."

As Ham speaks he visually is taking in the simple beauty of this woman and has to fight back the impulse to want her for his own. "I want to extend the opportunity to you and your sweet family to move into my city of Anat where I can personally oversee your needs." The oldest daughter is not bad looking either and in a few years would definitely be ripe for the picking, he thinks. "Your sons will be accepted into training of whatever field they choose. You will not want for any of the comforts of life – I so swear."

The girls are ecstatic over what their King is telling their mom. "Oh, Mother, what a wonderful opportunity for our brothers and for all of us. Can we move to the city?" asks Mia?

Ham walks up to Mariana and gently takes her hand, opens it and places a bag of gold pieces in her hand. As he touches the soft skin of her arm he quickly breathes in deeply, "Whenever you're ready, you have but to send word to me, and a place will be prepared for your family and you." There is a pause.

"How did Tabansi die?" Mariana asks, lips quivering, her eyes welling up with tears.

Ham clears his throat and begins his lie, his answer, "A snake bit him above his leggings on the right leg, the wound festered, and we found him already dead in a cave. We walled the cave up in his honor and left him there. He was such a great warrior, such a fine man."

"A snake?" quizzed Mariana.

"Yes. The bite was behind his knee where he could not remove all the venom by mouth."

"I see. Thank you. We will discuss your very generous offer and contact you with our decision. Must the boys join the military?"

"Not at all. Whatever field they choose will be open to them." Ham pulls out Tabansi's ivory handled knife and presents it to Mariana. "We found this near Tabansi's body and I knew it was something he would want you, or perhaps one of his sons, to have."

Mariana gently takes it from his hand, her tears flowing freely.

"I can sense your disbelief in not believing how one snake could have killed your husband and father of these wonderful children. Through all the memories of assignments I have given Tabansi, I too, had great difficulty believing it myself. But it is true. Well, I feel I have overstayed my welcome at your private time of grieving. Accept my sincere grief at your loss." Mariana nods her understanding. Ham exits, mounts and they all ride off, as the girls open the bag and they all 'oh' and 'ah' at the generous contents.

"Find your older brothers and bring them here. We have a tomb to find."

Ava asks, "Why, Mother?"

"Something is not right. A snake indeed," she sneers and watches the men ride away.

Nimrod and group have left the conference with the man, Kadenram, who drives the large flat wagon. The five men sleep in their clothes, each with a blanket provided by Kadenram. Behind the wagon is a small herd of sheep watched over by two of Kadenram's sons and their two dogs. The two dogs catch the eye of Nimrod and his group. Darting in and out, yapping at the heels of sheep that stray left or right and herding them back into the fold hour after hour amazes the young warriors. The two boys each carry four-foot long sticks that they occasionally use to tap the head of a sheep or the rear flanks, to help the sheep remember in which direction they should be headed.

Nimrod asks, "Where are you headed?"

"South down the Euphrates river past Babel," he answers.

"Never heard of Babel," Jared responds.

"It's no wonder," Kadenram answers. "It is the armpit of life, constantly being attacked and beaten by anyone's army of fifty men or less who have nothing to do," he laughs.

Nimrod and his group look at each other and grin. "The armpit of life," repeats Nimrod as he sniffs his own armpit and recoils slightly, to the laughs of his friends. "Sounds inviting." They continue chuckling as the wagon trudges steadily but slowly forward. Nimrod pauses and observes the landscape and then the sky. He looks back to where they've been and seems perplexed.

"Kadenram, pardon me for questioning you, but it does not seem to me that we are traveling south."

"Ah, you are right my young friend. I have one stop to make before I can begin my journey home. A thousand pardons for not asking you first."

"That's all right. It is we who are in your debt. A simple few days are not a problem. By the way, what do you do when you are home?"

"I am a trader. I take caravans of merchandise from the south and market my goods wherever God sends me."

"God? I'm not sure I'd trust Him to guide me."

"But why not, young warrior?" Nimrod's friends listen a little more intently, especially Jared.

"Lugal was one of the finest men I knew. God did not guide him from a murderer's hand. If God cannot, will not, do that, how can you trust him to guide you down a road?"

"As a great grandson of Father Noah, surely you know that God does not keep bad things from happening to good people. Am I right?"

"If I were God, I would." And so they rode in silence each absorbed in their own thoughts, examining their own beliefs.

As the sun descended into the light blue sky, Kadenram stops his team of oxen. He and his sons loosen the oxen's yokes, curry them gently, fed them and water them like pampered children. Soon dinner is ready and the night-time guards go out to watch for predators wanting a quick meal of ox or sheep.

"Can't the oxen fend for themselves against little wolves and mountain lions?" asks Jared.

"Yes, my young friend, they could, but why should they? They work all the daylong pulling us without complaint. Surely you do not think they then should spend the entire night fearing for their lives?"

"I hadn't thought of it like that," mused Jared.

"When one gives us their all, man or animal, do we not owe them a little in return?"

"Treating animals like humans sounds strange. But yes, we do owe them." Nimrod smiles as his good friend gets bested in the intellectual joust. "And how do you see that applying to us humans, Kadenram?"

"If I pay you a wage, do I then owe you anything after you go home for the night?" Kadenram's question is met by silence. He continues, "Only if you want that man to concern himself with your welfare as you go home. Who do you want guarding your sheep, your kingdom, a hireling or a shepherd? A hireling that closes his ears when he sleeps and does not, wants not, to hear the bleating of a threatened sheep when the wolves come in close: rather, do you want a shepherd? They are paid the same, yet the shepherd rises out of concern as he hears the frightened sheep."

Nimrod interjects, "Or a general who stays at the rear of the fight, eating his grapes and drinking his wine surrounded by beautiful women, rather than a general who walks the line checking on his troops and sleeps side-by-side with his men?"

"Okay", Jared says, "I give. I have much to learn about sheep and about men!"

"Yes, Jared. Much," smiles Zag.

At the break of day the oxen have already been hitched and the wagon moving when Nimrod and the others awake to the smell of breakfast. "We will be there today," announced Kadenram, as he sees his young friends stirring. "Come, let's eat!"

After breakfast Nimrod and friends hop down from the steady, plodding wagon and stretch. They then commence sparing with each other, trading partners as they change weapons: first with swords, then spears, then bows and arrows, then knives, all the while jogging to keep pace with the wagon. Kadenram was amazed with the agility of all the men and the ferocity with which they practice. Time and time again one would attack another and physically hurl their opponent to the ground or into a passing rock wall, with their weapon poised to strike a death blow. Only then do they stop and instruct each other on how to better attack or defend oneself in such a situation.

The men spend the better part of the day jousting and jogging and don't notice their arrival on the outskirts of a city. Nimrod looks up, "I know this place." No sooner had he said so than he and his men were surrounded by a good-sized group of soldiers with their swords drawn. "Ah," said Nimrod, "my father's city of Mahora." The soldiers escort Nimrod and his four friends to a small dingy building on the outskirts of the city where Cush is waiting to meet them.

"I asked my good friend Kadenram to bring you here, so I might apologize for my poor behavior when you told me of your plans to travel south. In search of your destiny, I believe you said?"

"Yes, Father, my destiny."

"And I have a favor to ask of you, and your friends. That is, if it will not interfere with your plans."

"And that is …?"

"There is a war about to be waged with a neighboring city. Would you, all five of you, help me train my troops?"

"How long do we have?" asked Fenchristo.

"About one week," answered Cush.

"Only a week? Father, I'm not sure what we can accomplish in only a week, if anything."

"Will you try?"

Nimrod and his companions look at each other with skeptical faces. "May we have a few minutes alone to discuss this?" Rising and exiting, motioning to his guards to follow, Cush leaves the five men alone to discuss their plans.

Jared is the first to speak, "Nimrod, a week?"

Fenchristo, "Why us, why now?" Who has been training them? Something doesn't seem right. Who will we be fighting, and how many are there?"

"And why are we fighting them?" asks Rayas.

"This is your father, Nimrod. Can we really say no?" asks Jared.

"No," says Zag. "You trust father?"

There is a pause as Nimrod thinks through the comments and questions. He crosses to the door and opens it. His way is blocked by a nasty-looking guard. "I need to speak with Kadenram," Nimrod states.

"He's gone," replies the guard with a goofy-looking grin on his face. "Gone."

The five men in almost unison, "Gone?"

Two more guards appear with their weapons drawn.

"Guess that answers if we can trust him," says Rayas as he draws his sword, quickly followed by the other men.

"That a problem?" asks a guard.

"Not for us," responds Jared. Jared steps toward the door with sword in hand, "Who told him to go?"

The guards are joined by several more of their comrades, and the sounds of swords being drawn is unmistakable, accompanied by a loud voice behind the guards. "Put down your weapons, you idiots," scolds Cush, "This is my son. Move! Get out of my way." Cush comes pushing through his men and enters the room. "Go away, you fools."

Guards follow Cush's orders reluctantly.

"This is entirely my fault, Nimrod. Please forgive me." Now there's something Nimrod was not used to: hearing an apology from his father. "I felt sure you would want to help me, so I told Kadenram to leave. He'll return in ten days. At least I have confidence you'll still be alive." Cush smiles a nervous smile. "I should have waited. I know. It was wrong of me."

Two apologies in one day: Nimrod wonders what the bad news is.

It isn't long in coming. Cush walks to a table and stool and sits, head down, dejected. "All I have left of my so-called army is a handful of men. We never were a large force, but lately I haven't been able to pay the men, so most have left. Moved to other cities. Just gone. Our little city is about to be overrun by men from the mountains. Bandits. Lots of them. Traitors."

"So it is not a war with another city, Father?"

"No."

"What about Grandfather Ham? Can he not send you help?" asked Nimrod.

"Do you know what it is like to have to ask your father … of course you do." Cush stops and looks at Nimrod and Nimrod can see the desperation in his father's eyes. "It's not just about asking for help; my father thinks I am incompetent. He thinks I am a failure. Asking for help, any kind of assistance, proves to him that he's right."

Nimrod looks at his friends and then utters, "We'll stay and we will help. Not because you forced us to, but because we want to. Assemble your men, we best start right away."

As Cush gets up and starts for the door, Rayes asks, "What size of an army do you have left?"

The men all look at Cush waiting for a response. He says nothing.

"Maybe he's adding all the numbers," comments Fenchristo.

"Father?"

"About one hundred and fifty," he mumbles.

"Zag not hear."

Cush repeats a little more loudly, "About one hundred and fifty men." The men are stunned.

Nimrod, "Assemble your men now, Father. To his four friends he announces, "We must work quickly."

Rayas, "Any of you women pregnant with boys?"

Fenchristo, "Now is not the time for your strange sense of humor."

"I was just hoping …"

"Ahhh! Enough brother."

Nimrod follows Cush to the door. "Jared, organize the men into groups of tens, fifties, and ah, well I guess that's about it. Select leaders for each group, the best fighters available. I must go and talk to my grandfather."

Cush leads Nimrod to a horse. "Nabu, he is my fastest. You should reach my father by sunset."

Nimrod hops up with the help of the horse's main and bridle. "I'll be back tomorrow. Just make sure your men follow my friends' instructions. These are some of the finest warriors I know." Nimrod signals the horse to leave, and it leaps forward like someone put a spear up its ... well, let's just say Nimrod barely hangs on as the horse streaks across the ground towards Anat. Nimrod looks back to see his friends convulsing with laughter at the sight of Nimrod and Nabu. They, and the town of Mahora, become a small blur as the horse charges on. Nimrod's mind moves ahead of even this speeding beast, contemplating how he will approach his grandfather Ham to send warriors to help defend Mahora. What could a son do to so offend his father that the dad would even contemplate allowing the son and his entire family, the whole population of a city such as Mahora, to suffer defeat at the hands of robbers?

Not just defeat, Nimrod mused, but the ravaging and pillaging of the population as he had heard from warriors who had seen and participated in the savagery of war. His thoughts turned to Semiramis and the two years he had to at least commence his 'destiny', as his father phrased it. His destiny was pushed out of his thoughts by the real life event of saving his father and his city from supposed annihilation in one week's time. Semiramis would have to wait.

Hour after hour his trusty mount Nabu flew as though this beast could sense the urgency of Nimrod's quest. His thoughts once again flew to the future and how he would certainly have a stable of horses such as this. If he lived.

Jared, Zag, Fenchristo and Rayas had done what Nimrod requested. The groups were going through extensive, exhausting drills with the bow and arrow, sword, sling shot, knife throwing, spear throwing and rotating who were the best in each weapon. Then, the best would help instruct all the others. Jared and his friends would instruct and refine the men's techniques. Over and over and over and over ... It soon became apparent who the true learners were, who wanted to better themselves and those who did not enjoy the exercises. It pretty well broke down into the older and more experienced being those who resisted new ideas the most. Know-it-alls, been there--done that, the "I've lived this long I must know what I'm doing, why change?"

There was a group of about twenty men who should have wanted their own men to improve, but obviously did not enjoy seeing these men having success. Why? Why would you not want those who potentially would have your life to protect in a battle not be as good as or better than you? Nimrod thought that we do find that to be the case in much of life. An example is when we steal other people's ideas and pass them off as our own. He remembered a time when he had an idea on winter feeding areas and summer feeding areas. He spoke to his older brother regarding the details and before long his dad called the family together to announce that Jasher, the older brother, had an idea about improving winter and summer feeding and how it would save the family money, time, etc.

Nimrod turned to his brother and looked Jasher right in the eyes. Jasher avoided his steady knife-like stare and ate up the adulation. The two of them never spoke of it again. Why, Jasher? Why brother? Why God, didn't you make it right?

God. Oh yeah, Him. Mr. do nothing unless it's important to Him. Forget the little guy. Forget Nimrod. Forget Lugal. Damn Him.

Zag threw his spear completely through the bale of straw target, while others bounced their spears off the same target as though it was made of stone. Even the older, wiser, more experienced warrior's ability paled next to Zag. And they now knew it. Zag would stand staring at his target, take three steps forward, winding up his hips and shoulders slightly and with a controlled grunt let loose the six-foot long spear. One could feel the unexpressed sentiment, "I'm glad the target is not me."

"Mind then body," expressed Zag. And when Zag spoke, all listened. Even the experienced ones squirmed. Even the experienced ones were no longer as stubbornly prideful. Kinda. Darkness halted the exercises. It was then that Jared requested that Cush provide torches so the men could train longer into the night. Darkness also found Nimrod in the home of his grandfather.

"Long ride from Mahora. Never did like that name, Ma-hor-a. Well, we'll talk tomorrow," said Ham.

"Can it then be at sunrise, Grandfather? I need to return to help train my father's troops," asked Nimrod.

"Sunrise? Perhaps we could talk now," grinned Ham.

"My dad has about one hundred and fifty men plus me and my four friends. He expects the battle to take place in six days. Will you help us?"

"Nothing like getting right to the point," chuckled Ham. He used his practiced, stare-into- space look, and then looked at Nimrod. With his brow furrowed, he closed his eyes, "What do you want me to do?"

"My father speaks of thousands that will attack." Ham snickers. "We are only one hundred and fifty – and five. What can you do?"

Ham grinned begrudgingly, "Won't tell me what to do? Smart, dear Grandson. Very smart. Were you in charge of Mahora I doubt this emergency would even exist. Your father is not very … Forgive me, Nimrod. Your father's abilities lie in a different area, not war. He's a good man, a good son, a good father."

"Please stop, Grandfather. My father is a weak man, a cowardly man, a brutal father. He makes it very hard to hold my head up high, but he is my father. I owe him this one favor. And with or without your help, I will stand by him, once."

"He does not deserve you."

"I don't know about any of that, Grandfather. Who is to say about who deserves whom, or what? Do you deserve great grandfather Noah? Do I? Did Lugal deserve to die at the hand of a coward?"

Ham grows restless with these comparisons, and for good reason, unbeknownst to Nimrod. "I will provide five hundred seasoned warriors at Mahora in six days. You are to be their leader, no one else. Is that understood? Will that do?"

"Understood, and thank you, that will do. That is most gracious Grandfather."

Ham rises, followed by Nimrod. "It's time for bed. Do not wake me on your way out tomorrow, at sunrise." He smiles and stops his exit, "You deserve far better than you have been given in this family. Far better." Ham exits the room. Nimrod retires to his bed unsure of all his grandfather meant, but grateful.

Nimrod was well rested for the 'flight' home, and the time also, passed quickly. He kept thinking that he had to get a horse like this when he became successful. Nimrod circled the city before going to the training of this small group of men. He had instructed his grandfather to split his troops into two groups and to push into the foothills north of the city and lie in wait.

Nimrod's force would be the bait and meet the bandits head on. Or …? His attention was diverted by the sounds of wild animals in a to-the-death battle. Off to Nimrod's right he saw a bear and a mountain lioness with two cubs looking on, locked in a dispute over a nearly-dead Fallow deer that was struggling to escape. Its hind quarters were still half- attached.

The lioness's frame was gaunt and several of her ribs were easily seen. Perhaps the need for her survival, as well as the survival of her cubs, helped turn the day, as the bear lumbered off licking its facial wounds from the lioness's sharp claws. She and her cubs settled in for a feast as the wide-eyed deer now stared off into eternity. Nimrod's mount was wild-eyed and shivering from head to tail from the sights and sounds of the battle. He urged Nahu forward gently until the feast was well behind them.

Perhaps his small army should attack the enemy at dawn, still using his grandfather's troops as back-ups. Attacking would have the enemy still groggy with sleep, with a dulled attitude regarding their expecting such a smaller force to be only a minor inconvenience on the field of battle. Thus by the attitude of overlooking, his army could kill enough of the enemy to further dull their attitude for dying. He would think on it further. He trotted Nahu into the practice area where his first army was preparing for battle.

Nimrod relayed the information to the cheers of his troops and friends. His father looked somewhat relieved and somewhat not. Favors from fathers can be expensive. Very.

"What's bothering you Father?" asked Nimrod, as he and his dad walked. "My father bothers me. In minutes he goes from my son Cush deserves what he gets for being incompetent -- to I must save him and his people because Nimrod asked. My father does nothing that will not benefit him greatly. So, the question is, what does he get out of helping me?" There is a long awkward pause as Cush and Nimrod ponder the possible answers. And Nimrod does not want to share his thoughts on the possible answers of his father's question, as he is not sure his father can handle it.

As dark surrounds the small army, Nimrod speaks to them. "We are training for a fight of survival of ourselves, our families and our city. Earlier today I watched a half-starved lioness defeat a larger, well-nourished bear for a meal of Fallow deer. As I watched the bear retreat from the fight I realized he must have calculated the effort and the pain, then decided he would live pain-free to fight another day. An easier day. A less stressful day. That is what we must do to our bear. We must make this fight so painful that the effort is not worth it for our enemy and they leave – to fight another day.

Our fierceness must be so overwhelming from the very first sound of attack that our enemy wonders what on earth is happening. There is a complacency that happens with larger, superior number forces that we must exploit in the first few seconds. Then, we must carry our aggressive spirit to our last sword thrust, our last spear lunge, to our last knife, our last arrow penetrating our enemy's heart. Then, and only then, will our enemy have but one desire – self survival. Then, and only then, will they not want to continue the battle.

We may very well look up and see faces that had been fighting next to us last month. Now, they fight against us. They took the easy way out. There can be no doubt on our part that this is war. No mercy for them."

There are some rumblings from the men, "No mercy."

Nimrod repeats, "No mercy."

More of us men repeat, "No mercy."

Again and louder, "No mercy!"

Men in unison and shouting, "No mercy."

"We will see you here at sunrise." They all disperse.

Three of the eldest of Mariana's sons have been searching the rocks and lower cliffs for signs of a cave that has been enclosed as their father's tomb. They have on leggings to keep the snakes from biting them, and they each have multiple knives on their arms and legs. The carcasses of several snakes can be seen dying in the sun on the heated rocks surrounding them. Tabansis in training.

They walk slowly, yet determined to find the cave their mother has commissioned them to find. They each have the strong, slim build of their father. There is no squabbling among them as to who is better, who is faster or why they are out here in the middle of a hot day. They simply work as a team, as they have been taught from birth by their loving, strict parents. And yes, strict is a sign of loving parents. The whining and crying of so many other children has been parented out of these young men. Their only thought of the moment is to do what their mother has requested.

On the fourth day of their mission the young men find a cave walled up with large boulders expertly stacked. As is evidenced by the earth in front of the cave, it is a recent work. They look at each other with an apprehensive feeling that asks, "What if this is really our father's tomb?" Thinking something is never the same as knowing, they kneel down. Aericas, the eldest, asks their God for the strength, physically and emotionally, to complete their task. They then proceed to remove each boulder off the top and lay each one out in the order that they removed it, so as to later close the tomb properly.

After they remove the first couple boulders the unmistakable odor of decaying flesh drives them from their task. Earron and Parahayker look their elder brother in the face and shake their heads.

"We cannot do this, Aericas. This is our father's grave, we're sure," gasps Earron.

"Perhaps so, Earron, and if this is -- was Father -- does not Mother have the right to know how her husband died?" questioned Aericas.

"Why would our king lie to her about how her husband died?" asks Aericas. They pause as they sit and stare at the tomb.

"Perhaps it would be best if you waited here then," says Aericas, as he collects himself and reverently approaches the cave and struggles to move the next boulder from the mouth of the cave. He grunts and is immediately assisted by two more pair of hands.

"Mother sent three of us and we will do as she requested," Parahayker says. With renewed determination they approach the opening and peer in, their mouths and noses covered with their shirts. It is then that they realize there is a mountain lion behind them, uttering a guttural dinner bell.

Chapter Three

Nimrod sends out three of the most seasoned troops who have found new ways of fighting difficult to accept, to scout the enemy camp. They leave two nights before the conflict is to begin.

"How do you know, Father, that the battle is to take place in two days?" quizzes Nimrod. "Why not tonight or three days from now?"

"I was sent a message by live messenger asking me to surrender myself, my army and my city. If I did so, the messenger said, we would be allowed to live, provided we laid down our weapons and offered no resistance. This I declined to do after counseling with the elders. These robbers, like most I'm sure, have a reputation of appearing merciful, but after surrendering, deal with the army and women very harshly. If we are to die, it would be better to do so fighting.

I did not tell you earlier but each family is armed with knives and swords and is prepared to fight to the death in the event we cannot stop this invasion. We are not of the mind to go quietly to our slaughter and let our women be raped. Each woman has a container of poison she will drink and feed to her children to keep from being raped and tortured.

Just before dawn the three scouts return and awaken Cush and Nimrod. Khammurabi speaks for the three: "The enemy is encamped at the top of the small mountain to the east. There are hundreds of smoldering campfires with tents and horses." As Khammurabi speaks Nimrod senses a slick, almost rehearsed presentation of the facts.

"Did you not see any lookouts or guards?"

"Oh sure, Captain Nimrod. We found one group of three men asleep, so we killed them."

"How?"

"We each took our sword and plunged it into the chests," bragged a second scout, Adad.

"May I see your sword?" Nimrod asked as he held out his hand. Adad hands him his sword and Nimrod examines it. "Your sword is clean, no traces of blood."

"Well we wiped our weapons clean on the clothing of the robber guards," chimed in Khammurabi, smiling and looking at the other two.

"In total darkness?"

"Yeah, in total darkness," responds Khammurabi defensively. "We are good at what we do," as his lips tighten.

"And what is that, exactly?" asks a suspicious Nimrod.

The three men stand in front of Nimrod, their hands on the hilt of their swords ready to defend their honor. Nimrod stands calm and relaxed. "I sent you into the mountains at night and you come back with your clothes completely clean, no dirt or brush, thistles or burrs on you, no blood on your sword or clothing. You're all well-rested, eyes clear, as though you slept in your own beds all night. And you take offense at me asking you some very basic questions?"

Nimrod turns to Cush, "Father, where did these men come from? They are not like your average soldier that you have in camp?"

"They were sent by my father to help with the training of my army. They've been here almost two years."

"Just about the same time as your soldiers began to abandon you?"

"Yes, but I don't see the connection between the two events."

"Perhaps not. There are, what, another fifteen men like these sent by your father, Ham?"

"Yes."

"And who pays them?"

"I cannot, anymore than the other men."

"Who pays you, Khammurabi?"

"We are not mercenaries, Captain Nimrod, we do not work for just money," states Khammurabi defiantly.

"Really?" says Nimrod as he slowly walks around the three. He sees a bead of sweat on the brow of the braggart, Adad, and the other scout, Puzur. He directs his question to Puzur, "Does your family live here in Mahora?"

"Ah, well, not in Mahora, exactly," answers Puzur.

"And your family, Adad, do they live in Mahora?"

"No, not exactly."

"Surely, your family, Khammurabi, lives here, yes?"

"Not exactly," murmurs Jared, Fenchristo, and Rayas, who have joined the others. They suppress a laugh.

"You told me, Khammurabi, that your wife's mother lives here and that you were staying with her until you could move your wife and children here, two years ago. You did tell me that?" Cush asks.

"Yes, I believe I did, Khammurabi stammers. "Look, I must start the last day's training for the men, what little there are. Can the questions wait until we're finished with that?" And he and the other two scouts exit.

"We will be right behind you," says Jared.

"Keep an eye on them, and your back," responds Nimrod as they four men exit.

"All is not right with these men, Father."

"Perhaps not, but I trust them. They have stayed by me through my city's trials. So what if Ham pays them. What does that mean?"

"'Our word is our bond' is what you taught us. Is their word their bond? Is it to you or to Grandfather Ham that their allegiance belongs?"

"Is it not the same, Nimrod?"

"If a man cannot swear allegiance to me and cannot die in defense of me, then his allegiance is to another. Whether that be to himself or another king is of no importance. He cannot be trusted by me. By another. By himself."

Aericas and his brothers spread out across the mouth of the cave. The idea is to force the lioness to select her target and the other two attack her while she has one pinned down. The lioness seemed to favor Parahayker, the youngest and the smallest of the three, so Aericas motions to him to take the center position with Aericas to his left and Earron to his right. "Tell mother I love her," Parahayker whispers as he shakes with fear. The lioness approaches slowly, crouched low to the ground, her ears back.

It is rare for a lion to attack a human, especially when she is outnumbered. With her ribs showing through her hairy body, it is obvious she is starving. Suddenly her two cubs appear and whine for mom to come to them. They too, show signs of not having eaten for some time. The lioness halts her advance toward Parahayker momentarily and makes an "I told you to hide and wait for me" message.

Then a lone wolf with half of its nose missing appears behind the cubs. It is obvious why the cubs did not remain hidden as their mom had ordered. The wolf grabs one of the cubs by a hind leg and starts to drag him off, all the while attempting to strengthen its grip on the cub by working its way up to the cub's throat. The lioness alters her attack now toward the wolf in an attempt to save her cub. She lunges for him as her powerful paw slams the wolf on the side of his head, momentarily causing him to lose grip on the cub. Both cubs run and find themselves behind the three men.

The wolf backs the lioness up in front of the brothers and her cubs. The wolf lunges in catching the weakened mother by her throat. It is obvious she has spent the last of her fading strength already and is helpless to further defend herself. She lies there as the wolf tightens his grip on her throat. It is a mother's worse nightmare, to die in front of her children, knowing they are next. In a flash, the three brothers descend on the wolf, Aericas grabbing the wolf by the head and slicing the beast's throat while his brothers thrust their knives into the wolf behind its front legs, hitting the heart from both sides. Within a few short moments the wolf is dead.

As the lioness struggles to her feet, her cubs run to her, licking her face and the blood on her throat. She painfully drags the wolf carcass over a small hill out of sight of the brothers. All that can be heard is the ripping, chewing and renewing of three lives. The three brothers renew their mission of removing enough boulders to allow them access to their father's body. As the three of them climb over the existing boulders they kneel and pray around their father's body. They have much to be grateful for this day.

As they arise they see where he was bitten by a snake as the flesh is still dark and swollen. There in the right center of his chest is one of his favorite knives, the black- handled one. Aericas removes the knife as Earron moans softly. His father was stabbed to death. Who would do such a thing? Aericas wipes the blood on his own loincloth. A thorough cleaning would have to be done later with water and a clean cloth.

With tears in their young eyes, the three boys struggle with the weight of replacing the boulders and the intensity of their emotions. Someday, someone would have to pay. This they did swear one to another.

The night before the battle, Grandfather Ham's five hundred troops arrive. Nimrod gives their leaders instructions, and they all sleep on their swords. As Nimrod is returning to his friends, he sees a fire in the camp of Cush's army and wonders why these men are up this late the night before the battle. He approaches the fire and finds all of Cush's men gathered, but not the men sent by Ham, including Khammurabi, Adad or Puzur. He hears one warrior captain state, "We may never return; therefore, let us tell the truth of our actions. No matter what is said this night, it is a secret, and no action or revenge may be taken."

There was a long pause until one warrior announces, "I stole the brown horse that Radar was missing. I sold it to a man in Arioch." The man sits and quickly Radar stands trembling and looks at the speaker, then sits back down.

Another pause and then another man announces, "I told a lie to King Cush when he asked me to run to Anat and deliver a message to his father, King Ham. I told him I was sick and could not go. But I was really too tired from staying up all night making love to Urtylergur's wife while he was on an errand for King Cush," he admits. Urtylergur stands and draws his sword and several men restrain him. He sits down moaning.

"I too made love to Urtylergur's wife," admits another warrior. Urtylergur's stands again with sword drawn. Again he is restrained and sits down.

"Me, too," says another voice from the dark. Urtylergur buries his head under his arms. "And I," adds another warrior.

"How is all this possible?" asks Urgtylergur, "My wife has been missing for several weeks."

"When your wife refused to sleep with me, I sold her to a man in Arioch," admits yet another voice from the dark. And so the night continued until all had told their truths.

The fire is put out and as Nimrod is leaving he hears Urtylergur ask quietly, "How much did you get for my wife?"

A voice answers, "A brown horse."

Long before dawn all are awakened as Jared, Zag, Fenchristo and Rayas quietly make their way through the camps, stirring all the men. Cush and Nimrod lead Cush's troops to the mountain path while Ham's five hundred take separate paths, half to Cush's left and half to his right. At the top of the small summit Cush and Nimrod halt their troops. Men with bows and arrows assemble to the front, as men and their slingshots wait behind them. The assault will begin with a hail of arrows followed by running troops using their slings with deadly accuracy, killing already wounded enemies and continuing the silent attack as long as possible. Once inside the enemy campsites, these men will then trade their slingshots and bows and arrows for swords.

The fight commences with light resistance. Only a few hundred men arise to meet the onslaught of men fighting to protect all they own. Zag leads the men of spears on an unmerciful assault behind the enemy's swordsmen, plunging their spears into all who stand in their way. The entire one hundred and fifty and five men fight to the center of the camp with but a few deaths and injuries. Where is the main force of the robbers?

On the back of each man's head, Nimrod had the women of Mahora sew a large white patch so all of his men would not mistake a comrade for a foe. Ham's five hundred men close in from the sides and the rout is on. Not one man escapes the trap. Arrows flying overhead of Cush's men reign down death on the half of the camp not yet engaged in the fight.

Thousands of arrows pour down followed by thousands of sling shot missiles, followed by heart-stopping screams from the attackers. These five hundred, not as well trained as Cush's troops, suffer more deaths and injuries then Cush's men. "No mercy," is the cry from Cush's men, and the glint from their eyes tells of the amazing transformation Nimrod and friends make in their minds--a lifelong and life-altering transformation. As the fighting progresses, Nimrod approaches the large tent at the center of the camp where the fighting has been the fiercest. Something about that tent seems familiar. As Nimrod walks around the outside of the tent, he notices something odd. There is a neatly sewn slit about four feet high commencing at the base of the tent. Hurriedly Nimrod runs to the front of the tent and peers in. It is devoid of humans and yet the appearance of the bedding suggests that the occupants have left in a terrible hurry.

This is not the tent of a general or a military man. And definitely not a robber. This is the tent of a family man. This tent belongs to Nimrod's great grandfather. To the Lord's prophet – Noah.

As Nimrod exits the tent, dawn is peaking over the mountain tops. He sees a group of Cush's men, the old, well-worn soldiers led by Khammurabi stabbing over and over a body on the ground. They utter happy and excited yells, until one of the men sees Nimrod and alerted the others. They all turn and have that bloody, excited lustful look in their eyes as they recognize Nimrod. Khammurabi, with his sword raised above his head as though attacking the enemy, charges at Nimrod. With bloody, filthy curses filling his mouth and the air around him, Khammurabi must have thought his band of brothers is charging with him as he is not the kind of man that would purposefully attack a man one on one. He is, however, much alone, as the others have commenced fleeing into the dawn's early light.

Alone, Khammurabi fails terribly at his attempt to kill Nimrod. Knowing what a coward this man is, Nimrod dispenses with him after a feign to the right and a thrust of his sword to the heart. As the coward lays dying and staring at Nimrod, Nimrod takes one of his daggers and stabs his assailant in the mouth. Nimrod takes great pains to clean his dagger on the cloak of Khammurabi and then his sword. While still in the grips of the death rattle, Nimrod spits in his face and walks to see who the fifteen men bravely killed. And in his mind repeats the question, where are the thousands of robbers? And why would they have been with a prophet of God? Is this Ham's repayment for helping his son, Cush? And what of Noah, who escaped this murderous plot? Does he know Ham had planned it all?

Aericas is followed by his two brothers as they enter their family's humble dwelling – a hovel by any standards. All the family is assembled for breakfast as the three men entered. Mother and the children stop their light-hearted chatter and stare at the brothers. Somewhere in the deep recesses of her heart, Aerica's mother still hopes that father is still alive. Mariana knows by looking at their unpracticed-art-of-deception that they had found Tabansi – and he was not alive. She weeps openly. She weeps long. She weeps hard.

There on the ground, body hacked to death with his limbs barely intact, face unrecognizable, lays Cush. All the terribly harsh memories of him from childhood to this present day are flushed forever from Nimrod's mind. Cush was killed by men who he believed were dedicated to him, to his well-being, to at least his office of King. Murdered. Slaughtered. He was soaked in his own blood. Nimrod is numb. His narcissistic mind slowed to a halt, like a slow-moving dance, disjointed thoughts slowly blur through his wide-awake brain. Noah, the patriarch of mankind, missing, and Cush, Nimrod's dad, dead.

Zag finds Nimrod sitting on the ground next to Cush. He says not a word. Jared and the others joined them in a silent memorial service. Soon all of Cush's troops join them, kneeling next to and around Nimrod, the exuberance of victory deadened by the gore of their King's mangled body. Several men use a blanket from a tent to carry Cush's crumpled dangling body parts to prepare for the short journey home. As they start home, ten of the soldiers who had hacked Cush to death have been captured and are kneeling with their arms tied behind their backs. They were mouthing gibberish to Nimrod's numb ears. "It was Khammurabi's order we didn't mean to … he was a decent man …"

Rayas asked Nimrod, "What shall we do with these men?"

Nimrod slowly turns toward the line of men, pulls out his twelve-inch knife and slits the throat of each man, with Zag, Fenchristo and Rayas holding the men still. But Jared does not. "This is but the beginning of payback for my dad, and for Lugal. Just the beginning, God."

Ham appears at the door of Tabansi's home. He knocks gently as his men sit on their horses' several steps away. Mariana had sent word for him to please come to her home. Ham thought she had decided to accept his offer to move to his city, Anat, to allow him to care for her. And, oh, how he would love to care for her personally. And her family, of course. Why else would she ask him to come to this God-forsaken place?

Aericas opens the door and invites King Ham in. Ham can feel the coolness of his attitude and is puzzled. Inside the home sits Tabansi's large family with Mariana front and center. Even the young children, tended by the older daughters, are puzzlingly quiet. Aericas offers King Ham a chair directly across from Mariana and all the children. There on a small table between him and Mariana lays the black bone-handled knife Ham had plunged into Tabansi's chest. Ham realizes why he felt such coolness from Aericas and the whole family.

"I lied to you," King Ham begins. He slips from his chair to the floor on both knees. "I ask for your forgiveness and from your family, Mariana." There is a long pause and then Ham began again. "I and my men searched for days to find Tabansi. He had been sent on a dangerous mission to scout out a large band of robbers who had been raiding, almost daily, herdsmen outside of Anat, killing families and stealing their herds, plundering their homes and destroying their crops.

We found Tabansi in the cave where your sons also found him. When we arrived he was dead. True, he had been bitten by a snake, but it seemed that he might have been recovering. What killed him was this knife." Ham points to the knife on the table. He puts out his hand close to the knife, but does not touch it. "We found it in his chest." Several of the children gasp and a few begin to softly cry. "In the name of all that is holy, if it takes a lifetime, I will find the man, or men responsible and they will pay dearly. Perhaps the robbers … I could not come to you with such a tale of murder, but hoped that by telling you he died from a snake bite, you would be better comforted. I was wrong to lie to you. I beg your forgiveness." Ham bows his head, on his knees with his hands together in a prayerful mode. Except for the gentle sobbing of some of the children, the room is deathly quiet. Could the family have possibly known that fifteen men were poised to take their lives too, if Ham gives the command?

Finally, Mariana speaks. "Please sit, dear King. It is not fitting that you should kneel before us." Ham sits. "Your story of a snake ending Tabansi's life did not ring true, and so my sons Aericas, Earron and Parahayker were sent to find out the truth. Thank you for your honesty, no matter how much it hurt to hear." She pauses. Mariana looks at her eldest three sons grouped together and they nod their approval to go ahead. "We would like to accept your generous offer of moving to the city and your offer of helping my sons to be trained in the livelihood of their desires. Is this still a reality?"

"Most certainly, Mariana."

"We do not want to be a financial burden to you any longer than necessary."

"It is I who will be forever in your debt, due to the service rendered by your husband. Now, when would you like to move to Anat?"

"Is one week from today too soon?"

"It is done. A week from today wagons shall arrive to take you, your family and your belongings to Anat." Ham's feelings of lust begin once again to flush his face and cause him to breathe in short, hot bursts. He rises to exit, "One week, then." He exits and goes to his horse. He breaths a great sigh of relief.

"Did they believe you, my Lord?" asks Adad.

"They are still alive, are they not?"

"Yes," he grins.

"Besides, what's not to believe? I told them what they wanted to hear mixed with truth too." A plan is unfolding in Ham's mind for the next phase: one guard and two robbers. Ham mounts and they are gone.

Kadenram is talking, the oxen are once again steadily pulling the large wagon, and Nimrod and his friends are once again listening to his stories with a smile on their faces. His stories are a small price to pay for his kindness. Jared, however, has not spoken to Nimrod since the execution of the ten men the night of the battle with the robbers. Jared too, had seen the tent and knew to whom it belonged. His prophet. His priest. His king. Zag, Fenchristo and Rayas are now caught in the crossfire of silence.

"In a few days we will be at Babel. I wish I could stay, but there is nothing there for me to buy or sell: a real armpit." The men smile. "What are your plans when we get there?" he asked.

Silence greets his question.

"I noticed you do not practice your arts of war anymore. Just tired?" No response as the five men stared into the distance. Not hearing. Not caring. Not interested. "I am very sorry about the death of your father, young friend. We had several interesting talks about life. It was he who taught me that part of living is learning to let go."

"And how long do I get to let go? A week, a month, years? Who is keeping score? You?" snaps Nimrod. "How long would it take you to let go if your best friend was murdered, then your father?"

"The ability, as your father taught me, to let go, requires humility. Without humility our trials produce resentment, a kind of acid for the soul. We must have faith that what God wants for us is also best for us. Trials are a form of preparation for the future."

"So God can take more and more from me just to see if I can take it? So I can pass some test He has for me? And for what? What lies at the end of this test? My death? And now my sons and my wife get to play the game too? When does it stop? Or maybe it doesn't stop; it just goes on and on until God tires of our family dying and then He can start on someone else!"

They ride in an awkward silence until dusk, when Kadenram and his sons prepare the oxen for the evening. Dinner is a quiet time this night. Nimrod does not join in for dinner and instead hops off the wagon into the night.

Kadenram tells Nimrod's friends, "I talk too much. But it is not good to walk alone here, especially in the night. There are many hungers hiding in the dark."

Kadenram's oxen and sheep begin to stir about nervously, moaning and bleating. One of his sons runs to him telling him that there is something in the dark scaring the animals. Kadenram lights a few torches, giving some to his sons, the others he mounts on hooks on the wagon. Zag, Jared, Fenchristo and Rayas sense the presence of something too and draw their swords.

As though out of the thin air they are surrounded by a band of robbers on horseback.

"Good evening, Kadenram. We are not here to hurt you or your family. We just want the gold and silver you Jews have collected for your trinkets from the towns around here. And to pay for the murders your friends here have committed against some dear friends of ours."

Jared speaks, "We are not murderers, and Kadenram is not going to give you his honestly earned money. Especially not to the likes of you, too lazy to earn a living."

"Very touching my friend. My name is Berosus. Should I start by killing a few of the children?" Some of his men dismount, hop up on the wagon and take positions around Kadenram's family. The children and wife sink to their knees with much whimpering and crying.

"Berosus, the coward too," hurls Jared. "I have a proposal for you, if you are man enough to accept. Choose fifty of your most gloriously gutless warriors, and we will fight them to the death. If we win, you leave empty-handed, except for the dead fifty men. If you win, you get Kadenram's money. No harm is to come to him or to his family. What say you?"

"Do I have fifty men willing to fight these braggarts to the death?" Berosus loudly asks. Immediately, over one hundred of his men leap from their mounts with swords drawn. They clear an area behind the wagon into which they wait for Jared and friends to jump into.

"Sorry," Berosus smiles, "I couldn't find fifty men. Will one hundred or so do? And yes, you have my word, according to your terms."

Jared stares at two of the men particularly, "I know you, Adad and Puzur. It took you and fifteen others to kill King Cush."

"Liar," shouts Adad. "We were not there that night."

"How did you know it was at night, traitor?"

"We, we heard."

"Be wary of these two, Berosus: they are liars, cowards, traitors and murderers. Hard to find those qualities in just two men. They pretended to be in the hire of King Cush and then turned on him and slaughtered him. And so am I to assume you are here tonight due to information they gave you?"

"That's right. Only because of them. They, however, accuse you of murdering King Cush and killing his guards who were in the service of the patriarch, Noah." Berosus gestures to his men to fall back, leaving Adad and Puzur alone in front of Jared, who has stepped down from the wagon. "But it does present an interesting problem, if Adad, as you say, you were not there then, how do you know these details regarding King Cush and the guards of Noah?"

The two men try to return to the ranks of their comrades but are blocked from doing so by their own men. "If you would turn against Cush, when will you turn against me?"

"Two against one, not your type of odds, Puzur, is it?" asks Jared. He draws his sword and begins to circle toward the two men.

"Berosus," yells Adad, "You can't believe this liar, this murderer!"

"But I do Adad, I do!"

The two men split up and try to get one of them behind Jared. As they do their little dance, Jared charges Adad and with one swift slice of his sword takes off his right arm, his sword dropping to the ground still grasped by his dismembered hand. Adad is left screaming in pain as Jared turns to Puzur, who is now attempting to back away, but is held in by his own army.

"Perhaps there is some honesty among thieves," Jared comments as he puts his sword through the heart of Puzur. As he does the rest of the hundred men move forward toward him and at the same time Zag, Fenchristo and Rayas fire arrows and spears into the closest group of robbers from atop the wagon over and over again while Jared fights two and three men with his sword. Bodies quickly pile up in front of Jared making access to him more difficult for the robbers.

Suddenly Berosus signals his men to stop by use of a loud whistle. They do so, not understanding why. The men turn to see Berosus on his horse, with Nimrod sitting behind him, a knife at his throat. Nimrod dismounts with Berosus and they walk up and onto the wagon. Nimrod motions to the two captains who have been guarding Berosus to come forward as well. Zag and Jared place a knife to each of their throats, and the army of men move back a few steps.

Those men who have been on the wagon are motioned to rejoin their comrades. Zag and Jared, along with Rayas and Fenchristo, tie the three men's hands and feet and then tie the three to each other, making it impossible for any of them to run away. From their feet a rope is looped around their necks and that rope is tied to a foot on Rayas, Fenchristo and Zag. There the three men sit rather uncomfortably in the back center of the massive wagon. They sit there all the way to Babel with several hundred men following at a safe distance on horseback.

When they arrive at the outskirts of Babel, Nimrod notes that not one alarm is sounded regarding this massive force approaching. Not one guard, not one soldier appears to question what is wanted. No wonder, Nimrod thinks, Babel is constantly being attacked and defeated. Those in charge of the city have to be idiots. No sooner had Nimrod and group arrived than a great cloud of dust appears, as if a dust storm might be headed straight for them. At least five hundred more mounted men surrounded their wagon and their leader. The father of Berosus rides up to the wagon.

"My name is Kish, and you have my son captive on your wagon. Let him go before you all die."

Nimrod walks to the front part of the wagon where Kish is and addresses the robber leader. "We will indeed let your son go, but only for a price."

"And that is?"

"We do not desire your money or your weapons. We desire your word of honor."

Several robbers chuckle at this until Kish turns his steely-eyed gaze in their direction.

"My word regarding what?"

"That neither you nor your men will come against Babel, its people, property or acquired property for five years hence. And that Kadenram will be free from robbers or revenge, forever. And no tribute money is to be demanded of him during that time."

"And this is what you desire for freeing my son and his captains?"

"That is all."

There is a great silence while Kish ponders the request.

"Keep my son and do with him as you will." Kish starts to leave.

"Ah, spoken like a true disciple of Ham the great." Kish stops and turns to face Nimrod.

"I am a thief and if given the chance, a pleasurer of women. I am not a murderer, especially of those of my own family." Pause. "I will consent to your requests providing you do not come upon me for that same period of five years."

"So it is said, so it is done," responds Nimrod. He walks to the edge of the wagon and holds out his hand. Kish rides up to him and clasps his hand and arm in Nimrod's.

"So it is said, so it is done." With that several robbers jump up on the wagon and free Berosus and his two captains.

Nimrod holds out his hand to Berosus, "Friends?"

"Not yet," smiles Berosus, "perhaps someday soon." With that the three men mount their horses and are out of sight in a matter of minutes. Nimrod and friends bid good-bye to Kadenram and family with their many thanks for helping spare their lives and money. Slowly the great wagon makes its way farther south.

Nimrod then turns his physical and mental attention to Babel, the armpit of life, where just now two half-dressed soldiers are making their way toward him. "Take me to your leader," Nimrod barks at them. The soldiers cower and bid him follow them. Through filthy, littered streets the party of five with their horses follow the two soldiers, noting the dirty condition in the streets from refuse, mainly animal and human waste.

"The armpit is about right," exclaimed Rayas, "only my armpits are cleaner. This is more like the crotch pit." Sand fills the doorways of most houses and shops with some residents shoveling the sand and stuff into the already overflowing streets. At least their shoveling of sand covers some of the stench of the other refuse. One could tell many of the people are unhappy with the dirty conditions, but also unable to solve the problem. Here and there some residents have set up a table and chairs, beds and cooking apparatus on the roof of their homes to combat the rising flood of trash in the streets.

The soldiers finally lead the group of five to a small one-level building that the two men said is the office of the garrison commander. Nimrod observes to himself that the commandant had positioned himself far enough away from the city entrance so as to keep himself from harm's way. The same conditions of cleanliness are evident as those on the way to his office, only worse. He lives in a pigsty. Even Nimrod's horse and the horses of the other four men keep snorting like they are trying to get the stench out of their nostrils.

Fenchristo asks the two soldiers," Where do the other soldiers sleep? This place is very small."

The two soldiers, Tyjeffiry and Cyrus, both enthusiastically respond, "We both sleep with the commander."

"But there can't be but one bedroom in this place."

Both are grinning, "Yes, just one. We sleep with the commander."

Finally getting an understanding of what they mean, Fenchristo groans, "But where does the rest of your army sleep?"

Cyrus responds, "In their own houses. If we need them, we just ring the bell." He points out a bell hanging outside the office door.

"And how many soldiers are there?"

Tyjeffiry interjects, "About sixty. We have four garrisons – north, south, east and west, each with about sixty men. We never need all of them at one time."

Nimrod has grown weary of this irritating conversation. "Where is your garrison commander now?"

Cyrus smiles. "This is his day to be home and service his wife and play with his children, eleven of them. The rest of the time he's ours," he grins proudly.

"Take us to his home." The two soldiers dutifully comply with his order. They commence down yet another dirty street only they are now forced to proceed single-file through the trash, sand and refuse. They stop in front of a humble home with kids screaming and crawling about like ants.

Cyrus addresses one of the teenage children as he flies by, chasing a naked younger brother carrying a bowl of food, "Where is your father?"

The teenager responds. "He's around the corner, taking care of business."

"Business?"

"You know, his other family." And with that he is off and running after the naked brother.

"I had almost forgotten. He has two families." So off they go, filing down another street and they find another humble home overflowing with life.

Tyjeffiry asks three children playing with a pet snake, "Where is your father, young people?"

They all point into the house as they continue their play. Cyrus taps on the door frame and announces their presence, "You-who! Commander Kiwayneid, it's Cyrus and Tyjeffiry."

A booming, blustering voice comes from somewhere in the bowels of the house, "I told you never to bother me at home! How did you find this house?" He stumbles half-naked to the door.

This long, skinny beanpole of a man comes to the door with his underpants disheveled, his balding head loosely covered with straight-stringy graying hair. His wife, possibly, is a pudgy middle-aged pregnant woman who can be seen peeking around the corner, putting on her clothes and shushing the children away from Kiwayneid. Their house is pitifully bare of furniture.

Commander Kiwayneid sees Nimrod and his friends, "Oh, well, look, I don't have the money here. Can you tell Kish I'll bring it to him tomorrow at my office? And why are you hunting me down at home? I always pay you on time."

Jared blurts out, "Kish, the benevolent, said you could use some good soldiers, and we should talk to you about trying out for your elite forces. You are the courageous Kiwayneid, are you not?"

"Kish told you that? Well, yes, I'm Kiwayneid. Tryouts? You got two arms and two legs? That's my tryout!" He laughs to himself and is joined by Cyrus and Tyjeffiry. "Actually, next week we have the competitions we hold every month or so for new recruits. Not too many show up, but all four garrison commanders will be there, and we divide any new recruits among the four of us."

Fenchristo, "We don't divide up."

"Well, you see, we have to keep the garrisons about the same size, and uh, five of you to one garrison kinda isn't fair. Right? You understand?" Kiwayneid is getting intimidated by the serious presence of the five men.

Nimrod asks, "I'm curious, Kiwayneid, Say Kish attacks your garrison with seven hundred of his men. What do you do?"

"Ah, well, I send one of my fastest runners like Cyrus or Tyjeffiry here"- - the five men look at the pudgy out-of-shape soldiers - - "to each of the other garrisons to send help."

"And how long does that take?" Fenchristo asks, "An hour, a day, two?" The five men chuckle slightly.

"Meanwhile," Nimrod asks, "what does Kish do? Does he wait for the other garrisons to arrive before attacking?"

"Well actually I don't know. He's never really attacked Babel. At least not at this gate. We are such a large city, ten to maybe twenty-thousand people, and growing all the time. We are a very prosperous city, a real thriving community with a well-trained army that, uh …"

Jared, "Yes, we see the prosperous, thriving people, and the well-trained," looking at Cyrus and Tyjeffiry, "army. So why then do you pay a tribute each month?"

Kiwayneid, "Each week. We pay him not to attack us, each week."

"So why doesn't your well-trained army just kill him and be done with paying this tribute?" asks Jared.

"Yeah, and why is your office so far from the edge of the city and not near where the fighting would be?" asks Fenchristo.

"And where are the lookouts who look out, you know, for trouble?" quizzes Rayas.

Kiwayneid has no answer for their questions. The answer is rather obvious: the leaders are cowards and the soldiers are soldiers in name only. They have not been trained to defend. To kill. To die. The group of five leave the commander, his families, and his two personal soldiers and travel slowly, single file through the streets of Babel. Dirt. Filth. Beaten down people. Street after street after street.

At one point Nimrod stops and asked an elderly woman who is sweeping and shoveling sand and refuse from her doorstep, "Excuse me, where would new families go to live?"

"Anywhere but Babel, young man. We have no army to defend us, no leadership to solve problems. Go while you can. Go before the weekly collection is due. That's this city's solution to everything. Tax, tax, tax. The government takes from the rich and takes more from the poor and gives to themselves. And what do we get? Crap, sand and more crap. The city should change the name from Babel to Bowel. She returns to her cleaning and the five men move on.

Zag, "Not good Nimrod. Not good."

"True Zag, it is not good. But did you notice there are two rivers – one right here on the east side of Babel and another river to the west, slightly farther away? You see that high ground to the north? That would be a great place to watch for enemies, a great place for a temple, or ziggurat, palace and a garrison. Did you notice the people living on their roof tops? The sand and garbage are filling the streets and houses. They simply need to build a second story in which to live, and an army that we can train."

"Guess we're staying in Bowel" comments Rayas. "It has everything we don't need to be successful."

The group travels on in silence until dusk. They camp outside of town on the northern high ground. Nimrod comments, "This place needs water from the river for trees and gardens. There must be people here willing to work; people who want a better life for them and their families."

Jared, "I did notice a brick factory on one street. It looked like they were quite busy. But why?"

"Tomorrow I need you, all of you, to help me build a sweat tent," asks Nimrod. "We will need rocks, water, cloth for the tent, and young sapling trees to hold the tent's shape. I must think. I must prepare for the military tryouts, for our new life here in Babel. Do not let me hear you call it Bowel again – please, my friends – no more."

Chapter Four

The group is up early and started collecting the items Nimrod had asked for. The trees are a good distance away, so Zag offers to ride to the woods for the saplings. Fenchristo and Rayas gather the rocks and then travel into town to find something to carry water in. Jared, too, returns to Babel and thinks of stopping at the brick factory to ask where he could find a tent maker. Nimrod stays in camp and prepares the ground for the sweat tent.

Jared arrives around mid-morning at the brick factory and is amazed at the millions and millions of stacked bricks everywhere. They are of various sizes from enormous that would take ten men or more to move, to regular bricks for homes or streets. "Why so many bricks my friend?" asks Jared of a middle-aged man mixing clay and straw and a black mixture he does not recognize. "I am Taydalor. Years ago the elders decided to build a ziggurat and commissioned our shop to produce the bricks. As you see we have the bricks, but no one has come to build the ziggurat, the Tower of Babel."

"Forgive me my ignorance, Taydalor, what is a ziggurat?"

"You do not know what a ziggurat is?" exclaimed Taydalor incredulously.

"You mock me, Taydalor."

"Oh no sir, please, I do not mock. I thought everyone ... never mind. It is a tower where- upon men may go to pray to the unseen, unknown God. To get as close as one may so our prayers may be better heard."

"And you believe that this unseen, unknown God will only hear your prayers if you are on a high tower?"

"Now it is you who mocks."

"No, Taydalor, I only seek to understand your ways. I, and my friends, are from the North Country and have traveled many days to Babel. In fact, I would be beholding to you if you could direct me to a tent maker here in Babel. A good one."

"There are several, my friend …"

"Jared is my name."

"Jared. The best is three intersections down this street, four intersections to the right and his building is on the corner. Omar is his name."

"My deepest thanks, Taydalor. We'll talk again regarding your unseen God."

"My pleasure young Jared, my pleasure."

"Omar the tent maker, unusual." Jared mounted his horse and followed Taydalor's instructions right to Omar's building. As Jared walks inside he is forced to step over and around many bolts of material, when he sees an elderly man stitching fabric quickly and effortlessly.

"Omar, my name is Jared. Taydalor the brick maker sent me to you. He said you are the best in Babel." As Omar turns in Jared's direction, Jared sees the man is blind and has a large grin on his face.

"Taydalor sent you?" I must go and see him and thank him for his kindness. What is it you need?"

Jared explains what he needs the material for and the dimensions. Omar seems familiar with a sweat tent.

"Yes, I can do that. How soon do you need it?"

Jared explains the immediate need and so forth and asks what would be the soonest Omar could have it ready.

"It sounds like your friend Nimrod is a man of God. That is good. There doesn't seem to be many of us left in the world. I will have it ready for you this time tomorrow. I will work through the night …"

"I would not have you work all night, Omar …"

"Tsk, tsk, my young friend. For a man of God I will gladly give up a few hours sleep. Business is not very good, and so I am happy to have the work."

They agree on a price and Jared leaves, notating mentally how to return for the tent. He cannot bring himself to tell Omar that this man of God is a lost one at the moment. Since the tent would not be ready until midday tomorrow, Jared rides around his new town of Babel. There are quite a few shops, most look unused for some time. There is one that had some interesting meat hanging in the open window, so Jared stops to find out what the man is selling.

"Greetings, young visitor, I am Sarsous, King of Jerk. Jerk, I call it. Jerk meat. I put it in a slow-cooking pot until all the juice is gone, hang it for several weeks, and then it will last for weeks, months, perhaps years. Problem is, everyone who buys it eats it right away and so I do not know if it really will last for years. It is excellent for long trips, perhaps even for soldiers. Not our soldiers, but real ones! It's light ..."

Jared stops the Jerk man, who obviously does not get many visitors. "What animals do you use for this Jerk?"

"Any animal you bring me: sheep, goats, chickens, oxen, cats, dogs, mice." He laughs aloud. "Just kidding about the mice. They are so small ..."

"May I have a small taste of the chicken?"

"Well, I don't normally give my meat away for free. But I guess ..."

"I will pay you, Sarsous. I do not seek something for nothing."

"In that case, cried Sarsous exuberantly, "try them all!"

Jared then takes a piece of each meat and pays for an additional large piece of each meat for his friends.

"God bless you, my boy. God bless you. This is more than I have made all week. Do come again."

Jared chews happily on each piece of meat, happy he did not have to chew mouse meat. Seeing the mice along the streets and what they are consuming makes him shiver, "Mouse meat, ugh." The cat and dog jerk meat are more tasty than he expected, though he much preferred the chicken and sheep meat. The Jerk man told him he would gladly jerk any animal he brought to him, and his price would be to keep a portion of each animal for himself. He would also do the killing and bleeding, etc. Jared finds a shop with a few vegetables and then heads for home, so to speak. That is, the high ground.

Nimrod places a ring of large boulders that would hold down the sweat tent. Large boulders, as anyone familiar with the desert knows, are required because of the wind and dust storms that seemingly come out of nowhere. Zag had been back for a few minutes and is helping Nimrod bend and tie the saplings in place. The sweat tent would be just tall enough for an average-sized man to enter crouched over and then sit for the duration. A ring of smaller stones is at the center of the tent where the fire would heat the rocks that are already stacked over the fire pit. Water in gourds have been brought back by Rayas and Fenchristo to pour over the rocks once they were hot and glowing, producing the steam for the sweat. All that would be needed is the actual tent material, and Jared informs Nimrod that the material would be ready tomorrow afternoon.

For dinner, Jared roasts the vegetables and surprises the men with his jerk meat. He tells them some of the meat is mouse meat and it sits there uneaten. He finally has pity on them and informs them that it is really cat meat. It goes down rather quickly after that with a few worried eyes watching Jared eat his, first. Nimrod shares with the group some of his ideas to make Babel a town people would want to move to. He speaks of having orchards and gardens that would be fed by canals from the river. Slowly the others begin to share his vision of the future. Slowly.

Jared lays there for the longest time, staring at the beauty of the stars and thinking of bringing his brother and families, his elderly mom and dad and brothers and sisters to Babel. Maybe after Nimrod's dreams become a reality, but now? It is all he can do to want to stay and support Nimrod. They are still distant in their conversations since the killing of the ten men and finding out they had almost killed the prophet Noah and his family. Then there was Cush's death.

The prophet had escaped due to a vision he had only moments prior to Cush's attack on his camp. An attack not orchestrated by Cush, but by his father, Ham. Had Ham really been behind the murder of his own son Lugal and the stealing of the birthright garments of Adam? Where are those garments and … His thoughts give way to sleep and to dreaming of his girlfriend, waiting for him. Two years …

Jared picks up and pays for the tent material. When he arrives at camp, all five men hasten to work on fitting the material to the saplings, moving the large boulders and placing them on top of the extra length of material around the tent's base. Most of the rest of the day is spent in the sweat part of preparation. The fire inside is lit, the rocks put in place and a chimney added for the smoke to exit. The gourds of water are placed near where Nimrod would sit and extra firewood is placed neatly in a pile so Nimrod would not have to move once he is in place.

The four men eat dinner and Nimrod prepares himself to enter the sweat tent. "Thank you, my friends, thanks for coming, for staying with me, for … thanks." And he enters the tent not to be seen, we think, for twenty-four hours: no food, no water for those twenty-four hours. The next evening comes and goes, twenty-four more hours. Then the third day. Toward evening, seventy-two hours after entering, the tent flap opens and out steps the stringiest, dripping wet, radiant man any of us have ever seen.

Little did any of us know that the radiance experienced by Nimrod did not come from God, the Eternal Father? Rather, it came from the god of this world, and the visions Nimrod had experienced of a new religion based on the worship of fire. We would find out much later that sacrifice, much like Christians must do, accompanies his new religion.

With military tryouts but a couple of days away, the group wants to hone their skills. While the sun is still asleep the following day, the men are awakened by a severe dust storm, and so they all head for the sweat tent to keep from having their faces and body parts sandblasted. The heat has long since dissipated, so by moving the rocks and gourds of water, the five men are able to fit tightly away from the storm.

The storm lasts for two days. Upon trying to emerge from the tent, they find their tent covered with sand. After considerable effort of digging with knives, gourds and bare hands, they are able to stand outside the tent and then crawl to the top of the sand. The only thing that allowed them to survive in such a closed area was the small hollow tree limb that they had used for ventilation in the sweat tent. The limb was originally two to three feet above the tent and now sticks out a mere few inches.

The tent is full of sand from digging. In the days that follow they would unload the tent of its sand, clear off the top of the tent and then move the tent to the top of the new sand level. The next storm may remove all this sand or add to it; it remains to be seen what nature had in store for Babel. For now, they need to find their horses and prepare for the tryouts tomorrow. While Nimrod still seems more mentally aware, the physical glow he had obtained in the three days has lessened. Upon finding their horses and entering town to obtain a few morsels of food, they find the prices of food have gone higher than the sand: supply and demand. On the way into town they notice many of the small trees cultivated by citizens are completely devoid of leaves. Devoid of fruit. Devoid of life. Welcome, young men, to the cycle of life in Babel.

It seems that everything revolves around the weather. While weather is important in most of the world, blowing sand is more of a real life-changer here. Stopper. Annihilator. The seasons of the year come and pass not like summer, fall, winter and spring, but by the day, hour or even minutes. And so food too comes and passes accordingly. Again, supply and demand.

Nimrod does not seem to be concerned with food. His sweat tent experience had changed him. He doesn't just seem more focused - - he is more focused and mentally thinks more quickly. Even his eyes gleam more intensely. Any fat he had lingering on his frame is gone. Stream-lined. He already had been a lean, mean, fighting machine, but now he oozes the lean, and the mean. He has shaved his hair on the sides of his head leaving just a tuft of hair in the center of his head from front to rear, making his angular head and jutting jaw even more pronounced. Fearsome. Warlike. The sky is clear and the air crisp in the early morning of the tryouts. The five are dressed in loincloths and sandals that lace partway up their calves. The four other men spend some of the early morning time shaving their heads to match Nimrod's. The effect on the other men gathered for the tryouts is impressive.

Some of the others are dressed like they are going to another day at work with robes that tie at the waist, hair that hangs in their faces, and few, if any, weapons.

The commanders each give speeches about serving their city and families, being the first line of defense, blah, blah, blah. Finally the agenda for the day is given. Each candidate would run around the perimeter of the city eight times, going up through the cliffs to the north, blah, blah, blah, blah. Nimrod and men put their weapons and other personal affects, with those of the fifty some other men, under the watchful eye of Tyjefferi, who grins at Nimrod as though he is his new, best friend, if you get my meaning.

While some of the candidates regard the run as a race, Nimrod and group know it is more a matter of finishing, with the fastest being top candidates as runners. To some, being a runner is important, as they are sent on various errands, secret missions for the garrison commanders and the elders of the city. In a real army you would be the first to enter a battle or a city and wreak havoc and devastation with your sudden arrival and unleashing of knives at army or city leaders. Many runners never come back, as they are caught, tortured and murdered before the bulk of the army can catch up with them. And they are off!

First time around the city the fifty or so men are in a fairly tight group, each feeling their way in deciding which part of the course is the difficult section for them personally. Going through the cliffs is mentally nerve-wrecking because the path runs along the edge that drops off some forty feet to a rocky bottom. While it didn't look like certain death if you fall, it would tear you up seriously and even more importantly, leave you out of the competition for quite a few months to come.

The line of candidates start to stretch out by the third trip around the town. A few that are wearing robes discard them and race a-la-nude. Interesting sight to see. Nimrod notices the number of young females increase significantly along the route after that. By the sixth trip only eight men are together at the front, with Nimrod and Jared among the eight. Fenchristo and Rayas are more to the end of the middle, and Zag is closer to the end group. In fact, he and another man are the end group.

There is one very large and well-muscled man who is almost dead last, yet still running with a young boy constantly by his side. He is struggling to keep his large-framed body ahead of Zag and laboring to even keep his body moving forward with but two laps to go. His young friend or brother, keeps urging him to stop so he won't hurt himself, but to no avail. Onward he trudges, slowly, painfully.

Nimrod remembers seeing the two of them at the beginning, but had paid them no mind. He did remember the younger boy helping the other tie his sandals and saying, "Puli, you shouldn't be pushing yourself so hard. What if you fall again and injure your head?" Nimrod now reflects on this man's perseverance and how he would love to have an army of men with this kind of determination. Nimrod smiled and realizes now why the large man spoke with slurred and stuttering speech. "Eyem dokay, Jessem. Eyem dokay." ("I am doing okay, Jessem, I'm doing okay.") A head injury. Still, Nimrod thinks, what a great asset his attitude could be.

Nimrod is on the cliff part of the run when one well-built, lithe man purposefully uses his hip and shoulder to bump Nimrod off the cliff. Nimrod stumbles and falls to his left off the edge. Desperately he seeks something to grab. A sharp, outcropping piece of rock stops his fall and is cutting his hand to pieces. His body is hanging in mid-air forty feet from the craggy bottom.

Fenchristo and Rayas have, unbeknownst to them, passed him at the same time that Jared hears his cry for help. Jared tries to get another competitor to stop and help Nimrod, but he waves his hand as though he could not be bothered. Jared leans over the cliff and tried to reach Nimrod. He scoots his body over as far as he can without falling himself. "Would what happened with my killing the guards affect Jared's desire to help?" thought Nimrod. Jared scoots even further and it is then he feels Nimrod's wrist. He clasped one wrist and uses his other hand to keep himself from falling.

He has himself in a stalemate. He has Nimrod by the wrist, balancing himself with his other hand but is physically unable to pull Nimrod's dead weight up even a few inches. It would just be a matter of a few minutes before either he or Nimrod would lose their strength to hold on. "Leave me, Jared, it's no use. Let go before you lose your balance and fall too. The fall will not kill me. Please."

"I can't, Nimrod. Please don't ask me to quit." Jared reaches over with his other hand to grasp Nimrod and his body slips a few more inches. Suddenly, someone has a hold of Jared's legs and is pulling him back away from the edge, and Nimrod too.

"Yhld on tite. I hlp." ("You hold on tight. I help.") Puli-ilu pulls with his mighty strength until Jared is safe, and then grasps Nimrod by his wrists above Jared's hands and literally pulls Nimrod straight up in the air. He steps back with Nimrod's feet still a good six inches off the ground. Puli-ilu steps back one more step and lets Nimrod gently back down on the ground.

Nimrod goes to Jared, "I owe you, my friend. Forgive me, please."

"So it is said, so it is done." They hug and then both turn to Puli-ilu to give him a gigantic group hug.

Nimrod, "Thank you. Thank you for my life." He and Jared hug him again and with that Puli-ilu lets out a big scream, and the two men step back unsure of what just happened.

Jessem explains, "This is Puli's way of releasing emotions when he is so full of them. He is very happy."

Nimrod looks at Puli-ilu and grabs his hand, "Let's finish the race together." By this time Zag has caught up, and so this group of five slowly jog around the course and finish together. When they come to get their belongings from smiley Tyjeffiry, Zag sees the competitor who nudged Nimrod, as the man seeks to sneak out of sight. Zag stares at him, "I not forget."

"Yeah, right, another retard," and the 'nudger' jogs away to catch up with a couple of his friends who are not happy with what he did. "C'mon guys, it was an accident. The jerk was trying to push me out of his way." They went on to the hand-to-hand competition after putting their weapons on their bodies. They take a sip of water and chew a piece of jerk cat. Meow.

At the end of the day it is obvious that the five men are at the top of this month's class. Cheers for them go up each time one of them bests another competitor, especially when the 'nudger' competitor loses. The cheering is loudest from that man's friends, against him. When it comes time for Puli-ilu to face the target for knife throwing, Jared runs over to him and gives him a quick lesson. Each man would all throw at a target painted on a bale of hay. After Puli throws the first of his six knives, all the competitors slowly moved farther away from the target. Puli misses the target, misses the wall behind the target, and to this day, the knife has not been found.

It was heart-warming and sad at the same time. This hulk of kindness would use every fiber of his great girth to attain success in everything he did. However, due to his fall as a youth, his brain and his motor skills, large and small, did not accord him any measure of success. None. Success, or more correctly the lack of success, in this manner did not deter him from trying. Consistently trying. Year after year after …

Puli-ilu attempted to qualify for the military and year after year, we would say he failed. He would say he was successful. He tried, he competed, and some years he even did better. But that isn't why he tried. That isn't why he tries. That isn't why he will try again and again next year and the year after that and … You get it. In almost all other parts of his life people recorded the results of Puli-ilu's efforts and measured them compared to others. By those standards – he was a failure. No one would hire him, or if they did he was fired the next day. He was labeled: retard, incompetent, stupid, slow beyond slow, a nothing, a waste of space, of food. Why didn't his parents just suffocate him as a youth and put us out of our misery? He made others feel awkward, uncomfortable. He slobbered when he ate, he spilled his drinks, and even wet himself on occasion when he got excited.

He would obviously never marry, never reproduce (thank God), never be useful to anyone for anything. Why in the world doesn't God release mankind of this embarrassing glob of flesh? This kind, thoughtful, loving-without-condition, never holding a grudge, low-maintenance-son-of-God piece of crap. Nimrod now owes his life to this paradox. Jared too, somewhat. Puli-ilu's family loves him, particularly his little brother, Jessem. So, when Puli lines up for his second throw, Nimrod applauds him and everyone else follows, albeit gently.

Puli-ilu is embarrassed, "Iknwgd," ("I no good")

Zag stands by him, "Yes, you good." Zag grabs his arm and shows him how to hold the knife, how to cock his arm and how to release the knife. Puli tries to follow Zag's instructions and this time he hits the wall behind the target. A cheer erupts from all present, except 'Mr. Warmth' the 'nudger' competitor who snickers loudly and shakes his head. His friends move away from him lest others think they agree with him. Puli-ilu hides his head in his hands in happy embarrassment. A couple of men slap him on his back. Puli readies another knife, trembling in anxious anticipation. This time the knife joins its brother far, far away on Shinar's plain. A collective "uhhhh" is emitted, followed by several, "You can do it, Puli," or "Don't give up" and "Keep your elbow in." A hush comes over the group and sweat beads appear on Puli-ilu's brow.

"Relax!" bellows Zag, scaring Puli by the force of his voice. Puli-ilu looks around with a wild look in his eyes. Zag feels like an idiot and repeats softly, "Relax Puli." Almost with his eyes closed and acting quickly he throws the knife. Silence, followed by the biggest roar ever recorded by mankind, Puli hits the target and the knife sticks, quivering like a newborn calf. Men yell and dance with each other. Even the garrison commanders are acting like little kids with Tyjeffiri and Kiwayneid dancing with each other. Jessem runs up to his big brother, and with tears streaming down his little face, hugs his brother. Several men grab this gentle giant and hoist him upon their shoulders and walk around as though he had just won the world's knife-throwing contest.

So, the question is, is this handicapped man really worthless? Why did grown, normal men cheer, laugh and cry over such a small success for a worthless idiot such as Puli-ilu of Babel? Puli did not take his last knife throw that day. He did not compete in spear-throwing, bow and arrow, sling shot or swordplay. Puli-ilu did not qualify for the military either. By all standards, he had failed again. But when he went home, he was carried and escorted by fifty-three men shouting and cheering his name. His little brother cried all the way home and over the next several months told and retold Puli-ilu of Babel's story to anyone who would listen. To everyone. And they all smiled a warm smile. Why?

The next morning a body is found at the bottom of the cliffs where Nimrod clung for his very life: the 'nudger' competitor. Yes, the same man who pushed, shoved and nudged Nimrod off the cliff to an almost certain maiming, possible death. The 'nudger' fell, yes, but when was his neck slit from ear to ear? His family could be seen loading his wolf-ripped body onto a wagon, wife and children, parents, as well as a couple of dogs, all mourning the death of a win-at-all-costs, dead-at-no-costs man. How then should we judge success and failure? And the win-at-all-costs some employ to get to the top, or the bottom, as the case may be?

Nimrod and his four friends are assigned to Kiwayneid's garrison. Forty-five of the other men are assigned among the other three garrisons. The remaining ten are recommended to try again in a few months, and to keep their clothes on. News of the five new men added to Babel's army spreads among the citizens of Babel, but most importantly, among the elders. One of the first things that happens in Kiwayneid's garrison is a new training program for his near-sixty men. Nimrod is asked to be in charge of the training, and after one week all four garrisons are assigned to Nimrod's training program. With just fewer than three hundred men in attendance, Nimrod and his group follow the same procedure as in Mahora. It is in the middle of the second month of this training that Nimrod receives some interesting visitors, one in particular.

The group of five have moved from the cramped sweat tent to a vacant house near the southern garrison headquarters. Haircuts mimicking the five are on the rise. In the early morning of the day the visitors appear, the five men are finishing breakfast prepared by their hired woman cook. Nimrod is the first to hear the sounds of many horses approaching the house. Fearing they are being besieged by an enemy, he and his four friends put their hands on their weapons as several warriors enter the house and put all five in a submissive position with swords and knives to their throats. While in this position a familiar figure enters the door. "My dear grandson," announces Ham, "this is not a very friendly greeting on your part." "Pardon, Grandfather," as the five release their grips on their various weapons. Ham's guards do not.

"The stories that come to me way up north are very intriguing. Way up in the mountains, families preparing to move to be near their sons, friends packing to find a better future, warriors wanting permission to follow some strange fellow in Babel."

"Grandfather, I assure you we are not recruiting people to desert you to follow us. I do swear."

"I believe you, Nimrod. I believe simply that the telling of your stories of success to your families is all that you are guilty of, and I hold no animosity toward you or your friends. I have really come to bring you items your father would have wanted you to have. I know because he told me so weeks before he died. I'm sure your mom agrees." Ham nods to his guards and two of them exit. The others put their weapons away. Four men return carrying two large chests and place them on the floor. Ham continues, "Many of these items are your dad's personal weapons, shields and the like." Addressing the four other men, "Would you mind if Nimrod and I talk privately?" His guards leave, but not Nimrod's four men. "Privately?" repeats Ham.

"You mean us?' questions Rayas. "We have no secrets, Lord Ham."

"Is Semiramis a virgin?"

"Ah, well, I don't …"

"Precisely, now leave." The four men exit outside.

"Sorry to be so abrupt."

Nimrod smiles, "They'll live."

"In one of those chests is a bundle of clothing tied together with some heavy string. I don't know how to say this, so I'll just say it. Cush stole this clothing from your great grandfather, Noah. There isn't any good way to give the package back without Noah thinking I stole it or, now, you. I suggest you just tuck it away for now and perhaps later you'll feel inspired as to how to deal with the clothes."

"My father stole these clothes from my great grandfather Noah?"

"I'm afraid so. For months he had been obsessed with his 'birthright', as he called it. And he would ask why didn't I want my birthright? Then, after the conference, all mention of his birthright ceased. I thought it a bit unusual but gave it no more thought. That is, until I came to see Cush, at his request. There, in his home, all alone, he sat in Adam's garments.

He asked me, "You like, Father?"

"A bit rustic, my son," I answered," but if you're happy … Cush ran out of the room and came back, followed by a servant dragging two sheep. Cush sat in a corner away from the sheep and commanded the servant to tie the sheep to the heavy table and then the servant left. At first, the sheep bleated and tried to leave. Then, your father got up and walked slowly toward the animals. They suddenly stopped their frantic movement and sounds. They just stood there. Then, the closer Cush got to them, the more submissive they became, lowering their heads and backing away from him. As Cush got closer, both sheep knelt down on all fours and finally lay down with their heads on the floor. They remained that way until your father left the room. When he came back without the garment, the sheep stood up bleating and again tried to leave. Cush untied them and they ran out. Supposedly, these actions had something to do with the Garden of Eden, Adam and Eve and who knows what other wives' tales. Guess that's about it."

Nimrod stares at Ham and after a long pause speaks, "You're telling me that my father, who hated conflict, devised this plan to steal these garments?"

"Yes."

"It sounds more like something you would do rather than my father."

Ham's face contorts and his icy stare examines Nimrod. "By your father's own admission." There is a long pause in which Ham contemplates killing his grandson.

"Which means he arranged for a man to scale the mountain wall, slit the tent, steal the garments and, (pause), kill Lugal, his own brother, and Lugal's servant." Ham looks very uncomfortable.

"Yes," Ham utters softly, "That is what I am telling you."

Nimrod is visibly shaken and almost yells, "And you did not immediately kill your coward of a son?" Nimrod is face to face with Ham. He falls to his knees in front of his grandfather. "My god, my god, my father killed my best friend, your son, and you did nothing?" Nimrod sits in a heap of the floor.

Ham reaches down and almost touches his head, "I only found out this information two nights before the war with the robbers. That is why I had him killed. Guess that's about it. How are things in Babel?"

The shift in conversation confuses Nimrod, "Ah, okay, I guess."

"If you do half the job here that you did in Mahora, Babel has found a great leader. Like I say, "If you work at it hard it's easy and if you work at it easy, it's hard." Ham exits, gathers his guards and rides off.

Chapter Five

The four men reenter their home and pass by the chests and sit. They are all quiet until Rayas speaks up, "So, Nimrod, is Semiramis …" Zag takes his fist and hits him on top of his head, "Not your business."

"Yes, Rayas, she is a virgin. Can you imagine any man taking advantage of her?" Nimrod is still in shock over the revelations regarding his dad as told by Ham.

"Or saying no to her!" Rayas responds' laughing at his own humor, but joined in by none. Changing the subject Rayas asks, "What's in the chests?"

"My father's weapons and personal items as well." Would you be so kind as to help take them to my room?" He gets up and stares out the door.

"But your room is the only one upstairs and they look very heavy," comments Rayas. "And why did you build a room upstairs? Expecting a lot of rain, Noah?" Again laughing at his own humor, again alone.

"Rayas!" yells Zag. Rayas grabs the handle on one end of the smaller chest with one hand, expecting to be able to move it rather easily. He cannot even budge the chest. He uses both hands and the chest barely comes up off the floor. Zag grabs the other end with one hand and easily lifts the chest a foot up in the air.

"Oh, right, you get the lighter end. Not fair, Zag."

Zag crosses to the other end of the chest and thumps Rayas on the head, "Move." Rayas scoots to the other end as Zag struggles with one hand and the chest does not move. He then uses two hands and barely is able to lift the chest.

"See! I told you. I had the heavy end." Rayas lifts his end with both hands with the chest barely clearing the ground. Zag uses one hand and lefts the chest a foot in the air.

"Joke," Zag grins. The other men are rolling with laughter, at Rayas's expense.

"Not funny, Zag. You hurt Rayas's feelings." Zag taps him on the head again with his fist.

"Lift, funny man." They lift and move the chest barely a foot before Rayas has to stop. They finally get to the stairs and disappear from sight, one step at a time.

"Not so fast, Zag, I think the weight shifted to my end. We hear a fist hitting a head. "Ouch, all right, I'm lifting." A few more grunts and groans and scraping sounds on the steps are heard. "I think ..." Rayas does not finish as we hear another fist hit a head. "Ahhh, no more, Zag. Geez, I think I'm getting shorter."

A man appears at the door, obviously a soldier and out of breathe: "Captain Nimrod, there's a group of men at the city gate demanding tribute. They said Kish sent them."

Nimrod, Jared and Fenchristo are out the door in a flash and onto their horses. To the soldier Nimrod asks, "Where is your horse?"

"I don't have one. I ran."

Nimrod to Jared, "Remind me to get horses for the guards at the gate." They ride off to the gate to find ten men waiting impatiently.

We hear a thud in the hallway with Zag exiting the house followed by a cry from Rayas, "Zag! My foot, you can't leave me here like this. Zag! I think my foot may be broken!" Zag crosses back to the unseen Rayas and we hear sounds of him dragging Rayas down the steps with a loud thud each time the chest drops another step, with Rayas moaning on each thud.

Zag appears dragging Rayas, who is limping with every step to get to his horse. The other three have left. "All you had to do was lift the chest, Zag. Now I am going to have to lift the chest up the stairs, again, this time with a broken foot, some damaged ribs and a sore head."

Zag goes to hit Rayas on the head with his fist and Rayas moves rather quickly out of the way, with no limp. "Wow, looks like my foot is healed," Rayas says as he grins and runs out the door.

"Payback, Rayas, payback."

"It's about time. Do you have the tribute? And what's with the funny haircut?" His friends and he chuckle. "Kish is not happy with you. You should have had the tribute ready weeks ago."

Nimrod dismounts, "Hmmm, weeks ago you say. How often do you collect this tribute? he asks with a slight, edgy smile. I'm new here."

"I don't know. What difference does it make, dimwit?"

"How am I supposed to have the tribute ready if I do not know when you want it ready? Besides, last time I talked with Kish, we had five years before the next tribute would be due."

"Five years? Liar."

Nimrod's smile fades and the cold look of an offended man takes its place. "Funny hairdo, and now I am a liar. You just don't know when to stop, do you, idiot?" Zag and Rayas appear. The ten men bristle with this insult. Nimrod dismounts as do his four friends. Soldiers and civilians are slowly gathering to watch. Nimrod is still simmering with frustration from his talk with Ham and is in no mood for this obvious liar and pretender: a man trying to make a quick, dirty, deceitful gain in the name of an honest, deceitful thief.

"If you want your tribute, cowards, come and get it." With that all ten men are off their horses with swords unsheathed.

"Hardly looks like a fair fight Nimrod," Jared comments as he slides off his horse with his sword unsheathed.

"True, but that's all the men they have so it will have to do,' replies Nimrod with a wry, tight-lipped smile. "Sit this one out, Jared, please." The ten men come at Nimrod in three rows of three behind their leader. In one quick movement the leader dies in the street and the first three men behind him are bleeding and dying from wounds in their chests and necks. Nimrod's sword snaps as it strikes the next robber's sword and all the men stop for a second.

"Gee, guys, guess I'm defenseless," Nimrod notes. As they grin and advance on him, outcome the leg and arm knives and, unlike Puli-ilu, Nimrod's knives find the throats of their victims, right-handed and then left-handed. Then, right and left together. Now, there are but two robbers left and they are not feeling very brave. They start to back away. Jared tosses Nimrod his own sword, "Which of you would like to live and tell your dirt-bag leader what happened today?" One of the men raises his hand and Nimrod slices it off above the elbow, which action is followed by a blood-curdling scream. "Be glad I am in a good mood." He turns to the other robber and kills him with a short fight, ending with a sword through the forehead.

Nimrod speaks to the one-armed man, "Now, go and tell all that happened. Do not leave out any details. Hurry so you don't bleed to death." The man starts for his horse. "No, you may not have your horse. Walk, run if you would prefer, but never return." Nimrod is right in his face. "Or I will kill you on sight. Am I clear?" The man nods in painful agreement. Nimrod cuts a strip of cloth from one of the dead men's clothing and ties up the bleeding man's bicep with a tourniquet. "Be careful out there, lots of snakes." Nimrod turns him and gently pushes him toward the desert. Before the man staggers off Nimrod places an animal stomach container full of water around his neck. "Bye, bye, now."

Nimrod turns to the cheers of the soldiers and citizens and he salutes them. Then he instructs several soldiers to get the ten horses and bring them to him. He returns Jared's sword to him and is congratulated by his four comrades. Several other soldiers collect the weapons from the dead and dying men.

"Don't bury these men," he tells those watching. "Drag them out in the desert a ways and pile them up for all to see." He indicates three men and tells them to go to the other garrisons and tell them what happened and to double the lookouts for the next week.

"Zag, assemble all the men from the four garrisons immediately. We have much to do before the dead men's friends return, if they return. Also, give these six horses to the other three garrisons for their guards to use when sending messages. No more running. We'll keep four here.

To the assembled soldiers, leaders and citizens who are watching, Nimrod cries out, "This is our city and we will show no mercy to those who seek to take it from us. NO MERCY!" Few follow his chant, "NO MERCY!" he repeats. His companions turn and urge the crowd to repeat, "No mercy." Again Nimrod speaks, "NO MERCY!" This time they all join in and chant, "No mercy!"

That night Nimrod and friends and the four garrison commanders wearing some odd looking hats, meet with the city elders to plan for the future. Other members of the community are present as well, to discuss various problems. As Nimrod enters the room, lots of applause and positive comments and thanks of appreciation can be heard.

The leader of the elders invites the four commanders and Nimrod and friends to sit up front. Several other citizens gladly give up their places for the men. "While there are other items on the agenda, we have agreed to let you speak first, in case you have life and death duties to attend to. And thank you. Thank you for your actions in defending our city today. Thank you and accept our heart-felt gratitude." He shakes each of the men's hands.

"Thank you, dear elder," Nimrod stands and begins. "My proposals, our proposals, are simple. We have around three hundred men divided in four locations to protect our city. We need three thousand men, even ten thousand, if we continue to grow." There is murmuring among those present as to the large number and costs of such an army. "I know that is much to ask of our humble town, much to consider. But for too long now Babel has been a joke among the other cities and our enemies. Robbers, like today, take turns to see whose turn it is to collect tribute money while our garrison commanders sit on their fat ..." he pauses, "rumps, doing nothing. In their defense, what are they to do with sixty or so men against five hundred to thousands of robbers? And our streets, dear elders, your responsibility, are like a trash dump. One has to hold one's nose just to walk our streets. Many of our homes are half full of sand or excrement with no plans that I can see to deal with the problem. I was told before coming to Babel that this city is called 'the armpit of life.' Our people have no pride in their city, no confidence in your leadership, no hope for their future. These three thousand to ten thousand soldiers will not be just for the occasional defense of our city, but will be at the front of the clean-up efforts, the rebuilding efforts and the leaders in building canals to bring us water for irrigation from the mighty Euphrates River. And that is but the start."

But," city elder Riplakish contends, "that could take years."

"You are right, dear elder. Years. How long will it take if we never start? How long will we stay alive without water? Who will want to come here and live in an armpit?" There are a few chuckles and nods of agreement. "I mean no disrespect, kind elders, but any journey of any length begins with the first step. Are you willing to take it with us? My friends and I can train the military; I have a vision for the future, and you are the brains behind the vision, behind the military. And when people see you putting your money and the city's money, where your mouth is, they will bless your names forever. Some will even name their babies after you, and so you will live on well after you leave this mortal state." The city elders smile an awkward smile at such a compliment and gently clap.

"And then, then, the citizens will want to know how they can help." Applause grows, even from the garrison commanders and city elders. As Nimrod continues to speak, the glow of the sweat tent begins to reappear, and it seems to all that his whole body turns white as he speaks regarding his view for the future. While it is not certain that the elders see the change, they hear the change. And the group of four friends witness the unmistakable change. Magnificent. Spiritual. Godly.

"My dear Captain Nimrod, many have come and gone in my lifetime with noble and lofty ideals, but few, if any, have stayed the course. You are talking of fifty to one hundred years of projects. Do we have the people for such efforts? Do we have the money?"

"Perhaps not now. But other cities have people, other cities have money. Much of it from their thievery from us. Other cities have creative minds that can solve problems if we but help them put their minds to it."

"To be sure, Captain, that is all true. But why would other cities send us men, money and minds to help poor Babel?" The four friends stand with their hands on the hilts of their swords. The garrison commanders take off their hats to reveal their new haircuts and they, too, put their hands on the hilt of their swords. "CONQUEST!" they yell, to the roaring approval of the audience.

Terah, one of the chief elders, rises to speak. He is a man of great integrity, and when he speaks, men truly listen. "Many again have come and gone: how do we know that you will be here to see these very excellent and lofty goals come to fruition?" Nimrod recognizes in Terah a wise and honest man and notates the value of this man for the future.

"You have asked, and rightfully so, will we be here, will I be here, to see these projects to their conclusion? I pledge to you, we pledge to you, the rest of our lives in pursuit of these and other goals to the betterment of Babel." This is followed by a lengthy applause from all present.

"Too long Babel has been the fighting arena for other cities, other armies, to decide how the residents of Babel could best serve their interests. As of today that is in the past. I checked with a friend of mine, a trader of goods from North Africa and he assures me that geographically, Babel is right in the middle of the future. After we set aside thousands of acres for personal gardens, with a small tax, areas for orchards, with a small tax, garden areas for commercial use, with a little bigger small tax, areas to grow crops for businesses that need hundreds of acres, with," in unison from the audience, 'a little bigger tax." Then a cemetery area, a garbage area, a hunting preserve for the wealthy, larger areas for herds of sheep, oxen, and cows – you name it. All with a small tax to pay for the development of each area and for the water you elders will bring to these areas.

Who owns the brick factory?" One elder raises his hand. "It really doesn't make money, Captain. I just try to keep as many employed as I can. These decent people need the income and I can afford to help them, so I do."

"That is about to change, my friend. Your good deeds are going to be rewarded. We will need bricks to keep the sand from absorbing all the water for our canals, miles and miles and miles of them, bricks for our ziggurat, our temple, our palace for a future king and queen. Bricks for a wall around this equally wonderful city to keep all within safe from robbers, safe from invading armies and safe from the wind. And our ziggurat will be the largest, tallest, the most wonderful ever built by man." The room is full of "oohs" and "ahs" followed by intermittent applause as Nimrod lays out his plans for the future.

"And the money, the people, the ideas? Like I said, other cities will pay for our improvements; other cities will send their men and women to work here, to think here. Now, think it over, dear elders, and let me know your wishes."

Someone shouts from the audience, "What is there to think over? Get it done!" This remark is followed with boisterous laughter and the chant, "Get it done, get it done."

The city elders do a quick back and forth conversation under the chant of "Get it done." As Nimrod and friends are preparing to leave, the city elders raise their hands to silence the audience.

"Our wishes, Captain Nimrod, are to fund you an army of five-thousand men," interrupted by enormous cheers, and arms raised by the city elders for quiet, "who are to begin immediately on cleaning our city streets and building a series of great canals from our mighty Euphrates River." This is followed by more cheers and then quiet, as an elder wants to ask a question.

"When will you start?"

"We will raid Calneh", and he pauses long and hard for dramatic effect, "tomorrow before dawn." Astonished comments and looks fill the room. "By wagon or forced march all the able-bodied men and women of Calneh will be here in Babel by noon. They will load every available wagon from Calneh with their own food and tools for the workers. The wagons from Calneh and from Babel will then be loaded with bricks from," pointing to the elder who owns the brick factory, "your factory.

Hire thousands more workers, you will get paid, and we will need more bricks than there are stars in the heavens.

Those wagons of bricks will make their way to the Euphrates where the men and women from Calneh, along with every available volunteer man and woman from Babel, will commence digging our first canal. By noon tomorrow our brightest minds will have determined where each section of gardens, cemeteries, garbage dumps and so on will be. These minds will be joined by the best minds, probably not very many, from Calneh," hoots and hollers from the audience, "to decide where the canals will be needed for the garden sections and so on.

These men and women from both cities will need food and water, elders; you must see to it by tomorrow noon. They will need shovels, pry bars and four-wheeled chariots to carry sand and dirt to pile along the banks of the canals. By piling sand along the banks, we do not need to dig as far down. We dig down ten feet and the banks will be twenty-feet high!" More cheers and applause.

"The bricks will be piled along the banks of the canal and then the wagons will return for more, all day long. Each wagon's first trip will also have workers riding or walking with it to the river. So when the wagon returns, only a driver will be needed. After the proper depth and width are achieved, the workers will then lay the bricks using bitumen to seal them. The canal off the Euphrates will need to be twenty-feet deep and thirty-feet wide. We will then dig canals off of it, the size to be determined by those bright minds of Babel, to the various orchard and garden areas and so on.

Each city's work force will spend three days each month working here and then be sent home. By then we will have a work force from another town. I'm not telling you which city, as someone may desire to inform a friend or relative of what's coming and thereby alert that city. This will continue until we have eight cities sending us men and women to do our bidding. Our people of Babel are to be asked to volunteer, donate if you will, one day a week to our projects. People like Omar, the tent maker, will be excluded. We can find some other way for him, and the others handicapped like him, to donate. You, the city elders, will be the ones to decide if someone is not able to work, etc. If a person is your friend or relative, you are to excuse yourself from hearing and deciding what is to be done in their case. Do not fail me on this, as this will be part of your legacy, and you should not taint it with selfish decisions." Perhaps by now some are realizing who is really in charge of Babel.

"Each month then, each city will send us workers for three days. Should any city not work hard, not send us all their workers, then their work load will double to six days a month. There is to be no beating of these men and women. They will be, however, under strict guidelines. Guidelines that will be enforced. That is to be one of the subjects for our garrison commanders' meeting once we leave here.

I do have a special request of the owner of the brick factory." He raises his hand. "My friend, Puli-ilu, is in need of a job, a job from which he must not be fired. Puli is mentally handicapped from an accident in his youth and is slow of speech, not slow of mind or slow of heart. Can you do this for me?"

The owner nods and says, "Consider it done. How much do I pay him?"

"I will be forever in your debt. Thank you. The pay is up to you. Having said that, it should be an honest wage. This is something I am not worried about with a man who has paid the wages of many men and woman for years because of his great love, respect and concern for their welfare. You are already a prince among men, my friend." Applause erupts from the audience, as they know this to be true.

"All of our people of Babel will be paid for any time they spend above their donation of one day a week. You decide the amount. Perhaps if this person is an engineer or such, the pay should be commensurate with his ability. The pay for those from other cities is that--they get to live. However, if someone has an exceptional ability, they should receive something additional. In fact, some may want to become citizens of Babel, and if so, they should be interviewed by you elders, and so on.

Anyone not working and without an excuse will be dealt with. Anyone beating a worker will be dealt with. Anyone taking advantage of the system in any way will be dealt with. That includes you and me, dear brethren. We must be the example, not the exception. We have the power over life and death and must not be seen as playing favorites, or finding a loophole whereby we can make an extra profit, and so on. Am I clear?" Nods of understanding come from the elders and from the audience. Unnoticed by most is the fact that Nimrod is in charge, not the city elders, although Nimrod respects them for their connections. After all, they have had a lifetime to do these things and have not. So, respect for them in this regard is extremely low for Nimrod.

"Let's meet each and every night for progress reports. Is that acceptable? Problems should not wait until evening and should be brought to the city elders, or my attention, immediately, if not sooner." General chuckling from all. "Where there is much to be gained, there is much to be expected, my friends. May we now adjourn? We have much to do tonight and tomorrow." A chorus of "yes" is heard and the meeting is adjourned. The city elders put their heads together and assign responsibilities. Several audience members are waved at by them and called into their little huddle for assignments. These elders know to whom they can go for help and Nimrod knows how to delegate. He did not tell them how to do, just what to do.

"Holy moly," says Fenchristo, as the five men walk toward the garrison nearby. "We will be forever training soldiers. Five thousand!" The men are deep in thought.

"We will need to organize our men into groups of tens, fifties, hundreds and so on," mulls Jared. "Each group must have a leader that is responsible to the next leader and so on."

"You like that, don't you?" comments Rayas.

"Like what?" asks Jared.

"And so on!" says Rayas with his humor still intact. Strange, but intact. The other three men just shake their heads. "What?" he says.

"Once we empty that chest in Nimrod's room, let's put my brother in it and give it to Sarsous, the jerk man."

"Hey, that's not funny," retorts Fenchristo.

"I don't know. He could make a lot of jerk out of a big jerk like you." All join in with their laughs of approval. "Probably wouldn't take any curing after he sliced you up in thin strips. You are good to go!"

Nimrod interrupts the frivolity, "You will be the leaders of the five thousand, and soon, I hope, of the ten thousand. Look at these men; we need good listeners, willing listeners and learners, good fighters, respected by the other men, willing to die to protect you and me, willing to take orders no matter what. That does not mean we want men who do not think. Some men need a little time to think things through, to see in their minds' eye what they are being asked to do. These men should then be able to lead their men into certain death and not blink. They will know by then that you will never ask them to go into a battle knowing there will be certain defeat, to be slaughtered. That, then, is your job, your commitment to them, to make good decisions so that they do not need to think, "Is this a good decision?"

We will need to dedicate one day a week to tryouts. We need a thousand runners with great knife skills. Anyone who fails is simply moved onto another discipline. And they do not need to finish the race for us to know who is going to make a good runner. Get in there and get them moving on. If after the first lap, or the fourth lap they are pooped, stop them: don't waste our time, your time."

"Once a man is moved on, do we fail him completely after knives, or do we give him a shot at all disciplines?" asks Fenchristo.

"What, after blowing the run, blowing knives, we simply ask him if he has strength in weapons we haven't seen? If he says "yes", take him right to it. If he is good, fine. If he isn't, then he's out," comments Rayas.

"Okay, says Nimrod, "but are there needs aside from fighting that he might be good for? I bring that up because I was thinking of Puli-ilu. I couldn't put him on the front line with any weapons and yet, look at his heart. Isn't there any place we could use a man with that great of a heart?" The group of men walk in silence until they are at the garrison commander's office.

As they enter Rayas says, "We could use a few good garrison commanders. Ours don't seem to think with their heads or their hearts." They all laugh.

In their meeting Nimrod points out that constant training will be the norm six days a week from here on out. Every week there will be a new conquest or two. The needs of the present will be stretched to the limits. Then he adds, "The next several months will be horrendous. We will be going from three hundred men to five thousand men as quickly as is humanly possible. These four men, indicating Zag, Jared, Fenchristo and Rayas, will be in charge. They will need your help. I know they do not have your experience and station as garrison commanders, and so I am requesting each of you give your permission, for them to ask your men to do things that you may think they should be asking you and not telling you.

Can you, will you, check your egos in at the door so we can all win?

"I will," answers Kiwayneid. "I can already see what I was and what my troops were, and, and", he pauses due to his emotions. "We were a joke. I was a joke. I couldn't have prevented an attack on Babel any more than I could have prevented my daughter Kama from catching a cold. These five men have treated me fairly and with respect, respect I did not deserve. So, you ask me to help you improve our ability to protect my Kama and everyone else in Babel by simply letting go of my ego, and it is a no brainer. You find someone else to do my job that is better, then replace me. You," pointing at the leaders, "have given me my chance to respect myself, and for that I will always be indebted to you. Anyone feel otherwise?" No one objects.

Nimrod continues, "At the end of several months I will be giving my input to the city elders as to which of you should stay and which of you should be replaced. How you react to these four men will, in great part, determine if I think you should stay or go. What I am asking is no small thing and I know it. However, it has to be done. I must have men willing and capable to do whatever it is I ask of them. Will you be those men?

I know, for instance, two of you think I am too aggressive, too pushy, too domineering. You're right. I am. But that is what I think is necessary for this city to get to its rightful place as a leader among the cities of this world and in a hurry. The leader. Now. Yesterday. Between wars, and there will be a lot of them, we will clean this city, we will watch over men and woman whom we have vanquished on the field of battle. We will kill those who do not respect us. Are you prepared to do this? The days of lying around the office, lying around at home, lying around at other women's homes, is over. The job you have is now a twenty-four-hour-a-day, six-days-a-week job. If you are not up to it or you think it is not what you want for the future, tell me now. There is no shame involved. I know this is a mighty difference from what you signed up for years ago. Let me know tonight before we leave what your decision is. Jared, you're up."

"We need to implement a system, weekly or monthly, where the best archer and the best on each weapon, can be challenged. This competition will keep our men on the edge of greatness, so they cannot sit back and basically say, 'Hey, I'm the best; why should I practice?' We need to tie in behavior so that they know that we want an all-around warrior, not just someone who can throw a spear better than anyone else, and someone who can pump ten arrows a minute into the hearts of our enemies. The rewards do not need to be fantastic, maybe just being noticed as the best this month would be good enough and an extra portion of their favorite beverage." The men all laugh a little. "Perhaps we make them instructors in their area of expertise. You ask men you respect what rewards they would honor, would train for, and would fight for.

Along with competitions, we need your input for future garrisons: size, functions, sleeping quarters for a thousand men who are on duty, horses, equipment, weapons, and communication methods between men and between garrisons. It has been mentioned that we need a retirement system. What do we do with injured warriors who can no longer serve due to those injuries or age? Are they even our responsibility? We need a court system for men who break the rules: little ones, big ones, ones that cost lives of fellow warriors, raping women, drunkenness and murder of civilians. What do you see as important, how should it work, who should be the judge or judges and should there be an appeal system?"

The meeting went on for hours. The important issue was tomorrow's attack on the city of Calneh and how it would happen. You could see the garrison commanders were nervous after Nimrod's announcement regarding their futures. They were also nervous because as garrison commanders they had always been in the rear with the gear, and none of them had actually killed anyone. None had actually led men into battle as opposed to sending men into battle much like the city council elders. The garrison commanders were among the first to realize that they were no longer in charge. So far their military experience was administrative.

Somewhere near the end of the meeting Jared says to his friends, "Wow, this is going to take a long time to organize and put these plans into action."

"Women?" Zag asks, meaning their women they left at home. No one responds.

"Not yet Zag. Soon, but not too soon," responds Nimrod. "If we send for them now, we wouldn't have any time for them, and that would really make them mad."

"Semiramis mad, not good," groans Zag.

"Jared," Nimrod remarks, "take charge of discussing with the garrison commanders how much room the northern garrison will need to house the three hundred men for a few hours tonight. I am sending out runners to alert them to assemble here in two hours. We will also need food and water for the trip to Calneh. Hopefully we can get supplies there for the trip home. We also need someone to organize the wagons for the supplies, weapons, gold, etc. that we will be bringing back.

"Fenchristo and Rayas, you concentrate on organizing our men into overseeing the captives coming back from Calneh and dividing the captives into wagon-fillers, wagon- emptiers, canal-diggers and brick-layers in the canals. Then, figure out how to get them back to Calneh in three days and then repeat the process for the next city. Take care to get the strong backs to dig the canal." Each of the men is silent.

Nimrod looks at them, "What's wrong?" No one wants to respond to him. "Commanders, why don't we take a break? You go on outside for some fresh air and let us discuss this amongst ourselves. The commanders exit.

"Ahhh, you're thinking Calneh has a large army, at least several thousand, and they beat up on Babel many times over the years."

"And we may get our rear ends kicked but good," adds Fenchristo.

"And it may take more than an hour or two if we do beat them, so can we then march the entire city back to Babel to work by noon?" adds Rayas.

"I've been to Calneh and timed how long it should take: it's not a problem," states Nimrod.

"We have less than three hundred men," notes Jared.

"Nimrod say. We do!" shouts Zag. Everyone stops and stares at Zag, whose face is red with anger that flows from his eyes. No reasonable man would argue with Zag when he is like this, and so the others shut up. Nimrod knows without the support of these four men there can be no success at Calneh. And while Zag means well, Nimrod also knows you do not win a man's heart simply by outshouting him or out bullying him into submission.

"So, we stay here and forget Calneh?" There's an uneasy pause as the others look at Zag. "Feel free to speak. Zag will listen, won't you?" Zag does not answer but stares at his three comrades.

"I do not feel as though our thoughts are even important, and it had been this way since the city elders meeting. I feel like you have made up your mind without consulting us. I guess I thought we were more important to you than that," states Jared.

Zag stands up holding his spear to steady him as his rage causes his whole body to tremble. Before Zag speaks, Nimrod crosses to him and puts his hand on his shoulder. Zag shrugs it off. "They are right, Zag, I should have consulted them and you. It was thoughtless of me. So what do we do now?"

"We sound the alarm, silently, assemble our troops and go to Calneh and kick Calnehian butts," Jared offers. His statement is seconded by Fenchristo and Rayas.

Zag looks at Jared, his eyes still blazing, "Zag not forget, Jared."

"Forget what, Zag? I don't understand why you are mad at just me? Am I not allowed to have an opinion regarding my own life?" There is no response.

The men assemble with their garrison commanders at the northern garrison. Nimrod addresses those assembled. "Warriors of Babel, you have been trained by the best warriors anywhere for many days, many weeks. Some of you have been paid for years, and this will be your first battle to defend Babel, defend its citizens, your families. Tonight we march on Calneh to pay them back for years of murdering and torturing that they have leveled in the past against our brothers and sisters. Tonight, we, the fiercest of the fierce, will show Calneh no mercy. Tonight we will realign the stars in the heavens. No longer will heaven or earth weep for poor Babel. We will put the fear of Babel in the hearts of all the world and heaven. 'No Mercy!' Jared and the others pick up the chant, "No Mercy!" They repeat it over and over until all three hundred shout it over and over.

A women's voice is heard from one of the homes nearby, "Can you keep it down out there, I'm trying to sleep? And good luck kicking their damn butts."

The army moves out, leaders on horseback, the rest on foot in a quick march, half-walk, half-run to Calneh. The runners go out before them, scout the city and report back every fifteen minutes. "There are no sentries, no guards on the south. The army is in two places of around five hundred men each. All other soldiers must be at home."

Nimrod continues the march and issues his orders through his four comrades. The army will split in half and push the opposing army's two halves toward each other with a small but strong group of warriors attacking each half from their rear. This small group will fight until the two halves of the Calneh army are pushed together and then the small groups will disappear. The two halves being pushed together will continue to fight, thinking they are still fighting the enemy, but in reality they will be fighting and killing each other in the confusion and darkness of night.

The battle goes as planned, and before the sun has poked its sleepy rays upon the blood-stained earth of Calneh, a long line of men and women could be seen winding their way to Babel. The sounds of children crying accompany the march for quite a while.

In Calneh, fifty four-wheeled wagons pulled by donkeys are collecting all the weapons of war forfeited by the surprised, sleepy and half-dead army of Calneh. Fifty more wagons are going house to house and shops, collecting all manner of food for those walking and working in Babel. The Calneh city elders and their families are isolated and put on large, slow moving wagons that would become their permanent homes. Ten of the small four-wheeled wagons are gathering all the valuables in the entire city. Some are successful in hiding their valuables this time, but not for long. The eyes and ears of the king would catch up to them in the near future.

Several merchants and leaders from Babel are put in place of the captured leaders of Calneh, even in their very homes. To the people who are left behind and the family members making the trek to Babel, the new rules of life are explained. "Those of you who refuse to work will have your children executed one at a time; those who seek not to fight will be executed. For each deserter, a member of your family will be found and executed until no more members of your family exist. Then, for each offense, a member of your city leaders' families will be executed. When they are gone, pregnant women will be found and their babies will be taken and executed. Next, if necessary, those new mothers will be executed."

The people on the march had riders going up and down the column explaining these rules too: "In addition to the rules explained to you, you who are in line marching will be kept for three days and then returned home. You will be fed while working and watered by your city residents. If they do not send food, you do not eat. You will sleep on the ground; next time bring a blanket. You will be returned home, and you will return in four weeks for three more days of work. This will continue until further notice, or until you die."

Up and down the line of men and women, scribes were taking names and names of family members still in Calneh. Any man or woman who has experience as brick layers are taken by wagon to the beginning of the canal, given tools and an extra ration of food. Any man or woman able to smith, or make weapons, is taken to Babel to duplicate the best weapons and returned to Calneh from Babel by wagon, instead of walking, and given an extra ration of food.

During the next three days any men willing to swear allegiance to Babel and fight in her army are escorted back to Babel for training. These men would be put in the front lines of any war, such as the upcoming one in Ereck. Those that survive are given the opportunity to live in Babel and have their family join them, permanently. The families on the large wagons are put to work making fine jewelry for the rich to buy in Babel. The gold and silver taken from Calneh and Erech are given to them after weighing and counting very, very precisely. Very precisely. Every gemstone, every fleck of precious metal is inventoried and then given to the head of the family on the wagon. The head of each family is given the opportunity to count, to inventory every item allocated to that family. A jeweler then is brought out to teach them the how-to-do of jewelry making.

These families are well-fed, they are told that no gemstone, no piece of jewelry, no fleck of gold missing or unaccounted for will be tolerated. Fingers and then hands would be cut-off. Once you are of no use you forfeit your life. So no child will be left behind, only one parent will be killed at a time, and then the process would start with the youngest child – fingers, hands, life. Once all the children are dead, the second parent would have the process start, again. Finally. No mercy.

The army now grows in numbers quickly as does the treasury. More public projects are planned and started, including a palace for the future king and queen. The money for each project is tucked away, no mortgages, if you will. All are paid for before the project is even started. The plans for a huge ziggurat are drawn up, the orchards and gardens begin to be plotted, the streets are cleaned by the new slave labor and the refuse taken to the newly designated valley for trash. Many homes have a second story added, as the sand is so deep that digging it out is no longer feasible. The doors and windows are boarded up and stairs to the second story are added. The population of Babel grows and soon a man from the south appears with a train of camels full of wares to sell to the thriving citizens of Babel. Kadenram!

At the end of the first year, eight cities are under control of the army; Calneh, Erech, Akkad, Resen, Calah, Khan, Ninib and Padan. Each of these cities has three days to fill for slave labor or involuntary civil service camp. Each city has its leaders placed on wagons that traveled incessantly. One of the city elder's full time job is to keep the wagons organized with random routes, gemstones, gold and silver and regularly assigned visits from a jeweler to assess the quality of the work being produced and to answer questions on how to become better at their jobs. Wouldn't want your wagon to lose its place in the kingdom to another wagon working harder or longer hours, would we?

Only the city elder, and certain military leaders, know where the wagons will be from day to day. Some wagons stay in place for two or three days or even a month. There is to be no rhyme or reason as to their comings and goings. Each family has sufficient tents and supplies on their wagon to sustain life for weeks at a time. They each had a fire pit, cooking area and utensils and personal hygiene area. Food and water are brought in every few days and visitors are even allowed, being brought to the family by army escort and taken back to Babel, each time blind-folded. While the visitors are there on the wagon they are expected to work. This is not a vacation for the family. Occasionally, rarely, a visitor desires to take the place of a wagon dweller, as a hostage, to allow that person to become an active member of society once again. And occasionally that replacement has to be killed just like the original dweller would need to be been killed.

The visitors to the hostage families are warned of the consequences of thievery. Should they be caught, they would become a part of the wagon permanently. Many times there are great amounts of tears shed by the visitors as well as the families they visited as they bid each other farewell. These visits become less and less frequent as the years wear on. Visitors are not carefully searched, at first. But it becomes necessary over time, as the military realizes that visitors, in some cases, don't really care about the punishments handed out, so to speak, once they are gone. Eventually, the search would include cavities and horses cavities, etc. You do not steal from Babel.

Searches are always carried out in public lest someone accuse the army of planting jewelry on a visitor. Guess who pays for missing jewelry that comes up unaccounted for along with the family? Oh yeah. Visitors, oh yeah. Romances are kindled between families and guards. Pretty daughters are used to get certain additional privileges a family may desire. And so the circle expands and continues, with the changing of the guards occurring frequently. Rarely, too, a guard would become a family member and give up his rights as a free man. Ain't love grand?

The next few years continue with the digging of more and more canals, sectioning of land, overcoming former enemies as well as winning the hearts and the minds of the citizens of Babel. All this, and the building of an army considered unbeatable, that now numbers in the tens of thousands. A well-trained, constantly training army with a waiting list of those desiring to serve in the Elite section of army. Desiring to serve not just their budding empire, but specifically Nimrod.

The elders call a special meeting in an outside plaza to accommodate all who wish to attend. And it seemed all of Babel desires to be in attendance. Puli-ilu and his family are there, seemingly all the many thousands of members of the army, the elders, the wealthy, shop owners like Omar, the blind tent maker, Sarsous the jerk man and their families. Sarsous could be seen passing out meat samples to the more affluent looking members of the assemblage as well as to the members of the army. And what army man could pass up free food? People could be seen in every corner of the plaza, in doors and windows, on the tops of the surrounding buildings. Children are sitting on the shoulder-tops of their parents and elder siblings' shoulders, all wondering why this meeting has been announced as so important for all.

The elders have been quite tight-lipped regarding the agenda for tonight's meeting, Nimrod mused. Normally, he would have been in on any meeting and its agenda, but not tonight. He and his friends, garrison commanders, some new to their jobs, and many military leaders sit to one side of the area set aside for the elders and their families.

Soon the elders arrive and take their seats. The din of so many thousands of people take a few minutes to subside but finally there is silence. The oldest elder, Riplakish, stands and welcomes everyone to this "momentous occasion." He pauses. "My fellow citizens, the city elders have asked you here tonight to consider the important matter …" and it is at this time a child screams out, "I want my mommy", to the laughs of many present. But not to Riplakish. His moment in the sun, his fifteen minutes of glory, is not to be shared with a screaming child. So he begins again. "My fellow citizens …"

"Get to it," someone hollers, "we ain't got all night."

"Ah, yes, well … to consider the important matter of whether or not Babel deserves a king." The entire congregation erupts in discussion, and some rather loudly and emotionally.

One voice can be heard above the others, "Speak up old man, what did you say about a wing?" The people chuckle around the really old man.

"I said," repeated Riplakish in a much louder voice, "we are here today to discuss the important matter of whether or not Babel deserves a KING!"

Another voice, younger and louder yells, "Not you, old man!" Another voice chimes in, "And who do you think should be this king?" A silent pause ripples across the crowd.

Riplakish responds, "We have here a list of worthy members of our community for your consideration."

He is interrupted by a large framed man, Puli-ilu, who stands and loudly proclaims one word, "Nimrod!"

"I'm afraid General Nimrod is not on our list ..." He is cut-off by other voices chanting, "Nimrod, Nimrod, Nimrod." Soon the entire assemblage, save a few whose names are on the list, are chanting, even screaming, "Nimrod, Nimrod, Nimrod."

Riplakish calls for order with his hands outstretched to ask everyone to be silent. "We have many experienced, longtime residents of Babel ..." Again he is drowned out.

"And with all that experience, did they defend the city?" The noise subsides somewhat and then the voice continues, "Where have they been all these years with filth in the streets? Did they defend the city against robbers or other cities attacking us? And now, they want the glory?"

"Hell, no," cries another voice.

And another, "Who brought us slaves to dig the canals?"

The crowd answers, "Nimrod!"

The same voice asks, "Who do we want to be king?"

The crowd continues more enthusiastically, "Nimrod, Nimrod." They chant in mighty unison, "Nimrod", to the point that some have to cover their ears as they chant.

Nimrod stands while his four friends, garrison commanders and troops cheer all the more loudly. People are banging their hands, pots, anything they can get a hold of, against the walls, their swords and shields, whistling and singing, cheering and yelling until some lose their voices. Nimrod walks to the table where the elders are sitting and majestically waits several minutes for silence to reign. He glows. As silence takes hold of the crowd he speaks, "Citizens of Babel, we came here, my friends and I, well over a year ago and pledged to our city elders that the five of us would consecrate the rest of our lives to improving Babel. Improve it for all, especially for the average person." He is interrupted by cheers, whistles and hoots. "I," he continued, "accept your love, the love of our army and especially the love of my four friends. These four men are more like brothers – they have stood by my side willing to face death, and they have faced death many times: they have dealt with the absence of their loved ones as well, to support my efforts, my dreams." He pauses deeply. "And so it is with great reluctance that I must say "no", to your most generous offer, to your deeply affectionate offer."

A chorus of "No's" is uttered by a stunned populace over Nimrod's rejection to be king.

"I was once told," Nimrod continues after silence is restored, "told that power corrupts and that absolute power, like being a king, corrupts absolutely. I do not have the strength to withstand that level of temptation. Do you?" The crowd mulls this over in muted silence. "What if I become corrupt? What if I fail you, my adopted brothers and sisters? What if I fail myself?"

"General Nimrod," questions the voice of Omar the tent maker, "what if you succeed? Is it worth the chance? For us, we had nothing, we were thought of by other cities as dirt, as nothing. We lived barely above our animals and now ... You have changed all that. You."

The crowd roars its approval.

"You gave us your respect and we love you for it. And we love the respect that others now pay us."

Cheers erupt again from the crowd.

"I am willing to take the chance that you will not allow yourself to become corrupt, that you will not hurt us, the ones you love and that love you."

"Yes!" another voice cries out, "my family will chance it too."

"And I," speaks another, until the air is filled once again with, "Nimrod, Nimrod, Nimrod," so that the entire, vast assembly is standing and chanting his name.

Suddenly Zag stands and a hush comes over the crowd. He kneels on one knee and silently bows his head. Others around him follow his example and within but a few minutes the entire assembly falls silent, each one with bended knee and bowed head. Each, except the city elders, who look at each other and then reluctantly follow suit. They are, after all, politicians. There is no noise among the tens of thousands present, even with the little children, that late afternoon. After what seemed like time being frozen forever, Nimrod speaks.

With tears in his eyes, he weeps unashamedly, he weeps and he glows and in a loud voice proclaims, "I will be your king."

And the crowd goes wild. They rise from their knees shouting, "King Nimrod, King Nimrod," and as they leave the plaza the chant can be heard all over Babel as those who had been present spread the news. Cheering. Celebrating. Confident. Ignorant.

Any not agreeing are smart enough to keep their disagreement quiet as to neither attract attention nor incur the ire of the majority. Any, included some members of the city elders and not just a few wealthy whose names are on the list and have not even been considered by the masses that night, a fact long not to be forgotten among the proud. Very long.

Chapter Six

A date is set in the ensuing weeks for the official coronation of Babel's first king for two months from the day Nimrod accepted the people's invitation. This is to be a glorious affair which the city elders hope would coincide with the completion of several canals from the Euphrates, and the mounding and flattening of the high ground north of Babel's city center for the ziggurat, named the Tower of Babel.

Not only are the hundreds of thousands of wagons full of dirt hauled to the grounds for the building of the Tower, it is also dirt for a temple to worship the city's idols and for a palace for their new king. This would be a palace that would stun the world in its breath-taking beauty and spaciousness. A separate canal is being dug to feed the many ponds associated with these grounds as well as the personal needs of the inhabitants of the palace, temple and Tower. The palace is to have hundreds of rooms, room enough to house endless wives, children, concubines and children, where getting-to-know-you would take on a whole new meaning, many times over and over and …

Formal invitations are being sent to each city that has been conquered, cities that are to be conquered, to the far away cities of Mahora and Anat and all the cities round about where Nimrod, Zag, Jared, Fenchristo and Rayas had families. Also, cities most citizens of Babel have little to no knowledge of throughout the present-day Middle East and the northern part of present-day Africa. Pharaoh Khufu of Egypt is wise enough to realize a new and violent empire is emerging to his north and has prepared to send his most trusted advisor to curry favor with this place now called Babylon, and its new king, Nimrod.

Just short of their self-imposed two-year mark, Nimrod, Jared, Zag, Fenchristo and Rayas make their way home. Nimrod's mind whirls at the many thoughts of the past two years as he rides along with his best friends. And then there is Semiramis. No letters, no friends coming to see if … or maybe … He has been morally true and he knows she has been as well. But, does she still desire to marry him? Desire to have his children? Share his new lifestyle? His religion? Leave her home? Forever?

To Nimrod, what he is offering her is all he had wanted for his entire memory of life. Is it what she wanted? Would the new life last? Would he make a fatal mistake that would cause some of the city elders and some of the wealthy to turn their backs on him, ask him to step down, force him to resign? There would be no room for complacency, no resting on his past achievements, only what have you done for us lately? Today? This afternoon? What about that "power corrupts" thing? Does he believe it could, would happen to him? Just how ruthless could, would he be? As ruthless as the God that destroyed millions and millions of His own children by drowning them to death in a flood--a flood that lasted the better part of a year? And left only eighty-two people alive. On a boat. The Ark. Talk about a power that corrupts!

Was slitting the throats of ten men who killed our father anywhere near as bad? Or of one man who tried to push you off a cliff? At least I faced my enemies face to face and didn't hide behind a wall of water that did my killing for me. I mean, that's what I would do if I were God? Kill face to face. Wouldn't you?

Nimrod's mind is in a frenzied state as he thinks of the future with Semiramis, their children, his friends and the contrasting thoughts of a religion free from the constraints of the God he now hates. How could he, Nimrod, now hurt the God that has so deeply hurt him? His plans formulate slowly as to how to turn the hearts of his followers from a God in heaven, to him, a god of this earth.

As the group travels on in silence, Nimrod has the thought come to him, "Am I a believer in Father Noah's God? In Lugal's same God? While Nimrod believes in a higher being, is that God? He knows he does not believe in nothing, as some fool's do. All he has to do is look around and see the perfection in nature, in the human body, and in what little Nimrod knows of the earth and sun and moon. All things seem to testify to him that there is a God, that there is an order in his small universe. But what is the purpose of life? Where do all of these millions of people come from? Is there an end in sight, or is there some giant baby-maker that would never stop--at least not until Nimrod and Semiramis are done! It is in this vein of thinking that absorbed the new King of Babel as he and his party round a bend that would take them to the small village they had called home. Upon the slight climb up to their homes, they notice a couple of older children running up ahead of them, yelling. Suddenly at the rise of the small flat plain where their homes are found, a large group of people are assembling. Behind them are men on horseback, who are soldiers, that seem to be hedging in the villagers. Nimrod and companions have the same thought, that some conquering force is taking their friends and families captives.

Then Nimrod recognizes his grandfather, Ham, as the leader of the soldiers, and his great grandfather, Noah, and some of his own family among the villagers. They are all there to welcome home Nimrod and friends, as they had received the good news of their accomplishments in Babel. Amidst the cheers and hugs and kisses of family and friends each of the five look for the girl they have each left behind, but to no avail. With all the happiness the men are enjoying, none of the five dare to ask regarding their young ladies.

Nimrod, Jared, Zag, Fenchristo and Rayas are led into the largest tent as night descended, for a great feast. The family patriarch, Noah, blesses the food and thankes God for the safe return of their loved ones. Grandfather Ham had procured the services of a few musicians and claps his hands for them to begin. It seems that the families have hired ten to twenty young women to serve dinner as none of the men recognize any on them. The women are dressed in full length robes and their heads are covered in flower-laden thick heads of hair that cascade over their shoulders and obscure their faces.

Those assembled desire to hear an accounting of the five men since their departure, and so one by one they recount the happenings of their journey. The feast and story- telling lasts well into the night with younger children falling asleep in groups watched over by their older siblings. When the men get to the part about Nimrod being asked to be king, the evening takes on a more solemn air. The adults lean in and the wizened faces of the elderly became concerned. Wrinkles around their eyes deepen and furrows multiplied. The five men notice the changes and their enthusiastic telling of their story dims. When Fenchristo finishes with Nimrod's acceptance, you would have thought someone had died instead of someone having been asked to be king. A long pause follows Fenchristo's account. Finally, Father Noah speaks.

"Nimrod, you must not think that we have feelings against you or against my son, Ham, or even your father, Cush, for being a king. We do not. I do not. Fenchristo has recounted that you refused to be king, citing the adage about power and corruption." He pauses. "It is true. What say you, my son, Ham? Am I speaking as just an old man?" Ham bows his head and shakes it side to side. "No, my father, you speak wisdom." With his head still down looking at the ground he continues. "No matter how hard you try, no matter how much you desire to do good, bad decisions, political decisions, personal want decisions break through here and there like wild flowers in the spring. And like the wild flowers, soon your decisions fill the hillside. You sit there some days seeing all the flowers, these decisions, and you think, did I make them for the right reasons? Did I send that man to jail, to death, because of what he did, or, did I do it because I did not like him?" Ham looks up and into Nimrod's eyes, "Like the men whose throats you cut."

Several gasps are heard from sisters and mothers. "And there will be more. I promise you. Good, bad, the decisions all blur together, and you become calloused. This wealthy man needs a favor, this woman ..." He stands and steps toward the tent door, "Let me know if I can be of any help, Nimrod." Ham exits, and with his troops they can be heard riding off.

Noah waits until it is once again quiet. "Ham has faults, many of them at times. But this night he has spoken truth." He pauses and with a heavy sigh begins again. "How do you think I felt when the water lapped at the sides of the Ark and it started to float away? I could hear the screams of my fellow human beings, some close acquaintances, neighbors, family. I could feel the reverberations of their pounding on the doors and sides of the Ark. Later, I could see bodies of tens of thousands floating, bloated and dead, with some of the great predator beasts of the seas feeding upon them. Millions and millions, dead. Eighty-two of us disembarked almost a year later. Eighty-two out of millions." Tears in his eyes and with a voice that falters he continues, "It was then that I pleaded, I begged our Father in Heaven: please, dear God, please, never ask me to do this again. Please." His emotions overcome him, and he just sits with the pain that you and I will never need to know.

His wife, Naiama, moves to his side and puts her head in his lap and tries to comfort him. "That's enough for tonight, dear husband." Quietly, reverently, the sleeping children are awakened, some carried by their dads, moms, older sisters, and brothers, and they all head for their homes. Nimrod and his friends walk to their families' homes, each with serious thoughts about the night's discussion.

Nimrod turns and asks as he's leaving, "Where is Semiramis and the girlfriends of Zag, Jared, Fenchristo and Rayas? I thought, I mean we though they'd be here tonight."

"They had to go to Anat," replies Semiramis's sister, Nukhush. Normally a very talkative person to the point of wondering if she had an off button one could push, it is unusual for her to be so tight-lipped. As Nimrod and men exit she adds, "They're all going to a wedding." They stop, waiting. She continues as though they're dragging the information out of her, "They've found some men that want to marry them. I can't tell you more. Oh, they are going to be so mad at me." Nimrod turns and looks at her with his hand on his sword and a look of disbelief. "Well, I mean I guess they figured you and, and them, I mean they, I mean all of you, together, weren't coming back for them or something, I guess. I really shouldn't be telling you, Semiramis will have my hide if she finds out I told you. You won't tell her, will you?" Nimrod and the others are already out the door. Nukhush calls after them, "You won't tell her I told you, will you Nimmy?" She'll be absolutely furious. You know her temper. They're all staying at my dad's sister's home. You know, Aunt Sudigas."

Nimrod is out of sight as she continues talking toward him, "Semiramis can be very cruel; I'm sure you have noticed. Maybe not toward you, of course, just not very forgiving. Oh, please, Nimmy, don't say anything." When Nukhush is really sure he's gone, she closes the tent flap and turns to one of the serving girls, "Think I did okay?"

Semiramis takes off her wig and hugs her, "You were beautiful, dear girl. I never thought your ability to talk would come in so handy!" The other four girls take off their wigs and overstuffed dresses. "They will be in Anat by sun-up. We better hurry."

"It was all I could do to not hug Zag. Oh, I hope he'll forgive me for lying to him," says Shamshi.

"Trust me, he will." And with that Semiramis and the other four girls exit the tent, mount their horses and ride off to Anat. As they ride a bit down the path to Anat, they are joined by Ham and his guards. And the plot thickens.

Just before daylight, Nimrod and friends are awakened by Mother Naiama. "Father Noah left already for Anat. He has several weddings to perform. I collected some clean clothes for each of you. I'm sure it was a long journey from Babel and I thought it would be best if you bathed and dressed before looking for your loved ones. You know, best foot forward and all."

Hot water in five large basins await the travelers, and after Mother Naiama leaves, the five men strip off their dirty and rather odorous clothing and proceed to bathe. Not a word is spoken among the men and yet what they are thinking blasts the air waves.

As they are finishing, Mother Naiama and Nukhush entered with steamy hot porridge and goat's milk. The five thank the ladies, eat and make a hasty departure with their weapons strapped to them. They give no thought to the rather formal wear they were given by Mother Naiama, they just want to get to Anat. This could prove to be a bloody ordeal, weddings or no weddings. As the men ride off, Mother Naiama, Nukhush and the few remaining women and children, each dressed in their finest clothes, giggling and laughing, board wagons for the trip to Anat. One small village left unguarded, except for a few mangy dogs, whose entire population is on its way to some weddings!

As Nimrod and group arrive in Anat, they ask regarding a wedding today and are directed to the King's palace. Once there, a group of men, soldiers, help them with their horses. The soldiers take their names so their horses would not be stolen during the wedding. They explain that robbers use occasions like this to steal horses and equipment. The soldiers ask that the men also leave their weapons, assuring them that the weapons would be safe in their care. And, of course, the weapons have to be inventoried for each man and so on.

The process takes forever, and Nimrod and men try to be patient, but one could see they are bursting at the seams to see who is marrying their women. Marrying, if those men live that long! The women helping the guards keep dropping weapons and putting their weapons with the wrong horse and so on. Finally, the inventory is done. As the five men try to storm off to find someone to kill, the women announce that the brides have requested those in attendance wear special clothing for the wedding. Out comes these fancy white and gold robes that Nimrod and men are asked to place over their frilly clothing.

All five protest, insisting they are not here for the festivities. The soldiers look menacingly at them and one speaks, "This is what Semiramis wants. And what Semiramis wants ..." the five men and other soldiers in unison said, "Semiramis gets." So, the five men put on the clothing.

"We look like girls," Rayas observes.

"Tell Semiramis," retorts Zag.

"Never mind."

By this time the wagons carrying the last passengers from the village have arrived, unseen by Nimrod and group. They are then escorted to an outdoor gathering place where hundreds of guests are waiting. "This could be awkward, Nimrod," ventures Jared.

From a small tent at the back of the congregation, Semiramis and the other four women appear. The women walk toward Nimrod and the other four men to giggling girls and comments about how beautiful each of the brides looks by members of the assembled visitors. Semiramis speaks to Nimrod and the four gullible saps behind him, "Please escort us to the front where Father Noah is waiting."

"Why are you doing this, Semiramis? Why? What have we done? The two years are not up," pleads Fenchristo. "Are they?" The five men and five women walk toward Father Noah.

"Where are these impostors that you have let take you from us?" asks Rayas. "They deserve to die!"

"You have betrayed us," adds Jared, with a forced smile on his face as he nods to the people assembled on both sides of him.

"Not happy," Zag added, "no, not happy, Shamshi." Shamshi begins to weep.

Nimrod searches the gathering. "Why do we have to wear these, these silly robes. No one else does. We were told everyone at the wedding had to be dressed this way."

They are at the front where five men stand with their faces obscured to the five men and the women. Nimrod and Semiramis are at the head of the five couples.

"Are these the men you intend to marry?" asks Nimrod. The five men turn towards the couples only to expose the five fathers of the women. "What the …?" says Nimrod. "Where are the men you are going to marry?" he asks in a loud voice. "Come forward, you cowards!" The entire congregation erupts in laughter.

Semiramis kisses him on the cheek, "They are all here."

Nimrod realizes the girls, nay the women, have duped them and but good. A ripple of giggles and laughter repeats itself in the congregation. Nimrod whispers what has happened to the others. Shamshi runs up the aisle away from Zag crying, "He doesn't love me. He doesn't want me."

Zag turns, helpless, watching her run away. "STOP!" he bellows and Shamshi stops, frightened. "I, I, I love." The audience reacts with gentle 'ohs' and 'ahs'. Shamshi cries even harder, turns to run and trips and falls. She is helped up by those close to her and escorted back to Zag.

"I marry, Shamshi. If you ..."

"Oh, I do Zag, love, forever," lovingly imitating his halting speech.

"Well, perhaps we should proceed, unless there are those who feel otherwise?" asks Father Noah. The five men look menacingly over the congregation. "Yes, well, I thought not." One by one the vows are exchanged, each bride is kissed, with the couple stepping to the side and so on, until all five are sacredly married.

Perhaps rather unheard of in our permissive society, but all ten of these men and women were virgins when they married. So, yes, the term sacredly married really applies: no condoms, no morning-after pills, no STD's, no abortions. This is the way God intended life to be lived. Sacredly. And the married couples go off to prepared tents, tents that are not too close to each other, and they know each other, several times.

A few days after the marriage ceremonies and all, the five sets of husbands and wives, meet to discuss their future.

"We want you men to be happy. We five women have already talked and decided that whatever you want to do, we will support you. Not because we have to, but because we want to. Sheepherders or kings, we do not care. We want to be with you, bear your children and grow old together, just not too quickly," Semiramis voices.

Jared holds Zamama's hand and smiles, "I know that the decision to go back to Babel is easy for me. I'm not the one they want to be King. I've enjoyed the life in a large city, being part of training young men to defend their homes, and seeing the fantastic change that has taken place: the people, for the first time in many of their lives, having pride in their accomplishments. I would like to continue what we've started."

"Me too," voices Zag.

"I guess the real question is, does Nimrod want to go back to Babel and be king, or do you want to be just a captain, or a general, in the army?" asked Fenchristo.

"In any case, it sounds as if we all want to go back to Babel, just with what job description, king, captain or general," says Rayas.

"You have so many great ideas for making Babel a better place," Jared adds. "Is it possible to continue putting those ideas into place if someone else were to be king? And it seems to me that someone will be king. Why then, not you? We will keep you on the straight and narrow, if the job goes to your head. If you let us." They all smile and gently laugh. Then they are silent waiting for Nimrod to respond.

Shamshi offers, "Father Noah and Ham have much experience. My father too. With great responsibility such as this, comes great heartache. Will the successes be worth the pain? I never thought before about what Noah described while being in the Ark and seeing millions of dead bodies floating … Then, God was quiet, for months and months. What were we told happened after Noah pleaded with God to not make him go through that again?"

Catalin hugs her Rayas and answers, "Mother Naiama told us God made a promise to Noah that a flood like this, almost ending all of humanity, would never happen again. The sign of God's promise is the rainbow, I know that it has taken all this time since the flood, one hundred and fifty years or so, for many people to feel comfortable with God's promise to even move a little ways from the mountains."

"Like living in the mountains would have helped in the flood that Noah lived through," gently laughed Rayas.

"What think?" asked Zag of Nimrod.

"I think," pausing and looking at each of the people present, "I would like to at least try, if, if you will be there to support me, to occasionally correct me." Nods of agreement and words of encouragement are spoken. "Especially you," as Nimrod looks at Semiramis.

"I believe Lugal and your father would support you too," smiles Semiramis with a thoughtful kiss on his cheek.

"Well then, let's pack and be on our way. The coronation, you said, is in three weeks?" Zamama notes.

"Just enough time to shop and find something to wear!" Rayas's wife Gechina laughs. The men just grin and groan. So it begins. It took three wagons to move their belongings that the five women had already accumulated, including the presents from the wedding. They all had to leave most of the live sheep, goats, pigs and chickens their relatives and friends had given them. The men had explained that where they live, there wouldn't be room for the animals. Jared had explained though that there was a man who took animals and jerked them, so he was bringing along some animals to be jerked. Kind of like food storage. The relatives seemed sad to have their gifts returned, although they did have a smile on their faces.

When they all arrived at Babel they were greeted by the city sentries at the northern gate to Babel. The excitement of having Nimrod and his wife present spread throughout the city in seemingly minutes. Several soldiers had been assigned to escort each of the couples to lodgings that had been prepared in their absence. The entire city was involved in decorating all homes, work facilities and the large, flat ground that now rose above even the tallest buildings in Babel. Not that that would have been hard to do!

Benches and chairs had been built for the coronation as well as awnings to keep the sun off the dignitaries. Thousands of benches, tens of thousands of potted trees each with a jug of water next to each tree for watering in the hot sun were scattered throughout the complex.

Every city contacted had responded with a list of those who would attend the great celebration. Even the Egyptian pharaoh Khufu was sending a delegation to Babel. Some cities, who had not been contacted, requested permission for them to send representatives for the occasion. All were greeted with a positive and enthusiastic welcome with an apology for overlooking them. Uniforms were made for runners and guides who were to assist visitors to various destinations and to show off the improvements already made, as well as those improvements planned for the near and not-so-near future. Soldiers wore a special purple and gold sash for all to see, especially prospective troublemakers, like the bandits who roamed the mountains.

Unknown to most, Kish and Berosus had been invited, but no word had been received regarding their attendance. Those with invitations would have to identify themselves to the security soldiers at the gates, and all weapons would be confiscated for the ceremony and returned on the way out. Soldiers patrolled the Euphrates River in large flat-bottomed barges, and groups of mounted soldiers patrolled the roads leading to Babel from as far away as one hundred miles in every direction.

Nimrod had gone to one of his 'invited guests' roaming the desert eternally on a wagon, and described a crown he had seen in a dream which was made of gold with a black cloth, covering his head. Nimrod would be the very first king ever to wear a crown. The crown would be done in plenty of time for the ceremony, right? It's not nice to fool with the king. Jared's family came later and found a place to live for Jared and Zamama as well as Jared's unmarried, reclusive brother and family. Jared's father and mother also moved to Babel and several of his brothers and sisters and families.

While the brother of Jared and family were a little farther away from the city center, than Zag and Shamshi and the others, they fit in quite well with the God-loving community that surrounded them. Jared's brother had become reclusive prior to moving to Babel, but now had become even more so. Few people saw him and even fewer spoke with him. He had premonitions that most always turned out to be correct. In one conversation with Jared, he warned his brother not to get to close to Nimrod, hinting that there was a very dark side to him.

Nonetheless, this brother felt it his duty to move to Babel to protect his brother, Jared. He explained that his being reclusive, as some thought, would be of a great benefit to the family in the future, and he asked Jared to say as little as possible to Nimrod regarding him. He also was known to have exceptional spiritual powers in restoring people's health. Much like a modern-day muscle-testing chiropractor, no doubt.

Coronation day arrives. The electricity of excitement was just below the crackling point. Some residents of Babel were actually short of breath as they sought the best position for watching the parade of important people that would wind itself through the city, culminating on the high ground north of Babel. Room was scarce even in a huge area as had been built up, pounded, watered and pounded again foot by foot, city block by city block. Unbeknownst to most, even long-time residents and members of the city elders, construction had commenced underground for the temple and palace.

A series of underground drains were all but finished, allowing water to run off all four sides of the built-up ground. Along with these drains were the secreted tunnels that had been dug at night for protection of the workers from the elements and potential enemies, hence the nighttime work. Oh yes, and from prying eyes of anyone, period.

The tunnels ran under the Tower of Babel ziggurat, the temple to the unnamed gods, the future palace of the King and Queen, multiple wives and families, concubines and families and the huge ponds and grassy playing and lounging areas for royal get- togethers. I wonder why all that would be a secret?

Kitchens were planned in each of these projects and they were to be underground as well, to minimize heat, noise, smells and interactions with the very important personages that would be practically nonstop in their goings and comings, and stuff. The foundation for each of those major buildings had been set with enormous rectangular granite blocks each the height of a tall man, the width of a tall man and the length of two tall men. Shaped and squared at the quarries high in the mountains, each block took months to prepare. Many wagons had been broken and several teams of oxen had been destroyed pulling these enormous stones. The concept of the giant wagons used for captive families had been recognized and employed for the stones carved out of the mountains.

Teams of forty oxen were then used to pull the giant wagons with lumber from felled trees placed on the path from the mountains to the raised ground. These full-sized trees, side by side, were for the wheels of the massive wagons to roll on, keeping the wheels from digging into the soft earth. Before the lumber was employed, the first wagon made it down the slight downgrade from the quarry before the wagon came to a permanent rest with the six-foot round wheels completely below ground encased in soft sand.

Once at the site, thousands of men and oxen pulled on the foot-round diameter ropes extending on two sides of the granite blocks. Hundreds of trees had been felled to create the ten-inch round logs that were placed across the path to act like rollers when the blocks were pulled. Men and oxen were there all along the route to move the rounded trees to a forward position once the block had passed.

Hog grease was slathered on every roller log to facilitate movement of the blocks. Only the absolute strongest men of Babel, or I should say her strongest slaves, were used. The conquered cities now numbered in the twenties. The first several layers of each building would be granite and then the rest of the buildings' layers were to be of hardened bitumen bricks. The cost, in terms of money and time, was so enormous that only the first few layers could be of granite. The pits for the ponds were already dug and lined with bitumen bricks to keep the water from being absorbed as quickly into the ground. Today, Coronation day, the children had much fun running up and down the sloped sides with occasional tumbles, scrapes and tears.

The canals were finished for filling the ponds and were going to be opened today. The deepest pond at thirty-five feet was for the army to practice water maneuvers, the second pond was twenty-five foot deep and no one was sure what it was for. Well, at least those who knew were not saying. There was a connecting canal from this second pond to yet another pond which was about fifteen foot deep and then more ponds of ten feet deep for water to be used in the palace for personal needs and for watering vegetation around the various structures.

Suddenly, a blast from the military bugles was sounded, children were promptly warned to clear out of the ponds and the gates damming up the water miles away were opened. In a matter of minutes water started seeping into the ponds. In an hour or so the water was coming in a strong, steady stream. Kids were still testing their ability to run in the water and escape the ponds, but now were chastened by soldiers with their purple and gold sashes.

Parents were asked to be more responsible for their children, as swimming was not the strong suit of most desert dwellers. Yes, parents were actually chastised for not properly overseeing their children. It'll take a while for that concept to sink in, I know. Of course, it helped that the chastisers were soldiers with swords.

Then the unexpected, yet expected, event occurred, with a five-year-old slipping and falling into the thirty-five foot deep pond, which had maybe only eight to ten feet of water in it. Onlookers tried reaching the child by people clasping arms together in a chain, only to have the last adult loose contact with the chain and now two people were flailing around in the pond. These are people who do not put their heads under in a tub for bathing, let alone go swimming. It was wicked to watch, helpless to help, as they both succumbed to death by drowning on such a glorious day as this day of Coronation. Their bodies were ultimately retrieved and the families left for home, unnoticed by the hundreds of thousands gathered.

There were no complaints filed about the lack of handrails around the ponds, no lawsuits about the untimely arrival of troops with bloated animal stomachs for flotation, who ultimately retrieved the bodies. Just serious reflection on how the parents failed to properly supervise their child, and how incredibly brave the older cousin was to give up his life trying to save another family member. It was rather like two fleas on a hound being eaten by the hound: no big deal except to the fleas, and except to their families.

Babryanifi, envoy of Pharaoh Khufu, had a front row seat. Just prior to the ceremony commencing, he dismissed his two fan bearers so as to not obstruct the view of those behind him, a rather magnanimous gesture, considering his position of importance in Egypt. But, to his credit, Babryanifi recognized he was not in Egypt and scored big points with the Babylonians, as they were now becoming known as. The right man for the right job, one might say. It is of importance to note that there were no interpreters present, necessary, or even thought of. The earth's inhabitants all spoke the same Adamic language, while expressing it differently in writing, depending upon each area's ability with an alphabet. The Egyptians were thought woefully inept, due to their laborious system of drawing pictures on everything to communicate. Babryanifi was soon accompanied by other leaders of equal importance, at least to them, from various countries, cities and religions. Yes, Father Noah was in attendance, but not Ham, Japheth or Shem. This was a faux pas not soon to be forgotten by Ham.

Among such notable dignitaries were also found Zag, Jared, Fenchristo and Rayas and their wives. Queen Semiramis had a throne next to, lower than and two steps behind that of King Nimrod. After all, she was just a woman. She had not fought and won war after war, killed many enemies, offered new and innovative ideas for canals and so on. She had not, as of yet, even produced a male heir to the throne of a king who was not yet a king. But she suffered through all these things quietly. She had a very good memory, as the world would find out.

But for now, this was her husband's, her lover's, her equal half's day before the world. Over time she would earn grudging respect of all, as the power behind the throne. She exemplified the adage, "The hand that rocks the cradle rules the world", putting to rest the whining and crying of women worldwide who pouted about no respect. She asked, "Who in the world raises your children, teaches them values such as respect? If you do not get respect, then you do not deserve it," she commented on several occasions. "As far as I know, one hundred percent of mothers are women; therefore one hundred percent of children's nurturers and teachers are women. Do your job."

All the kings and all the kings' men were in place when the triumphant trumpets announced that the parade had reached the high ground. From the back of the gathering of the hundreds of thousands came first members of Nimrod's Elite fighting force with their side-shaved heads, swords and royal purple and gold sashes, hundreds of them. They were followed by the city elders resplendent in all-white robes and gold sashes, followed by many hundreds of the wealthiest and politically powerful, and now politically castrated members of Babel, each in their choice of raiment and each with a red-and-black sash.

Puli-ilu, Omar the tent maker, Sarsous the jerk, Kadenram and many lesser merchants who had befriended Nimrod and his band of brothers, were each wearing their best clothing, topped with a blue and red sash. These men were followed by the religious leaders in the community: idol worshippers, fire worshippers, of whom we will hear more of later, God lovers such as Noah, pharaoh-worshippers and many others. They could not agree on a color sash, so they wore none.

Finally, on a litter of brilliant white and gleaming gold, with plush plum purple flags on each of the four sides of the cover over his head, carried by forty volunteer Elite soldiers, sat Nimrod. He sat wearing a gown of pure white that contrasted well with his dark skin, with slippers of gold cloth, and neck and wrists trimmed in gold thread. He waved enthusiastically to the crowds, not like some beauty pageant runner-up, as they stood when he passed them. The crowd was standing and cheering at the top of their lungs for the man whom they chose to be their king. He seemed serenely at ease with all the pomp, almost humble. And so it went until at last the litter was set down on four white, gleaming blocks of granite, and Nimrod was escorted to just below his throne. Semiramis was already seated on her throne but rose when Nimrod stepped out of his litter. The chief elder of Babel motioned to the gigantic crowd to be seated. The elder thought to himself, "I wish getting the people to be quiet at the town meetings was this easy!"

Babryanifi knew that his standing and sitting at the proper time did not tarnish his rank as the number two man in all of Egypt: it in fact enhanced his image. Courtesy never really is out of fashion, and respect for another's position, even if not for the person, counts. Terah approached, as he held Nimrod's crown of gold and black. Riplakish spoke, "This Coronation of Nimrod, the mighty, as the first King of Babel is a result of one hundred percent vote by the people of Babel in favor of this action." His last few words were drowned out by the cheers that erupted as he spoke. "In less than two years, Babel had come to mean and represent success: success on the battlefield over cities and people who for hundreds of years beat upon Babel and its armies like a drum, with no thought of our welfare. Today represents a reversal of those conditions." Cheers, cheers and more cheers resounded from all corners.

"Today, we are Babylon!" The audience stands and waves anything within reach, cheering for themselves. One out-of-town invitee turns to Babryanifi and says, "A rather pompous and braggart attitude, don't you think?" Babryanifi looks at him and responds, "It isn't bragging if it is so."

Riplakish continues, "Now it is our former enemies who pave our canals, build our ziggurat, our palaces, and fight on the front lines of our wars. And we owe all this and much more, as you will see in the future, to this man," pointing to Nimrod. "Nimrod, the mighty."

More loudly and longer than any cheers so far offered by the crowd, the celebration of their king goes on. Cheers from the crowd turn into chants of "Nimrod, the mighty, King of Babel." Riplakish acts as the cheerleader as he uses his hands to keep beat with the chanting cheers. This goes on for minutes after minutes.

Way back in the crowd near one of the huge foundation blocks of granite stand two unchanting men, unapplauding men, and unhappy men due to the crowd noise. Kish says to his son Berosus, "Looks like we have found a worthy opponent in King Nimrod."

Berosus responds "Are we going to kill him on the battle field or in his bed?"

"I promised him five years of peace. I gave my word. I did that for you. So, it is for you to use the next three years to plan his death. Then, all this will be ours. In fact, I might give him another five years, things are going so well!"

They laugh together and give a weak, "Hoorah for Nimrod," and leave.

Riplakish settles down the audience with his hands pushing down, "Thank you my fellow Babylonians and most distinguished visitors. I want now to turn the time over to Terah, our most noble city elder." He gestures for Terah to come front and center as he steps back.

Terah does so and pauses, waiting for absolute silence. "Thank you, my friends. Thank you, Babryanifi, and to your pharaoh for sending you to our king's coronation. We look forward to many years of trade and mutual exchange of ideas." Babryanifi acknowledges his remarks by a nod of his head. "I have worked and waited for many years for someone so strong, so sensitive and kind, so full of ideas to come to Babel. We have seen others with ideas, but not with the pulsating drive to accomplish those ideas as we have seen with General Nimrod. It is sad, however, that it is so necessary for the use of force to create change, but that is the world we live in. We are here with a former captain, a former volunteer soldier, to crown him our king. Soldier to captain to king in two short years." Again the crowd takes over with cheers and chants. Finally, the noise subsides and Terah continues, "I can barely wait for the next twenty-two years!" Again the crowd goes wild, "Nimrod, Nimrod, Nimrod."

After they quiet down, Terah turns to Nimrod, who stands next to Terah.

"The city elders are, after today, a thing of the past in power and authority. We want you, Nimrod, to continue to represent us well, to continue to take up the challenge of Babel against all our enemies. Will you do that?"

"Yes," answers Nimrod.

"Will you heed the needs of the poor and afflicted?"

"Yes."

"With every fiber of your being, will you deal honestly with all citizens of Babel, of Babylon, whether rich or poor."

"Yes."

"Whether a man believes in the true and living God or in some other form of worship, will you conduct yourself without prejudice when a grievance is presented before you?"

"Yes, I will Elder Terah."

"And will you, your army and any representatives, treat each of us with dignity, honesty and respect as we have need to come before you?"

"Most certainly."

"I hereby crown you King of Babel." The crowd once again deafens the ears of the hearing. All across Babel the people can hear what they have been waiting for, for hundreds of years. They have a king. The people on the raised ground start cheering and dancing even as Terah places the crown upon Nimrod's head. The roar grows even more deafening as Nimrod takes his place on this throne, kissing Semiramis on each hand and then on her lips. Nimrod motions to his guards, and they move Semiramis' throne forward, even with Nimrod's, as they both sit holding hands. The feasting begins immediately as thousands of men and women appear with trays of fruit and vegetables, trays of meat and trays of breads. The contents of the trays are quickly devoured and followed by even more trays of food. The wealthy and visiting dignitaries including Father Noah and Babryanifi are served separately from the masses. Trays of beverages follow those of food until even the most ravenous appetites are quenched.

For hour upon hour the celebration continues with food and drink continuing unabated. When dusk comes, thousands of torches are lit and set in place. The ponds are completely full and shimmer in the torch light. At dusk also come musicians who start to play the resonating beat of drums accompanied with the sounds of harps, lyres and fifes. Unnoticed in all the celebration is the disappearance of the King and many of his Elite bodyguards. In an underground meeting room still under construction beneath the Tower of Babel, King Nimrod presides over a meeting of some five hundred strongly committed citizens both male and female. Committed to Nimrod.

"My friends, this is but the first of many meetings we will have over the next hundred years." Some light laughter. "I am going to be King longer perhaps than some of you may live. I have asked you here tonight to be the very first of many, as my 'eyes and ears' throughout the kingdom. Some of you may be asked to relocate in some of the other cities we have recently conquered. Some cities we have yet, but will, vanquish." Happy laughter and excitement at feeling they are the first to hear, the first to know these things. "Some will think of you as spies. I think of you as part of the ten thousand eyes and ears of the King. Will you be my eyes and ears?"

Resounding "Yes, my king!"

"My scribes will go among you, taking names, issuing you passwords and signs. They will teach you how to recognize others in your city from our group. We need to know if you have relatives or friends in other cities that can be trusted." Nimrod stands to leave. "I will meet with you again." His Elite soldiers fall to one knee and cross one arm across their chest as King Nimrod prepares to exit the room, and they chant together; "May I die rather than turn against my king." The people kneel and cross their arm across their chest and repeat, "May I die rather than turn against my king."

Chapter Seven

It is not long until the "eyes and ears" of the king prove their worth. In the town of Akkad, three families have had ongoing "health issues", in that these three families consistently have members not show up for their mandated three days labor in Babel. Zag is assigned to look into the problem. He and twenty of his Elite soldiers with their side-head shaven trademark ride to Akkad. On the outskirts of town, Nimrod's city administrator awaits them. A runner has been sent to alert him of Zag's coming. Along with the administrator are a mousy-looking man and his wife, in chains. As Zag dismounts his horse he walks to the man, with his back to the administrator. The man motions with his left hand by touching his eyes with two of his fingers; Zag smacks him on the right side of his head and sends him sprawling to the ground.

"Tell me or die," Zag threatens the man in chains.

"He's, he's told me …," the administrator starts, but is silenced by Zag's raised hand in his direction.

Zag points his spear at the man on the ground and repeats "or die." The man proceeds to tell Zag that the three families have been storing up food for some unknown reason. "And, and they have packed most of their belongings and have them hidden in a small windowless bedroom. The three families are friends with each other and look to be in very good health. I believe they are preparing to run away. They only send one or two sons to work to keep suspicions off of them. But they are enemies of our great king."

Zag extends his hand to the man, helping him to his feet. In the hand of the man are now several gold coins, unseen by anyone else. The man and woman are released by Zag's men, and the administrator leads the way to the homes of the three families, all of whom live side-by-side-by-side. Zag's men round up all members of the families. They number one hundred and twenty-six. They are then herded to the center of Akkad and forced to their knees, hands tied behind their backs. The moms and dads, older brothers and sisters are separated into groups apart from the younger children, twelve and under. All residents of Akkad have been assembled to watch.

A lesser-ranked leader, Nuradad, of Zag's troops, pronounces the sentence. "You who are about to die have dishonored our great king, King Nimrod." He motions for several of his men and they stab to death all the older girls by placing the blade of their sword between their breasts and pushing down into the women's hearts. Many screams and cries are heard from the children and men. The three moms are simply beheaded after watching their daughters die. Several of the brothers stand and curse the soldiers and Zag for killing their sisters and moms. Other soldiers come forward and hit the brothers in the head with the butts of their swords, stunning them or knocking them momentarily unconscious. The brothers are then beheaded, but not the fathers. Again the cries of the children are heard. Gasps from the assembled citizens can also be heard.

Nuradad continues, "You were asked to only work three days a month in Babel. Now, each man and woman of Akkad will work six days a month for one year to make up for the work these families did not do." The soldiers mount their horses, leaving Zag and the administrator.

With one swift thrust of his spear Zag kills the administrator. "You failed," utters Zag.

Zag mounts, and he and the soldiers ride off, leaving one soldier behind. The soldier addresses the assembled citizens, "I am your new administrator. I will not die for you. Clean up this filthy mess!" He unties the three dads, who in turn untie their crying children and go home. They number sixty-one. The rest of the people gather carts and take the bodies outside of town to the town's burial zone. In one mass grave they bury all of the sixty-five. Before, however, all jewelry is removed from the bodies and delivered to the new administrator.

On a large cart somewhere in the desert carrying the leader of Akkad and his family, one person must be selected, by the father, to die as well. The body of his blind, ten year old daughter is found one morning in the public square days later in Akkad. The message – work like your life depends on it, because it does.

The temple is completed with its huge magnificent altar, upon which several water buffalo could be sacrificed at one time. The thrones for a King and Queen and one additional seat for a high priest are located behind the altar. A chute has been installed near the altar for the disposal of sacrificial remains, the cover of which can be opened and closed by two men. There are vessels containing water and more containing a powdery substance used for enhancing smoke and flame near the altar. Another very large vessel contains oil for rubbing on the sacrifices to shine the skin and make it crisp. The oil also is used for keeping the chute slippery, aiding disposal of the remains.

Multiple entrances from below and outside are available for priests, dancers, musicians, and additional animals, for use in worship services and other needs. These have been well thought out. Seating along the two long sides of the temple accommodate several hundred worshippers and lesser priests and their helpers. A raised platform is at the opposite end of the altar for presentations, et al. Above the thrones behind the altar rising some thirty feet above the floor, in magnificent red and black kiln-fired tiles, is the image of the "Great Red Dragon." While resembling a large snake, it also combines the fabled wings and claws of the Dragon and would become known as the "Fiery Serpent."

In front of the Dragon is a woman with twelve stars in her crown that the fiery breath of the Dragon touches. This represents the devouring fire to which human victims, especially children, were to be offered in sacrifice. Better yet, infants would be even more of an acceptable offering at the altar. Many of these decisions came in private conference with Nimrod, Semiramis, Thoth, and Tashshigura-mash.

Each person's idea feeds on the ideas of the others, including the rationale as follows: when the fruit of a woman's body is thusly offered, it is for the sin of the soul.

A principal of this God's law, which would become required by Jews and Christians too, is that the priest will partake of whatever is sacrificed in a sin offering. Huh?

Therefore, the priests of Nimrod, or Baal, are required to eat of the human sacrifices. Henceforth would the term, Priest of Baal, be known as a devourer of human flesh. On the opposite wall from the Dragon in brilliant yellow and orange kiln-fired tiles is the Sun known as "Shemesh," that is, "the Servant." It occupies the entire wall with flames which seem to burst out of its center, consuming all present, with a menacing serpent wrapped around the center of the Sun. The head priest has already been selected by Nimrod and Semiramis to officiate in the temple ceremonies. His living quarters, as well as many other officials, are in the lower chambers of the temple.

Nimrod has been fascinated with these ideas, some of which he has gleaned from a city subordinated by Babel, and by his visions while in the sweat tent of fire worship. The head priest has many talents for idol worship, though his knowledge of fire worship is understandably lacking, lacking because Nimrod is the first to have conceived of it in the sweat tent. The priest, Tashshigura-mash, is a quick study. Very quick. Very brutal.

All this has occurred under the guidance of Nimrod's minister of religious worship, Thoth. Only the workers necessary to tile the inside of the temple are allowed inside. Those hundred or so men would, over a period of two years, simply cease to exist. No eyes. No ears. No witnesses.

Now, it so happens that after the incident at Akkad with the three families, Zag is involved in disciplining one of his soldiers who is working on the canals, for raping a slave woman. The soldier had been admiring this particular lady as she worked, and mentally had convinced himself that she had feelings for her. When she was alone, he made his move on her. Instead of willingly participating with the soldier, she fought him and she died. Another slave, her teenage son from Calneh, reported the incident to the army captain in charge and he, in turn, reported it to Zag. Zag is flogging the soldier, and he flogs the man so hard that he breaks his back, and the soldier shortly thereafter dies. Zag is brought before King Nimrod. The King has no recourse but to punish Zag and strip him of his command as General of the Army. He is demoted and Jared is put in his place.

"Since you are my General, I too must pay for your sins. You acted on my behalf – so it is said, so it is done. Place him in a prison cell until sunrise. Assemble all my leaders in the temple, no outsiders are to be in attendance. The punishment will be ten stripes." Zag is taken away.

"Early the next morning Kind Nimrod arises and gets dressed in a humble robe he has a servant bring him, a robe such as a poor man would wear. Semiramis stirs, sees the worn, dirty robe and gently asks, "What is my husband in costume for this day?"

Nimrod walks to her, kisses her on the hand and forehead, "It is nothing, my love, I must preside over a whipping this morning and do not wish to bloody my royal clothing." With that he exits.

The great temple is over-filled with war-hardened generals, captains, lieutenants, each who have witnessed many deaths, many beatings, and so their attitude is more of a festive nature rather than somber. No one is really aware that it is Zag who is to be punished. I mean, come on, the General of the Army being flogged? If they knew it was Zag, most figured the King would have found a way out of punishing his General. At the end of the great temple hall where presentations are to be held, is a table with restraints attached. The high priest is present with a hood on and a cat-of-nine-tails whip in his hand. Each end of the multiple strands of leather has a piece of sharp granite tied to it. It is a flesh-eating machine.

King Nimrod enters and immediately all conversations cease. He is wearing his royal robe over his other worn-out robe, his crown on his head, a somber look on his face. Zag is brought in the hall just as King Nimrod sits on his throne. A hushed, startled buzz goes through the assembled group as they see Zag in chains. Zag is escorted the length of the hall to the table and priest. The guards proceed by stripping Zag of his garments, and as they go to tie him to the table, the King raises his hand. The assumption is King Nimrod will still find a way to spare his best friend, his most fierce General, from this punishment.

King Nimrod drops his royal robe on the throne and walks down the steps and crosses the length of the hall to Zag. He motions for the guards to remove Zag from the table. Nimrod removes the worn and dirty robe leaving his body completely nude. Again a little buzz goes through the room. Before he lies down on the wooden table, he looks at Zag and then in general at the audience, "He but did my bidding," and lies down. He motions to the stunned guards to strap him in on both his hands and feet, which they hesitantly do.

Zag is bewildered, "No, my king," as he seeks to approach the King. The guards keep him a foot or two away from King Nimrod, not sure what they should do. The hall is grimly quiet. Nimrod nods to his high priest and whispers, "Ten." Immediately the whip comes down forcefully and the priest counts, "One!" Nimrod moans and all can see the ripped skin. This is not a publicity stunt: their King is truly being whipped.

Down comes the second strike of the whip. Zag is wild with frenzy, "No, me, no, my King." He throws himself on top of Nimrod to prevent the priest from continuing.

"No, Zag. It is as it should be. Remove him." The guards pull Zag back a step or two and he falls to his knees.

"Three." Nimrod moans louder and his hands seek something to grip and find only the restraints, which he grabs. Zag crawls to him, clutching one of Nimrod's hands.

"Four", with the flesh popping and rising like miniature volcanoes of pimpled flesh peeling away each time the whip strikes.

Tears well up in Zag's eyes, "No."

"Five," cries out the priest.

Zag cries out a lone, mournful cry that reverberates around the room. All the men are silent and some turn their heads away from their king.

"Six," the priest announces. Zag's fingers clutch Nimrod's hand so hard that Zag's fingers cause the King to bleed.

"Seven," as Zag's tears fill his eyes, and he emits a cry that comes from the depths of his body and his soul.

"Me, not my Lord. Me."

"Eight," and all that can be heard is Zag's scream. Behind the men surrounding the table twenty-men-deep, can barely be seen a blue hood, the hood of the queen accompanied by two of her servants in the doorway. Many of the men have tears in their eyes from the whipping or from the reaction of Zag; it is not possible to tell for who their tears emanate.

"Nine," relentlessly counts the priest. King Nimrod's body goes limp as Zag continues his agony. Even the priest is having a hard time finishing his task. As his hand twitches and shakes, he pauses longer than normal.

Before the final blow, at the top of his voice and all through the "ten", Zag emits the sound of death, the sound of soul-wrenching pain, the sound of repentance, the sound that will never need to be repeated by him.

"Ten."

Just the crying and moaning and short bursts of screams, all sounds from Zag, can be heard as all exit like ghosts from the great hall, quietly, reverently, where screams will be the norm in but a few months.

The Queen has already exited.

Zag is taken back to his cell.

The guards quickly extricate the King from his restraints and his physicians surround him, motioning to the guards to carry him to his bedroom. There they clean his wounds, apply ointment, wrap him with bandages and give him a sedative in water. Semiramis is by his side holding his hand and weeping.

Outside the temple are many hundreds of troops and citizens who have expected someone to be punished and know not the facts. "How was it? Did he get what he deserved for killing my friend?" asked one man to the cheers of some fellow bystanders. "Did he?" he repeats. The military men push past him forcefully, but not brutally, with tears in their eyes.

"Aye, son, he got that and more," one captain responds. The crowd cheers.

The physicians give King Nimrod another potion to drink that will dull the pain considerably.

Zag lies on the floor of his cell moaning, "Me, me, me."

A king pays for the sins of his followers: a sight rarely seen by mankind. A lesson not soon to be forgotten by thousands of military souls in Babel. A king put his life on the line for one of his followers. And as the story travels all across Babel, a lesson unfolds not to be lost upon tens of thousands of others. A lesson that turns the hearts of even the greatest foes of King Nimrod soft, for a while. This is a prototype of things to come in two thousand, four hundred, thirty and three years.

King Nimrod survives the day, as does Zag. The relationship they forged would never be broken. Zag would never again give offense that would, could, be attributable to his King.

Nimrod's goal now is to involve all mankind in the art of Fire-Worship. Whoa! Wait a minute! What happened to sweet old Nimmie, great grandson of the prophet of God, Noah - - the man who ruled forcibly and yet justly with his army for Babel and its many conquests? One doesn't just jump from worshipping the true and everlasting God to Fire-Worship. Does one?

I don't know. How long did it take some of the greatest men of all time to switch from quiet and unobtrusive to their defining life's work: great men like Stalin, Lenin, Hitler, Idi-Amin, Mussolini, Genghis Khan, Kublai Khan, several Chinese Emperors, Aztec rulers galore. The list is almost endless. The numbers of the sacrificed in the hundreds of millions.

The above-mentioned men achieved their great successes each in less than what, thirty, forty years? Nimrod lived for over four hundred years! What the mind can conceive, man can achieve. Especially with a little help from our dear, warped, deviant brother Lucifer. If you do not believe in him you truly do not have a clue regarding life on this earth.

Okay, but what has brought this change on in our man, Nimrod? As you already know, it started with the death of his friend, Lugal, and then the murder of his dad, Cush. Nimrod would never let go of the idea that he has somehow been the one wronged by the deaths of these two men. He never accepts the teachings of his wise Great-Grandfather Noah regarding life after death, never accepts the idea that God would not just step in and save all righteous people from bad things. He never accepts the concept of God would cease to be God if He interferes with men's desire to do bad and that if He does, God would be playing favorites and would therefore cease to be God.

When he killed those ten soldiers he began the process of setting himself up as god, setting himself up as the righter of wrongs by use of revenge.

But what about marrying the beautiful, the virgin, the headstrong and seemingly righteous Semiramis? Surely she has the power to sway Nimrod. Absolutely! And she does. This is the most murderous tandem ever known to man. Her thirst for power begins the day of Nimrod's coronation when she sees hundreds of thousands literally under the influence, the spell, of her husband Nimrod. Her signature of death would find those who oppose her with a cup of sand poured down their throats, filling their mouths and suffocating them. Let them eat cake? Starving begins to sound like a great way to die, no?

But, what causes some people to be this way? Don't we all have tragedies to face in this life? I am not completely sure. When you find out, tell me and I'll write another book! The black comedian, Flip Wilson said, "The devil made me do it!" Do you believe him? Do you believe the devil, or God, or ??? can make you do anything?

When Nimrod laid on the whipping table to take the ten stripes for Zag, what was he thinking? Like the King of Kings? Physically it knocked him out, but mentally he became Satan incarnate. He loved it, thrived on it, and relished the thought of taking one for the … Yeah, that intense. Snuffing out a few lives like in Akkad is nothing: like eating a few grapes before breakfast and popping those with your teeth and feeling the juice explode in your mouth. Or making an omelet. Can't make that omelet without breaking a few eggs, right? That powerful. That inspiring. That addictive.

Now, to signify to the world how great, how glorious King Nimrod has become, the eternal flame is instituted on the eastern side of the temple. This flame burns day and night, lighted by the virgins of Babel, a very unique and select club of young women who have distinguished themselves with the priests over a period of time. Women trained in the art of, of well, uh keeping a hot flame hot, so it wouldn't even flicker. Day and night, year after hundreds of years they, uh, toil.

And each year in April, men, women and animals are made to pass through the fire. This is a ceremony performed in the temple, at night; a ceremony that purifies, where Nimrod raises many, many men almost from the dead. Passing through the fire represents obtaining a new life from sin, regeneration from spiritual death to spiritual life. So we say, Nimrod raises sinful men from their dead lives, almost, to sinless new lives. This is celebrated, of course, with the burning alive of human infants. This is what enables Nimrod to pay for these sinful lives with great, eager help from the core of virgins. The closer to the womb, the fruit of the woman, that the sacrifices are, the more powerful is the ability to pay for a man's sins, so goes the theory. Thus is born the concept of Fire Worship, the religion of Nimrod and Semiramis. But where to get willing participants who would give up their infants for sacrifice? Ah, there's the catch.

Soon after the temple opens to the special few, homes in Babel are slowly adopting snakes as the people's sign to King Nimrod that they approve of this form of religion. They do not know regarding human sacrifice, just that the Sun is really important, that Fire has a great deal to do with it, and that snakes, serpents, are part of it. So, snakes are the logical choice, as Fire and Sun are not practical choices to have in the home.

The snakes begin to be found nestled about the home's altar. Now you have to have an altar too, and like a dog or cat, the snakes could be petted by visitors. The serpents creep about the home, slithering about the cups of the guests. In hot weather, ladies would use them around their necks for the purpose of keeping cool. Showing off to neighbors is not unheard of. Couldn't hurt to have a few witnesses of one's desire to please the King either. Of course, these sacred serpents are also good for making war on rats and mice.

But as they live a charmed, sacred life, no one dares openly lay violent hands on them. They multiply fast and become a replacement nuisance for the rats and mice. If one does tire of their presence, one best bury their sacred little bodies deep in the dry desert sand lest the eyes and ears of the King find out.

When the priests leave the temple for excursions into the city, they are always accompanied by assistants carrying long poles with live serpents wrapped around the pole. In the years ahead it becomes the habit of the inhabitants of Babel to kneel momentarily as the priest and the serpent pass by.

Good King Nimrod soon starts a school for public administrators on how to conduct the affairs of the kingdom in the towns and cities being conquered and new cities that he is having started. Yes, King Nimrod colonizes areas of his domain to increase taxes, to increase the population and to increase the ability to grow crops. To help the population in his colonized cities grow, certain fruitful women, with their polygamist husbands, who have proven their ability to have male babies in almost litter-size numbers, are paid a healthy stipend.

Then, at the age of eight, the young men would undergo a series of tests to determine if they have the skills for religious service, for administration, science, for warfare or some different jobs in the ever-increasing army. There are many other schools organized, including engineering, math, and the arts and so on.

The palace living quarters for the King and Queen are completed soon after the temple. The hundreds of additional rooms would soon follow. While the temple remains relatively empty as King Nimrod, high priest Tashshigura-mash, Semiramis and Thoth, the religious minister, devise their final plans for Fire Worship, the palace is becoming a hive in full bloom.

Among the first court cases to be heard by King Nimrod in the palace common law chambers is one brought before him by two wealthy citizens regarding a slave who has been sold by one and purchased by the other, supposedly.

"Your Majesty, it is so wonderful to have a man of your experience to hear our little squabble of a case. Thank you so much for your time. It is a great honor ..."

"Could we please get on with the specifics of the case? Though I do thank you for being so enthralled with me and my abilities without having experienced them first-hand."

"Well, as I was about to say, your Majesty", (not having appreciated being cut-off even by the King), "I sold this man-slave to my friend and the slave refuses to work for him. The slave claims he is mine and cannot be sold! He told my friend, and I quote, "You are not my master and I shall not work for you!"

King Nimrod looks over the black slave from his throne and the two nervous, pale, wealthy men -- men who obviously had never been told no and did not expect to be told so today. "Where did you purchase this very well-proportioned slave?"

"I, uh, well, I didn't exactly purchase him, your Lordship, he came to me rather as a payment of a debt."

"What kind of debt?"

"I won him in a game of chance, horse-racing, Majesty. But what earthly difference does that make? He is mine to do with as I please!"

There is a rather unhealthy, silent pause as the noise of his comments reverberate in the common law chambers. Had this man lost his marbles?

"You feel," King Nimrod said icily, "it is your place as a wealthy citizen of Babel to tell me what difference something makes because, because you have money?" An attendant to the king whispers something in his ear.

Realizing he has irked the king, the wealthy man begins to sweat and back-tracks. "I said that rather poorly, my King. I humbly apologize."

"Yes, it was said poorly. And I do not accept your haughty, pitiful apology. I assume your nasty attitude is one of being offended by me being a 'nobody' one day and a king the next. While you, why you've been a wealthy man since, oh I don't know, since your father died four years ago - - inherited money, the worst kind. Pompous ass. Money not really earned by the sweat of your own brow. It is more like the sweat of your large, fat buttocks trying to get in and out of a chair.

While you may be someone of standing out there, I am the someone of standing in here," raising his voice, "Am I understood?"

"Yes, yes, your landlord, landship, lordship."

King Nimrod turns to the second wealthy man, "Now, you tell me, sir, about this purchase."

"Majesty, I too won this slave in a game of chance, horse-racing too." My wife and I have had our eye on him for some time as he is an outstanding, uh, worker."

Nimrod raises his hand to stop the man, "Your wife noticed he was an outstanding worker? Your wife visits the fields or granaries or stockyards to watch muscular black men work?"

"Ah, no, not exactly. I guess she, she ..."

To the slave King Nimrod asks, "What exactly do you do for the women of these men?"

The slave looks him in the eye and kneels before speaking," It is Chiamaka's essence that they want, for their wives, their daughters and their personal maids."

"Is there anything Chiamaka would rather be doing, or are you happy spreading 'your essence' from flower to flower?"

"These women are fat, they are ugly and they smell bad. I would rather spread manure than be with them. Truth be told, I was a warrior in my homeland of Africa. I would rather be in the service of my King fighting his enemies, fighting the enemies of Babel, of Babylon, Great One." He prostrates himself before Nimrod.

"Unfortunately, my friend that cannot be. The law is very specific. You have been brought before me for denying who your master is and for not working for that master. While I believe you and your desires, you are owned by this man", pointing to the second wealthy man. "You hereby stand convicted." King Nimrod snaps his fingers and one of his elite soldiers brings him a knife. "You sir," pointing to the second wealthy man, "are to cut off the slave's right ear, as he has been convicted of lying about you being his master."

The slave, Chiamaka, has not moved and is still laying prostrate on the floor.

"But sire, don't you have someone to do this sort of thing? I, I can't do this."

"The law is again quite specific, in that it says, "the master shall cut off his ear, not the King or the King's appointed person."

The Elite soldier goes to the man and extends the knife to him. The wealthy man clumsily takes the knife and looks at it.

"I would caution you, citizen of Babel, to make sure this is the right slave you are about to maim. Should this be a case of mistaken identity, I mean you know how all foreigners can look alike, you would be in jeopardy of having your right ear removed and your right hand that committed the offense."

The two wealthy men hastily confer and number one speaks to the King. "Perhaps we were a little too quick to judge. He does strongly resemble another of my slaves. Would you be so kind as to pull his pants down so I can see his … uh, his" gesturing, "you know, his …"

"No, I will not subject him to public scrutiny like that."

"Then may I ask if you would be so kind as to allow us to withdraw our petition, and we will look into the matter further?"

Very pointedly and coolly King Nimrod speaks, "He is or he is not, which is it?"

"The second wealthy man speaks, "He is not."

"The former slave Chiamaka is free to go. Refund these men their petition money. Next!"

The two men can be heard arguing on their way out of court, "What is wrong with you, 'he is not'; we've lost a lot of money," says number one. "Yes, but that is better than me losing my ear and hand, if you are wrong."

The slave speaks as he rises and is untied, "May the God of rain, wind and fire bless your house forever, good King."

"In a few days General Jared will conduct Babel's yearly tryouts for the army of Babylon. Perhaps you should attend."

Smiling he answers, "So it is said, so it is done, my King."

Another part of the hive activity is the addition of several children to Nimrod and Semiramis. True to her promise of many children for her husband, the queen tirelessly produces male heirs and next-generation female queens.

"My dear king and husband," began Semiramis, "have I pleased you all these first years of marriage?"

Nimrod looked at her quizzically, "Have I given you reason to think otherwise, my queen?"

"No, my husband, not at all. It's, well, I have something on my mind and I wish to tell you about it. First, I thought I'd find out if there is anything I could do that would make you pleased with me more."

"And that is …?"

She motions for him to sit as they pass one of the beautiful ponds outside the palace. "We will need an abundance of infants for the temple ceremonies, once the temple is fully functional, right?"

"Ah, yes"

"And we wouldn't want our children to be used, even though they would be the highest form of sacrifice possible, would we?"

"I agree."

"And it wouldn't really be prudent to steal children from our population of mothers here in Babel, or even from any of our conquests. Word would get around and it might put you in disfavor with our people."

"I hadn't thought that far ahead, but yes, that makes sense."

"Well, what if we had a royal baby-making service that was almost as pure as our own children?"

"A royal baby, what?"

Semiramis slides close to Nimrod and takes his hand in hers, "A royal baby-making service!"

Nimrod looks at her bewildered.

"If you were to take, say, a woman or two from each of our conquered cities and marry them ..."

"Semiramis, I don't need any other women in my life. I have you. I only love you ..."

"I know, but this isn't about love. It's about babies for sacrifices that our new religion needs. Not yours and mine, but of other women you make pregnant with your magnificent essence."

Nimrod gets up and walks a few steps with his back to her, "You want me to marry other women, get them pregnant and then sacrifice those children?"

"Yes!" Semiramis exclaims and claps her hands, "What do you think?"

"I've never known any woman except you, I ..."

"I know you love me. I'm not concerned about that, silly. This is just sex. I will keep track of who is pregnant, who is fertile, who is ready to get pregnant. I'll have women who take the babies from their mothers to nurse them, raise them. Every second baby from the same mother will conveniently die from some complication at birth. Each mother will have a couple of children who live and some that die. You just visit the women when I tell you and get them pregnant!"

"I'll be honest. I could never share you with other men. How can you ..."

"I am not sharing you. This is just ... just sex. Business. And our religion. Our life. If I had sex with other men it would be just to further our future, for business, for sex, for religion."

"If another man touches ..."

"Oh my silly Nimmie, this is just an example. You are the only man for me, forever. I have no need of anyone else. Just think on it."

"Think about two or three other wives?"

"Well, I am thinking more like two or three hundred."

Nimrod sits down like a sack of mud, "Hundreds? I feel tired just thinking about making all these women happy, the problems, the complaints …"

"I will take care of all that. I can even arrange for each of them to take a sedative before you visit them. They'll just smile and say thank you after you've spread your royal essence."

"Spreading my essence among hundreds … And you're okay with this, really?"

"Well, I plan on arranging your schedule so I am available to you too!" She cuddles with him. "Why don't we go inside and I'll help you come to a, conclusion?"

They start to go back inside the palace and Semiramis continues, "We can notify each city that, uh, uh, to improve relations, so to speak, with your city, the King has decided to marry two, no, maybe four royal women of your city. Please arrange your prospective ten choices for an interview this coming week. Or something like that. I'll work on it, later. You just let me do the arranging, okay?"

"Hundreds," Nimrod says, disrobing.

Zag stands before thousands of young men ranging in age from sixteen to forty at the break of day. Nuradad speaks for him. "Welcome to this year's tryouts for the magnificent army of Babel, the finest fighting force in the world." Cheers from the men. "Today is the tryouts for runners. If you have tried out before, this being your second time, it will be your last. If you have run this race twice before, please stand to the side." A few men do. "You are still eligible for the army tryouts in the weapons section such as for knife-throwing, spears, bow and arrows and so on. We are seeking a few good men in each area.

Lieutenant Zag will oversee tryouts for General Jared, and the Lieutenant's word rules. If he feels you are disqualified, you are. There are no appeals. If you cheat, you are permanently disqualified for life. And God help you – as Lieutenant Zag will not. So, it's a beautiful day here in happy valley; let's get started.

Six times around the city, you will follow the poles with the royal purple banners attached. You may not receive any aid for any purpose at any time during your run. Your times are not being recorded, but the position in the race is. Each of you has six identification markers on a bracelet numbered one through six. As you come around this final turn of each lap, drop the marker in the correct barrel. Barrel marked one – first lap. Barrel marked two – second lap, and so on. Do not drop the wrong number in the wrong barrel or you are disqualified.

There are tables with water in mugs just past the number barrel, thousands of mugs. Take one, two, as many as you need each lap. There are twenty huge wagons positioned around the course. If you feel like you need to stop due to fatigue or injury, find a wagon and a physician or his assistant will help you. The race for you is officially over. All others must finish the race by sundown. No exceptions. The race belongs to the swiftest and those who endure to the end.

Any questions?" There are none. "Ready," Nuradad signals for a horn to be blown, "Begin." And the runners are off.

Some runners have come a long distance to be in this race, including three young men from Anat. They are Tabansi and Mariana's oldest sons, Aericas, Earron and Parahayker. Their mother finally married King Ham and has so far produced two more sons.

Seems like step-daddy Ham found the three men responsible for the death of Tabansi: one guard and two robbers. The men had conveniently had their tongues removed and so they were unable to defend themselves, to provide alibis that they were truly hundreds of miles away from the cliffs at the time of Tabansi's death, that is, his cold-blooded murder. So, they were publicly executed, thus bringing to a close this tragic episode among the members of the human race.

Mariana's attention was for their little half-brothers, and their step-father's attention for the three of them, was, well, a step-father's affection. True to his word Ham had placed them in his army as runners, but without any training, very low pay and a lot of inattention. Having heard of the phenomenal successes being achieved in Babel, they came seeking their place where they could be recognized for their efforts. And in doing so, be trained in the art of running and knife-throwing like their father. God-loving men, like their father. Willing to die for a king worth dying for, unlike their father.

Most runners have come from Babel. So it is with Chiamaka, the slave released by King Nimrod. Built like a cheetah with powerful shoulders and upper body and slim waist and powerful ripped legs, he would be a great addition to Nimrod's army. Zag is well aware of this young man and watches him with great interest. So many had tried with much talent and physical prowess before, but few had the heart to go with the talent. Zag would see.

Chiamaka and the three brothers wait for the runners to settle into a pace and then find the pace to their liking behind the first few hundred men. Six trips around the city is a daunting task, since the city has expanded more than twice its size since Nimrod had ran the course several years ago. Being first on the first trip around is not important. These particular four men had, on the day previous and with other serious runners, jogged around Babel to get a feel for the distance and the terrain. They had calculated the time necessary to accomplish this day's task.

None of the four men speak to others, while some chat with their friends during the first trip. On the second trip around, the chatty ones have fallen well off the pace. Chiamaka's mind is occupied with thoughts of his possible future in the army of Nimrod. And so the time passes quickly. The three brothers have thoughts of the past and their family far away and of their father.

The third trip finds the lead group thinning out considerably to about one hundred men, with the course now full of various-speed runners the entire distance around Babel. There are no chatty ones left. The twenty large carts are starting to fill up with quitters.

The distance around the city is about thirty miles a trip with the most difficult part still being the up-and-down of the hills to the north side. Coming down the hills is as painful, with the constant jarring of the descent testing the calves and thighs at every step.

One man stumbles and loses his footing in front of the three brothers, and they jump over him simultaneously. The men behind them are not so fortunate and three more men hit the rocky ground, ending their race. The lesson here is not lost on the other runners around them, and distances between runners grow. Day dreaming has its price.

At the beginning of the fourth lap, every man is grabbing water both to drink and to pour on their heads to combat the stifling heat. In the first two laps those behind the leaders do what the leaders do. If those in the lead drink, it seemed they all would drink. And, in the first lap, few leaders did drink and so the rest would follow. Except the three brothers, the slave and a few others: they would drink a little each trip and pour a little on their heads too. Habits they each had developed in their lifetime that were proven to work. Why would men assume that leaders in a race know more about your needs than you do? Something all of us seem to do from time to time. You go with what got you there, not the fad of the month.

What has become of Jared, Fenchristo and Rayas? The two brothers are captains, while Jared is now the General in charge of all the armies, in Zag's place. Jared tries to allow Zag to continue most of his duties albeit unofficially. Jared knows Zag is a very proud man and wants to keep him on his best side. This is not an easy thing to do with Zag.

The three men oversee the training of the more than ten thousand troops, now closing in on fifteen thousand. Training is a six-days-a-week job, not only for the new recruits, but also for keeping the most experienced men sharp. Jared has become known as the King's strategist in war. He is in the process of assembling thousands of animal stomachs from all over the expanding kingdom. Why? We'll find out soon.

Jared's family has moved to Babel to support him. Zamama, his wife, his fourteen children, and others are desirous of a future of more than raising livestock. However, raising animals in an ever-increasing population like Babel's is now a full-time and prosperous job.

Fortunately, Jared's family has settled on the outskirts of Babel near the area designated for the raising of animals. Jared has insisted that along with edible beasts, the family also start raising horses and oxen. Being a forward thinker Jared knew the value of these beasts of burden, and so his family has already purchased top of the line breeding stock shortly after their arrival. They have quite a goodly number of horses and oxen ready for sale when the large carts are being built for transporting granite and for the families wandering the desert. Each cart requires at least twenty to forty oxen and the need for horses was constant with the large numbers of the increasing army.

Jared's brothers and sisters also follow him, especially one brother of whom the family rarely speaks. He is an older brother who seems reclusive, more so since they have moved to Babel. The brother of Jared, as he comes to be known, is an extremely righteous man who receives strong feelings and impressions from his God; feelings such as the ones he shared with Jared concerning Nimrod.

"You must be very wary of confiding in King Nimrod about religious matters and regarding me. He is not the man you grew up with. He will soon seek to destroy the people of God, my brother," offered the brother of Jared.

"Nimrod, my brother? Hardly", laughed Jared, thinking his brother may have become a bit paranoid regarding unseen persecution. "As you say, I have known him all my life. If it will make you feel better, yes, I will watch for signs of change."

"Nevertheless, be cautious."

"Yes, Mahonri."

"Please, Jared, no names."

"As you wish." Jared could see the seriousness and hear the seriousness of his brother. He also knew from past experiences not to trifle with his feelings." It's strange, thought Jared. Here is my brother living in the shadows of life, and yet he is beloved by all his family and those near to the family. Jared had seen his brother place his hands on the heads of people and cure them from various sorts of difficulties, from infections to broken limbs, to conditions people had from birth.

And when the brother had given verbal advice such as his warning to Jared about Nimrod, he'd never been wrong. Never. But Jared has little time to worry about Nimrod, as he has been made aware of impending conquests and needs to prepare his troops for yet another battle. Also, he is to prepare thousands of his men to ride horses and at the same time shoot bows and arrows as they attack their enemy.

While horses were indeed common, obtaining thousands is not. Then, where does he keep them, train them and feed them? Plus, thousands of men would need tens of thousands of arrows, shields, bridles and quivers. The list seems endless. He has runners searching every city as far as five hundred miles away for horses and breeders of horses.

One area that seems very promising is a place called Arabia. They have horses such as the one Nimrod had ridden in Mahora, his father's favorite horse, Nabu. These horses are fast, high spirited and hard to find. Hard, because no one wanted to sell breed mares to outsiders. He had contacted Kadenram for his help. As of yet Jared has not heard back from him.

He has already requisitioned every maker of bows and arrows from every city within the kingdom to fill his needs. It would take at least six months to have the supplies and equipment to train his men and prepare for war. Then, he has to prepare stratagems to conquer the cities on his list.

Of course, Jared's personal contact with Nimrod is extremely limited lately and he has no knowledge of the purpose of the new temple. And Fire Worship. And Nimrod's new religion.

The recruit runners are just ending their fourth trip when Zag sends one of his Elite to the race course to request one runner to come and see him. This man, unbeknownst to Zag, is a cousin to Zag's mouthpiece,

Nuradad. Zag has seen this man come around a bend in the course before the barrels and tables and appeared too fresh for his fifth trip. As the man passes the barrels for the identification tags, Zag sees him very smoothly drop several markers in the same barrel at one time, a clear no-no.

When the soldier brings the runner, a strong-looking, muscular man to Zag, the runner feigns great fatigue, holding his side with one hand as though he has a pain in his right hip. Nuradad and the runner exchang a quick, concerned glance as the soldier brings the runner before Zag. Zag whispers another order to the soldier and off he goes to the barrel where the markers has been deposited.

Meanwhile, Nuradad asks Zag, "General, what is wrong?"

Zag responded, "He cheated."

"My general, are you sure? While I know him not, this is a very well-built man, and he'd make a good addition to the army. Why would such a man cheat?"

The soldier returns and privately places the several markers in Zag's hand.

"He cheated." Zag shows the multiple markers to Nuradad and his cousin, Shahmanesor. "Cheat!"

Chapter Eight

Nuradad hits the runner on the side of his head, knocking him to the ground. "Great general, I will personally punish this man."

"Name?" questions Zag.

"Shahmanesor," answers both Nuradad and his cousin simultaneously. Nuradad realizes his mistake immediately, "General, uh, his name is on the markers."

The markers are still in Zag's hand. Zag looks suspiciously at Nuradad, "Punish, now."

Nuradad takes a small hatchet sized axe and lays out his cousin's fingers of his right hand, spread apart on the floor of the great wagon in preparation of cutting one of the fingers off. Two guards hold Shahmanesor in place. Nuradad holds his cousins left hand down and prepares to swing the small axe when the whooshing sound of a full-sized axe whizzes past Nuradad's left ear, severing both the left hand of Nuradad and the left hand of Shahmanesor. Both men writhe in agony with screams of pain and blood squirting everywhere. Hundreds of men on the wagon look on in horror. Nuradad looks at Zag with pain and hate in his eyes.

"Liar. Cousin!" Zag shouts at the two men. "Cheat," he yells at Shahmanesor. The two men take a cloth handed to them by a soldier, wrap their left arm stumps and stagger off. "Nuradad, no more!"

The screams startle the runners nearby, as they are preparing for their sixth and final lap. Chiamaka has moved to the front of the small pack of fifteen runners with Aericas several runners behind. His brothers Earron and Parahayker have dropped quite a distance behind him, and yet will still finish in the top seventy-five runners out of the four thousand starting the race.

Nuradad and Shahmanesor cross the path of Aericas, their blood dripping on the ground, as the two men scramble to find a physician. Both men will live and then must pack a few belongings before leaving Babel forever. Soon the entire army will hear of their offenses and the men would then be fair game to any soldier wishing to cleanse the honor of Babel.

With all that soldiers have to contend with - - murder, even rape, plundering and pillaging, drunkenness - - and then to have their honor stained by another soldier's lies and cheating. Would lying and cheating be enough to incite them to murder? Is it possible?

Makes one wonder as to the logic of it all. Why not just shun them? Shame them to leave Babel? They already have been punished with the removal of their hand. What good will they be trying to support themselves or their families? Ah, their families. When Nuradad reaches his home and tells his wife and children what happened and that they have to pack and quickly, none of them move a muscle. One by one those old enough to understand what had transpired, turn their backs on their husband or father until he has left. Same at Shahmanesor's home. The two men should feel fortunate: had this occurred in a couple thousand years in a town called Sparta, the men would have been found dead, with a kitchen knife in each of their backs, a knife lovingly stuck there by their dishonored wives.

Today, it seems, we look on either of those two scenes with the attitude of, "What's the big deal?" Then we make them the CEO of a large company who gouges out the financial eyes of his investors, gets stock options and a golden parachute. Or President. Then, the outraged citizens storm the streets protesting that ... a bit late.

The stifling heat of the day has passed and soldiers can be seen helping convulsing bodies to the great wagons. The agony of other bodies with their leg muscles knotted up so tight they are unable to walk and having to be dragged, crying in pain to the wagons, tugs at the heart strings of all around them. And yet the runners run. Hundreds will finish today, many hundreds more will be finished today, not making it to the finish line. Not willing to quit. Not ...

These many hundreds excite Zag. These are they that he will mold into machines for Nimrod's empire. No, they will not be Elite runners. They will be, however, the leaders of the masses, the heart of the heartless army. The never-say-die guts of the empire. These are they that when left in that circle drawn in the sand, would die in that circle rather than reach outside for easily obtainable food or drink.

Thousands of years from now a noble author would put it thusly, "To thine own self be true, and it must follow, as the night the day, thou canst not then be false to any man."

These are the warriors Zag smiles over. Well, we think he smiles. Maybe it is gas.

Of the four thousand men that started that day, four hundred and fifty finish by sundown. This includes the three brothers and Chiamaka, who finishes first. Eight hundred have to be helped home in the dark after they are taken forcibly off the course. Fifty-five men die. Forty-seven are permanently disabled due to the rigors of the race. Two thousand, six hundred and forty-eight quit and live to fight another day.

Yes, the race could have been made shorter to five, four, maybe three laps. Maybe the organizers should have waited for a cloudy day. Perhaps all the men should have been given a ribbon for at least trying to finish and all could have been declared equal winners. Then, maybe all those men could have felt good about themselves.

Maybe no one would have died. No one would have been crippled. No one would have spent a lifetime preparing for this achievement. Maybe all the late sleepers, beer guzzlers and want-a-be's could have had this same achievement without the lifetime of preparation. Maybe each of us should climb a fifty-story building, jump and fly to the moon. We'll give you a ribbon for trying, for finishing, for providing us with an example of "Stupid is as stupid does." Will we ever learn?

Zag, it turns out, married a woman any of us mere mortals would die for. No, she isn't the 'looker' that Semiramis is. She isn't the bright and bubbly, house-duster, clothes-cleaned-and-neatly-folded, every-hair-in-place wonder woman of Babel. She is simply a woman who loves her man, who makes him feel appreciated, who ignores his obvious faults and yet seeks ways to encourage him to be a better dad, a better husband. Shamshi welcomes Zag home every day with a smile and a long, long hug. Each of their eight children stand in line behind her to kiss and hug their dad. And Zag returns each and every kiss and hug lovingly. He learned that from his wife. Zag's home is truly his castle.

What happens at work, stays at work, and whatever happens at home, stays at home. Zag is able to live a very compartmentalized life. Zag loves his wife. He loves his family. He loves his King.

Shamshi had been brought up in a home where her father drank excessively. Beat his wife excessively. Beat his children more excessively. There were few tears when he died, falling drunkenly under the wheels of a neighbor's heavily loaded manure wagon. What tears were shed were for, "Thank God, it's over." Shamshi was sent to live with her aunt who had married but never had any children and wanted help around the house. Shamshi's mother needed the income, and so Shamshi moved several towns away to live with her aunt and husband. Her head danced with all the ideas she had for helping her aunt.

She had her own little room in the back of the house, away from all the noise of her aunt and husband arguing. There was no window in her room, but Shamshi did not complain. The first day there, Aunt Entressia and uncle Jacobar found a few things for Shamshi to do: cleaning the floors, dusting, helping with meals. She fell asleep immediately from her honest day's labors and the long trip. She did not first awaken to the sounds of someone slipping into bed with her. It wasn't until it was over that she started to cry.

Life went on like this for four years. Knowing her mother needed the meager income, she never complained. Then, at a get-together of young people in the town square, she met Zag: big as a building Zag. She no sooner smiled at him then Aunt Entressia whisked her away to their house.

"What do you think you are doing? Embarrassing Uncle Jacobar and me like that with your whoring ways with that gigantic freak of a man. Shame on you!"

"At least he doesn't do to me what my own uncle does to me at night, when you are asleep."

Enraged, Aunt Entressia beat Shamshi with a broom and sent her to her room. There was great yelling that night that could even be heard in her room. There was yelling and crying that night, all night, from Aunt Entressia's room. At least there was no visit from Uncle Jacobar.

On errands to the shops for fruit, vegetables and clothing for sewing new dresses, Shamshi would catch a glimpse of Zag working with other men building a new home, a new shelter for someone's animals. Each time Zag would nervously smile at her. Then, one day Uncle Jacobar and Aunt Entressia went out of town for a relative's wedding.

"You are not to leave this house," Aunt Entressia warned. Uncle Jacobar just glared at her for telling his secret. Shamshi knew things were going to get worse; it was just a matter of time. All the neighbors and church members thought Uncle Jacobar was such a wonderful man. He would get up in meetings and speak so eloquently about God and His angels.

Zag appeared at the door while Shamshi busied herself cleaning the house. When she turned and saw a man in the doorway she froze, stumbled backward and moaned, "No, Uncle Jacobar, please, no!"

Zag stepped toward her, "Not Jacobar, Zag."

Shamshi crumpled to the ground sobbing, "I'm sorry, Zag, I thought …"

"He hurt?" Zag asked.

"Yes, Zag."

"Me sorry. I go." And Zag exited.

A few days later Aunt Entressia arrived home from the wedding and went straight to her room crying. Shamshi dared not ask what had happened or where uncle Jacobar was. It was several days before Aunt Entressia came out of her room. When she did, she would not look Shamshi in the eyes.

"I knew what Uncle Jacobar was doing. I pretended to be asleep, but I knew. I was weak, afraid of being alone. But it's over now. I hope someday you will forgive me."

"Where is Uncle Jacobar?"

"Dead. On the way home from the wedding, not far from here, he went for a walk before coming to our tent to go to bed. I heard this sound like someone gasping for air and choking, then a weak, far-away moan and a thud. When morning came I looked for Jacobar and he was nowhere to be found. I gathered our things and placed them in the wagon and started the short drive to home. Suddenly, the horse reared up and snorted near a cliff. I looked down and there was Jacobar's body at the bottom. Then I came home."

"I'm sorry, Aunt Entressia. So sorry." They hugged.

The next few years went by peaceably. Zag came by frequently, delivering unordered food, helping around the house. Then he told Shamshi that he needed to leave for two years and would she wait for him.

"Yes, Zag. I wait." They smiled at each other and Zag took her by the hand and kissed it, the first time he ever touched her. Then he left. When he came home, as you know, they were married. A year later their first child, a boy, was born: Zaggai.

Aunt Entressia met an older man who yearned for companionship. They were married and lived happily for many years.

The divisions in the military as to what group each man belongs to is becoming more physical. What makes a soldier "elite?" So, King Nimrod, General Jared, Zag, Captains Fenchristo and Rayas and the now eight garrison commanders meet to discuss the topic. Each garrison commander has about two thousand soldiers, some of the best runners, some of the best in each weapon category. Do we centralize all of one group here or there, and what about new troops? Do we place them all together for the first year or more or …?

"General Jared, before we begin," comments King Nimrod, "I would like to announce our decision to the rest of our military leaders. General Jared and I have decided that Captains Fenchristo and Rayas should no longer be captains." A little buzz runs amongst the leaders. "They should instead be called General Fenchristo and Rayas!" An enthusiastic round of applause is heard and several "Atta boys, way to go, congratulations, etc."

"While General Jared is the head army general, Rayas and Fenchristo will be the next in command. We will announce our decisions to the troops tomorrow. Along with that, we have also decided to name two new captains. One has been with us for quite a while and one is rather new to us, though he has had extensive experience elsewhere. Our two new captains are Zag and Chiamaka." The reception of these last two is less than enthusiastic, mainly for Zag.

"Men, what should we do with our troops?" asks Jared. "Some of them like the haircut with the shaved sides, regardless of which group they are associated with. Is it okay?" again asks Jared.

Rayas responds, "When the four of us chose to follow Nimrod, uh, King Nimrod, sorry boss, we did it to emulate our leader, to choose to show our combined belief in his decisions. It wasn't a fad. True, it really made us stand out and perhaps that's important. What I'm saying is that each group should have something that identifies those soldiers with that group. But it should not be each soldier deciding what he wants to do."

Fenchristo asks, "So, is there a so-called highest group and if so, what is the highest recognition?"

"How can we decide what group is the best, the most valuable to an army? Everyone is important. All parts make up the whole," offers Jared.

"Perhaps," begins Rayas, "we should not think in terms of best or most important. Perhaps we should simply give an identification to each branch or group within the army. An overall excellence in all areas could then allow a soldier to apply for the Elite group, as we call it. A group that defends the King, our generals, leads us into battle and guards important positions like the palace and so on."

"I like that," says King Nimrod. "Elite."

Jared agrees, "And this would be a relatively small group, high moral standards, tough tests of weapons, with physical stamina and determination."

"Glad I'm not applying," kids Rayas.

Fenchristo adds, "And just size or muscle development is not a measuring stick. I mean, there aren't many Zags in the world." All the men laugh and agree. "And if a man has a weakness he can still be admitted, say on probation, but he must correct the weakness in a certain period of time or he is moved elsewhere." Everyone enthusiastically agrees.

Garrison commander Nazibugas chips in, "Yeah, well, when General Jared talks of high morals, it sounds like we're looking for a bunch of religious nuts. I drink, so I wouldn't qualify?" There's an uneasy pause.

"If your drinking causes you," notes General Jared, "to do things that would reflect poorly on our king, then, yes, you wouldn't qualify. But if you drink and control your drinking and not beat your wife and children, then by all means, you qualify."

Nazibugas stands belligerently, "General or no general, you aren't telling me how to live my life, how to treat my family or anything else!" A very tense pause ensues.

"Then do not apply to be an Elite," responds Jared. "If high moral standards bother you, by all means stay where you are."

Nazibugas lunges for Jared but is tripped up by King Nimrod. He gets up a bit woozy as he has already been tipping back the bottle this morning.

"Leave," announces King Nimrod.

Not knowing who has told him to leave he starts, "I'll leave when I am damn …," the words get caught in his throat due to Zag's hand cutting off his air supply.

"You are fired," says General Jared.

Nazibugas stumbles out, leaving the group of leaders unsure as to what should happen next.

"Leaders of Babel," states King Nimrod, "it is important that we walk the walk like those whom we ask to follow us. The role of a leader is more than sending men to die. Men must feel that those who send them are worth dying for. Clearly commander Nazibugas was not one to die for. How do our men feel about allowing only the Elite to have shaved-sides-of-head haircuts?"

Rayas, "Good."

Jared, "I agree with General Rayas." All the others express agreement too.

"Then," continues King Nimrod, "what is to be the number of our Elite forces?"

Another garrison commander, Abasi, offers, "A few hundred, perhaps."

Rayas, "Five thousand?" The others look at him quizzically. "Okay, maybe, two thousand?" Pause. "One thousand?"

Jared, "Let's start with five hundred. We can see if there is enough interest in being the best, being the first in battle, the first to die, defenders of our King and our city."

"Yes," agrees King Nimrod.

"Then, if we find that enough men desire to be an Elite, we can raise the number. But probably not to five thousand!" All chuckle at Rayas.

"Hear, hear," echoes the group.

"I believe," says Fenchristo, "they should all train together, sleep and eat together when on duty."

"I agree," adds Abasi. "Who shall be their leader?" No one speaks.

"I think it should be," Rayas comments, "one of the garrison commanders, and he should have a separate area from the other commanders and train as General Fenchristo has suggested."

"Perhaps," smiles Fenchristo, "we should have a contest among those wishing to be the Elite commander." Lots of chuckles and then silence.

"Any takers?" asks Rayas. Several hands go up, Rayas and Fenchristo included, with four garrison commanders. "Six of us. What say you, General Jared?"

"Tomorrow at daybreak, gentlemen."

And so the meeting went. Men by their expertise with weapons will be divided up among the eight garrisons. Runners too. These men, in their respective weapons group, will still be trained together one day a week. All troops are to be divided into groups of tens, fifties, hundreds and five hundreds. Leaders are to be determined by tests with weapons.

Runners are to train with knife-throwers and then with other runners for stamina, distance and speed. All Elite candidates are to be interviewed by King Nimrod and General Jared. The Elite are to be divided up into runners and weapon groups too. They will then become the trainers for the rest of the army.

General Jared is to continue with his job of strategy and tactics plus oversee the new weapons group of bows and arrows on horseback.

The army now has need of a new garrison commander. That will have to wait until after tomorrow when six men compete to be commander of the Elite.

Zamama is busy preparing the dinner meal for the family when she hears one of her youngest sons, five year old Lufian, talking with two of his friends, William and Paz, in the doorway to the home. Lufian is drawing in the dirt with a stick, "Your sister Tonya sure is pretty, William, and I like her 'cause plays with me." Zamama pokes her head, unseen, around the corner with a smile. She returns to her cooking still with one ear on this conversation.

William answers, "I guess."

Paz asks, "Have the mosquitoes visited her yet?" Zamama pokes her head again with a perplexed look on her face.

"What 'squitos', Paz?" William asks.

"Mosquitoes," Paz corrects William's mispronunciation, "Mo-squi-toes."

"Oh, you mean those things that bite you?" asks Lufian.

"Yep, those." Have they visited her?" asks Paz.

"I don't know. Why would 'mo-squi-toes' visit my little sister?" questions William.

"My dad was talking with our neighbor and said my mom had mosquitoes bite her," and he gestures to his chest. The boys all check their chests for bites. Zamama is biting her lip to keep from laughing aloud. She understands now what the boys are talking about.

"Dad said they must have been small mosquitoes," William continued.

"Golly," said Paz, "I can't imagine how big the mosquitoes must have been that bit your mom, Lufian." Zamama is in hysterics on the kitchen floor.

"What's the big deal 'bout mosquitoes?" puzzles Lufian.

"You know, they bite you and your body swells up around the bite," William offers. There's a poignant pause with sounds of muffled laughter ... The boys turn and look, but no one is there. "Oh," Paz and Lufian say together.

"Dinner's almost ready Lufian, the boys will have to go shortly," Zamama says with breaks in her voice from trying to control her laughter.

"Okay, Mom," Lufian responds. "I don't care about mosquitoes, I think she's pretty," Lufian adds.

"Yeah, well you've never seen her without her clothes on. Then you wouldn't think she's so pretty. You know, she doesn't have one muscle that sticks out on her whole body. Not one."

"That's terrible," says Paz.

"I do!" says Lufian and he makes a muscle on his bicep.

Paz looks at his own very small bicep closely, "Do you think mosquitoes could help my muscle?"

Lufian responds, "I don't know. How old is Tonya?"

"Don't know. Maybe six or seven. Why?" asks William.

"Just wondering if I was too young for her."

Paz is still looking at his bicep, "When do the mosquitoes come? At night maybe?"

"Dad didn't say. Night, I guess." William replies, "Why?"

"Maybe we should stuff things in our bedroom doors so the mosquitoes don't bite our chests," Paz offers.

Lufian looks in his shorts, "Can they help ..."

"Okay boys," Zamama blurts out as she enters the room, "time to go home. See you tomorrow." The boys say their goodbyes and leave.

Yelling after them Lufian says, "Let me know when the mosquitoes visit Tonya."

Lufian sees tears on his mom's face and asks, "You okay, Momma?"

Zamama shakes her head and wipes the tears from her eyes, "Yes."

That night Zamama recounts the story of the mosquitoes to Jared as they lie in bed laughing. Jared says, "Paz was right about one thing: those would have been some big mosquitoes ..."

"Jared, honestly, you men are all alike." Silence and then Jared makes the sound of a giant mosquito, "Buzz, buzz."

A voice from another room calls out, "Mom, you okay?" Lufian asks. Jared and Zamama giggle.

Jared awakens in the early predawn hours to leave for the contest among the six men. Zamama has already been hard at work preparing him breakfast. They eat in silence. Jared is holding his wife's hand, "I'll be late tonight." He kisses her and exits, "Go back to bed and get some sleep."

"I'll try," she responds.

From a distance she hears, "Buzz, buzz."

"Very funny she mumbles, General Nuisance."

When Jared arrives at the garrison holding the contest, there is already a large number of on-looking soldiers: soldiers who have heard the word of officers actually having to compete for a job, like them. Captain Zag and the seven garrison commanders arrive shortly after Jared and to all of their amazement, there are eight, not six, men in the main practice area preparing for the contest. Two have their heads covered.

General Jared asks the men to stop their warm-ups and stretches. He asks, "Announce who you are and your present position."

In turn they announce, "Abasi – garrison commander, Fenchristo – General, Rayas – General, Ortzi – garrison commander, Zigor – garrison commander." The other two men seem hesitant to uncover and announce who they are.

"Gentlemen, please comply with my request: name and position. The first man uncovers his head, "Nimrod- King." There is a huge explosion of comments from the hundreds and hundreds of soldiers assembling in the arena.

"Well?" says Jared to the last man. He uncovers his head, "Berosus, second in command to Kish, the robber King, and ruler of all these lands."

Several men can be heard and seen unsheathing their weapons in preparation of attacking Berosus. General Jared holds up his hand to calm his men. Jared goes to King Nimrod, "Your majesty, this is not possible. What if you were injured or killed? The whole of Babylon could be lost. Please, please my king, please rescind your decision."

Nimrod turns to Berosus, "When the eyes and ears of the King reported what this whelp and his cowardly father had planned for today, I could hardly sit by. I will not rescind my decision."

Zag walks up, "I fight."

Berosus seems amused, "A giant of a man or a midget of a king. It matters not to me."

Zag, Nimrod and Berosus draw swords. Behind them and all around them can be heard hundreds of swords being drawn, including the other six contestants. Berosus is surrounded.

"Now, who is the coward? There still are not enough of you for me to change my mind, cowards!" More swords are heard being drawn and men are beginning to approach the eight contenders.

A voice rises above the din; "Berosus! Berosus! What are you doing? I gave my word."

"But, Father, I did not!"

"I gave my word. If we do not honor our word what is there of value?"

"We are thieves, Father, robbers!"

"Is there no honor among thieves as is commonly thought? Are we not still men? And if you win this contest to be the commander of the Elite, what then? Will you fight to protect the King of Babel? Will you train these men to the very best of your ability to kill any and all who come against him? Will you kill all those men who stand ready at this very moment? Will you kill me?"

"I, I …"

"Who can know when your word can be trusted, my son? You cannot say I will lie here, but not there, to him but not to him and then expect loyalty from … whom? Honor from …?"

Kish addresses Nimrod and gives him a token bow. "It matters not who commands your troops. None of you have the cunning, the craftiness, the cold-heartedness to best me, my son or my men. You are all too civilized. So please, select whom you will. Your best shot really is my son, but he is no longer available. Are you?"

"You are right, Father. I cannot train these men to kill those men outside of Babel. Forgive me for nearly dishonoring you." He kneels and kisses his father's hand.

"Forgiven. And now King Nimrod, may we depart in peace?"

"You may," and they exit to the sounds of many hundreds of swords being resheathed.

King Nimrod turns and watches the two men depart. Within minutes the rumble of thousands of horses can unmistakably be heard. King Nimrod turns to the thousands of men replacing their swords in their scabbards. "Are there some who have left their post at the gates of Babel and left the entire city at risk?" More than a few men disappear immediately.

"Is there no one among us who is fierce enough, cunning enough, cold-hearted enough to lead my Elite into battle, into hell itself?"

There is much conversation with little movement. Then, one man walks slowly toward the King: Chiamaka. He kneels before his King and kisses his hand. King Nimrod bids him rise.

"Before I came to your kingdom, I was a prince among my people, a warrior, a leader of men. I taught the ways of war to my people. I can, I will teach my brothers of Babel the dark art of murder, the dark art of secrecy of death handed down from my father's father. I am here today because of jealousy among other leaders in my country, jealousy I did not expect, jealousy I will someday repay.

These things I will teach for the greatest king on this earth. He kneels again to a huge roar from the crowd.

"Let the competition begin!" King Nimrod proclaims, as he has Chiamaka stand.

General Jared, "Against our best advice and wishes, our King will compete." Cheers erupt from all around the arena as thousands more citizens and soldiers gather. The sun is up as the combatants square off in sword-fighting. As one man is defeated, he holds up one hand to show he is yielding. He then sits away from the action.

The fighting with swords goes on for several hours until two men are left - - King Nimrod and Chiamaka. Both men have sweat streaming down their faces and off their bodies. A cup of water is offered to each man and after consuming, "Begin!" shouts General Jared.

Each man circles the other until Chiamaka seemingly stumbles and King Nimrod rushes in to "kill" his opponent. When the king is about to raise his sword, Chiamaka throws a handful of dirt into King Nimrod's face, rolls toward the king and places his sword under the king's chin. The king raises his hand. Jared and all the other leaders breathe a huge sigh of relief.

There are many boos for Chiamaka's win by "cheating."

The knife-throwing goes to Rayas, as he records nine out of ten kills to his target against Abasi's eight out of ten.

One event for Rayas. One for Chiamaka. The bow and arrow event starts at twenty paces from the target until half, four men, are eliminated. The final two men are King Nimrod and Chiamaka. They are to shoot from sixty paces. Each man has five arrows. The center ring is worth ten points, a second ring five points and zero points after that.

King Nimrod goes first and fires a ten. Knowing what side their "bread is buttered," the entire arena applauds and cheers their king. When the crowd subsides slightly, Chiamaka fires a ten and quickly fires his second arrow without hesitation and it, too, is a ten. A modest applause follows.

Silence awaits King Nimrod's second attempt. His second shot is on the line between ten and five. Zag and Jared run to the target to get a better look. "Five," shouts Jared, which is accompanied by a chorus of very partial boos.

The king's third and fourth arrows find the center as does Chiamaka's

King Nimrod has but one arrow left and it hits the dead center of the target to yet another round of cheers and applause. The arena is dead quiet as Chiamaka fires his last arrow. A five. The arena erupts once again for their king. Perhaps Chiamaka is a politician as well as a warrior. They each get a half of the event.

The spear event is won by Rayas.

The score stands, one and one-half events for Chiamaka, one-half event for King Nimrod and two events for Rayas.

The sling shot contest has a dead animal's head on a stick that a man moves back and forth across the arena. The man holding the sticks is behind stacked bales of hay. When a hit registers, the head literally spins on the stick.

King Nimrod wins the event. The contest is down to the last event, with the winner being the champion.

"The last event is our newest", announces General Jared, "the bow and arrow from horseback." The announcement is followed by lots of 'ohs' and 'ahs' from the crowd. Each of the other two contestants left has his favorite mount brought in, except Chiamaka.

"Where's your horse?" asks Jared.

"Chiamaka does not own such a fine thing."

"Use mine," Jared offers and signals for his horse to be brought in. Chiamaka takes off the blanket and pats the horse on his face. He then gently breathes into the horse's nostrils and kisses its forehead.

"This is a very fine horse, my general."

"He thinks so," laughs Jared and they exchange smiles.

Jared announces, "The only contestants left are King Nimrod", big cheers, "Chiamaka", slight applause, "and General Rayas", strong applause. "Obviously, whoever wins this event wins it all. Each competitor will ride the opposite way the stuffed animal goes. Each will have three shots."

The competitors already eliminated have taken seats as judges on both ends of the bales of hay, three on each end, close to the targets, for judging hits and misses.

King Nimrod goes first and records one hit, two misses. Chiamaka records two hits and one miss. Everyone is on their feet, cheering and applauding as Rayas starts his turn. First shot is a hit. Cheers erupt and his horse flinches from the noise and rears up on its hind legs. Rayas calms his horse and signals he is ready. Rayas charges ahead and the cheers from the crowd get louder. As he is about to shoot, his horse again flinches causing the shot to go astray. Shades of Puli-ilu! Little by little the crowd, the competitors and Rayas realize his last arrow is sticking out of the chest of Rayas's brother, Fenchristo.

A bewildered look is on Fenchristo's face as he sinks to his knees and falls face down on the dirt. The hush of the crowd is permeated by the scream from Rayas as he runs to his brother. It is too late. Fenchristo is turned over by Rayas and stares at him, "Tell Gechina I …" and he is dead. Rayas rocks his brother back and forth repeating, "My god, my god, oh my god."

It was decided later that Chiamaka would be the first commander of the Elite under the supervision of General Jared and Zag, a decision that would be looked upon later as a real turning point in their personal association. Rayas's horse is found dead the next day with an arrow through its head. The family requests a quiet, personal funeral. So it is said, so it is done. Catalin and Rayas agree that Rayas should marry Gechina so she and the two boys could have a home with a dad. Rayas is to never know Gechina. Abasi is made a captain and takes over Fenchristo's troops and two new garrison commanders are found as replacements for Abasi and Nazibugas.

Even in a world with a dictator king, death does not take a holiday.

King Nimrod has decided to tour, incognito, some of the facilities in Babel and starts off at the brick factory. When we first encountered this factory, there were but a few people employed there, and the acres of the factory spread out with literally millions of bricks, of all sizes and shapes. Bricks were stacked as high as a human could reach, row after row after row of them. Today, as a hooded King Nimrod walks through the yard, there are but scant piles of hundreds of thousands of bricks, fresh from their molds, fresh from the curing process. As soon as bricks, or tiles, are ready, wagons are waiting to take them to their destination. Millions of bricks had been used for the canal building and millions more would be needed for more canals and other present-day projects, let alone the projects for the years to come. That does not even count for the different shaped and different sized bricks to be used in the construction of buildings.

While the acres of ground are not gorged with bricks, they are full of workers, forms and materials to be used for the making of various bricks. Thousands upon thousands of bricks are prepared every day, being made by thousands upon thousands of slave laborers.

True to his word, Nimrod has made the owner of the brick factory a wealthy man. Very wealthy. Very generous. Very righteous.

And it so happens that this day the owner, Berakhiak, is there on his monthly visit to hand out awards, bonuses and recognition for workers and their accomplishments. Men and women flock to him to say hello, thanks, and to shake his hand. Nimrod has never seen such a spontaneous outpouring of gratefulness as he is witnessing this day.

Berakhiak seems to know the name of each worker and asks how this man's wife is doing after her bout with a sickness, this one just had a baby, another has fallen and broken his arm and should he be back to work so soon, and so on. Finally, all the hundreds of workers are assembled, not including the slaves from Calah, Ninib or Padan, who continue their labors.

Baskets of fruit are given to men, or the women themselves, whose families have given birth that month, baskets to those who have returned to work after missing a few days work and baskets to those who have lost someone that month.

Awards are given to those who have not missed a single day of work, awards for filling in an extra shift for a fellow worker, awards for a team of workers who have exceeded expectations for numbers of bricks made that month. Awards are presented for trainers whose trainees exceeded expectations. And then, the award for employee of the month and supervisor of the month are announced.

A huge roar of approval goes up for the woman announced as employee of the month. Then a great hush descends on the workers, as Berakhiak announces the supervisor of the month – Puli-ilu! His fellow workers applaud and shout his name. Puli hides his grinning face as he make his way to the front to accept his basket, his yellow sash and a small bag of coins. Tears are in the eyes of many as Berakhiak raises Puli's hand in the air for a man so gracious, so kind and hard-working.

When the workers quiet down Berakhiak speaks, "When I first hired Puli, I was concerned about his ability to perform the work. I was concerned too, that he might hurt himself on some of the tools and equipment. I soon found out that my concerns were really judgments out of prejudice about handicapped people. What a great blessing it is to have Puli-ilu as one of my workers. I am so grateful to Heavenly Father for opening my silly mind and eyes to see the worth of the human soul. I hope you all feel the same."

Applause and cheers follow his remarks. Surprisingly the applause is coming not just from the assembled workers but also from the hundreds of slave laborers. Nimrod's heart is touched.

King Nimrod removes his hood but for a moment to get a fresh breeze on his head and that is all it takes. Puli-ilu catches a glimpse of his King and shouts, "My King!" just as clear as day. Those who hear him turn and see King Nimrod. Puli hands his awards to a fellow worker and as he nears Nimrod, he falls to his knees and upon bowing his head, he hits it on the ground and splits open his forehead. With blood trickling down his grinning face he starts to chant, "Nimrod the great!" It is soon taken up by all the workers and Berakhiak. The slaves do not join in.

King Nimrod crosses the few steps to Puli-ilu and helps him to his feet. The blood still trickling down his face, King Nimrod takes a cloth from a worker and wipes the blood as best he can. All the while Puli is leading the chant, "Nimrod the great." Arm-in-arm the two men walk to the entrance of the factory grounds.

As Nimrod exits and waves goodbye, the chanting fills the air.

Nuradad and Shahmanesor live. Deep in the mountains they nurse each other back to health while deep in frenzied thought as to how they will extract their revenge, revenge for the wrongs they supposed were done to them by Zag, Nimrod, and Babel in general. They know of other dissenters who are dissatisfied with the great Nimrod, dissatisfied with the success and attention he receives as the savior of Babel.

So, little by little, they make forays into Babel and attract followers who come to the mountains with them. They visit conquered cities and find those unhappy with being slaves. In Akkad they take not only husbands, but whole families, back to the mountains. Administrators can do very little when the entire family disappears over- night. But another child from the city leader's wagon shows up dead in the city square a few days later. The sins of the parents are visited on the children after all. This growing little group could now formulate plans to destroy or disrupt the public projects of the great king Nimrod. And if they are careful, their work will be labeled as that of Kish and Berosus.

King Nimrod is taken by a group of his trusted Elite and some wealthy citizens to a mountain retreat. They have all been working on a private game reserve for Nimrod that stretches for miles and miles in any direction. They have posted markers every so often to warn others to stay out. They also find berries and plants that the animals prefer and nurture those plants within the reserve.

And so today, the king is taken to his preserve to hunt. Beaters are supplied by the Elite and the game is driven toward Nimrod and his wealthy benefactors. Nimrod kills several animals, much to the applause of all: mountain lions, gazelles, fallow deer and two Arabian Oryx.

His Elite are about to skin the animals, as is the custom, and leave the carcasses when Nimrod stops them. He asks, "Have you ever eaten the meat from these animals?" and the Elite and wealthy answer "No." None have. Perhaps not generally known at the time, but Nimrod is the first to eat the wild animal's flesh in the annuals of history. "Well, let's start a new tradition with this new hunting preserve. We kill it; we eat it."

And so the animals are packed on the backs of the horses, much to the horses' dislike, and are taken to the palace. There, the animals are taken to the royal kitchens where master chefs are instructed to prepare the animals for a feast in honor of King Nimrod and his wealthy friends: wild animals for wild men.

So it is said, so it is done. Meanwhile, the wealthy men are taken to the temple's lower chambers to be entertained until dinner by the dancing and frolicking virgins. Oh yeah.

As Nimrod relates the experiences of the day to Semiramis she is pleased that Nimrod is happy with the surprise that's been given him. Then, Nimrod goes to a closet in his bedroom and uncovers the skins his grandfather Ham has given him. He sets the package on the bed and stares at it. "How could anything make hunting better than it was today?" he muses. Actually, he thought, it wasn't much of an adventure with fifty men beating drums and cymbals, pushing the animals toward him. Perhaps, he thought, he should try going hunting without all the men, just him, and the skins. Next time.

Chapter Nine

A messenger interrupts his thoughts with news of Kadenram and his huge caravan approaching the city. The caravan would be here tomorrow around noon. Nimrod smiles. It is like his birthday all over again each time Kadenram appeared. Nimrod could hardly contain his enthusiasm for tomorrow. Semiramis laughs at him, "A grown child on the outside, a handsome, goofy child on the inside."

Tomorrow comes and Nimrod leaves his palace in search of Kadenram and his treasures. Once found, Kadenram sees him and they embrace each other. Kadenram steps back and greets him with a polite bow and Nimrod again embraces him in a manly hug, "There is to be no bowing between us, my old friend. Now, what have you brought me?"

"Well, I know you have crocodiles, but not like these. These are twice the normal size and have been bred to be extremely aggressive, if that's possible with crocodiles!" They both laugh.

"Look at the size of these monsters, what wonderful creatures." Nimrod instructs Kadenram's men as to the pond they should go in and they leave with instructions to tell the queen what they are doing.

"Now", says Kadenram, "for the most beautiful killing creatures on earth." He leads Nimrod to several cages where Nimrod sees four young black panthers.

"Oh my, Kadenram, these are marvelous, absolutely marvelous: one male and three females?" Kadenram nods yes. "Leave the cages in the shade over near the palace, and my men will take them to my hunting preserve."

"May I make a recommendation, young majesty? You may want to keep these two blacks here at the palace for show. I have seen them trained and then chained to the throne elsewhere. They make a very effective crowd control measure for those who might take offense."

"You are absolutely correct, dear friend."

"Now, the elephants: the massive movers of mounds of heaven or earth. One of them can do the work of six to ten oxen. They are fantastic animals and so very gentle. As with each of the other animals, they include their trainers as well."

Kadenram takes Nimrod down the caravan to hundreds of glass windows being unloaded, each made for palace windows. Nimrod motions for several of his soldiers and instructs them where in the palace the glass is to be taken. Kadenram motions to his men to follow and install the glass windows.

They go on to the precious metals, of pots and pans and, more importantly, weapons.

There are beautiful, highly polished and light-weight weapons, bows and arrows, light -weight spears, knives of unusual shapes and sharpness and more.

Then, Kadenram presents musical instruments from Africa, Asia and Arabia, each with its master musician who will teach the musicians in the palace of King Nimrod.

Beautiful black women are next, skilled in the art of manly happiness, who need no instruction manual or trainers: Two dozen of them as brides-to-be for the King, with smiles of gleaming white teeth.

"Fabulous, absolutely fabulous, but how did you know?"

"Your queen, my lord. Your queen sent me word. I do have a few surprises more, if you are willing."

"I'll have to conquer a few more cities, but never mind. What have you possibly left as a surprise?"

Kadenram takes him around a large gathering of camels, and there are twenty of the most beautiful Arabian stallions Nimrod has ever seen. Nimrod's breath is taken away, and he kneels on one knee and watches their flowing manes and skittish foot movements.

"Stallions," Nimrod whispers.

"Not just stallions, good King Nimrod," as Kadenram moves around yet another clump of camels, "brood mares, fifty of them."

"Fifty? But where, I mean, how ...?"

"Do not ask, dear friend. I do not want to lie to you." Kadenram laughs. Nimrod has tears in his eyes as he hugs Kadenram.

"All this you must pay for," Kadenram jokes, "but these, these are a gift from me to you." He goes to a camel and produces some of the oddest looking stones Nimrod's seen.

"Stones?"

"Oh no, dear king, not just stones, glowing stones. It takes nine years to produce these stones. They can be used in your palace for nighttime movement, and in your ziggurat, once it is built. Now, if you can find deposits of Barite, I have a man who will move here and teach you the delicate and laborious art of making them."

"Then it is settled. By your next trip I will find the Barite."

"And I will bring the artisan with me upon my return. And his family."

The two men go inside as the sun sets just as dinner is served.

Puli-ilu and his ten-year-old brother Jessem are closing up the brick factory for the night with Jessem wearing Puli's yellow sash and holding his basket and bag of coins. They chat as the sun begins to set and as they slowly walk towards their humble home.

"Kng nrd, hgd m, hgd m!" (King Nimrod hugged me, hugged me!) Puli exclaims, smiling with a big welt on his forehead.

"You are so lucky, Puli. The King hugged you?" Jessem repeated.

"Hm gd mn brtr." (Him good man brother.)

"Yes, Puli, he really is. He got you this job too."

"Yth. I lv hm." (Yes, I love him.)

As they walk Puli dances in the street and the two brothers laugh and talk. Unbeknownst to them they are being followed. At a dimly sunlit part of the street where the shadows grow deepest and just two streets from their home, a voice behind them is heard.

"Oh Puli, you're so lucky, so strong, so stupid," the voice laughs and is joined by several drunken laughs.

The voice continues, "How did you get to be so big, so ugly, and so stupid?"

The other four men laugh, mocking Puli's retarded laugh.

Puli turns to Jessem and whispers, "Rn hm, nw Jesm. Gt hp." (Run home now, Jessem, get help)

"No, Puli, I don't want to leave you."

"Ge NW." (Go now.) Jessem leaves with his hands full of the basket and coins. As he runs he drops the basket and then the coins crying, "Help, Father. Help."

The five men circle Puli, their shaved heads shimmering in the dimming sun light. One of them staggers, trying to run and catch Jessem. Jessem's young legs outdistance the drunk and so he returns to his comrades, "I couldn't catch the kid."

"Get him, we can't have no witnesses." As the soldier turns to run after Jessem, Puli-ilu trips him and the soldier falls hard, hitting his head on the side of the building, causing his head to bleed. He gets up slowly and draws his sword.

"You're a dead man, you moron," as he turns to stab Puli. Puli brushes the sword away with his hand, cutting his hand on the blade.

The other four men draw their swords too.

The bleeding mean speaks, "We just wanted to have a little fun, you freak, but you, you made it personal."

"Yeah," adds his friend, "This is all your fault."

One of them rushes Puli, narrowly missing Puli's stomach. Puli smashes him in the head with his fist, knocking the man down.

Another Elite soldier charges him and Puli grabs his sword, ripping it out of the soldier's hand, but deeply cutting Puli's hand. Blood is dripping from his hand as the three other men land their blows on Puli's massive, unprotected shoulders.

Puli grabs one of the men, lifts him above his head and throws him into the others. The soldier's friends accidently stab him as they try to catch him.

"Kill him, kill him for me," the wounded soldier screams.

The four men attack Puli like piranhas attacking their prey. Cussing and yelling obscenities, they chop Puli to pieces, hacking and stabbing him long after he is dead.

They stop when they realize Puli-ilu is no longer moaning. They grab their injured comrade and limp off into the twilight, still cursing filthy obscenities at Puli's dead body. One of them turns and staggers to Puli, kicking him ferociously, "Damned brainless piece of filth", he utters, still kicking his head and groin. "You no good piece of crap." He pees on Puli and leaves.

Jessem, his dad and six of his older brothers, can be heard screaming down the street, carrying knives and pitchforks. They run up to Puli's desecrated body and immediately the dad grabs Jessem and hides his head. Jessem is screaming, "Puli, Puli, I ran as fast as I could. Puli!" Puli, the gentle giant. The supervisor of the month. The idiot.

Puli's mangled body is carefully carried home. Jessem is inconsolable. His crying has left him unable to walk. One of his older brothers carries him home as he moans and pauses in the dark, "It's my fault, God. Take me." "Puli yelled at me to go. I shouldn't have listened." Pause. "God, will he ever forgive me?" The pause is punctuated with giant sobs from his small body. "I'm a coward. Oh God, I'm a coward." More sobs accompanied by tears from his brother. "Why did God let those men kill Puli. Doesn't he care?" "Why did they kill Puli? Why Puli? He never hurt anyone." His soft crying and moaning kept the other men verbally quiet as you could hear only their footsteps.

People poked their heads out to see what is happening and gasp as they faintly make out the body of Puli-ilu. Word spreads quickly and many people gather at Puli's home by the time his brothers and father reach the front door.

Men who never raised a weapon toward another man are fierce in their hatred toward the army when they learned of the five soldiers' murderous acts. Men swearing under their breath line the streets of Puli's neighborhood. Religious men. Family men. Men who had themselves even once questioned the worth of this soul, of an idiot, of a moron, of a halfwit, of a stupid person like Puli-ilu of Babel.

The men, the dad and the brothers, who have been so tight-lipped all the way home, know the emotions that are to come at home. They have been bracing themselves the entire way home. Bracing for the tide of a mother's love gone mad by the pain of suffering for such a noble child of God. No child knows the pain a mother bears due to the actions of her children. That is, until they themselves become mothers or parents.

Full grown men bracing for the loud sound of a fish breathing under water, bracing for the crash of death of a giant tree in the forest when no one is listening, bracing to hear a mother's heart snapping in two for one such as Puli-ilu of Babel.

News reaches the palace as the deep black of darkness descended on Babel: news of a handicapped man's passing that adds fuel to the fire of a best friend passing, of a father's passing. All for no apparent good reason other than God has willed it so.

Unlike the friend or the father, Puli has five men who could be, would be, found, judged and executed. Yes, they are remorseful, very scared out of their minds with fear at finding they had killed a man close to the heart of their King.

Perhaps you feel some sympathy for these men who have committed this murder while under the influence of alcohol, some compassion for men who have been extremely brave in defending their kingdom against all who would seek to destroy it. You might have some understanding how men could want another person dead because that person is imperfect, or some thankfulness even for having rid the earth of a slug, of a cheap counterfeit of a real man, of a goon not deserving of the food and water it took to keep it alive.

Perhaps you would be kind enough to explain those feelings of sympathy, compassion, understanding and thankfulness to Puli's mom.

The next morning in the central square of Babel there are five posts sunk into the ground with the tortured bodies of the five Elite soldiers hanging from those posts. The men are barely still alive, their feet spread wide on a platform attached to each post about eight feet above the ground. Each man has his hands tied above his head and to the post. In the middle of the platform is a five inch hole centered directly below each man's privates. Through that hole has been forcibly shoved an eight-foot spear up through each man's anus, through his intestines, stomach and has rested just below each man's throat.

During the night, a wagon and six Elite soldiers have visited Puli-ilu's home, petitioning his mom and dad on behalf of King Nimrod and successfully removing Puli's body. Puli is then taken to the temple and is placed on a platform opposite the altar. Several dozen infants have been procured from other cities and the high priest and accompanying virgins are readied for the ceremony. The fire is heated up under the altar, the musicians are assembled and then enter the King and Queen.

For hours the high priest invokes the spirit of Baal to bring Puli-ilu back to life. Tashshigura-mash lights two of the babies as candles, one at the head of Puli and one at the feet. The screams are unbearable to listen to for many present. They stop playing their deep vibrating drums, they stop their mesmerizing dance and chanting to Baal and, for a moment, recoil at the sight and sounds of human candles.

Yes, they thought they could bring Puli back to life. Did they ever consider the quality of life he might have? If they were successful, what would happen to his hacked apart limbs, the wounds to his heart and hands? He was already brain-damaged from early childhood. What new conditions would he have to suffer with, if the priests and virgins were successful? Why, then, would they even attempt this spiritual resuscitation to his frail body, mind and spirit? Ego. Not Puli's. Tashshigura-mash's. Semiramis's. Nimrod's.

Ego.

They did not care regarding Puli-ilu's quality of life, just if Baal would grant unto to them the power of life and death. Death, of course, was easy. Ask the five Elite soldiers, now all dead and rotting in the hot desert sun.

What would the world say about Nimrod and Semiramis if Puli walked out of the temple – alive? Who cares if he was a vegetable, a zombie, a body full of tormenting, agonizing pain with broken and unusable limbs? Who really cares?

For three full days and nights the sounds and sights and screams continue, now impervious to all. No signs of life register in Puli's poor body. The only sign of change is the smell, somewhat covered by the enormous quantities of incense and the odors emanating from the massive amounts of burning wood.

The writhing, sweating bodies of virgins dancing to the mind-bending sounds of various drums rising and falling in volume and tempo may have had their effect on the various priests dancing with them, as 'pulsating' couples, from time to time, and then again dancing, but not on Puli-ilu.

As the king and queen look on, sometimes joining in to 'pulsate', it is otherwise obvious that the dead would remain dead. The only thought they have is, what is missing? What is keeping their Puli dead? There must be an ingredient that they have overlooked, something Baal has failed to communicate to them. Something they failed to hear. To observe. To do.

Each day the family of Puli-ilu comes to the king, humbly asking for his body so they might properly bury him. Each day they are turned away. On the fourth day the King grants their request.

The body is returned. His body is cleansed with much holding of breath and even more incense. His flesh is now turning colors and fluids are starting to ooze from various openings.

The evening of the fourth day his body is ready. Dressed in all white Puli is laid in the front room of his family's home. Many well-wishers, friends and relatives alike have paid their respects. Berakhiak has come with several of Puli's coworkers. Many more are soldiers and leaders including Zag and Shamshi, garrison commanders and lastly, the King and Queen of Babel.

After the last well-wisher has left, some leaving flowers and small gifts, a pouch is discovered with a vast sum of money, enough money that the family could live on for a lifetime. No one has seen who had left such a magnificent gift, and yet all know it was the teary-eyed King of Babel.

The doors are closed, the windows shuttered and then from a back room two figures emerge. The dozens of family members stand or sit around Puli's clean, beautifully pure body, men and women still weeping for the beloved human remains of a spirit well received in Heaven by friends and family who have gone on before.

Jared mingles with the family sharing hugs and kisses while his brother walks to Puli and gazes at him, tears dropping every few moments. Tears, not for death, but for the pain this dear son of God suffered in his last few hours on earth. Jared's brother looks for Jessem, but cannot find him. He knows Jessem was there and that is enough.

"My brother," Jared announces, "would like to give Puli a blessing. If you would simply hold hands with someone near to you so as to form a complete circle, Maho ... my brother will commence." The family members do as requested. When they are ready Jared's brother bows his head.

A hush comes over the already quiet room: a hush that only comes at sacred moments, a hush unknown to most of the world this is a hush that cannot be mandated by religious rules, one that cannot be forced or imposed by churches trying to obtain a state of reverence.

Jared's brother places both of his hands on the forehead and hair of Puli's head and pauses for what seems like minutes. His eyes are closed. Unseen by those present is a peaceful smile that covers the brother of Jared's face.

"Dear God, Maker of All," he begins. Thanking God for life, earth and the Heavens he pauses again. "Dear Father, one of your finest sons lays before us, a son who never complained about his lot in life, a son who brought joy to all, all except the few who had hardened their hearts to the purpose of this earthly life: those for whom life was a chore instead of a blessing." He does not condemn Puli's killers. He continues, "His spirit has resided with thee for three days, and now we ask thee to return Puli to his family here on earth. His work here is not finished. He has yet to raise up righteous sons and daughters who are to preach the gospel of Jesus Christ by example, as did Puli."

There are gasps and other emotional reactions from the family to such a request. "We ask thee, kind Father, to restore every limb, every violated area of his body, every part of his mind to their proper state. We know all things are possible with thee, Father in Heaven. According to thy will that must be done, and not ours, we pray in the name of the unseen, the unknown Savior of the world, even Jesus the Christ. Amen." This is followed by a smattering of "amen's."

There is utter silence in the room with many disbelieving, averting looks cast in Puli's direction. From a corner of the room can be seen the hoping-against-hope face of Jessem. He would give his very soul, his chance at life, to see his brother rise from the grave and be replaced by his body. Gladly.

Yet, there is no external movement, no sign that what this man has asked, according to the will of heaven, is to be. Everyone has their own time table they consider correct about the time for something to occur. That time has passed for most, except Jared's brother, and God.

The wait for the impossible is excruciating, with the weaker-willed, the less experienced, giving in first. Their sighs are like saying, "Well, I knew it wouldn't work. I mean, I wanted it to, but oh well, let's bury his decaying body. Boy, I am hungry."

That's when the impossible occurs. It begins with a moan from Puli's lips. Those farther away think someone near Puli is playing a trick, a not very funny trick at that. It scares the living … you know, out of all who are close to Puli's body, and some of them jump back, while others grab for a hand from anyone to hold onto.

Before all present, his broken body begins to heal, the gashes from swords disappear so much that people rub their eyes as though their eyes are playing tricks on them. His severed, his broken and twisted bones straighten and heal. A gentle sighing emanates from his lips, not a sigh of pain, just a gentle sigh of relief.

Puli sits up and those closest to him practically knock over those in their way, so they can put a little distance between themselves and the moving dead man. They love Puli, they want the best for him, they just don't have any experience with dead men rising.

When Puli put his legs down over the side of the table, he smiles and says as clear as day, "Why are you all staring at me?"

Jessem shrinks down to the floor, his teary-eyed head in his hands, his quiet sobs marring the silence. All the self-imposed quiet, all the honest desires of wanting to trade his life for his brothers, break through his little, sobbing body. He doesn't see his brother rise and cross to him. He only feels a hand reach for his head and stroke his hair gently.

"I'm okay Jessem. You did what I asked of you. You have nothing to be ashamed of, or guilty of."

Full-sized sobs of love consume Jessem, as his brother picks him up off the floor and hugs him to his own body. "I love you, Jessem."

Haltingly comes the response, "I … love … too."

By now the entire room is engulfed in happy tears. The relatives take turns hugging Puli and then his dad and mom embrace him and a new wave of tears began. Jared breaks up the moment, "Puli-ilu, you and your entire family must pack and be gone in the next hour. The King will desire your lives. He does not like being shown up. Since he failed to bring Puli back to life, he will not look kindly on someone, a man of the true and living God, having done what he could not do. I do not have time to explain more fully. Just know that my brother has seen these things. You have seen this night how God works through him. Trust now; he knows what is best for you.

I'll tell the King and your neighbors that living here with the memories of Puli was too great, and so you decided to leave forever and took Puli's body with you.

I have written down instructions for you to follow to another town very far away. Read it and then, burn it. The eyes and ears of the King are all around us. Speak to no one. The money Puli earned will more than compensate for the flocks and herds and the losses you will incur. The money the King gave you will keep you for many years. You must never visit Babel. You must never tell anyone of your life here. Never. Now, go and pack and leave. God bless you."

They hug and say their goodbyes. In just less than one hour the entire family is loaded onto wagons and horses and headed out of town.

The ziggurat, the Tower of Babel, has been on the back burner for many years. The construction of the canals has taken precedence in order for the city of Babel to have food for the many thousands who are now being attracted to this prosperous city on the Euphrates. Then, there is the palace for the King and Queen and the expanded royal family that now included one hundred wives, babies and nannies.

Then again, there is the expense of the Sun/Fire Temple and the mysterious goings on inside. The army, nearing fifteen thousand well-trained and seemingly invincible, also consume much of the empire's time, energy and money. Dozens of cities have been conquered, tens of thousands of conquered citizens now trudge their way to and from Babel each and every day of each and every week of each and every month of each and every year – after year – after decade. Meanwhile, many dozens of large carts traverse the desert carrying leaders and their families of those dozens of conquered cities.

Nimrod has not been seen, for the better part of a week, with all matters on his schedule being cancelled until further notice. Withdrawn deep into his palace, no one has seen or heard from their king. Semiramis comes out periodically to announce that the king is in mourning for his friend Puli-ilu and will not be available until further notice.

Semiramis, obviously disturbed by her husband's retreat from life to the seclusion of his hidden room off his bed chambers, would sit by his bedside for hours rubbing his muscles and his head, gently coaxing him to speak to her about something, anything. But he speaks not a word.

He lays in his bed twenty-four hours a day, his eyes closed to occasionally half-open. Semiramis tries to have him drink a potion to alleviate his anguish but Nimrod would not. He eats but a piece of fruit now and again that is pressed upon his lips, with moisture dripping down his chin. Then, he would gently vomit his food back up. After a couple of days, she quit trying to get him to eat. He drinks, rather sips, small amounts of water and then rests some more.

Semiramis knows he is suffering from defeat. Although his affection for feeble-minded Puli-ilu is genuine enough, Nimrod is in agony over not being able to raise Puli from the dead. Each day for three days and nights Nimrod and his priest Tashshigura-mash, his minister of religion, Thoth, and his beloved wife chanted, prayed and sacrificed. The final count for infant sacrifices came to twelve candles and twelve baked over the giant alter – all to no avail. They would have sacrificed even more but they ran out of meat. What's one to do?

Well, that's how they consider it – meat. Callous, I know. But c'mon, it's no worse than today, is it?

I mean, we sacrifice infants by the millions each and every year because women can't keep the 'arches of gold' closed. So, we affectionately go to our doctors and have the offending meat ripped apart limb-by-limb out of the body and throw it into the trash.

But, you say, at least we don't worship some idol, some god of the underworld. Really? In the name of what god do we perform abortion? (Pause) Uh, I'm waiting. You are not one of the few who still cling to the hope that there is no God, right? If you believe in God, surely you do not ascribe to killing His sons and daughters to relieve one's discomfort, like constipation or gas. If you are among the few who do not believe in God then, Nimrod wasn't wrong in considering babies as meat.

The question for Nimrod and Semiramis is, why? What had the King and Queen done wrong? Was the head of one child facing the wrong way? Should the sacrifices and candles have been all males? All females? What had they missed in their late night training sessions with Baal?

Was it me, thought Nimrod? Was I not fit to lead the raising of the dead ceremony? Should I have let Semiramis conduct the sacrificial ceremonies? Was Puli-ilu not a worthy candidate to be raised from the dead?

What would his faithful followers think of their God on earth failing like this? Should he go out and eradicate Puli's entire family as payment for their failure of providing a worthy subject to be raised, and then, ultimately, Nimrod's? Would Nimrod have to teach them all a lesson about his divinity? On and on the second-guessing ate at Nimrod until the seventh day.

He wakes up and smiles at his faithful wife, knows her several times and leaves the room to bathe and clothe himself in some of his most resplendent robes. He eats a modest meal. His mind is clear and the first order of business is to send out a squad of his most Elite to round up Puli's family for slaughter, for payment for their unworthy sacrifice that they had sent to Nimrod, for polluting the sacred ceremony with their base filthiness. The purge would begin there, but there would be more. All involved in the failure would be made to pay.

Well past the five years agreed upon by Nimrod and Kish, the battles for leadership have been minor, very minor. Troublingly minor, as Nimrod reflects upon it with his military leadership. "I want you to devise a plan, General Jared, for eradicating any threat from these mountain robbers, Kish and his clownish son, Berosus. Tell me what you need and it is yours," Nimrod announces.

"A summer home near Egypt would be nice," the general smiles. Nimrod does not. Snickers from the other men present are stifled when they see Nimrod's reaction.

"First, my king," continues Jared, "we need to know their numbers, their main location or locations, their general habits of attacks. Then, we need information regarding their methods of warfare, as well as other questions I need answered. This would be possible if we had members of their band who were allies with us. And please, my king, forgive me my frivolity. I meant no disrespect."

"Forgiven. And as hard as it may seem to believe, I have several eyes and ears among them who are loyal to me, men and women. I will arrange a meeting for you with them, as you require. This will be best done at night and away from Babel. I will inquire of them where and when they feel it would be safest for them. General, you must not ask any questions of them for identification or so forth. This is for their security. Am I understood?"

"Yes, my king. The sooner we can meet the better, in terms of my planning an assault on them."

"I will contact you with a time and a place shortly, General. On another matter, what of this other group of thieves and misfits led by Nuradad and Shahmanesor?"

"My king," responds garrison commander Abasi, "their group is growing a few hundred per year, and so far they seem content in minor attacks on canals and such, trying to disrupt our daily life. I do not think they pose much of a threat."

King Nimrod walks over to him, "There is no such thing as a minor attack, Commander Abasi. Large things always start as small things. General Jared, eradicate them, every man, woman and child."

There are murmurs from among the men and then Jared speaks, "Sire, we have never made war on women and children. How ..." He is cut off by Commander Zag.

"Do it!" Zag shouts and stands defiantly facing Jared.

Jared stands, "I will not kill women and children. I would not kill your woman, Shamshi, or your son Zaggai."

"Not Shamshi. Not Zaggai."

Both men stand toe to toe, Zag's huge frame looming over Jared. "They are somebody's Shamshi and Zaggai," says Jared grimly.

King Nimrod interrupts them. "Zag, sit down. You sit too, General. Jared is right. Take the women and children prisoners – we'll deal with them later. Understood, Zag?" Zag breaks off his stare on Jared and grunts, "Understood."

"We have those loyal to us among the women, and for the moment my anger got in the way of my judgment. I will arrange a meeting for you at a later date." He pauses and goes to his chair and sits. "Gentlemen, it does no good to quarrel and argue amongst ourselves. Zag," Zag is still in his hate stare at Jared. "Zag!" the King says more forcefully, getting Zag's attention, "there must be room for disagreement and discussion. But once we have done that and a decision is made, all must be in agreement. End of discussion. End of opposing points of view. If you cannot do that, General, then we have a problem."

"I have never gone against you, my king. Never." Jared responds.

"See that you keep it that way." There is an uneasy silence among the leaders. Nimrod continues, "We will be starting the construction of our city's ziggurat next week, and we will require the service of many of our men in providing security among the slave laborers and the volunteers from Babel. I have asked the engineers to provide us with a model of the ziggurat," he motions to one of his guards. The guard disappears and returns with four men carrying a large platform covered with a cloth.

The men place it on a large table and then exit. Even with the cloth on the model, it is obvious that there is a very tall building under it making the model look like a modern- day rocket. Nimrod uncovers the model and all present are taken back with the height of the ziggurat and the surrounding beauty of the walls and staircases leading to it, the palace and the temple.

"Stunning," says one man.

"Absolutely beautiful," offers another.

Jared touches the ziggurat, "It must be a mile high, my king."

"I wish. It is but a mere three thousand feet: easily seen for miles on earth and in heaven."

Jared starts to laugh, and then realizes Nimrod is quite serious. "I'm sorry, your majesty. I was not laughing at you, just the immense height of this prayer tower. It is incredible."

"That's fine, my general. On another matter, my friends tell me that Puli-ilu's body and his family have completely disappeared. Do you know anything about that, General?"

"Yes sire, somewhat. It seems from what I can gather from friends and neighbors that the family was so distraught over Puli's murder that they decided to leave Babel forever. The daily reminder of Puli, the well-meaning questions of friends and neighbors were more than they could bear. I believe they took Puli-ilu with them, but to where they went, no one seems to know. I personally searched their homes and could find no clues, knowing you would want to know as much as possible about your friend. I believe they just wanted to go somewhere and quietly start their lives all over. I do know they left all their animals and herds behind, and the animals have been claimed by grateful friends and neighbors." He pauses.

"Thank you. I will find them, General, you can be sure of that."

"But, if I may ask, why? They have done nothing wrong that I am aware of."

"You are right, Jared. Forgive me. Now, how soon can we count on moving on the mountain robbers? Weeks – months – days?" And so King Nimrod skillfully guides the conversation away from Puli-ilu. Nonetheless, Jared could see in his king's eyes, revenge, and Jared knows his brother was once again a heavenly guided man. This is even more reason to keep his brother secret from the king, secret from his Elite emissaries and secret from the king's eyes and ears. Jared could not help but compare his friend, his king, Nimrod of today, to the man he knew just a few years ago.

Jared muses over the change in Nimrod, not realizing the deep-seated hatred Nimrod had developed for God. Nimrod's hatred, like most people's, is born of a self-centered belief that how Nimrod thinks, has to be right: self-centeredness, pride, self-aggrandizement, the inability to accept things in God's plan, the sense that Nimrod knew better than God. Hence, when Nimrod could not bring Puli-ilu back to life using human infant sacrifices, he turned his defeat into a deeper resentment, a deeper hatred for God. Had he known of Jared's brother's success, Nimrod could have easily killed every last member of both Puli's family and Jared's. Why? Revenge. Foolish, childish pride. If I can't have it, do it, then no one can.

And so Nimrod deflects Jared's 'why' for the moment, but the hunt and payback is just beginning. Damn God. Damn Puli. Damn Jared. Damn his brother. Damn everyone.

A time and a place for the meeting of General Jared and the eyes and ears of King Nimrod among the robbers is set. Jared is to take five hundred of the Elite, with him as a caution due to his rank, and then travel after dark to the rendezvous, in case of any unforeseen happenings.

The near all-night ride is uneventful and gives Jared time to think regarding his relationship with the King, the immense amount of success the five men have enjoyed since coming to Babel, the untimely death of a dear friend, Fenchristo, the resurrection of Puli and so on. He narrows his thoughts down to his own success on the field of battle using strategies that he devises for the army. Thanks be to my God, he reflects.

As they ride closer to the meeting place Jared has the distinct impression that he and his small army of Elites are being watched.

There is no outward sign, just that skin-pimpling feeling one gets from time to time. Jared has learned to trust those feelings and begins to wonder if he is riding into a trap. But, he argues with himself, these are the eyes and ears of the king, some of the most trusted men and women on earth – for Nimrod.

Chapter Ten

Jared sends word for his captains to ride by his side, and they devises tactics for deploying the Elite once they arrive at the meeting place.

Jared recalls the tactical meeting he and Nimrod had prior to his leaving and wonders if the king may have been correct in wanting Jared to take one thousand Elite soldiers. Jared had reasoned that that huge number of men on horseback would really attract attention, especially at night. Just the sounds and vibrations would be heard for a great distance on the flatland of Babylon.

He laughed to himself at the thought of his tender wife's feelings when he explained the necessity of this night-time meeting, and how her brow furrowed deeply on her kind, loving face. She let the pretend pout cross her cheeks and lips as he told her he'd be gone for several days, and then she let her fingers do the walking up his arm as she exclaimed, "Oh what shall I do while thou art away for all that time?" Jared hugged her and replied, "Perhaps you could spend a little time with our eighteen children."

"I've often wondered why we have had so many children so quickly, and now it's clear. You've been planning this get-away for many years, and to keep me from temptation, we've had a large family!" She crossed away from him, feigning being distraught. Then she turned her head and winked at him as she disappeared into the bedroom.

"General."

Jared smiles into the night, remembering walking to the bedroom.

"General," the voice persists. Jared realizes one of his captains is calling him.

"Yes Captain Zarek"

"There's the hut."

"Deploy your men as we discussed. Stay alert, Captain."

"Yes, General."

Jared dismounts and notices several other horses tethered nearby. He opens the door and goes into the small, farm-style, one-room hut. The lighting is a single candle in the center of the only table. Seven of the eight chairs are occupied. The people are all hooded and remain silent as they await the General. The atmosphere in the room is not one of fear, just one of guarded caution.

"I do apologize if I have kept you waiting. It was not intentional." Two of the men exchange the money they had bet on whether the General would arrive on time.

"It's not a problem, General. Let's get on with the meeting so we can leave before the sun rises."

"Very well. And thank you for coming. I realize the risk each of you has taken in being here tonight. Your King has asked me to relay to you his thanks as well." Pause. "How many men does Kish have at his command?"

"Five, maybe six thousand," one voice answers. Others agree with low tones and nods of their heads.

"Are they all in one main camp?"

"Two main camps, General," another voice adds. "And it would take fifty-thousand men to defeat them."

"Why is that?"

"The way to the camps," adds a tall, large and well-muscled man, "is through the mountain cliffs, where sentries are camped day and night with rocks and boulders by the thousands, waiting to be hurled down on any advancing enemy."

Another voice adds, "There are thousands upon thousands of spears, bows and arrows and sling shots stored under waterproof wraps the entire way above the trail."

The large man adds, "At certain spots giant boulders are resting with large pry bars already in place that would take ten men to push and have those boulders roll down the cliff and crush men, wagons and horses, which in turn would block the trail. An army, what's left of it, would have to dismount and crawl around and over them to advance."

Jared is impressed with the preparations as he shakes his head, nodding here and there with the information he's being given. "What of the soldiers' training?"

The large man continues, "Kish has spared no expense in finding the best men in the use of each weapon to train his men. They are very good, and the whole army trains constantly, much like, I understand, does yours. And these men are brought up here for a month or two at a time and paid very handsomely. When they leave, the hood they wore when they came up here is replaced, and they return to Babel to train your men. Moon-lighting, someone called it, making more money during that time than they do all year long at their regular job."

"What's their weakness then? You make it sound like they are invincible?" There is a long pause. "You mean they have none?"

"I think they are invincible, up here. Get them away from their strongholds and it might be a different story," says one of the hooded men.

"If they have a weakness," adds another voice, "I believe it is their leadership. Not so much Kish, but his officers. Kish trusts no one, and so he keeps all decision-making to himself. His officers do not feel that he trusts them, as he never allows them to comment on his plans, his strategies. I believe that their loyalty to him, because of this, is very thin. Cut off the head and the snake will die."

The big man says, "I never thought of that, but you may be right."

The questioning went on for hours, with each man present supplying vital information regarding the robber band.

"Why haven't they attacked Babel? The five-year truce has long, long since passed."

"Easy," answers the large man, "Kish wants Nimrod to do all the work before he comes to take it from him. I don't think Kish ever expected Nimrod to accomplish such fantastic feats as he has done, so why stop him now? I believe that once the Tower is completed, that may be the thing Kish is waiting for. The canals, palace and temple are done. And the addition of the Arabian stallions, large cats in the palace, the huge number of women Nimrod's made his personal baby-making machine make Kish, and especially the pathetic Berosus, very anxious to take over. There are also several spies in the Elite, and one garrison commander who will help the army peacefully give in, once Kish attacks."

"There's a meeting in Babel in four days where Kish's eyes and ears are to be in attendance. That meeting possibly could give King Nimrod much more information."

Suddenly there are sounds of fighting heard outside the hut and one of General Jared's captains comes rushing in.

"General, we have been surrounded. What would you have us do?"

The large man removes his hood, "My, my, General Jared, the King's right-hand man, looks like you are impaled on the horns of a dilemma!" And he laughs and laughs. No one else joins him. The voice is that of Berosus, son of Kish. "You remember those five to six thousand soldiers of my father? They're all outside and very anxious to make your acquaintance." Berosus pulls out his sword.

"Seems to me," says General Jared, "you should have waited until your daddy was here before announcing your presence." Jared and all present in the room draw their swords. "You must be a big disappointment to your daddy."

Jared's Captain goes to Berosus and takes the sword of a perplexed looking Berosus. Captain Zarek ties Berosus' hands behind his back, "You think Daddy will give up another five years for you?"

Berosus responds, "I don't know, but you'll not live to enjoy those years if he does. Either way, you and your men are dead. You'll be slaughtered here and your bodies delivered to your king on stakes, like the three men who murdered the king's idiot friend."

"Captain Zarek, go out and tell our men to hold their positions, do not attack. Also tell the leaders of the robbers that we have Kish's son hostage." The captain starts to exit. "Captain, light a torch and have one man stand on the hut and wave it back and forth five times. Exactly five times from left to right, slowly. Understood?"

"Yes, my general, left to right five times." He exits and the sounds of his announcing Berosus as a hostage can be heard. Also heard are some of the moans of robbers commenting on their leader's brain-dead son.

Kish appears at the door of the hut. "General Jared," he sighs a deep sigh, "I am Kish, and that, that is my son." Kish has a steely-eyed look about him as he gazes at his son. "May I speak with him?"

"You may."

Kish motions to Berosus to come to him and he does so reluctantly. "Berosus, you have caused me much grief with your stupidity, but this takes the cake."

"Father, I am so sorry, I don't know what I was thinking. But we've got King Nimrod's General of the Army. I just couldn't wait any longer! Nimrod will give us anything we ask. We've won!"

Kish looks at his son with a long quiet stare. "And you? What will I give them for you?"

"What?"

"Once again you are their hostage, Berosus. What must I give them to keep you alive?"

"I hadn't thought of that."

Kish kisses Berosus on both cheeks and then pulls out a knife and stabs his son to death before anyone can react. "I'm sorry my son, stupid is as stupid does", he says with tears in his eyes and gently lowers his son to the floor. Jared and the others are stunned.

"General, you will pay dearly for the death of my son. You," Kish points to the others in the room, "you, will pay even more. Slowly, very slowly."

Kish backs out the door and joins his men. Jared and some of the others exit the hut. Suddenly, the noise of many thousands of soldiers riding in fills the early morning air. Fourteen thousand and five hundred to be exact, attack the five to six thousand, and the other five hundred defend General Jared and the spies in the hut.

The slaughter continues until well after the sun comes up. It continues even after some of the robbers begin to throw up their hands in defeat. And then they are forced to pick up their weapons until they have no hands to throw up. It continues until all five to six thousand robbers are dead. Completely dead. Stabbed over and over dead.

Only Kish is left alive, barely, with multiple wounds and bleeding from head to toe. Every robber is then examined to make sure he is dead, again. His horse and his weapons are taken away, and the bodies are left to bloat in the heat of the desert sun.

Jared signals to one of the men who had been in the hut to come to him. "Your name?"

"Dalziel."

"Dalziel, will you come with me to Babel? You are no longer needed here."

"Yes, my general."

General Jared signals for one of his captains to come to him. "Captain Bittor, take your one thousand along with the wagons, and immediately go to the robbers' stronghold. Women and children are to be taken back to Babel – on foot. It should take you at least four days.

"But General, we could be there with a forced march in two days, I'm sure."

"I know Captain Bittor, but I need time to set a trap for the spies who are among the Elite and the people of Babel. No word of this battle must reach Babel for four days. None of your men may return to Babel for four days, is that clear? If anyone even asks for a special release, take their name down and pass it on to me later."

"Yes, my general."

"Good. Send out word for all the other captains to meet me here in one hour. Then, on your way, seal off the mountains so that none can escape. None. Have every woman account for every member of her family. Use the threat of harming the youngest to get your information."

"The threat only, General?"

"That's right. You know we do not make war on women and children, unlike some others. Do you need more men to go with you? I know not how many warriors may still be in the camps."

"I know, General Jared. And no, my thousand should be sufficient."

"No one must be allowed to escape or even be left alive to pass on any information. Check and recheck the dead, check every niche, every possible hiding place. Take two of our spies in the hut to help discover any caves or special hiding places. No one can be allowed to make it to Babel before the next four days are up. No one.

"I understand, General, I really do."

"Yes, I'm sure you do. There are spies among us here, Captain, and in Babel. Those still in Babel must not be warned of this battle and the death of all their comrades. Just a reminder, no rapes, Captain, no ravaging."

"The men know."

"Just remind them, and that the penalty is their own death and that of their families. There may be a few women who would seek to gain favor by being, friendly, shall we say."

"The men know that too. But, I will remind them." Captain Bittor grins.

General Jared puts his arm around his captain "This is why I have chosen you time and time again for these types of missions. Battle after battle there have been precious few calls for concern with you and your men. You are my right arm." They shake hands and the Captain is obviously pleased with this compliment.

"Send me Captain Lionel, and then make haste for the mountains. Once the camps are secure, take your time in seeking out any who would hide. Go now. And take two of our men from the hut."

"Yes, General." Captain Bittor laughs as he starts to leave.

"Something funny, Captain?"

The captain stops and looks at his general. "It's just that I've never seen you so nervous over a few spies. And repeating yourself."

"It is not the few spies that are my concern; it is what they may do to our men and our families once they know all is lost. What bothers me is their so-called code of being killed before being captured, or killing all they can in repayment of their impending death, in destroying all around them, including women and children.

I am even more concerned where each one of our military leader's life is common knowledge.

I know this band's complete disregard for the sanctity of life which was literally beaten into them day after day as rules, memorized and recited as prayers to Baal, Their forced way of living, walking, eating and praying as the only way to their heaven – that bothers me."

"And now it bothers me," replies Captain Bittor. "The fact, too, that my wife and children live on the outskirts of Babel, as well as other members of my family, bothers me: such easy prey."

"Then do your job as though your very life depends on it, because it does."

"Permit me to take an additional two hundred men with me to protect your family and …"

"No captain. No special favors. No drawing attention by out of the ordinary measures that could alert Kish's eyes and ears that something unusual is afoot. Just your most earnest prayers on their behalf would be sufficient."

"So it is said, so it is done. I hope our God is good at keeping secrets."

"Like there is going to be a flood!" smiles Jared.

"Oh, boy." Captain Bittor exits and immediately Captain Lionel appears.

"We have a meeting, my general?"

"First, Captain Lionel, I need you and twenty of your best of the best of the best warriors to accompany me back to Babel. Please see to it. Time is of the essence. You and your men will be charged with getting Kish to Babel, more specifically, to the King. Alive! Once the King tells you what to do with Kish, then you and your men are free to go home. Under no circumstances are you or your men to talk to anyone regarding this battle, Kish, or anything else about the last few days. Understood?"

"Understood."

"Any questions?"

"No, my General. I'll have the men ready in a matter of minutes here in front of the hut. So it is said, so it is done."

Jared grins and slaps Captain Lionel on the back. "See you in Babel."

Kish is a marvel in that he should be dead, with all the wounds he sustained and with all the blood he had lost, and yet there he is, lying on a litter, grimacing in pain.

No sooner had Captain Lionel left than Captain Bomani and two of his men come running in a full sprint to General Jared. "General, Captain Lionel has been stabbed to death. One of our men greeted the Captain and then stabbed him repeatedly before he even fell to the ground. The man was caught by these two soldiers and killed immediately."

General Jared is visibly shaken. "One of our men? Lionel was one of our finest leaders. Who is his next in command?"

"I am General, I'm Captain Bomani."

"Well, Captain, if Captain Lionel trusted you, I can do no less. Take twenty men and escort the robber Kish to the King's palace. Talk to no one of these happenings. Stay with me in Babel; we have lots to do."

"Yes, my general." Bomani and men exit and prepare Kish for the journey to Babel.

The other captains have assembled and General Jared gives them their marching instructions.

Wagons are dispatched to go to the stronghold of the robbers and all weapons, thousands upon thousands of them, are taken back to Babel. Anything of any value is also taken to Babel and would be divided up among the fifteen-thousand soldiers.

The women and children of the robbers are given their choice of coming to Babel and living as loyal subjects of King Nimrod or joining their husbands. Few choose to join their husbands, deciding that they would rather live to raise their family, raise them with a hatred of Nimrod and all he stood for. They then walk back to Babel under the watchful eye of the Elite.

The pregnant women would be taken to the palace to await the birth of their children, and then they would be allowed to join the regular citizenry of Babel, never again to see their infant children. Just a high mortality rate, they guessed.

Zaggai has never seen his father strike his mother. He has never heard his father even raise his voice to his mother. So why is it that

Zaggai is growing into such a belligerent young man, cursing his mom, never in front of his father, and shoving her out of his way when she would reprimand him? Is it because his father is a man of great power, both physically and with his position in the army?

Zaggai is an example for his many brothers and sisters, and his actions are starting to be imitated here and there. It is when Zaggai begins twitching and having distorted facial expressions that Shamshi consults her friends. She knows telling Zag of his son's poor behavior would have an immediate physical consequence for Zaggai, and she is not ready for that conflict.

Zamama is visiting one day and Shamshi decides to confide in her. "Zamama, I don't know what to do anymore. His brothers say they have found him killing small animals, even torturing them to death."

"Who have you discussed this with?"

"No one. Unlike you, we have no family, no circle of friends to talk with. Zag has grown very distrustful of Jared and I don't know why."

"I do, Shamshi. It's Nimrod. He's changed, and Zag never has questioned him, especially since Nimrod took that beating for Zag."

"But Zag is such a wonderful father and husband. Why would he dislike Jared?"

"Jared stands up to Nimrod and Zag sees that as Jared being disloyal. I …" She hesitates. "I have to tell you that Zag has done some very serious things for Nimrod, Shamshi. I'm not sure if he and Jared will ever be friends again."

"And what of you and me? Can we be friends?" Shamshi weeps.

"Always." They hug and shed a few tears together. Shamshi walks away a bit.

"Zaggai is nearly a grown man, a very large and strong young man. I know something is wrong with my son, so what do I do?"

"Would you mind if I talk to Jared about him? I'll make him promise not to say anything to Zag or Zaggai or anyone else. Promise."

"I, I guess."

Suddenly one of Shamshi's oldest daughters runs in crying. "It's Zaggai, Momma. He hit a neighbor, old man Gyurka, with his fists, and the man is unconscious, lying in the street."

All three women run out of the house. Others have reached the old man first, and he is coming to.

A neighbor blurts out, "Shamshi, this can't continue. Gyurka did nothing to harm Zaggai. Anymore the whole neighborhood lives in fear of Zaggai and his temper."

Shamshi reaches Gyurka and cleans the blood from his face with her dress, "Oh, Gyurka, I am so sorry." She cries and rocks him back and forth.

"It's not your fault, my dear. Zaggai is such a good boy, a bit big and strong. I don't think he meant to hurt me. I stumbled and fell into him and I think I scared him. That's when he turned and hit me. He ran off crying and shaking."

Shamshi and Zamama spend the next few hours looking for Zaggai and could only find one man who had seen him running towards the mountains, screaming and pulling out pieces of his hair.

When Zag comes home, there is no hug or kisses from his dear wife. He finds her curled up in their bed, sobbing. All the children are huddled together in one room, crying and afraid.

"What?" asks Zag forcefully. And then softly, "What?"

"Father," said Tiflumany, the oldest daughter, "it's Zaggai, "He hit Gyurka and ran off into the mountains. Mother and Zamama have been searching for him for hours. Please make mother stop crying, please. She never cries like this." She goes to him and gives him a long, sobbing hug.

King Nimrod is on his throne, absolutely exhausted from the day's proceedings. So many needing help. Needing wrongs righted, the weak versus the strong. Favors done. A guard comes in and whispers in his ear.

"Send him in." The guard exits and returns with the wise and aged city council member, Terah. Nimrod motions for the guard to leave and bring two chairs. Nimrod comes down from the throne and sits next to Terah. "My friend, I hope I can call you that."

"Certainly, good King, certainly."

"I never imagined so many things one person in charge must do to keep the kingdom rolling along."

"By all accounts, my King, you are doing an excellent job. What complaints there are, seem to be born out of jealousy, rather than of you doing a poor job."

"Jealousy? Ah yes, probably among the wealthy." Terah nods his head and smiles.

"Terah, I have asked you here today to consider coming to work for me. For Babylon."

171

"Forgive me, your Majesty. I fear I have little to offer you in my frail season of life."

"What you have is very much a product of all the years you have spent getting to this season of life, as you call it. I do not need you to lead my troops into battle." They both smile. "I need you to oversee the day-to-day running of the kingdom. I need your advice, say, as to how best to deal with the wealthy."

"Your majesty, I am flattered, but …"

"Please Terah, let me finish. I noticed in working with you as an elder of Babel, your compassion, wisdom and gentle diplomacy with people. I lack some of those qualities. I need someone to oversee the daily problems brought before me, the long term problems of how to grow the empire, what is fair, what is foolish. I need you to be my Grand Vizier, my number two man."

"I am completely taken by surprise, your Majesty. I thought perhaps I was called here to help with, I don't know, with …"

"Please, go home, speak with your wife, mull it over and come back in a day or two and we'll discuss it some more."

"Your Majesty, I know it is a small thing. Perhaps trivial to you, but … but I am not married."

"My dear elder Terah, with all your wisdom and age I just assumed you were married and had a large family."

"No sire, no wife, no children."

"Forgive me, Terah, if I have offended you."

"My goodness, dear King Nimrod, you could never offend me. That is not in your nature."

"Thank you, dear friend. Your position with me would give you power and authority over all in Babel, in all of Babylon, save myself and the Queen. This would also give voice for the wealthy to speak of their legitimate concerns. I do not need you to be a military man. I have very capable men for that. I need you to help me improve the kingdom, to help me reach out to those outside of Babylon, to hire competent men, to hear the concerns of the general population in our courts and so on. Will you at least consider it?"

"Yes, my King." Terah exits, obviously overwhelmed by this offer.

"And Terah," Terah turns and faces the king, "start looking seriously for a wife. You are a fine-looking man, wealthy and very intelligent. You have much to offer a woman."

"Ah yes, much to … if you say so, your Majesty. But how … where?"

"I have one or two women in my harem that I believe would be extremely interested in getting to know you. Would you mind if I speak to them about you?"

"You would do that for me, sire? I ... well, yes, I suppose I could meet with them, one at a time of course."

"Of course."

"For dinner, perhaps?"

"Yes, and Semiramis and I would be pleased to dine with you, kind of a back-up for you if you get nervous."

"Splendid my King, splendid" Pause. "When?"

"I, uh, well, let me speak with the Queen and see what she thinks and I'll contact you. Any night when you're not available?"

Pause as Terah thinks. He nods his head left to right as he says, "No, just about any night will be fine."

As Terah once again prepares to leave, the King puts his arm around him and walks a few steps, "A wife will give you so much joy, and you'll feel a sense of completeness, a sense of fulfillment." Just then several children can he heard outside the room from which they are exiting screaming and running. One of the guards picks up one of the four-year-old girls and holds her suspended in mid-air.

"Shhhh!" orders the guard, "The king is having a meeting."

"No," pouts the young princess, "I won't, and you can't make me. Nobody can make me: I'm a princess." At which time she starts screaming again, joined in by the group of other children, totally perplexing the guard, who finally slaps her on the bottom and puts her face right up to his.

"I said, shhh!" To which she stops screaming and tears begin to flow as she hugs the guard.

"I love you too," she whispers. He lets her down and the group runs off screaming all the more. "But I am a princess and I can scream if I want to."

"Yes, my King," responds Terah, "joy and completeness."

Nimrod watches him leave, "Never can have too many eyes and ears among the glutinous, wealthy whiners."

A guard approaches Nimrod, "Sire, Kish is here."

"What of his army?"

"All dead, sire, every last one of them, except the women and children."

Nimrod crosses and sits on his throne. Kish is brought in, still in his bloody clothes. The guards exit.

"My, my Kish. You don't look well. Guess my men got carried away."

"I thought perhaps you had changed your mind, and I was to die with my men."

"Now, now, we had an agreement and I always honor my agreements, honor among thieves and all. You delivered your army and I spared your life. I have prepared for you a wagon laden with gold, weapons and food, five beautiful women and a driver. You are to drive south until you reach the ends of the earth – never to be heard of again. Agreed?"

"Agreed, now get me to a doctor. I am feeling faint from loss of blood, please."

"Of course. Sorry to hear about your son."

"He was a liability. You know how it is. A doctor, please." A doctor comes in and administers a potion to Kish. He is dismissed and several guards come in and lift the litter. They carry Kish behind King Nimrod through secret corridors into the temple. The altar fires are burning bright and now Kish is feeling no pain. The fires are bright with no apparent sacrifice in sight. Until now.

King Nimrod turns to Kish, "Yes, sweet liabilities."

Zaggai is found lying on the ground and is taken by two men on horseback deep into the mountains. There, his limp, barely breathing body is dumped at the tent door of Nuradad.

"Big fella, kinda young. He's bleeding from hair being pulled out around his temples," one of the men offers.

"Was he tortured?" asks Nuradad.

"Don't know, boss. He looks familiar. It looks like he's been wandering around up here for a few days."

"Put him in the medical tent and put a guard with him, just in case."

"Okay." The two men drag Zaggai off.

Over the next few days Zaggai's fever keeps him in a semiconscious state. One of the young women watching over him takes a liking to him and offers to stay with him. She puts fresh water compresses on his forehead and cleans the blood from his head. She listens to his incoherent ramblings and strokes his hair.

When Zaggai comes to, he does not remember who he is or how he came to be in the mountains. His new girlfriend leads him around camp like a lost puppy.

"Hey, Lenka finally found a man that's not too particular?!" a man laughs with his friends as they sit by the fire pit in the early evening.

Lenka says to Zaggai, "He hurt my feelings." Zaggai goes to the man and picks him up off the ground and throws him into the fire. The man yells and hollers in pain, as several of his friends help put out his clothes that are on fire.

"Anything else you want to say to me, ugly?" a smiling Lenka asks.

"Not with your stupid goon nearby."

"His name is Bouhous."

"Whatever, and your name is dirt bag when he leaves."

Lenka starts to tell Bouhous (Zaggai), "He hurt …"

"All right, all right. I'm, ah, sorry, Lenka."

"At least he treats me with respect." She turns and takes Bouhous by the hand and they walk to her tent.

"You see what a little respect could have gotten you?" murmurs one of the man's friends.

"Yea, yea, I'll get some, again, with or without respect, you watch."

"Nuradad doesn't go for that kind of stuff. You know that."

"Like I care what Nuradad goes for. He's a one-arm coward, like his cousin."

Terah, and a fellow elder of Babel and his wife, are talking about King Nimrod's offer when they are interrupted by a persistent knock at Terah's door. Terah excuses himself and opens the door to find Riplakish beaming, with a face full of knowledge regarding Terah's visit to the palace.

"Well, tell me, tell me everything the King said," as he pushes his way into the house.

Terah looks at him, astonished, "How could you possibly know about my trip to see King Nimrod?"

"He wants you for a very important position, doesn't he? Well?" To the couple visiting he says, "Pardon the intrusion, folks. It's not just the king that has eyes and ears. Money buys eyes and ears." So, he sits himself down in the chair vacated by Terah, "What did this ignorant buffoon want of our most esteemed city elder? Please, please, please, I won't tell a soul." The couple roll their eyes at each other like "right." Keeping a secret was not strength of Riplakish, and having already poisoned the well with his characterization of the King as an "ignorant buffoon", Terah knows he could not tell this man the truth. But, what to tell him?

It is his friend's lovely, white-haired wife who shocks Terah with her answer. "The King wants Terah-bear to make a list of all the wealthy and influential men in Babel and whether or not they are loyal to him."

Riplakish is taken back by this announcement and struggles to find the right words to say, "Well, you, you know, I was just kidding about the King being an ignorant buffoon, right? A joke? Look, I must be going. Give my warmest regards to our great King." And with that Riplakish is gone.

General Jared and his twenty men and Dalziel arrive in Babel the day before the meeting of the traitors who work for Kish.

Jared scouts the meeting place with Dalziel and then stations his men around the neighborhood. The place is a vacant, rundown house in a poor part of Babel. There are children playing in the streets, but Jared reasons, by nightfall they should be in their homes and not in danger when the fighting breaks out.

The spies of Kish are smart to use the night to meet, so as to keep their identities safe.

The day of the meeting Dalziel cautions, "General, these men will realize their lives are forfeit if they're caught. They will do everything possible to escape. Either way they know they are dead men, and dying here at the edge of your sword is a lot better than going through hours-upon-days of torture when they can be forced tell us if we have missed anyone."

"Of all the men I really want, it is this so-called commander. I can't believe I have helped select someone to train and lead our troops who is a traitor to our King."

"You're wondering how you could have seen what's in a man's heart, General? That's good work if you can get it. Perhaps you should be the next Noah."

"Ah, no, not that, anything but that!" They grin slightly and Jared puts his arm around Dalziel. "It's not a pleasant business we're in, at times, is it Dalziel?"

"No, General, but the outcome when we do our part is a pleasant thing: freedom from oppression, freedom to live our lives to our choosing. Don't you think?"

"It gives one pause to ponder what if ... " as his voice trails off.

"What if, General?"

"Yes, Dalziel. What if you or I were Kish or Berosus and felt King Nimrod was oppressive?"

"But he's not!"

"That's our opinion. I'm just saying, being the devil's advocate as it were, when I view the other man's point of view, it gives me pause to ponder, what if? I am not saying you and I are wrong in our support of our King. I'm just saying you and I shouldn't condemn those who do not agree. Now, to kill and rape because one disagrees, that's another matter."

"Do we rape?"

General Jared sighs, "I hope not, I certainly hope not, Dalziel. If we do, it makes us no better than the robbers, does it?"

Dalziel nods his head in agreement. "I guess the killing part is all dependent on how it is done then. Is that right?"

"I believe so. If you kill to subjugate that's one thing. If you kill to stay free from terrorism, that's something else. And even then, is it what God wants you to do?"

A soldier, a runner, is seen quietly running down the street and stops where the two men are hiding like they are standing out on the street in plain sight. Jared looks at Dalziel and shakes his head and Dalziel just grins.

"General, we've sighted several men wearing hoods that are headed this way." The runner then exits and really hides.

Dalziel, "Let the games begin."

Three men separately make their way to the rendezvous house. Each is extremely cautious in his approach and each enters gingerly. Soon, another three men join them, again doing so with extreme caution. Their caution testifies to their understanding of the serious nature and consequences of their actions. Another two men make their way to the house. With the growing absence of sunlight, there appears a flickering light within the house. It would seem that all that are coming are now present.

Chapter Eleven

As Jared is about to give the signal to close in, in the dim evening light several more figures make their way down the two streets that intersect in front of the suspect house.

Several men can now be seen moving on the roof tops around the house and more men, out of our sight have sealed off the back of the house. Another few men, the rest of the twenty that came with General Jared, now press their bodies against the houses leading to the meeting place.

When General Jared sees that the trap is tight, he leaves his place of seclusion and immediately one of his men shouts out, "You're surrounded!" causing Jared and others to freeze. At the same time four men come running out of the house and try to escape. One is killed and the other three run back into the house. Jared hears a shuffling of feet inside the house.

"Gentlemen," General Jared announces, "It would be best for you if you came out and threw your weapons down."

He hears the sounds of tight-voiced muffled comments behind the door and it seems to him that some want to give up their weapons and come out – but do not. A voice comes through the door, "How do we know you just won't kill us if we choose to surrender?"

"You don't, but this is General Jared and I am known for keeping my word. As part of your deliberations, you should know that Kish, Berosus and all five thousand seven hundred and eighty-five of your fellow robbers are dead. They died four days ago. You no longer have any friends alive to help you. You have no one left for which to keep your secrets. I advise you, for the last time, to throw down your weapons and come out. If you don't, again, you have my word, we will come in and get you."

More huddled, intense conversations take place. The door opens just a crack and some swords and knives are thrown out. A couple of men start to make their way to the door when one announces, "General, I was asked at the last minute to fill in at this meeting tonight. My commander said I should take notes and bring him the information ..." A scream emanates from the house and the man falls forward, with a little help from his friends, having a large knife stuck through his back and protruding out his stomach. Two of Jared's men drag him over to the General as he lays there dying.

"Who is your commander, soldier?" The man tries to say the man's name but only blood pours from his mouth. "Time is up gentlemen. What's your decision?" More scuffling in the house with a couple of more screams. General Jared gives the signal for his men to enter the house. The men break down the door and to their surprise all the men are dead. Three plus the man outside have been stabbed in the back; the others have committed suicide.

The hoods are removed and Jared and his men attempt to identify the eight men. Several are quickly identified, the others are a mystery. A wagon comes to the door and all eight are loaded on and taken away under the watchful eye of twenty to thirty curious neighbors. The dead men are transported to the palace.

General Jared gathers his men together. "Who yelled out, 'You're surrounded'? "No one offers a hand. "One of you said it, mind as well admit it." No hands.

"General, it was Captain Bomani. I was right behind him." All eyes focus on the Captain.

"Is it true?" The Captain will not answer. "If you do the crime, Captain, you also must do the time. What say you?" Still no answer. "Everyone makes mistakes Captain, why can't you admit it?"

With a hate-filled look on his face that contorts all his facial features, he stops staring at the ground and takes a step towards the general, but is stopped by several men around him. He strains against their hands and arms, "I hate you, you filthy coward. You call yourself a General, but you are a monster: you and your so-called King. It has been all I could do to not kill you every time I looked upon you these last four days. Kish was my uncle. He was a true man. A true general. A true king."

"Take him away. The King will want to talk to him." Jared waits until Bomani is led away and then announces, "We are still missing the garrison commander. And now, we may never know his true identity."

Within a few hours all the garrison commanders are assembled at the palace to look over the remains of the eight men. Along with those already identified, the commanders are able to identify all but one. The one who said he was filling in and only taking notes. No one claimed him as part of their regiment.

General Rayas, a wee bit ragged-looking these days, comes forward with several of his men and stops to look at the dead men. He looks over the one man not yet identified and proclaims, "This is one of General Chiamaka's aides."

"Rayas, are you sure? Chiamaka?"

"Quite sure, Jared."

All the men are released and go home except General Rayas. Within the hour General Chiamaka arrives and is told of the evenings events and that one man was identified by General Rayas as an aide to General Chiamaka.

"It's true, General Jared, "General Rayas has correctly identified him. His name is Dertelli, Captain Dertelli. He was recently, like in the past month, picked by me to be an aide. His commander, Commander Abasi, recommended him very highly as to his organizational skills. I had no idea he was a robber. You have my word, General. And I did not assign him to a meeting tonight to take notes for me. I will investigate the matter with Commander Abasi, if you wish."

"Very well, General. Please conduct an investigation with Commander Abasi and then the two of you report back to me in two days. We leave for the land of the giants then and I would like to have this wrapped up before we leave."

"Yes, General."

The brick factory owner, Berakhiak, had been notified by a runner that King Nimrod has decided to tour his facility. Puli-ilu was but a fading memory for most, but not for Nimrod.

Puli represented Nimrod's first defeat. True, the personality of this injured man was infectious even for Nimrod, and yet, Nimrod wanted some form of closure, so he came to the factory where Nimrod himself had been instrumental in obtaining Puli's first real job.

Berakhiak did not know why King Nimrod desired this tour of his facility. Had he done something wrong? Did the King think was he hiding some deep, dark secret? Berakhiak sweated for two days, worried the King was looking for a reason to confiscate his brick factory. That idea had been the brainchild of Riplakish. Berakhiak was a godly man and needn't have put himself through such mental machinations, but the rumors he had heard, primarily through Riplakish, regarding the Temple, regarding Zag and missing persons, and regarding the stories of those who had opposed the King weighed heavily on his mind. These stories, along with more stories of entire families sent to live on a wagon somewhere in the vast deserts. So what should be of concern and what should not be of concern?

And so it was with these worst-case scenarios roaring through hBerakhiak's mind that King Nimrod, alone, appeared at the main gate to the factory where thousands worked six days a week to provide bricks for the many projects the King required of his people.

Berakhiak bowed profusely before his King, as Riplakish had explained he should do, and was lightly chastised for his profusion.

"Dear Berakhiak, all these years we have known each other, please do not treat me so officiously, as distantly unrelated beings. I am a man, like unto you. I was elected King so very graciously by a majority of the people of Babel. I was not born to the office by lineage, but I dare say, I am of the same lineage as your own, and I seek to remember that daily. I am grateful for what you did for me, for Puli-ilu and for the countless thousands of others that have come to you seeking employment, seeking to just eat and live one more day.

If anything, it is I who am deeply indebted to you. You made the last years of my friend, Puli-ilu, the best years of his entire life. You treated him fairly, without pity, but with dignity. For that I will always be in your debt. Always. Now, so that I may have a better understanding of what you do here, please take me step-by-step through the process you have developed."

It was about then that Berakhiak knew he had to stop listening to Riplakish. In fact Riplakish was about to hear an earful from Berakhiak. "My King, you honor me deeply. With regards to Puli, he was a boon to his family as well as to me and my factory. Did you know that adding bitumen to the brick to further waterproof them, was his idea?"

"I was not aware."

"First, one must have four-parts clay to one-part sand mixed thoroughly together with water. The only place I know of for many miles is here, for the right type of clay. Sand, is well, sand. It is everywhere and now, thanks to you, dear King, water. All the water one could possibly ask for is at our fingertips.

Over here is one of twenty mixing pits requiring two hundred workers where we combine the clay, sand and water. For special bricks such as those used in the canals, we reduce the amount of water and substitute in bitumen. This rich, rather shiny ingredient causes water to run off the bricks rather than the water being absorbed. Any brick will partially repel water, but bitumen just makes the bricks do so even more.

We have our people, ten people to a spoke and ten spokes to a wheel, hold onto the spokes of this wheel and just walk around and around in circles, while others hoe the clay around to help mix the ingredients."

"Like making a giant pie!"

Berakhiak laughs, "Yes, your Majesty, I suppose so. Well, once a pit is considered well mixed, other men and women come in with shovels and forms and then fill the forms for that particular sized brick. Other workers quickly remove all excess clay and make sure the four sides are filled in completely. There are twelve bricks per board and the workers remove the boards to this area," he gestures as they walk, "where the tops are made smooth and then a worker marks each brick, NIMROD/BABEL, before the bricks are moved to a drying area. The bricks are laid out one-inch apart in rows of five hundred bricks. Sometimes, we'll have upwards of a thousand rows."

"That's around five hundred thousand bricks."

"Yes, Sire. And that's just for that size or shape brick. They are turned daily for two weeks and then loaded onto these one-wheel carts called brick carts, and the bricks are taken to those funny looking shelves we call a brick clamp.

This is where we stack the bricks one-inch apart, row upon row up to fifteen-feet high, ten-feet wide and thirty-feet long. One brick clamp will have approximately forty thousand bricks, using all four sides and the roof of the clamp covered. Every so often a brick on the roof is missing where the water vapor is allowed to escape. As you can see with this clamp, there are three large holes on the longer side and two holes on the smaller sides, the ends. Inside you can see large stacks of wood being prepared."

"Why not just lay the bricks out in the sun and let the sun do the work?"

"That's a good question, your Majesty. For the first two weeks that's exactly what we are doing, but the temperature isn't high enough to harden the bricks. We stack all these bricks on the brick clamp to heat the bricks to around two-hundred-and-fifty degrees all day and all night for two more weeks."

"All that just to make the bricks hard?"

"Well, kind of. You see each brick has about one pound of water in it, and we need to heat the bricks to remove the water. Before the clay and sand are mixed, many hours are spent cleaning the clay and sand of anything that doesn't belong there: twigs, small insects, small rocks and so on. If we don't cleanse the clay and sand of foreign material, when it heats up, the material will pop and cause the brick to have a hole in it."

"From just two-hundred-and-fifty degrees heat?"

"No, but after the two weeks of two-hundred-and fifty-degrees of heat, we change from just wood-burning to coal-burning that allows us to get the heat much higher – around two-thousand degrees."

"Two-thousand degrees!"

"Yes, Sire and for two more weeks – night and day. At the end of that period of time the bricks need another week just to cool down so the workers can touch the bricks."

"I noticed over here that most of the bricks are reddish and black while some are gray and others, such as these," and he reaches out to grab a brick, "are really black and rather rough-looking."

"Yes, your Majesty, we call them clinkers because of their rough, black exterior. The grays were on the outside of the clamp, the black, rough bricks were right in the middle and the reddish-black ones were all over."

"What causes the reddish color?"

"That would be due to the small red flakes in the clay we call iron. During the heating, the small red flakes melt and the whole brick turns red. When making bricks with bitumen, it's much harder to see the red."

"What's next, Berakhiak?"

"The bricks are taken and laid out for cooling for one more week and then workers with brick carts collect them and we store the bricks over here for whatever project they were made."

"And what project are all these hundreds of stacks for?"

"These would be for the ziggurat."

"Some of these bricks must weigh hundreds of pounds!"

"Yes, your Majesty, they do. They'll be used to place on top of the granite blocks coming from the quarries for the foundation. Some parts of the ziggurat will have rooms, and the walls will be thirty-feet thick to hold the weight of the building. We're told that this will help keep the heat down, the privacy up and the strength of the walls constant."

"Yes, Berakhiak, each item is important due to the sensitive nature of some political discussions. Also, this will be the tallest ziggurat in the history of the world. The part you and your seemingly unimportant bricks play is in reality, rather enormous."

"If I may ask, what political discussions might there be?"

"If I tell you, I will have to kill you." A slight, uneasy pause and then the King smiles. "Uh, that's a joke, Berakhiak."

"Oh, good one, your Majesty, good one." Berakhiak is still not sure if it was indeed a joke.

"Each city, even each nation, will send delegates to the meetings for nations to discuss our future, what steps we may want to take for security, for expansion. Some cities may need to be censored for actions that do not fit with peaceful people. If that does not help a nation see the light, then military action may be required to get a nation to comply with the majority opinion."

"Suppose a nation wants out of this group, as they are too warlike and want to do things their way? What then? Can they just leave?"

This last remark draws a steely-eyed response followed by, "They will comply."

"And if they do not want to even join this, uh, this …"

"United Council of Cities."

"Thank you, this United Council of Cities, what then?"

"I don't know, Berakhiak. We've not come up with such a scenario. You raise some excellent questions. Excellent. May I return us to your bricks?"

"Forgive me, your Majesty. I have offended you and I did not desire to do so. I'm afraid my curiosity got the best of me."

"Not a problem, old friend. Just rest assured that what is discussed in the Tower of Babel, stays in the Tower of Babel, especially before final votes, final decisions and so on." Getting back to the bricks, I see that you have thousands of enormous stacks of wood and just as many stacks of that glittery black stuff. Why so much?"

"Each brick clamp will use sixty stacks of wood in each two-week period. We presently have ten brick clamps in one phase or another of heating or drying. Obviously the large bricks you pointed out earlier must dry and heat differently than the smaller bricks."

"I am impressed, Berakhiak, very impressed. And you do this all year long?"

"There are times when we do not have as great a call for bricks, particularly when the weather turns cold: cold by our standards, not wintery, snowy cold like in the higher mountains. It is then that we mix our sand and clay, cleaning it and storing it for warmer weather. We also stock the firewood and the black, shiny stuff, coal, for later use in preparation for the warmer weather and the activity the warmer weather brings. And then there are the dust storms. The coal is what really helps us get the temperature to 2,000 degrees."

"No need to explain my friend. Dust storms can be horrendous. What's the longest you've seen a dust storm last?"

"Oh my, let's see. Before you were named King we had a storm that lasted eight months, day and night. It literally changed the landscape of Babel."

"Eight months. Incredible. And I thought the one we had several years ago was bad and it lasted only a few weeks."

"We've been very fortunate over, give or take, the last hundred years. Hardly anything compared to that one I mentioned."

"Oh yes, why is NIMROD/BABEL on the back of each brick?"

"We are very proud of what you have accomplished since you've been King, what we have accomplished. We want all to know of that pride."

"In turn, Berakhiak, you make me proud. Thank you."

"It has been truly a pleasure to serve you my King. And may I add, everything is not always perfect. When those times come, please have the confidence in your people to work out any problems that may come our way. You have continually done that and I hope you will continue to do so in the future."

"I will take that under advisement. To sum up my brickyard schooling for the day, it takes about two to three months to produce a batch of quality bricks, correct?"

"Yes, Sire."

King Nimrod starts to walk towards the entrance where he started his tour. "Do you ever hear from Puli-ilu or his family?" It is obvious that Berakhiak is startled by the question and he struggles to answer it in a positive manner.

"Sire, Puli is dead … his family, his family is gone. I haven't seen or heard from any of them since the viewing of Puli's body in their home.

I understand their grief was so great at the vicious cause of Puli's death, they just couldn't bear walking the same streets where he was murdered, and they just picked up and left.

"Yes, that's what I heard too. Thank you again, Berakhiak." Nimrod shakes hands with Berakhiak and walks out of the factory.

With that King Nimrod not only exits the factory, he exits another part of his life. The work continues on behind him, but what of his search for Puli-ilu? The saying, "In the mouth of two or three witnesses, all shall be established" has taken hold. The King would no longer seek the whereabouts of one Puli-ilu.

In a far distant city days later, Puli and his family were two streets away from the King's questioners. Puli and family had frantically been packing their belongings and were prepared to leave under the cover of darkness. How the King knew where to look for them, they knew not. But, the King's men were there in their little village. Members of the family had been watching the progress of the King's men for days. Then, and without warning, one of the family came running to Puli's home. "Puli, they're gone. The just packed up and left. People on the next street said a runner came to the King's questioners and told them to return to Babel, the hunt was over."

Puli and family and select friends embraced in joy-filled hugs and tears. Then they, very solemnly, knelt and gave thanks to their God for continuing to watch over their family. They rose and with their bags already packed, left during the night to a land much farther north of Babel. The God of the universe watches over his children, especially those who seek to do His will. Anyone seen an idol do so? Thought not.

Now, on to the mystery man and Commander Abasi: King Nimrod no sooner arrived at the palace from his tour of bricks than General Jared and Chiamaka were waiting for him. "My King," began General Chiamaka, upstaging General Jared, "the news I bring is not very good. My most trusted Commander Abasi is dead by his own hand. I had sent word for him to meet with me and General Jared, when a runner came back to me saying he had found the commander in his office at the training grounds hanging from the ceiling. There was no note, no signs of a struggle, just his body hanging there."

"While that is certainly not proof of his guilt, it is a very strong indication, my King," added Jared.

"Thank you both. We'll speak more of this later."

Chapter Twelve

"Seems to me Thoth, our King grants these so-called people of God far too much leniency."

"How's that, my dear high priest?"

"Well, just look at how he treats that General Jared. He doesn't have serpents in his house and Nimrod says nothing. Poor Zag is demoted for doing what any good General would do in chastening his troops, and then the Christian, Jared, is chosen to replace him. Jared does not come to the meetings at night with all the other Elite leaders. He doesn't have the special marking on his foot or behind his ear, and why?"

"I guess he believes in his own religion. He doesn't fight against us and our religion. Why not just let him be?"

"You cannot just let good alone, Thoth! It spreads, like a fungus. Soon, others will want special consideration."

"Does he know of our sacrificial ceremonies?"

"Humph, I doubt it, or he'd complain about that too. Ah, the man and his kind give me a headache. On another subject, Semiramis had guaranteed me that all the babies she brings us are deformed or defective from birth, and that is why we shouldn't feel bad about them being sacrificed. It is their only way into heaven, as they are second-class beings at best. We are doing them a favor. Quite honestly, I couldn't care less. I hate the little rug rats and the more we can put out of my misery, the better."

"King Nimrod doesn't complain about us to her, does he?" asks Thoth.

"Not that I have heard. You just can't trust those in charge to be honest with the help. That's my experience. When you smell the rats deserting the ship, you'd better be up front leading the charge or you'll be in the rear getting stomped to death. I have my eyes and ears, dear

Thoth. I mean, look what the King did to Zag! And he's his favorite general. His favorite! No, you and I can't really trust anyone. We'd better stick together, or it may be our turn to be stuck. We'll be stuck in a barrel and thrown out with the trash, like Zag."

"You have to admit we have a pretty cushy life though – all the drink we can handle, all the potions for aching muscles known to man."

"Ah yes, those marvelous potions. Thanks to Kadenram. They are fantastic! And all the women to make our muscles ache we could possibly ask for," moans Tashshigura-mash. Both men laugh the crude laugh of the crude.

"True, true."

"And now we have all the residents of Babel, and all the residents of all the little conquered towns, kneeling as we pass by with our snakes on a pole."

"Ewww. I hate those little buggers."

"You are a genius, Tashshigura-mash, a bloody genius."

"Well, thank you, Sir Thoth, you're very kind and very perceptive." They both laugh at their own genius. "But then again, here comes Jared and his so-called Christians. They do not kneel! And does Nimrod do anything about them? No! It makes me sick. Suppose others catch on to being a Christian, not having snakes in their homes or not having to kneel before us? What then?"

"Perhaps I should mention this to the King and at least get him thinking about it. Nothing too strong at first, just by-the-way, for your information, Sire."

"Great, Thoth, very good. Nimrod does not like to be pushed. Yes, just a little by-the-way, good, very good. And we keep our eyes and ears out for some incident that we can pounce on and say: see, this is what we've been afraid of."

Zag and Shamshi are on their way to a get-together at Jared's and Zamama's. Zamama has invited them over, not knowing why exactly Zag has such an intense dislike of her husband. She and Shamshi have become excellent friends and just want to sit and talk to get to know each other's family better.

As they are walking Zag emits, "No like." He is carrying a small bouquet of flowers.

"It's just a few hours, Zag. For me?" Shamshi stops walking and looks into his eyes. "For me? And for me, you'll be kind to Jared?"

"For you."

A drunken soldier makes his way past them. He has the Elite soldier's haircut. He bumps into Zag. "Sorry there, big guy. The street keeps on moving. Hey!" He looks up and up to Zag's face. "Aren't you Ziggy, or Shaggy, the washed-up General?"

"Name Zag." He raises his fist and is stopped by Shamshi.

"Yeah, right, how'd you know? Hey, why ain't you headed for the temple for our meeting? Gonna be lots of pretty girls there as usual. Lots of heart-pounding music."

"Go home."

"Nah," he burps, "gotta keep the King happy. All those snakes, virgins and screaming babies."

"Stop!" yells Zag. He grabs the man, now face-to-face. "King sees you – you die."

"Oh yeah, I almost gorfot. King does not like drunks." He stands there staggering and wobbling. Zag turns him around.

"Home. Say sick. Live." Zag pushes him gently.

"You're a great gob, Zorb. Thanks." He stumbles into the dark.

Zag and Shamshi walk a ways, not talking. "What did he mean about your meeting?"

"Not for me." They walk a ways again.

"What did he mean about snakes?"

"Not know." They walk some more.

"Virgins?"

"Hot tonight."

"Screaming babies?"

"Shamshi! That work, this home. Hot, very hot."

"Since when are virgins a part of work? Whose babies are screaming? Do you have another family?" Shamshi is near tears.

"Ahhh, kill him."

"You didn't tell me you had a meeting tonight," Shamshi whispers through her tears.

"Not for me."

"We'll talk later." Zag moans the moan of the damned as he knows talking later will be very painful for him. Shamshi knocks on the door. Jared and Zamama open the door and all exchange pleasantries. It is obvious Zag and Shamshi have had a difficult walk over to Jared's house. Zag offers not more than a grunt for Jared and a head bow to Zamama. Zag hands her a small, squished bouquet of flowers.

"Thank you Zag, They're, ah, beautiful. And thoughtful. She puts them in water while the others find chairs around the table. There is an awkward silence while they wait for Zamama. She brings a few treats of dates and figs and some water and cups to the table.

Zamama asks, "Did you have a nice walk over here?"

Simultaneously, Zag, "Yes" and Shamshi, "No." Pause.

Jared, "Ah, good. Good."

Zamama, "Eat, eat Zag. Drink, water."

Shamshi mentions, "I don't think I mentioned to Zag that you don't drink, ah, drink, drinks."

Zamama tries to explain, "No Zag. Just water, goat's milk. No drink drinks." A pause ensues which is only broken by the chewing of treats and Zag taking a large slurp of water.

"This water?"

Jared responds, "Yes, Zag, water."

"Not bad."

Kids can be heard running and giggling somewhere in the house.

"They're supposed to be asleep," Zamama explains.

Shamshi responds, "Don't worry, we understand. Right? Zag?"

He has a mouth full of treats, "Hmmm."

"So how are your kids doing? Zaggai is your oldest?"

"Yes, he's the oldest and then we have another ten. And you?"

"Well, we've been here thirty years, which would be twenty-four children. Right, honey?"

"How many?"

"Twenty-four," whispers Shamshi.

"All here?"

"Yes, Zag," responds Zamama.

"Busy, very busy," says Zag.

"Zag!" whispers Shamshi.

"No. House. Busy." Zag moves his arms around, making buzzing noise. Jared and Zamama break out in laughter at the buzzing noise like a bee.

"What funny?"

"It's an inside joke, a family joke. Bees, buzzing, mosquitoes," Jared offers.

Zamama nudges him, "Jared, no. Honestly." She is embarrassed.

Jared whispers to Zag, "I'll tell you another time." There is a lull in the conversation and each goes to munching of the snacks.

"What's this meeting, Zag, and you are missing?" inquires Zamama.

Jared is confused and offers, "I haven't any idea sweetheart, honestly. I know of no meeting scheduled for tonight."

"Me confused, too."

You are the general of the army, aren't you?"

"Yes, my love. Perhaps we could discuss this later, after our guests leave. I promise to look into it tomorrow. Will that be okay?"

Zamama hugs him, "Sure, mon general."

"Moan general?"

"It's something I heard from Kadenram, the merchant," Zamama responds.

"Moan?"

Having broken the ice a bit, the foursome relax into general conversation about their families, jobs, and the future. But always Shamshi seems to point the conversation away from their children, especially away from Zaggai. Her look of sadness does not go unnoticed by Zamama and Jared.

After a pause Jared adds: "I've said something to upset you Shamshi, I'm sorry."

Shamshi begins to cry. "What's wrong?" asks Zamama, and Zag gets this bewildered look on his face, as he does not do well with his wife crying.

"It's Zaggai. He had a fight with an elderly neighbor and ran away from home. We haven't seen him for several weeks."

"I didn't know. What can we do to help?" offers Jared.

"Our problem," Zag says, obviously on the defensive.

"Zag, we do not want to pry," says Zamama. "We just want to help."

Shamshi continues, much to the discomfort of Zag, "He's been changing over the last few years, getting very emotional, very explosive: toward me, toward his brothers and sisters, towards pets. Then he struck our neighbor. This isn't our Zaggai. It's like someone or something has taken his place." Zag is about ready to explode.

"We go." He gets up and heads for the door.

Shamshi looks at him through her tear-filled eyes, "Zag, that's rude." Zag exits the house and Shamshi excuses herself and hurries to catch up with him. Jared and Zamama look after them from their doorway.

"They only want to help."

"Know weakness. Use hurt me."

"Jared? Hurt you? No Zag, he's not like that. Zamama is not like that either."

"Hurt!" Zag cries out. There is a considerable pause. Shamshi takes him by the arm as they walk.

"I love you, Zag. I not let them hurt you."

"You like Mom. She not stop Dad. Not stop hurt."

As they walk Shamshi was thinking about her dear husband and what he had told her of his youth. Of how his dad had very little patience, and drinking made it worse. Zag had always been a little slow to answer questions, not slow of mind, just slow of speech. He had to choose the right words, and so his demeanor was made to look as though his brain was defective. This pausing drove his dad absolutely nuts.

"He get even; he let other kids hurt."

Shamshi put Zag's conversation in her own words: "Zag said something to an older kid, larger kid and he chased Zag home. Zag almost made it to the front door but he tripped in front of the house and fell down.

The other kid jumped on him and pinned his shoulders to the ground, facing his house. The kid proceeded to punch Zag time and time again. Zag turned to see his father watching them. Since his father did nothing, the kid went back to punching Zag. Zag remembers yelling out, "help, Father," but his father kept on eating a piece of meat saying, "You gotta learn to defend yourself sometime."

When the other kid ran out of strength to punch Zag anymore, he got up and started to leave. He returned and kicked Zag in the face and then left for good. Zag crawled into the house crying and bleeding from his mouth, his nose and his eyes. Zag's mom cleaned him up and put him to bed. Zag remembers his mom crying in her bed asking his dad how he could allow such a thing to happen. He slapped her and told her to keep her mouth shut.

That was one of the few times Zag's brothers and sisters treated him kindly. They smuggled little treats into him now and then, they did his chores around the house, even though his father would yell at them and slap them around for doing so.

"You'll just make him a weakling his father yelled. Let him get up and do his own chores." I guess Zag's swollen face made them want to help him more than their fear of their father.

Zag's dad liked to create two teams with his kids and then ask questions about everything, anything. The winners would get a piece of candy to split among them or an extra portion of dessert. Questions like, "how many people were there on the ark?" And then he would call out a name, always Zag's, if he thought he didn't know the answer. "What were their names, alphabetically?"

"C'mon Zag, c'mon son, spit it out! Hurry, fast, what's the damn answer! What is it? What is it? What? What? What?!" With his voice getting louder and his face right in front of Zag's, his spittle would splash onto Zag's cheeks and eyes.

"Zag would start to stutter and, and his, his mind would go blank trying to be fast, but it was no use. No matter what team he was on, it always lost because of Zag. Then, even his brothers and sisters started calling him the same names his dad used.

"Hey, bird-brain, think, think, think! Pea-brain, what's the problem Dumb-dumb the numb-numb." One night my father was eating a piece of meat at dinner and started to choke. He stared at Zag to do something, but Zag just calmly watched him gag and choke to death. Zag remembers saying to him as he grabbed Zag's shirt and pulled Zag right in his face, "I can't, too stupid, remember?"

From that time on Zag could only put one or two words together and he still couldn't make his brain and mouth work together and form complete sentences. By then Zag was large enough that his family stopped picking on him for fear he would hurt them. And he would. And he did. And it felt good.

Not as good as the time they found that bully kid who beat Zag in front of Zag's father, dead at the bottom of a cliff near our home. Now, that felt great!

Then Zag noticed other kids, other people, who had a defect, or a problem, had people who picked on them too. So, he started doing away with the trouble makers who preyed on the weak. Hurting them never felt bad, never seemed wrong. He never let other people get close to him, never allowed them to know his business, for fear of their using any information they'd get about Zag to hurt him.

Zag never wanted to give another person the opportunity to make fun of him, to hurt him, that is, until he met Shamshi. He knew deep down she would never do that to him. And she never has. She is a good person. A good mother. A good wife.

"I love Shamshi," murmurs Zag.

And so they walked in silence all the way home.

Zag waits for Jared to say something about Zag's problems in the various meetings they have. It never happens. True to what his wife had said, Jared and Zamama are friends, good friends. Zag finds out they have been searching their neighborhood for a lost boy, and then they ask several, older family members to ride into the foothills looking for a lost boy. No one finds Zaggai.

It is also sometime after that evening with Jared and Zamama that King Nimrod calls Zag in and interviews him in front of Jared and the other generals. What for he does not know. General Jared stands up and speaks of the great progress Zag has made in his treatment of his men. Jared also makes sure those present know that Zag is the finest fighting man he, Jared, has ever served with and that he would gladly serve under Zag anytime. Then the General sits down. King Nimrod looks at each of the men and Zag sees all but one nod his head yes as in approval of something. Then they dismiss him. He, Zag, is now a general once again.

Zag goes home and confides in Shamshi what had just happened. Shamshi jumps up and down, hugs and kisses her huge husband, and giggles off and on all through the night. The children hear the commotion and run in to be told the good news. Much like their mom, they jump, laugh, hug and giggle on behalf of their beloved dad. They then leave to give their parents time to be alone.

"Why good? My life not good. I not good. Why?"

"You do not need to be a perfect man for good things to happen to you. I believe Zaggai will come home. I know you are a great man. I know we have two very, very good friends, and those type of friends do not waste their love and friendship on bad people. On losers."

Zag ponders on that for many weeks to come, as he respects greatly his wife's opinion. He even starts wanting to be a better person, for her.

At the same time Semiramis has also become a better friend lately, and so Zag spends more time helping her than pondering. Even he, though, could tell that their friendship is only because of what Zag could do for her, and not because she wants Zag to be a better man or a better human being. Actually, she likes what he is and does not want him to change at all. And Zag ponders this as well.

With the number of new wives and concubines fast approaching one hundred and fifty, Semiramis is in her glory running her mini-kingdom. She has called on Zag to help with the one or two who are defiant to Semiramis's wishes. He has no remorse in holding down those insignificant wenches to the ground as Semiramis administers her dose of 'medicine' to the worst offenders – a cup of the desert's finest sand. She knows she can depend of Zag to discreetly remove the remains via the temple's altar. Barbequed wench and down the chute they'd go.

Zag is becoming less the unconscious killing machine, with the advent of good friends in his life and the consistent efforts of his loving wife, born of her great love for her scarred, human husband. The concept of right and wrong is starting to take place once again, and the almost pleasure he has taken in destroying life is slowly eroding. It seems the old adage is true; the more wrong decisions one makes the less able that person is to make good decisions. Conversely, the more correct decisions one makes, the less wrong decisions one is able to make. Thus, Zag is caught in the dilemma of good versus bad for the very first time in his adult life. Morals. They can be a real pain in the –conscience! And you thought I was going to say … shame on you.

The gigantic task of building the steps and massive walls that are to surround the palace, temple and ziggurat is now beginning to bear fruit. The labor force has now tripled what it once was as the hauling of stones and bricks up the huge main staircase has drained every ounce of strength from the forced labor core as well as the volunteers from Babel. Even the army has been organized so that each soldier dedicates one week a month to working on the ziggurat, walls and grand staircase. From the old ground level in Babel there are three hundred steps to reach the ground level of the temple grounds or the palace complex, as it is now known.

On the inside of the wall surrounding the Palace complex is a stairway and lower wall, that soldiers patrol day and night to keep the royal family safe. Regular bows will not shoot the arrows from the wall to the ground with any force without the arrows literally floating to the ground due to the huge distance. So, General Jared and his group of expert engineers have devised giant bows and arrows to do the job. The bows are six-foot long and thicker, and the arrows three- foot long.

The soldiers assigned to these weapons are among the strongest men the army can find. Even the recruiting techniques have a special section dedicated to firing these weapons. Once trained, the arrows fired from these bows can pierce the skull of any animal alive from the top of the wall to the ground, hundreds of feet below.

Because the arrows are so expensive to produce, young boys are paid a price per arrow for returning any arrow they find after the archers have finished their daily practice sessions. The boys have to carefully extract the arrows from the bodies of the animals: lame oxen, diseased sheep, donkeys and the like that are herded up around the Palace complex for target practice.

The five hundred special archers have their own competitions amongst themselves. The weekly champions can select the virgin priestess of their choice for a Saturday night date or a cash prize. Men! Don't they ever change? Grow up? Mature? Nope.

The yearly overall winner gets to choose one of the King's concubines to marry. Or a virgin, if he so chooses. If he is already married, he still may have a second or third bride. If that is not the prize he desires, he too may take a monetary prize instead. There are the prizes for monthly winners, yearly runner-ups and so on.

The archers decide what the prizes should be, thus making them much more invested in the competition. And as King Nimrod and General Jared have found, competition breeds excellence far more than fear will ever do. Don't misunderstand: fear has its place. When someone is in fear of losing one's life, fear is a great motivator. But not in competition.

King Nimrod is in his Public Court when he is advised that the city elder, Terah, is in line to speak with the King. Nimrod tells the runner to escort Terah to his private chambers nearby. As Nimrod finishes with the case before him, the court clerk announces that there will be a brief recess, and the King will return shortly.

"But I have been waiting for hours, your Majesty. Couldn't you just hear my case so I can get back to my bakery and then adjourn?" asks the pushy, overweight baker. The King stops his exit and turns to the baker, "My goodness, how inconsiderate of me to need to go to the bathroom just when it's your turn. I'll just tell my bowels to wait a little longer before they burst all over the courtroom. Is that what you desire of me, dear baker?"

"Well, no, Majesty, I mean, I thought someone else, not your bowels -- I'll just wait here, quietly, until you return. I'm sorry, your bowelship, I mean ... the King holds up his hand, the baker stops and the King exits.

The baker mops his brow and goes to retake his seat. Someone has taken his seat and an argument ensues, until finally the baker sits on the man who took his seat, slightly crushing the skinny man. He groans and offers to move if the baker will kindly stand. The baker does and the man limps off.

King Nimrod enters his chambers, and Terah stands and bows slightly to greet him.

"No, no, dear elder, there is no need of such formality between the two of us. Please sit, go on, sit." They both take chairs and at the same time, Nimrod dismisses the guard.

"I, well, I've thought considerably about your offer, my King, and I have one or two questions before I decide."

"Very well Elder Terah, please ask."

"If I become a member of your distinguished court, do I have to convert to your religion of light?"

"No, no, dear elder, you are free to worship as you please, as are all residents of Babel. Why would you worry about that?"

"I do not want to seem unkind, but those that seem to flourish in your courts, in your administration, all seem to have embraced your religion."

"It is true some have, but it is not a requirement. You know of General Jared, and he is a God-worshipper, as are quite a few others. If you should want to know more, by all means, I would be pleased to discuss religion with you at any time. What else would you like to know?"

"Must I marry?"

"I beg your pardon?"

"I was at your military awards ceremony last month when several of your soldiers were awarded new wives and I thought …"

King Nimrod laughs gently, "No dear elder, what those men did was optional. They did not have to marry or marry multiple wives. I want solid family men running our city, men just like you, but I do not force men to marry."

"Oh, good. And lastly, lastly, well, I'm not sure how to present this question. But, do I get paid for the work you desire me to do? As a city elder my efforts were all voluntary and part-time. I assume my duties here will be of a more full-time nature."

Smiling, "Yes and yes. Yes, I need you full-time Monday through Friday with an occasional Saturday. Never Sundays, but perhaps an evening here or there, like the occasional Saturday. And your pay should allow you to live quite comfortably, with even a paid vacation several times a year."

"Several … wow. I am prepared to accept your most generous offer, my King. I would very much like to help you with the affairs of the kingdom, if you still want me with all my human frailties."

King Nimrod stands and grasps Terah's hand, "Of course I still want you as my Grande Vizier. I can't wait to turn over the Public Courts to a wise veteran like you. And as time goes by, I will want you to become more and more my second in command in many other areas of government.

You will have aides to offer opinions based on what I have decided in the past, only as guidelines for you, not as hard and fast rules. I want you to feel free to render fair and honest verdicts as you see fit. All I ask is when in doubt, postpone your decision, council with me and then return to issue your verdict. Does that sound fair?"

"Absolutely, I can't wait to get started. When do you want me to start reporting for work?"

"Tomorrow morning. I would like you to sit with me for a day or two so you can see how I do things. And then, I'll leave you be."

"Wonderful, dear King: until tomorrow morning. Good day" He exits. Kind Nimrod motions for his clerk and instructs him to have a second throne brought in for tomorrow. He also instructs his clerk to take copious notes for the first few weeks of Terah's take- over so he, King Nimrod, may monitor Terah's decisions. The King takes a deep breath and reenters the Public Court, motioning to the baker to once again come forward.

"Your Majesty, I hope everything came out as you expected. I mean, that you're time out was productive …"

"Please Baker, get on with it."

"Yes, your Majesty. I have been accused of allowing rats in my granary, and this man," he points to the one he sat on earlier, "says he found a rat in a loaf of my bread." The man holds up one partial loaf of bread and one scrawny, half-eaten rat.

King Nimrod addresses the man with the rat. "What do you want?"

"Yar Lardship. I want that he replaces the loaf of bread without a rat."

"That's it?"

"Yup."

The baker looks like someone just beat him up, "A whole loaf of bread, for free? Look at the half of the loaf that's missing." He grabs the loaf and rat from the man. "And the extra protein from the half-eaten rat!"

"Enough!" King Nimrod hollers over the baker, "Give him his loaf of bread. You sir," motioning to the man, "give the baker his bread and his protein." The man does so. "Now, Mr. Baker, you eat the protein. And you can start by taking a bite of protein – now!"

"But sire, I'm allergic ..."

"You now owe him two loaves of bread."

"Two whole loaves?"

"It's now three!" The baker gingerly takes a bite of the rat.

"Next case." The two men exit with the baker gagging. "You know, you get rid of the fur and it's not so bad. I should charge more for the meat."

Word has been received at the Palace that Nimrod's mom is dying, and she would like to see her son once more. Semiramis is with him when the messenger presents his purpose for being in Babel.

"So, my husband," as she strokes his hair and rubs his head at the temples, what are your wishes? Shall I make ready and accompany you to say goodbye to Elka?"

"I think not, my wife. You are the only one in whom I'd entrust the power of the kingdom for any length of time. It would not do to give anyone even the smallest of chances to foment unrest in the absence of both Babel's King and Queen. Even our beloved high priest, Tashshigura-mash, or Thoth, our minister of religion, have moving up the ladder of success on their minds. I am torn between having you by my side and leaving the kingdom unguarded. What think you, my dear? Am I getting paranoid?"

"I had not thought about whose hands in which to leave Babel in our absence. My first thoughts now would be of General Jared, in whom I think you could be one hundred percent sure of his loyalty."

"This is true. No doubt about it. My only reservation is that he is such a good man, that the intrigue of politics would be much above his head. He is a noble man, but I think too innocent for the job."

"Perhaps so, my dear. Which means you have no such misgivings about my abilities. No misgivings as to my innocence?" She nibbles on his ear.

"You are turning my words, dear wife. You have the mind capable of running any kingdom anywhere in the world. You can be ruthless and unforgiving as, uh, I don't know, me. It took me awhile to realize that my dear wife from Calneh, who was found dead in the desert, had not swallowed that cup of sand voluntarily or by mistake."

"She would not fulfill her wifely duties as I had instructed. What was a queen to do?" Semiramis smiles and embraces Nimrod in a passionate kiss and lingering hug.

"So my queen, will you be offended if your king wanders off to say farewell to his earthly mom?"

Semiramis kisses him even more passionately, "Just be sure to hurry home, my dear, as I await you and you alone."

They hug and kiss and walk to their bedchamber to say goodbye in their own intimate way.

"Perhaps I should take our son Tammuz with me."

"Excellent idea, my King. It's time he had some exposure to the inner workings of the kingdom. Seeing his father, the King, spending time with the King's Mom, on her death bed, perhaps bequeathing her last earthly possessions to an estranged son, whose dad attempted to murder Father's Father, the prophet Noah, only to be slaughtered by the King's dad, Father Ham? What an excellent opportunity for Tammuz to be introduced to the inner workings of such a dynamic family."

They disappear into their bedchamber giggling and laughing like two recently married, innocent little lovers.

"I'll leave in the morning."

Tammuz was both startled and excited by the news that he would be accompanying his father on such a special event as the death of his Grandmama.

"Gee, Dad, thanks so very much for inviting me to come with you. I am deeply honored," he shares as they leave the palace with two hundred Elites.

"My goodness, son, think nothing of it. I'm sure the family wants to see the kind of young men we grow in Babel. Just be sure that unless I tell you to speak, you keep your mouth shut."

"Absolutely, Father, you have my word. I won't embarrass you. I promise. Mother said …"

"Son?"

"Yes, Father?"

"Please stop talking for a while. I have a splitting headache already."

"Certainly Father. I'm sorry you are in pain. I've had headaches before and I know what you must be …"

"Son!"

"Yes?"

"Now."

"Certainly."

A pause as they ride on in silence.

"Father, how long until we get there?"

Nimrod moans in real pain.

A few moments later, "Do we have anything to eat?"

An Elite captain, who has overheard their conversation, comes over to the aid of his King.

"Tammuz, would you like to ride at the front of our column, and ask the guards there some questions?"

"Oh yes, Captain Zarek. Father, would you mind?"

"No, my son. Thank you, Captain. I am in your debt."

"Not at all, my King. I have little ones at home and know how they are."

"He's thirty, Captain."

"Oh."

They ride in silence. It takes several days for them to reach the tent of Nimrod's mother. Nimrod's older brother, Jasher, meets them as they ride into the little village.

"Dear brother, we had no idea there would be hundreds of you. I don't know where I'll put you all, or how to feed them? Where would you like Tammuz kept?"

"Far away, dear brother, just far away. My men will be fine. They are used to fending for themselves. Just keep your unmarried daughters close to you, very close. And your wives, grandmothers and so on. How's mother?

"She has good days and then … You know, I'm sure. She asked to see you the moment you arrived. It is late afternoon; if you want, we could wait until morning."

"That's fine, Jasher, lead me to her. Perhaps she'll find comfort in knowing we have honored her request to see me as soon as I arrived."

"Very well." Jasher leads Nimrod to their mother's tent, where the atmosphere is somber. Jasher takes Nimrod inside, and those waiting on their mother are gestured by Jasher to leave for a few minutes. Elka is sleeping, and Jasher awakens her to tell her that Nimrod has arrived.

Elka opens her eyes slowly and smiles slightly as she focuses on Nimrod. All exit to leave the two of them alone with Jasher.

"It takes my death to get you to come to visit, does it?"

"I'm a sorry excuse for a son, Mother. I, I have no real excuse for waiting all this time. After Lugal and then Dad, I ..."

"Ever since your father died ..."

"He was murdered."

"All right, ever since your father was murdered ..."

"By his own father."

"Can a dying mother get a word in here?"

"Sorry, Mom. Sometimes people want to forget what really happened. I will never forget what Grandfather Ham did. And he then tried to kill his very own father, the prophet?! What is wrong with him?"

"I do not know, Nimrod. And that's not even the worst of it" There's a pause.

"Mother, are you sure?" asks Jasher.

"Not the worst, Mother? How could anything be worse?"

Elka looks at Jasher and then, "Noah and Ham had it out one night. A brutal argument over just what you said. They both got to drinking and yelling, shouting at each other. Noah took his clothes off and was running around naked yelling at Ham, recounting the many mean things Ham had said and done. Noah fell down on the ground and passed out. Ham was furious and went over to his father, kicked him, grabbed him, and made Noah sit up against a tree stump, but Noah just groaned and fell back to the ground, inebriated.

Ham was incensed. Then, he went into Noah's tent and Naima was asleep. Ham ..." Jasher looks to Elka and she motions for him to continue, "Ham, he, uh, pretended to be Noah and knew his mother."

"He raped his own mother?"

Silence fills the tent.

Jasher speaks, "No one knew until after the baby was born. The baby, Canaan, just didn't look like any of us children. In fact, he was the spitting image of Ham."

"I'll kill him. Hurry up and die, Mother, so I can get to my Grandfather's death."

"Nimrod, you came here to have me hurry up and die? You want I should die now? Nimrod, listen to yourself."

Nimrod stops and realizes what he has just said. He kneels at his mother's bedside, "I am so sorry, Mother, and I did not mean what I said. I can't believe what pain one man can inflict on a family."

"So anyway, this poor son of Noah and Naima wanders around, everyone knowing what he is and all. Everyone except him. Noah has told everyone to leave Ham alone, that God will deal with him. Noah has his hands full dealing with Naima and Canaan. What a terrible mess for such wonderful people. Naima is just beside herself: She is just sick with grief, having mothered a son by her own son and not even knowing it. She thought it was Noah."

Elka starts to cough, and a doctor and a nurse hurry back into the tent to help settle her down.

"Could this please wait until later, after Elka has had some rest?" the doctor asks.

Elka waves them off. The doctor and nurse then exit with worried looks.

"Look, Mom," starts Nimrod, "I can come back tomorrow and we can talk some more."

"Now, Nimrod, now." She pauses. "I've heard some disturbing stories regarding you and a new religion, a religion that worships the devil. Is this true? Is this even possible?"

"I have found a religion, mom, but, but we do not worship the devil."

"Then what do you worship?" A long pause.

"We worship the sun; we worship the warmth of fire."

"You worship fire? Does fire answer your prayers? You were born with the belief of a Savior, of a God that created the world. If you believe in anything else, whose religion is it? You think God creates multiple religions for His children to worship? Choose A if you need warmth, choose B if you …"

There is only silence in the tent.

"What does fire have to do with families, or with the purpose of life? Nimrod, to whom do you pray?"

More silence.

"I know you were deeply hurt, frustrated when Lugal died, was murdered. But Nimrod, the murderers will answer to God, and He can punish them much more than you can, much longer. Leave it to God. 'Let vengeance be mine, saith the Lord.'"

"We pray, Mom, not to anyone in particular, but we pray. You wouldn't understand."

"You know we sacrifice the best of our flocks, of our herds, to the unseen God who has yet to be born, the Son of a God who created us, a Son who will be sent to earth to pay for the sins of all mankind. And so we offer up, in similitude, as perfect an offering as we can. What do you do?"

There is a giant pause after Elka speaks.

"We offer up sacrifices too, you know, burnt offerings -- for a person's sins. We offer up, things."

Elka gets a horrifying look upon her face as though she has been told what Nimrod has really been offering to his god. Her face goes pale, as if she would run out of the room, if she could.

"What things?" She sits up straight in her bed. "What things?" she yells. "Oh, my God."

"I can't tell you."

Elka sits there quivering and suddenly slumps over. Nimrod goes for the tent door and motions for the doctor and nurse to come in. They come running in and see Elka. They lay her back in her bed and make her as comfortable as possible. Nimrod exits sweating and unnerved by his mother's reaction, as though she already knew and only wanted him to admit what he did. Was his conscience still active? Did the sacrificing of live, human infants actually bother him? Torturing them. Killing them. Lighting them on fire?

Chiamaka, his Elite commander, came to him and saw his King was visibly shaken. They walked together in silence for some time, the evening shadows beginning to crowd out the daylight. Chiamaka trailed his King in silence as they walked, having learned a long time ago not to intrude on the thoughts of a King.

Semiramis had a very average life growing up as one of the many daughters of a shepherd family. She wanted for very little: one might argue what could she really want living in a tent, moving with the herds from season of the year to season of the year? Occasionally, she would walk the fields with her older brothers and listen to their stories of the occasional attack by wolves and such. She always looked up to her brothers, who spent much of their lives away from the hustle and bustle of family life, and the squabbles of siblings.

Sometimes she had thoughts that it would be well worth fighting off a few starving wolves just to have several minutes to look at the stars and contemplate her life. Alone. Without twenty or thirty brothers or sisters running around constantly, interrupting her thoughts. The only real alone time she had from baby-sitting, cooking, cleaning, washing and brushing many sisters' hair was when she had to, well, I mean that personal, personal time when she had to visit the human waste dump tent.

Most people hurried in and hurried out, attempting to hold their breath the entire time. Semiramis found that if she brought a scarf scented with her favorite flowers wrapped around her nose and mouth, she could stay in the out-tent for up to an hour! Of course that meant putting up with the occasional upset parent or sibling needing to use the facilities. While there were multiple holes in the 'ole out-tent, there were times when the need struck multiple children at the same time. Like a half an hour after dinner, lunch or breakfast. Woof!

She met Nimrod at a church conference much like the one where Nimrod told her he'd be gone for two years. She knew, even at the tender age of twelve, that she loved him. He would be among the young men jousting with swords, spears or arrows, besting all but a few. Zag was never beaten with the spear.

It was just the way he smiled at her. He didn't show off when jousting or sparing. He never kicked an opponent when the other man was down. In fact, he always helped them up, grabbed their hand and put his arm around them and gave them his "better- luck-next-time" speech. It was almost an honor to be defeated by Nimrod.

Over the following years she watched him at conferences. She knew he knew that she knew he knew she liked him. And he knew she knew that he knew he liked her. Once in a while their eyes met briefly, and that was all either of them needed. Their unspoken love one for the other grew over the years. Both were in young adulthood before words between them were actually spoken. Semiramis broke the ice, spoke the first words, and expressed her feelings. She smiled and said, "Is that all you can do -- fight?" Romantic, I know. Unforgettable stuff. Nothing like the stuff girls give their guys these days with the "I'm available, always open," signs they symbolically wear around their necks.

Semiramis is walking with two elders who come from a powerful city to the south. It is early evening and the sun is setting on the magnificent palace grounds with the shimmering water of the ponds. The army is just finishing some exercises in the deepest and the largest pond, with men laughing as they float on inflated animal stomachs.

The next pond is shallower and is emptying its contents of royal wives and royal offspring, who have been wading to release the tedium of hot days after hot days: little kings and queens enjoying their childhood, watched over by nursing nannies and pregnant mommies whose own childhood now seems a very distant memory.

Each of the women nod their heads in honor of the queen mother as she passes.

The next pond is guarded by several Elite soldiers to ensure no one inadvertently goes in to feed the twenty-foot crocodiles, major giant killing machines that Kadenram brought from a river called the Nile. Semiramis smiles at one Elite guard in passing. After the threesome are in the distance, he gathers together several other guards and they ask the women and children to quietly hurry as they leave the wading pond. Each soldier assists several women and soon the pond is empty.

The one guard spoken to by Semiramis disappears and several minutes later reappears. He whispers something to several of his fellow Elites and they take up positions around the wading pond.

The one rather overweight pompous elder is expanding on the virtues of his city and the magnificent work performed there in gold. The other elder seconds his sentiments to the queen, who acts impressed.

"So tell me dear Elder Etan," Semiramis addresses the pompous one, "why are you reportedly talking against my husband and Babylon?"

"Oh, well, my queen, I am not sure I would categorize my feelings as against King Nimrod ..."

"Why?"

"It would seem he speaks of freedom and friendship, of peace, and then when anyone opposes him, that city is the next to be sacrificed in a most brutal manner."

"Hmmm. What can I do to, stroke, your feathers?"

"I beg my Queen's pardon?"

"Surely, there is something I could say, or do, that would soothe the savage beast," she coos, touching the chain hanging from the folds of his neck, "to help you champion my husband's, Babylon's, causes. Please, tell me, and it is yours." She stands toe-to-toe with Etan, as he begins to sweat profusely and is short of breath. He looks at the other elder, "Yakov, my friend, tell our Queen there's nothing that can dissuade us from opposing oppression and tyranny ..."

"I am not so sure, Etan, there is nothing ... and oppression and tyranny are such harsh words to use in front of our Queen."

Semiramis turns her back on the two men and walks toward the wading pond with the two trailing behind her.

"Yakov," in hushed tones, "where's the support you promised?"

"I never promised to support insults of the Queen or her husband!"

"I had no choice! I will not lie to her."

"You better learn how, dear Etan. I do not think the Queen takes lightly you calling her husband, the King, a tyrannical and oppressive dictator!"

"Dear Queen," starts Etan, "I apologize for speaking so frankly and rudely. I did not mean to do so."

Semiramis is at the wading pond and with a look at the Elite guard, dismisses him. When the guard is gone, she disrobes and stands on the edge of the wading pond. The light is nearly gone from the sky, and the two men step back away from her, unable to stop gazing on her nude body.

"Join me in my wading pond, dear Etan?" He timidly disrobes, with his folds of flab not quite as appealing as the queen's delicate body, and steps up on the edge of the pond. He looks back at Yakov and then steps into the pond, his left hand raised to help Semiramis step into the pond. She does not take his hand but stands there smiling at him. "Goodbye dear Etan," and at that moment a twenty-foot crocodile rises slightly out of the water behind Etan and grabs his right thigh, dragging him under and proceeding to do the death roll.

Blood is splattered everywhere. The quiet, serene shadows of evening are pierced by the gurgling screams of an outspoken fat man. Semiramis just stands there in her regal stance as though she's overseeing a piece of theatre. Within moments a second crocodile joins in for dinner and Etan is no more

Yakov hands Semiramis her robe and the two of them stroll across the walkway to her bedchambers. "You were right again, dear Yakov. Now, for your reward." She smiles and places her arm around the elder as they enter the palace bedchambers.

"I am forever at your command, my Queen. No need to fear of my change of heart toward our godly King. I will gladly bring you any news of Etan's replacement and his disposition towards King Nimrod."

Before the Queen, at the Public Court, came the issue of a guard killing a young man outside of the palace compound.

"Your Majesty, it was the middle of the night. There was no way to tell if this was an intruder, a member of a larger force ready to attack, let alone a ten-year-old boy. I saw a candlelight movement at the base of the wall and fired my arrow. Immediately the light went out and I could hear no other noise. In the morning a squad of guards went out and found the young man dead, with two used arrows in his grasp."

"Thank you. Where is your supervisor?"

"Here, my Queen. I am Captain Erik."

"Sounds innocent enough. What have you to add?" A pause. The Queen senses his uneasiness. Captain?"

"During the night this guard, along with several others, had been drinking and competing by shooting arrows at dead animal's eyeballs. The eyeballs shine in the moonlight at times and make great sport. When someone sounded the alarm in this guard's sector, the same group saw the candle as another form of competition."

"Killing a ten year old – competition?"

"To the guard's defense, it was not possible to tell if this could have been an intruder …"

"An intruder, like an army attacking the palace? Using candles to find their way?"

"Ah-hem. Shortly after the alarm was sounded, it was retracted. Exactly to your point of an enemy using a candle. Unfortunately, this guard and his friends had already started their competition. Due to their state of stupor from the alcohol, they did not hear, or chose not to hear …"

"I swear, your Majesty, we did not hear the 'all clear' signal. I swear."

"You were drunk on duty?"

"Yes, my Queen. We had snuck a skin of drinks up to the wall. We had been on duty for over a year, your Majesty, and nothing ever happened at night."

"What do you not understand about not drinking while on duty?" Silence as the guard weeps at the thought of the boy's death.

"Are you married?"

"Yes, your majesty."

"Children?"

"Yes, four boys and two daughters."

"Any ten-year-old boys?"

Hesitating, "One boy is eleven."

"Give him to the family."

A scream can be heard from the audience as the guard's wife, and the mother of their eleven-year-old boy faints.

"No, please, your Majesty. Is there no other way?"

"Give him to the family or kill your son. What will it be?"

"I will take him to them, your Majesty." He drops to his knees.

"You are hereby relived of your position as a palace guard and as a member of the Elite forces. Should you, at any time hereafter, be found drunk while on duty, you will die. Is that understood?"

Sobbing, he shakes his head, "Yes."

"That is all. Bring the boy to the palace this very day. Next."

The captain guides the former guard out of the room with the wife still sobbing in shock.

The sun still had not set as Chiamaka and Nimrod stopped and sat on the edge of a small cliff overlooking a fertile valley with a herd of sheep bleating in the distance. They ate some jerky while some younger boys were playing a type of tag. The shepherd and his dog rested in the grass, keeping an eye and ear out for predators looking for a quick meal.

Suddenly, in the valley a voice could be heard whooping and hollering, scaring the sheep en masse towards the shepherd: Tammuz was running around like an overgrown, half-brained shaggy dog, trying to catch a sheep. The sheep dog growled and barked at him at first, until his master quieted him.

Nimrod watched his thirty-year-old son running, chasing sheep without a care in the world. Here Nimrod was wishing he could trade places with his mentally under- developed son, the son he had been trying to avoid the whole trip. It gave Nimrod pause to ponder. What had he done with his life? With any luck at all, his mom would die so Nimrod would not have to again face her, knowing the question she would want answered. "Who was the idiot now?" he thought.

Memories of his conversation with his dad regarding being a shepherd flooded his mind. For the moment at least, Nimrod wished he could go back to his simple life. He hung his head between his knees and vomited.

Chapter Thirteen

The nurse hesitatingly approached Nimrod with Chiamaka looking on. "Your mom would like to speak with you, one last time. She said to tell you she will behave herself and that you shouldn't fear speaking with her. But hurry sir, there isn't much time left."

"Thank you, said Nimrod, and the nurse turned and scurried back to Elka's tent.

"My Lord, Chiamaka ventured as they turned and walked toward the tent, "may I speak freely?"

"Please do."

"At a tender time such as this, perhaps honesty is not the best policy. Allowing your mother to pass on calmly, with dignity in her offspring and hope for their future, may be the way to go."

"Lie to my mom? Chiamaka, that is impossible. She has a keen sense about her for these things. We, her children, gave up trying to lie to her years ago. She sees right through our lies, our half-truths."

"Then perhaps you could throw her off by speaking of others and their propensity for gossip and pumping up their half-truths at your expense."

"Hmmm, perhaps you're on to something there." The nurse exits the tent, obviously emotionally disturbed. Just a few steps from the tent the two men stop as the nurse approaches them.

"It's too late sir, your mother just died. She said to tell you, to tell you for the killing of innocent children, she hopes you will burn in hell. Her last words," and the nurse is looking at the ground, "were that you leave here immediately and neither return to her tomb nor to your dad's ever, ever again. I'm sorry to tell you this, sir, but these were her last words." The nurse turns and reenters the tent.

Chiamaka grapples for something to say, "I'm sure your mom did not speak so harshly as …"

"Oh, I'm just as sure that she did." Nimrod spits on the tent door flap. "Let us leave this place. Her wish is gladly my command. Gather up the men and my idiot son and please, keep him away, far away from me on the ride home. The ill mood I am in, I could kill him and be glad of it."

"Yes, my King." Chiamaka goes and prepares the men, and Tammuz, for the return trip to Babel.

"What did I expect from such a God-worshipping family? So this is Christianity, is it? So self-righteous, so hypercritical with their way being the only way; not able to compromise, not able to accept points of view different than their own as though their way is somewhere set in stone as the only way for the entire world's population."

Nimrod rode along in silence and all those around him did as well. This would not have been a good time to gain the attention of the King for any reason. Promise.

Somewhere near the end of the second day riding toward Babel, King Nimrod and his men are set upon by several hundred of the followers of Hadeon, a Calneh city elder who had long ago been imprisoned on a cart in the desert. Hadeon and his family had been imprisoned for over twenty years, and this group of men felt that Hadeon and family had served their time honorably and should be set free.

"We simply want you to take our grievances to King Nimrod and gain us an audience. If we were to just appear one day, it is our feelings that he would have us all killed for opposing him. We do not oppose him, we just want him to hear what we have to say, and we will live with his decision." The leader, Ronnre, then handed Chiamaka the scroll with their grievances written on them.

"I am Chiamaka of the Elite forces of King Nimrod: do you not see the predicament you present to our great King, King Nimrod? If he grants you your request, you will but embolden others to take other men of Babel hostage, like today, and that would cause King Nimrod even more trouble. No, I'm afraid we cannot do as you have requested." With that, Chiamaka prepares to ride off.

"Chiamaka, you are in no position to tell us you refuse to do as we have asked. There are nearly four hundred of us against perhaps one to two hundred of you. Besides, we are not taking you hostage. We are simply giving you our written request to then forward on to your King

Nimrod. I mean, twenty some years he has kept my grandfather captive. Surely, there is an end to the punishment for his crimes of defending his family, his city."

"I am a commander for the great King of Babel and yet I cannot speak for him. Having some experience with the good King, I can, though, assure you he will not look favorably upon your request. Especially today, he is really in a stinking bad mood."

Chiamaka drops the scrolls in the dirt and his horse steps on them. "It is best that you and your men move on before you give our great King reason to inflict personal and permanent punishment on Hadeon, again, and members of his family, again, as partial payment of your crimes, again."

Ronnre draws his sword, followed by the sounds of Chiamaka and his men drawing their swords, and the followers of Ronnre drawing their swords. "Good Chiamaka, we had no wish to make this a conflict, but your hostility and low-life disrespect leaves us no alternative but to teach you some civility and good manners."

"Yeah, good luck with that," responds Chiamaka. "May I tell King Nimrod who you were, and your whatever father's name?"

"I am Ronnre, grandson of Hadeon, of the great city of Calneh. I will inform your king that you, Chiamaka, died bravely and gallantly for him, albeit, stupidly, as there was no need of this conflict."

King Nimrod rides to the front of his men and is addressed by Chiamaka. "Good King Nimrod, this is Ronnre, grandson of Hadeon of Calneh, and he is here today to die for his grandfather. I, Chiamaka, would prefer to not die today, but as your Elite commander I am prepared to die as are all the men around you, should it be necessary, your Grace."

King Nimrod addresses Ronnre and his men, "Chiamaka has well spoke my position on freeing your grandfather. Please say whatever godly prayers you need to, and prepare to die. You tire me with your pathetic mumbo-jumbo of sadness."

A pause.

"What, no 'help us god to defeat this barbaric host of infidels', no 'may the better god-lover win', or 'we worship the true and eternal god so we will be victorious' speech?"

Nimrod, "Save him and ten of his men— kill the rest, sacrifice them all to Baal. Attack!"

Immediately two hundred Elite soldiers unleash a barrage of arrows upon the four hundred poorly-equipped and trained men of Calneh. The Elite quickly emptied their quivers of their twenty arrows, dropped their bows and charged the remaining forces, unleashing another barrage of spears. As the enemy threw up their shields, one hundred of the Elite formed a wedge and drove into the center of the enemy, while the other one hundred circled behind the enemy and drove a wedge in from behind.

As the Elite slaughtered the men between them, they caused a group on the left and on the right to become separated. Then came the close-quarter combat throwing of knives at the uncovered heads and necks of the hundred or so remaining enemies. Knife, after two hundred knives, time and time again. Then came the swords. Efficient. Bloody Quick. Slaughter.

With three quarters of the enemy already destroyed, the Elite turned their forces on the pitifully-trained enemy on the left and destroyed them, all but their leader and ten of his men, whom they took prisoner. They were made to walk all the way to Babel tied, each man, to his horse's tail. Each time his horse needed to defecate, that soldier would be showered with his horse's residue.

The three hundred and ninety bodies were then stripped of weapons and food. Any valuables were strapped to the horses they rode in on. Though some of the Elite were seriously wounded, none died. The bodies of the enemy were piled up and left to bloat in the hot desert sun, each having been stabbed several times to ensure no trickery.

The most vicious soldier that day was the King, who fought like a mad man, a man possessed of demons. Was he killing his mom, his family, his god – or himself? He did not put down his sword until Chiamaka, his Elite commander, came over to the glossy-eyed, blood-covered King and said softly, "Enough, my King." King Nimrod's troops bowed before him as he turned and stumbled his way to his horse. Admiration beamed from the men's faces along with not just a little "'thank god I didn't have to fight this man."

Several days later Hadeon of Calneh and his family were found and treated to the parceling out of the body parts of eleven of their family and friends. Slowly, deliberately, each man was cut into pieces and thrown around the huge wagon. Not a word was spoken by the army, so as to not distract from the screams and begging for mercy from the unfortunate eleven. The grandson, Tupac, was saved for last.

One of the young sons of Hadeon ran off the cart with a knife in an attempt to kill Ronnre – to put him out of his anguish. The young man was stopped, stripped of his clothing and flogged ten times, after the grandson was dead. Each event was choreographed for the maximum effect on the survivors. The heads of the eleven were attached to poles that were then mounted on the wagon.

The family worked thereafter without one word being spoken, without the body parts being collected or buried and with the stench of death in their nostrils for eleven days. Then, without warning, the huge cart rolled away. Many days later all the surviving members were released at the Calneh town square into the waiting arms of their family and townspeople. Then, the huge cart rolled away looking for yet another family to entertain. The heads were dumped in the town square as yet another reminder of the Axum, "resistance is futile."

The family of Hadeon had bug-eyes, with horror permanently painted on their burnt faces forever, a testament to that city of the gruesome death of over four hundred of their young sons. This was a family not soon, not ever, to forget what challenging the King costs, a city that would never again challenge the King. Ever. Mission accomplished.

Upon arrival at the palace, the Queen comes to see her husband and son dismount. With the aid of Chiamaka and Tammuz, Nimrod staggers toward his wife, passing by her as though not seeing her. Tammuz supports one side of his father and Chiamaka the other. As they pass the smiling Queen, whose smile quickly fades, Chiamaka puts his finger to his lips to tell the Queen not to speak to King Nimrod. She stands there helpless. The Queen of Babel is unable to help just one man.

Is Nimrod tired? Yes. Bloody – yes. But the real strength zapper was the interview with his mom. And she died hating him, hating what he had become. And he in turn, now hates everything. Anything. More intensely than ever.

It takes Semiramis seven weeks of constant night and day nursing to bring her husband back to his almost normal self. It takes lots of powdery potions to relax the King's mind, lots of stroking and caring, lots and lots of love. Nimrod loses a tremendous amount of weight, and over the next few months walks with the aid of his most trusted advisors and, of course, Semiramis. Chiamaka has filled her in with the details he knew from the meeting with his mom and is there every day with his King.

Semiramis has run the kingdom flawlessly in the mental absence of her husband. It even seems some prayed for the swift return of their King, due to her unrelenting attention to details. Even General Jared grew tired of having to appear before her on an almost daily basis to report the status of acquiring horses, feed for the horses, arrows and so on: a world class micro-manager, a world class "pain where a pill can't reach, only an enema."

She has tried keeping the many wives and concubines on schedule by using Tammuz. That has proven to be a disaster. All he wants to do is talk and play silly hide-and-seek games with the women. Rarely does he achieve the purpose for which he has been sent. That plan comes to a screeching halt. The stockpile of new infants is already plentiful, so there is no harm in waiting for Nimrod to fully recover. And in time he does, but the emotional scars would never be fully recovered from. Never. And true to Nimrod's nature, someone would have to pay for his pain.

Jared's plans for attacking Tukulti are complete. He determines that this city on the Euphrates with high walls of dirt mounded around half the city and fortresses well-defended on top of those walls are nearly impregnable. Yes, they could be taken, but the cost in lives for Babel's army would be horrendous.

The second half of the city was bordered by the Euphrates, a natural defense with relatively little muscle defense needed from within. It is, therefore, Jared's plan to mobilize twelve thousands of his troops outside the walls with daily barrages of flaming arrows and sling shots, seemingly probing for a weak spot in the city's defenses.

Each time a foray was made, Tukulti's defense shifts ingeniously to cover the attack, keeping Tukulti's army's attention focused on those troop movements of General Jared. One night, Jared's army lights torches and approaches the city walls from three points. True to character, Tukulti's generals shifts all their manpower to those three spots. Trumpets could be heard telling the troops with their system of short and long blasts what to do and calling up all the city's reserves.

Flaming arrows are shot by the thousands in these three spots. Meanwhile, up river, three thousand Elite troops, who have been training for months in the largest and deepest Palace complex pond, float down the Euphrates on inflated animal stomachs to the shores of the now-deserted river defenses of Tukulti. By morning all three thousand troops are inside the city and are prepared to strike. All three thousand land, except the handful who fail to properly steer themselves into the landing area. They are somewhere near Egypt by now.

The river troops ready to attack have more recently donned copper helmets lined with a leather cap underneath. By the dawn's early light, the copper helmets make the soldiers appear more brutish, more animalistic as the sun bounces off the helmets. It is hard to focus on the individual men. Then, each man has darkened his face with black soot and charcoal, making their appearance even more frightening, as they purposefully slobber their way to the city's front fortifications.

Soon all twelve-thousand men outside the walls begin grunting and making noises like great apes, with their grunts growing louder and more vicious sounding. All the while they bang their shields against their six-foot-long spears. Attention along the wall shifts as the three thousand make their way stealthily through the deserted streets. All residents have already shut and locked their doors and windows so as to not be confused with any intruders.

Dogs bark and growl as the three thousand run uncontested through the streets, slaughtering any animals in their path. A little four-year-old boy opens his front door, chasing his pet dog. "Come in here, Hanza. Don't you bite this nice man."

One of the soldiers has compassion on the boy and his dog, fairly gently kicking the small dog to the side of the street, right to the boy. "Get inside before you and your dog get hurt, kid."

"I'm not afraid of you, and my dog is not afraid of you either." The dog can be seen peeing profusely on the boy's clothing. "Why'd you have to kick him, mister? He's only a puppy? Would you like it if I kicked you?" The boy's dad's arm reaches around the half- open door and pulls both the boy and the dog inside.

"Thank you, sir, for sparing my son. Thank you."

As the boy is being dragged inside, he could be heard saying, "But dad, he kicked Hanza. Aren't you going to do anything to him? Make him apologize?"

The soldier stands about six-foot-four inches tall in his sandals, covered with soot and charcoal, topped with a menacing copper helmet and a six-foot-long spear in his hairy, oversized hand.

"I think he has learned his lesson, son. We'll let him go this time."

Meeting no resistance in the streets, the three thousand begin to increase their running speed toward the front walls, grunting and banging their shields with their spears. They are upon the defensive-minded soldiers of Tukulti within minutes, thrusting knives by the hundreds and thousands into anyone who moves. This is followed by round after round of slingshots from the river troops, as the outside twelve thousand begin hacking their enemies to death at the top of their makeshift ladders, using their swords.

Fifty of the Elite river troops run for the main gate, making short work of the few men who have been assigned to guard the massive gates. Once the gates are then opened, the Tukulti army is in full slaughter mode, as there is very little they can do against fifteen thousand murderous souls of the empire.

No soldiers are spared. King Nimrod's grand entrance into Tukulti is preceded by one hundred four-wheeled chariots carrying men, weapons and supplies into the conquered city.

The residents are rounded up into the town square and asked for their chief elders or their king, to come forward. No one moves. So, several soldiers proceed to line up twenty men and women and children and have them kneel and face the thousands of residents.

"Is this your city elder or king?" asks an Elite captain. No response. The captain signals to a soldier and he decapitates the first person in line. Screams followed by several women passing out begin.

The captain moves to the woman who is next in line, "Is this your elder or king?"

There is some uneasiness and shifting but no one comes forward. The woman is beheaded, followed by more strident screams from the residents.

A voice shouts out, "Where are you, you rotten coward?" No one comes forward.

"I can do this all day; can you?" asked the captain.

A voice shouts out, "He's hiding with his sons in that house over here," as he points to a house a few steps away. Several Elite soldiers break down the door and find a trap door under a rug. In the hole are four men who are dragged out into the square.

"Which of you is the elder or king?" asks the captain. The three younger men look at their dad.

"Why are you looking at me? You …" pointing at one of his sons, "you know you're the king."

Several voices in the crowd shout out, "Liar, coward".

The true king of Tukulti is taken forth with his sons, and the other women, children and men are sent back into the crowd. This has all taken place as King Nimrod enters the square, which is followed by a huge cheer from his soldiers and even a few from the residents of the city.

"So Sir, you are the leader of this town?" asks King Nimrod.

"No, no I am not. It's one of them," pointing to his three sons.

"Ah, one of them," and King Nimrod moves towards the three men.

"No, dear King of Babel," a voice cries out, "that man you have before you is our king, the lying, disgusting pig that he is."

King Nimrod, "Assemble all his family members in front of me." The town's people point some out; some come of their own free will. A giant wagon enters the square. "All members of this man's family, please get on the wagon. You have nothing to fear."

The family members do so, spitting at their leader as they do. King Nimrod motions as the driver starts to exit, to stay where he is. The crowd is standing in front of the wagon.

"Normally," says Nimrod, "I would grant unto you the opportunity to declare your support for me and for Babel. But frankly, I can think of no place in our kingdom for such a treacherous dog who would sacrifice his own son to save his flabby life."

With that, King Nimrod draws his sword and beheads the city leader, to the cheers of the man's hometown crowd and family. Now the cart driver is given the signal to proceed out of the city. Soon there will be very little to cheer about. The rules are ready to be read to the inhabitants of Tukulti, including such rules as working for six days a month in Babel. The cart rules are being read to the members of the family, who will live there for perhaps the rest of their lives. Rules for the city include: the time to and from Babel are not part of the six days required. Walk quickly.

The carts of valuables and weapons have already left the city. Behind the workers leaving already for Babel were carts full of food to sustain those workers for six days. Long days. Hot days. Back-breaking days. Like all the other conquered cities it would be up to the average citizen to organize the food for the workers for their next work period in Babel. One month to nourish the crops and meat sources for the many thousands whose lives depend on their friends. Young family members and the elderly have to have the food necessary to sustain the workers. Mere children are out hoeing and weeding and watering and harvesting so that their moms and dads can stay alive to come home to them.

The literally hundreds of thousands of arrows shot at Tukulti have been mostly collected and placed on the weapons' wagons. The young boys and girls have been told a reward will be given by the administrator for each arrow found thereafter. Hundreds of arrows are found and turned in during the ensuing weeks.

One family of eight young children come to the administrator with one hundred and sixty-five unbroken arrows. The administrator takes the children into another room with a table full of gold pieces, fresh fruit and rock candy. Asked to choose what they want as a reward, the children all stand staring at the rock candy as their oldest brother speaks.

"We cannot take the candy, dear brothers and sisters. We need to think of mom and dad and our oldest brothers in Babel. They cannot eat gold or candy. So, we must take the fruit. Do you agree?" With tears in their eyes each nods their head, and so they carry out the allotted amount of fruit in exchange for their arrows.

As they leave, the administrator takes a small piece of rock candy for each of the children and gives it to the eldest. "You have chosen wisely, young one. Be sure to keep your eyes and ears open for things I should know about, won't you?" The oldest boy nods his head, quickly takes the candy and distributes it to his younger siblings.

"Thank you, Sir, we will be sure to keep our eyes and ears open for you."

And so it begins in Tukulti.

"General Jared!" a voice rings out as the General is walking home. "General!" the young man persists. The General is surrounded by a small group of his soldiers, some assigned as his guard for the evening, and some live in the same direction, and some just like being around a General. The General looks at who was calling him, but does not recognize his face.

"Who is that man?" he asks one of his captains, "I don't recognize him."

"That's Parahayker, General. He's a runner with a couple of his brothers. They are really good; fast and have endurance too. This one is taking math and science classes. Don't know anymore."

"Bring him to me. Let's see what he wants."

The captain signals for Parahayker to come to him. The captain searches him quickly for weapons, finds none, and takes him to Jared.

"My General, thanks for seeing me. I've tried several times to meet with you, but your aide insists you are too busy."

"What can I do for you?"

"Me? Nothing. It's what I think I can do for you and for the army and Babel. I have this idea of how to enlarge Babel to the East." You can see some of the men trying to figure out where East is, and others realizing there is a river in the way.

"East? That's called the Euphrates river, son."

"Yes, sir, I know, but please hear me out. Isn't it a shame that we can't live and work on the other side?"

"I guess. I never have thought about it, but okay, it's a shame."

"I've figured out a way so we can – live and work there as part of our great city."

"Really? Do we just move the river?!" Jared asks jokingly.

Parahayker thinks the General knows of his plans. "How did you know, General?"

Jared sees the young man has taken his remarks seriously. "I was just joking. What's your name?"

"General, Parahayker, General. My name is Parahayker. And yes, we do move the river, just temporarily. Right now there isn't any way to put down supports for a bridge. But I've figured out how to do that! We dig a separate river path – half on one side of the existing river and one half of a new river path on the other side. Now, the river can continue to flow. When the areas where we need to place the bridge supports dry out, then we dig our support holes."

There is a lot of scratching of heads among the soldiers who do not have a clue of what Parahayker is proposing, but General Jared gets it. "What makes the river just follow the new path we dig, instead of staying where the river already is?"

"I almost forgot. We go upstream a little ways past the new river paths we dug, and we dump huge boulders in an inverted "V" shape, kinda like an "A" without the vertical line, and that gently guides the river to the new path!"

A pause as the General listens and thinks. All of those with him have been drawn into the presentation and are thinking too. Not quite understanding as completely as Jared, but thinking too.

The captain asks, "Can we do that? Move an entire river from where it's been for thousands of years?" No response.

A voice from the group of onlookers chirps, "General, if I understand what Parahayker is proposing, yes. Incredible as it seems, yes!"

"And think," continues Parahayker, "of all the land that we can irrigate for more crops, orchards, and water for homes, sheep and animals of all kinds."

"And horses and oxen," muses Jared. "Come with me to my home and draw up the plans for such a project."

Parahayker hands him the plans he has already prepared: charts with the depth of the supports, width and depth of the holes, the size of the actual bridge, etc.

"Oh, you are prepared. The King is out of town right now, but as soon as he returns I'll make an appointment for you and me to speak with him. If he approves of it, and I think he will, it will probably have to wait until the ziggurat is finished."

"Thank you, General. Thank you so very much." He rushes off to tell his brothers and family members. Ham, having tired of Mariana as a new plaything, has moved her out of the palace to a small shed of a home on the outskirts of Anat. Her three sons in Babel, having learned of Ham's disaffection with their mother, travel to Anat and convince their mom to move to Babel to be with them as a family once again. This time they have no need of Ham in their lives.

Ham does not mind, as long as his sons by Mariana stay with him. Mariana is free to move, along with their daughters, but there will be no financial support for them from Ham if they do so. So much the better, thought Aericas and Earron, as they never completely trusted Ham. They still have lingering feelings that he lied about their father's death, but have no facts. No evidence. No witnesses. Ham, the man, wins again.

When King Nimrod returns, he has been quite ill for well over two months, General Jared bides his time. When the King is well-recovered, he arranges a meeting in which King Nimrod becomes very enthusiastic about the river and adding more land to the already bustling and prosperous city of Babel.

This young man, this engineer, architect and inventor is destined to be a favorite of the King. But like most inventors, this may be both his first and possibly his best idea for the kingdom. However, Parahayker would now be bound for life to King Nimrod.

In fact, the King likes the idea enough that he commissions Parahayker to start the project immediately. Nimrod allocates six-thousand 'involunteer' laborers, three- thousand volunteers of Babel and one-thousand soldiers to oversee the 'involunteers' and general need of horses, wagons, oxen, and tools for the bridge/river project.

The first few years are spent digging. Digging. Digging. And did I mention, digging? Once a narrow part of the Euphrates river close to Babel is selected, Parahayker, and other engineers, map out the width and depth of the temporary river and the distance inland on each side from the existing river. The dirt is piled high on each side from the existing river in preparation for the future of returning the dirt to its original place.

Once the temporary river beds are completed, the second huge task begins of hauling boulders to the river, placing them on barge-like boats, and with teams of oxen on each side of the river, pulling the tremendous weight of the giant boulders. They must be dumped in the river at a precise point, so they would be stacked upon the first boulders, and so on.

Several more years pass and the boulders are now being loaded upstream and brought downstream, the oxen now being used to slow the barges once they come to the now visible pile of boulders in the "A" wedge shape. The original river is now a mere stream, as each addition of boulders slow the stream to a trickle and the river bed begins at last to dry.

The river becomes quite the tourist attraction for people from all over the known world: an absolutely brilliant masterpiece of engineering, and that is without a bridge being in place. Meanwhile, the temporary river bed takes the Euphrates past the bridge-building point, and no one downstream would have ever been able to tell the difference in the flow of the river. The drying process takes another two years, and the forms for the supports are now being dug.

During the past few years, crews of workers have been sent to the mountains to find the largest and straightest trees. The trees have been stripped and left to dry near the Euphrates for several years, after which they are brought to the holes that have been dug. The trees are then coated over and over and over with bitumen to further waterproof them. Each massive hole takes six gigantic trees to fill, and then sets of trees are banded together with cords soaked in bitumen over and over. The massive trees tower over the banks of the original river and will later support the planks and handrails of the thirty-foot-wide bridge.

The dirt is filled in and packed down around each set of tree supports and then more boulders are brought in to surround the base of the sets of tree supports.

The hand-hewn planks are lashed into place over flattened trees that span the original support trees and run from one side of the Euphrates to the other -- a fantastic wonder of the ancient world.

Once all the construction is completed, the task of removing layers of boulders upstream commences. Large nets made of rope are wrapped around the boulders, and once again the barges and oxen are employed. This time they drag the huge boulders off the pile, until there is but one level of boulders on the bottom of the Euphrates.

Then, the work begins to fill in the two temporary rivers with the mounded earth that, years before, had been left from the digging of the Euphrates temporary rivers. The digging of canals on the east had already commenced years ago, leaving the area nearest the river until after the bridge construction has been completed. The land has already been divided into living areas, gardens, orchards, farm land, grazing land for herds, trash and human refuse dumping, etc.

Of course, garrisons are constructed to protect this second half of Babel, and more soldiers are employed to protect this new section of Babel. There is no need to replicate the palace or temple or The Tower of Babel, a tower which now thrust its height toward the heavens, an awe-inspiring sight for all the peoples of Babylon.

Sightseers come from hundreds, even thousands of miles to see this new edifice, this new monument to the unseen God of Adam. At least that is what most people choose to believe. In reality, of course, King Nimrod had this ziggurat, this prayer tower, this Tower of Babel erected in his perverted hope of killing Adam's God.

Once the very top of the Tower is completed, Nimrod, with a few of his most powerful archers, would take their large bows and arrows to the top at dark and unleash hundreds upon hundreds of arrows into the heavens each night. King Nimrod's hope is to find an arrow with God's blood on it. This ceremony, this ritual, is performed each and every night of each and every week of each and every year. Rainy weather, windy dust storms or any other weather does not deter the doggedly determined and devious Nimrod from his dastardly desires.

The spent arrows are gladly collected, in the light of day, by the young residents of Babel. The story of their young, dead friend grows into a myth, and time has kept the newer hunters of arrows from ever attempting to find arrows at night, at least not with candles. The resting place now for many of the arrows is not in the rocks and valleys surrounding the palace grounds, surrounded by gigantic walls and hundreds of archers. Arrows would be found in the land north of the palace complex, where the young men and women only have to brave the creatures of the mountains that come down, especially at night, looking for food. It takes the chomping and mutilating death of several young entrepreneurs before the night-time hunting of arrows completely stops.

As to the myth of the young arrow hunter killed by a drunken guard, he is almost deified, due to his uncommon bravery and not as well-known at first, his heroism. When the young arrow hunter realized what was happening, he used his body to shield the body of his younger sister who was with him. She was there to hold the candle and hold onto the arrows the young man found, thus leaving his hands free to scramble through the rocks looking for more arrows. A marker is erected by the soldiers to commemorate the sad event that one of their own had helped to memorialize. Needless, perhaps to say, the reaction time to any disturbance in the night is slowed considerably, so the soldiers could make doubly sure what their target is.

More sharp, craggy rocks are brought in to fill in any level areas at the base of all four sides of the palace grounds walls, to make any movement a suicide mission for perspective enemies.

Rumors of giants in a faraway area of the mountainous region north of Babel, hundreds of miles away, begin to intrigue King Nimrod. Along with the giant men are rumored to be giant animals – especially eagles. Nimrod then puts General Jared and his young engineers to the task of how to defeat such human beings, and how best to trap some eagles to bring back to Babylon. They are commissioned in secret and told this would be a mission for several years in the future. But as we already know, when something occurs in Kind Nimrod's mind, it does not always stay years in the future. Especially not after some of his eyes and ears report finding a very large dead man in the foothills near their city. Under cover of night Nimrod has the body brought to the temple, where his remains are closely guarded, studied and toasted.

Nimrod's runners are successful in finding barite in the mountains to the northwest of Babel, several days journey at best. When Kadenram returns for his now yearly visit, true to his promise, he brings a family of Barite-stone purifiers with him. Not only do the elderly man and wife come, but six of his sons, wives, and their children come also.

A list of materials needed is given to King Nimrod, along with requirements for living such as homes and food, is provided to the

King. All is fulfilled. In a matter of months thirty wagons full of people, materials, tools and food are on the way with one hundred single Elite soldiers. The soldiers would be a permanent part of the settlement for protection. They also would provide the little colony with meat from the mountains. Every twelve months the Elite soldiers are replaced by another group and so on.

The new group would also be accompanied by many wagons of food and tools: tools to replace the broken, worn-out ones used in the mining and smelting of the Barite-glow stones. Once the stones are mined and smelted, it takes nine years to produce a batch of glow stones. Nine years.

First, the stones are placed in the palace for night lights, then in the temple and living places for the head priest and minister of religion. Next, the stones are placed in the interior halls and rooms of the United Cities Council members in the Tower.

Each and every city or nation under control of Babylon is requested to provide a contingent of representatives authorized to make decisions regarding the running of the towns and nations. Peace-keeping efforts are also involved after the disarming of peoples; solving disagreements without war is also a main point of the council member's decisions.

Needless to say, some of these issues are moot points in regards to Nimrod. Once he decides a city was a "problem" he finds a way to justify his conquering said people. With the unknown help of Semiramis, there seems to be very little opposition to many of Nimrod's proposals.

Of course, those who represent Babel are headed by Terah, with King Nimrod making an appearance every now and again. Terah, of course, has strict instructions as to what is acceptable and not acceptable. He is also to take copious notes as to who said what, who supported certain amendments, new rules and their attitude. Mysteriously, those who are the most vociferous in their complaints, whining to downright opposition to King Nimrod, retire, move or just disappear.

And so this new cooperative leadership experiment headquartered in Babel's Tower and run by the master ventriloquist and puppeteer, King Nimrod, began. If anyone has hoped that Terah would be a good influence on Nimrod, they will soon be disappointed. Terah, as you will remember from your Old Testament Bible studies is the father of Abraham. Yes, this is actual, even factual, but not yet. Such is the magnetism of Nimrod that Terah is drawn to, uh, shall we say, the dark side.

Terah is soon to actively participate in some of the less offensive temple ceremonies, has already purchased some lovely snakes, and has championed King Nimrod to all who would listen. Those with whom he goes to church have started avoiding the elder statesman, with the unspoken sentiments that the dear 'ole boy had lost some of his main marbles, or is no longer playing with a full deck. Even Riplakish realizes Terah is fast becoming a lost cause and stops coming around to find out what King Nimrod is up to. When he does, Terah would lecture him on the good that Nimrod has accomplished and how he, Riplakish, should be honoring the position Nimrod holds as King, even if he finds the person or his politics, at times, objectionable. Guess that's even good advice in our time. I mean, for the average person, right? You – me, we're uh different. Exceptional even. What's the rule for this – do as I tell you, not as I am doing?

Over time Terah finds King Nimrod and his friends much more open-minded than his own people. Wonder why that is? Is it right – fair? Hmmm. So, Terah reports faithfully, Nimrod listens intently, kindly, patiently, and Semiramis befriends the friendless and feeds the crocodiles. And support for Nimrod just climbs.

An expedition of one hundred men to the northern mountains looking for giants has ended. We don't know how or what they found or … it just ends. The men, the horses and equipment never come back. No trace of them is ever found. Ever.

The harem increases to two hundred and fifty-six wives and concubines, and the infant mortality rate grows as well. Many of the nursing moms dry up with nothing to do, in spite of the large number of births occurring among the King's harem. Everyone just assumes the old gene pool wasn't what it used to be. The temple trash bins, however, are overflowing and are being emptied more and more frequently.

There is yet another young lady who does not see eye to eye with the Queen, our lovely Semiramis. This woman stands toe-to-toe with the queen regarding being a broodmare, as she calls it: Antandra.

"I didn't come to Babel to be the King's whore. I am here to represent my family and my village and expect respect even from my King. And you, my Queen." (You know, respect for the office even if not for the person.)

"You, dear child, are married to the King of Babel. Whores are not. You have been given fine clothes to wear and a very beautiful place to live. You have servants to fulfill your every need. How is any of that disrespectful?"

"My family was forced to have me be part of the group of wives from my village, my Queen. Where's the respect there?"

"My husband, the King of Babel, is not responsible for your family or your village's selection process, Antandra, is he?" No response. "I expect the courtesy of a response, dear girl."

"No, my Queen, he is not, but he is responsible for the conquering of my village, the abduction of our elders and families' which included my intended. And here I am, one of over two-hundred-and-fifty breeders for the King to have fun with."

"The King does not simply have fun, dear girl. He is preparing the world for the future by selecting the best physical and mental specimen from among his male children to be his heir. His daughters he expects to be queens at the side of royalty from all over the kingdom of Babylon, and beyond."

"Very well my Queen, but I want nothing to do with the breeding of future heirs or queens. I respectfully decline to have the King come and make love on me, period. Can you respect that?" The Queen stares at her with visions of sand floating through this girl's mouth. And then …

"You will respect your wedding vows. The King is not scheduled to 'visit' you for several months, but since you have made such an issue of respect, and so on, he will be in your bedchamber this very night. And he will visit you every week until you are pregnant with his child." The Queen walks up to her, "And should you not produce a child, you will be cast out. And trust me, you will not be fit to be even a whore. Do we understand each other?"

Antandra stands in Semiramis's face, "I understand. But I will not participate – not tonight, not next week, not ever. Do you understand?"

"Just make sure you wash off the sheepherder's stench from that body of yours."

They stand there staring at each other. The Queen claps her hands and a guard comes in and half drags Antandra away, with her still staring at the Queen. Semiramis claps her hands twice and a female attendant appears, "There's been a change for the King's schedule for tonight. Prepare a potion for Antandra, who will receive her King. And I don't care if the guards have to hold her down and break her teeth – she will drink the potion, and you will have her cleaned, dressed and prepared for the King. Now go." The female attendant leaves.

"This is much more satisfying than even a cup of sand." Semiramis laughs gently. "She will rue the day she defied me. I can do this each and every year of her life."

Terah is addressing the many men present who represent over one-hundred cities. Many are hand-picked by King Nimrod's city administrators and have been told to be silent in most meetings and let the new cities' representatives speak.

"We have such a great opportunity to make a difference in our world today. King Nimrod has given us this marvelous building in which to meet and has the foresight of a great leader to allow us all to gather here to make the rules under which we all desire to live." A gentle ripple of applause and foot-stomping follows.

"He wants us to develop a constitution by which we can govern ourselves and our cities." Another ripple of applause. "He desires, and hopes that you desire, peace, financial stability and prosperity for all." A more thunderous applause, hooting and hollering by most. A few are skeptical or are not yet completely converted.

"Thank you, thank you. It's time for us to break into our committees. Our attendants will guide you to the proper room. We'll reconvene here for lunch in a few hours."

The delegates follow separate attendants, who wear different-colored sashes for each committee and lead the delegates to their conference rooms in the Tower. As the delegates are leaving, other workers are moving chairs and bringing in tables and flower decorations, replacing the chairs and then placing placards at each chair. Terah is in conversation with an upset individual.

"There will always be mistakes, Enoka, my friend. We are just beginning to feel our way through the process."

"But why must I sit next to a man on a committee who has warred against my people for years? How can such a person be a part of peace?"

"If you can show the world tolerance for even one who has so mistreated your people, imagine the good that does for the whole of humanity."

"I, I will, perhaps, but he doesn't even act as though there is a problem!"

"I will speak with, with, Mr ...?"

"Zorian, Zorian of Nur."

"I will speak with Mr. Zorian and tell him of your concerns. I'm sure he will feel just terrible. Enoka, give him a chance."

"Very well, if you will speak to him and he will try, I will try."

"Thank you. Now off to your committee meeting." Enoka and Terah exit and Terah sends an attendant for Zorian of Nur so that he, Terah, may speak with him. Another man stomps up to Terah who greets him with a handshake and a smile.

Zag is in charge of a meeting of captains where they are discussing problems and solutions.

Enoka is speaking. "Gentlemen, in our preparations for battle we have a lot of injuries. I'm sure it is due to the intensity with which we practice, trying to imitate real battles. Any suggestions on what we can realistically do to lessen these injuries?" There's a pause. Zag motions to Enoka to continue. "The General has given this matter considerable thought, but would like your feelings on a solution. Also, we have many cities, many men whom we have conquered, that we don't feel confident letting roam around completely unguarded. So, a lot of our time and man power is taken up guarding these men, in case they decide to cause our King trouble."

"Too much time and effort, if you ask me," offers Captain Leksi. "We should have killed them all on the field of battle when we had the chance."

Zag forcefully bangs his fist on the table, "Not finished."

"Sorry my General. It's just maddening."

"General Zag, would like you to consider the following possibility. There are also quite a few men who were injured by our army in battle who live here or in other cities throughout the empire. These men, as well, are a drain on our resources.

What if," Enoka's eyes start to sparkle, "what if, these men were to be used in our practices? We could practice against them, and any injuries they sustain would be of relatively no consequence. Might even help us keep these untrustworthy men's numbers down. Thus, this could save our troops from as many unnecessary injuries and, like I said, if some of these men die, oh well. What do you captains think?"

"That's absolutely brilliant, my General. Brilliant!" says Captain Leksi.

"Would these men be armed with real weapons or just practice as human sacrifices?" grins Captain Wit.

Captain Enoka answers, "They would be armed, like us, and expected to fight vigorously. If we find some worthy to be in our army, they would be given the choice of swearing allegiance to our King and to Babylon, or continuing as they are."

"How," muses Captain Ruka, "could we possibly know if they can be trusted? Some men would swear to anything just to get out of cleaning their own home!" General laughter.

Enoka continues, "General Zag is proposing that for those men willing to fight for Babylon, they and their family must be moved to Babel. Whether that be a wife and children, a mom and dad, or a distant uncle and family, matters not. The family would be our insurance of a man's sworn loyalty to being sincere. He screws up and the family members die, and then the man."

"Just be sure'" adds Leksi, "not to include step-dads!" That comment meets with a roar of approval and laughter. "Course, step-dads may be the reason some of us enjoy killing so very much." A few more laughs, etc.

"On a more serious note," adds Captain Varian, "I'm not sure many men would be willing to put their lives on the line with these new, uh, recruits, supposedly having their backs."

"At first," comments Captain Enoka, "they wouldn't be in a position of protecting our soldier's backs. All of these men would be on the front lines of our assaults. Should they survive and prove their ability as fighters as well as their loyalty, then they could be placed in the regular ranks of troops."

"So, first," comments Captain Ruka, "they are trained to fight with, say, the sword, put into practice scrimmages with our regular troops and if they can survive that, their reward is to go to the front lines in a real battle. I love it!" "And then," says Captain Leksi, "they get to move into the regular ranks of our army."

"I'm not sure any of us could have made it that way," offers Captain Varian. A few chuckles follow.

"That's true," says Captain Enoka, "and that's why we would not be looking at large numbers graduating to the regular army."

"Is there a downside to all of this we are not seeing General?" asks Captain Wit. Zag and Enoka confer.

"It certainly is possible that if this group becomes large enough that they could try and rebel against us. But then, every member of their family would immediately face execution, and they themselves."

Captain Wit, "What if some of them are plants from a robber band, and all we're doing is training them to come against us with their friends?"

Enoka is obviously tiring of the same questions in different forms, "Look guys, its 'poop or get off the pooper' time. Are we going to do this, learn as we go, solve problems as we get to them, or not? I want these men to have the best chance at success as is possible, and at the same time keep from killing and maiming our own men in practice. Does this sound like a system that will do that?"

Mumbling among the captains. "Look, I think if we handle this right, we minimize the chances of rebellion, minimize our injuries, and possible get some quality recruits for our efforts and not just a scheme to rid the kingdom of troublemakers or hanger-oners."

"Here, here," say several captains.

"Are we agreed then?" Unanimous raising of hands and vocal "ayes."

"Then, General, your plan is accepted. Who shall we put in charge of it?" Several captains smile a big, broad smile at Enoka and his shoulders slump. "You dirty dogs."

General Zag, "Enoka. Done."

"It will take a couple of months to organize the new "recruits" and make sure they have adequate training on different weapons, gather the families to Babel of the men who qualify or volunteer and so on. When you have ideas that come to you, send them to me via a courier." His speech is followed by verbal "here, here, atta boys" and the like.

"I will need two volunteers for help in training and interviews." Suddenly the room is quiet and all seem to be occupied with something other than direct eye contact with Enoka.

"Thank you, Captains Leksi and Ruka. I appreciate your willingness to help."

Together the two men object, "Hey, I didn't ..." Down comes Zag's fist. "Meeting over."

"Maybe our slogan should be," offers Captain Wit, "a few good men."

Chapter Fourteen

King Nimrod enjoys donning a cloak, a wig and some unusual clothing. Thus disguised, he would go to many different cities. This time, he ventures to the city of Ninab that he and his army had conquered. He would walk through a city's main square and rest for a few minutes, watching the very young play games. He observes the young adults engage in their mock swordsmanship with friends, seeing who could impress the young ladies the most. Older members of the city would keep an eye on their children -- all just like when he was growing up in what seemed to be a thousand years ago.

Invariably someone would engage him in conversation about this or that and soon the conversation would turn to politics. King Nimrod plays the part of a visitor from a foreign land and feigns ignorance regarding Babylon. Since all languages are still the Adamic language, an accent or foreign-language vocabulary is not needed.

"You have never heard of Babylon?" exclaims one older gentleman. "You truly must live a sheltered life. This is the greatest civilization ever to exist on the earth. Our King has carved out a Garden of Eden in the desert by building thousands of miles of canals for irrigating our personal gardens, our herdsmen and our orchards. Have you been to Babel?"

"No, kind sir, I have not."

"Ah! You must go there and see the greatest ziggurat in the world. The King's palace, the beautiful ponds, the Temple, all are jewels to behold. You must go there, you must." The elderly man shuffles off with the aid of his wife, and a son and can be heard exclaiming, "He's never been to Babel. Can you figure that?"

"Neither have you, Father."

"Well, no, but I've heard the stories, my son."

"Yes, Father, it was I who told you the stories."

"Oh."

A young couple stops a few paces from Nimrod and their conversation can be heard by him.

"In two years", he says, "in two short years I will have enough sheep to start my own herd, and then I shall ask your father for your hand."

"Please hurry, I think my father has been talking to one of the elders in town. His wife died and he is looking for a younger woman to take her place, to clean for him and start another family."

"Maybe I should go to Babel and join the army. Perhaps I could earn more money faster. What do you think?"

"I don't want you to be in the army. What if you die? King Nimrod is always attacking cities and fighting other armies. You could get maimed. When will he have enough so the world can stop fighting?"

"What if I just spoke to your father and asked him to wait for me to have the sheep I need to pay him for your hand? Do you think he'd give us time?"

"I don't know. We haven't any money, and the man father is talking with is very well off. I mean, he's nice enough, I guess. But he's lived his life; why can't he let us live ours?"

She cries and as they start to exit, Nimrod motions for the young man to come to him. He does so, leaving his intended crying and bewildered.

"Young man, I couldn't help but overhear your conversation. Do not wait two years: I know what that is like. There are too many unknowns; Marry this beautiful, precious young lady now. Here is an early wedding present from King Nimrod." He hands the young man a small purse full of gold pieces and motions for him to return to his woman. He does and as he opens the purse he faints. The girl runs to him and looks in the purse and she faints, falling on her man.

"Hate to say it, but there's a match made in heaven." Nimrod walks over and helps them to their feet and helps them stumble down a street headed for her home. The girl stops and runs back to Nimrod and plants a big kiss on his lips, hugs him, cries on him and runs back to her man. The man does the same thing and finally the two exit the square as a rowdy group of four men approach Nimrod.

"Hey old man," one of them calls out to Nimrod, "Got any money?"

"No young man. I was robbed on the road this very morning by four men very similar to you. "Where's your policemen, your army, your town administrator? Help," he calls softly. "Help!"

"Whoa! Old man. We didn't rob anyone!"

"Don't you have anything to do besides bother old people?" faking being old.

"Like what? Big fat 'Limprod' has taken everything from this city. He makes all of us work one week out of each month in Babel, for what? Him, his two hundred whores and for what? He took all our gold and valuables; he then takes our most excellent women. Who needs two hundred wives? What can you do with two hundred that you can't do with one? Then he comes by each month and steals from us again."

"What do you mean, each month he steals again?"

"His Elite soldiers, about thirty of them, come to the city and the administrator. The administrator says we have to give these guys all our jewelry again, our best sheep, oxen and cattle. Doesn't this great king ever beat us up enough?"

"When do they come?"

"What do you care?"

"Just curious, my young friend."

"About the first week of each month, always in the evening."

"Thank you. Oh, and what do they look like? Clothing? Hair? Face?"

"Yeah, Toko." One of his friends chips in. "They all had those weird haircuts, 'ya know, the center shaved to the bone with the sides fairly long."

"The center shaved, you're sure?"

"To the bone, old man, to the bone," Toko adds.

"Did anyone stand out in particular?"

"Yeah, one was a lot younger than the others, like you being a lot older than us. Weird, you know?"

"I can hardly imagine that much weirdness."

"And a heck of a lot bigger!" chips in one of his friends.

"Yeah," Toko continues, "and he talks like his brain was stuck. Imitating, "Give. Go. Bye." All the others laugh and imitate Toko.

Another adds, 'He keeps on twitching and talking to people that aren't there. And, and he has a chain around his waist that one of the other men holds. The chain when they wanted to move or go somewhere. It isn't pulled hard, though. Guess he doesn't want the big guy to be mad at him. Really weird."

Immediately King Nimrod knows who they are imitating – Zaggai. Excited, "Which way did they go when they left?"

"Right." No one gets the joke. "You know, the old man said "when they left" and I said, "right. Ya know; left, right, left, right. Marching?" Still no response from anyone.

"I thought it was odd," Toko continues, "that they didn't go toward Babel, they went toward the mountains (he points north) up where the big guys live."

"The big guys?" Nimrod quizzes.

Toko, "The Giants. I ain't seen them, but people have stories about them."

Nimrod reaches into his left pocket and pulls out a little bag with gold pieces. He hands the bag to Toko, "You have been most helpful, my friends."

"Hey! We was helpful too, old man," another of the group responds, as he tries to reach into Nimrod's coat pocket. Nimrod quickly subdues him by knocking him to the ground and holding his fingers apart and one foot in the man's armpit. "Now, now, let's not be greedy, friend." The man is whimpering in pain, "But you're supposed to be old."

"Your friend will share, I'm sure. He has that trusting look about him."

"You talking about Toko?" one of the men comments, laughingly. Toko rewards him with a fist in the gut that doubles the man over. He just sits there on the ground rocking and groaning.

Toko has opened the bag, "Wow! I thought you said you were robbed?"

"That was my right pocket; this was in my left." A grinning Nimrod slaps Toko on the back. "You know, right, left – marching!" Nimrod laughs to himself. "Never trust old people: they can be very devious." Nimrod starts walking away. The two are examining the contents of the purse, the third and fourth are examining their hand and fingers and gut.

"Holy cow, we're rich. Maybe he's got more!"

Toko slaps him too, "Think about it. He didn't have to give us anything. Now, we can afford to chew our brains out."

Nimrod whispers to himself while shaking his head, "That shouldn't take long."

His second friend adds, "Hey, old man, each of them had a tattoo on the left side of their neck, ah," trying to think, "just below and behind the ear."

"Of what?" Nimrod asks.

"The ear on their head, like mine. The thing you hear with." He's been enjoying the night a bit too much.

"Some kind of animal, I think," adds Toko. "I'm not sure." Hey, we're on our way to a party, old one: Care to join? Gonna be lots of joy weed."

"Joy weed?" quizzes Nimrod. "That's what you're on now?"

One of the group responds, "Yeah, we got started early. You know, the early birds and the worms?"

"Yeah," injects Toko and hands some to Nimrod, "you chew this for a few minutes, and joy to you and me!" They all laugh and leave down one of the lesser traveled streets.

"Joy, baby, joy," is heard as they disappear.

When King Nimrod returns home he is met by a very distraught Semiramis.

"My dear wife, as he removes his wig and clothing, please tell me what has you so upset? Did I do something to cause your heightened state of anxiety? If so, I've got something," he pulls out some Joy weed, "that should help." He obviously has sampled the product on his way home. "How is it that kids find this stuff before us adults?" Giggling.

"No, my dear," with a puzzled look on her face due to his light-hearted and giggling condition, "I knew you'd be gone for a few days overseeing the kingdom: it's not that. While you were gone someone violated our personal bedchambers …"

Even though foggy, Nimrod immediately begins to become concerned, "Have you been harmed, in, in any way."

"No, no dear husband, it's not that."

Nimrod kisses her and pulls her to him. "Anything else I can deal with Semiramis. So tell me, what is it?"

"Someone broke into our chambers and stole the package you had wrapped up and covered over with your hunting clothing.

Nimrod heads for their bedchamber, holding Semiramis's hand. He goes to a corner where the "package" had been secreted.

"How would one, anyone one, know of this package's existence, let alone the value? I've told no one about it. Even you do not know the contents, do you?"

"No, Nimmie, I do not. And I've never had occasion to discuss it or answer questions about it with anyone."

"So, that leaves a small list of people, or is that a list of small people," he giggles. "Sorry, who would have known what to look for and where to look?"

"The maids couldn't have possibly known what was in the package, though they would have known where it was."

"And never have I told anyone of its existence, let alone what its value may be, which makes me believe this theft must be the work of my dear old grandfather, Hammy-poo."

His witty humor convulses him into a state of laughter. "Hammy" giggle, giggle, "poo."

She waits a few seconds before attempting to continue, "Ham?" More giggles from the peanut gallery. "Oh, this is impossible. Darling husband, King of the modern world, isn't he the one that gave you the package?"

"Yes, my dear wife. He gaveth and he taketh. Never underestimate the devious doings of one Ham, son of one Noah, one son of a … Yes, the more we talk of it, the more I am convinced it was he." Nimrod laughs a real belly-gusher.

Again Semiramis awaits her King. "What is so funny?"

"I hope he wears it without checking it out first. Oh please, Lord, let it be."

"Why?"

"Because he stole an imitation of the garments of Adam, not the real thing! Many years ago Zag and I determined that if those garments, the skins, were really endowed with special properties, gifts, powers, what have you, we should protect them. Therefore, we set about finding animal skins to match them exactly and had them sown exactly like the originals and then wrapped them exactly in a like manner, exactly." Giggle, giggle.

"That's what the thief thefted, a bunch of worthless animal skins. I wish I could be a fly on the wall when someone tries them out." He lets loose a belly full of laughter.

"What are the skins supposed to do?"

"Can you free up your schedule for a few days this week?"

"I am free even as we speak."

"Good. Tomorrow I want you to accompany me on a hunt: a day to get there, a day to hunt and a day to return. That should give us plenty of time to experience the power, the force of the skins."

Early in the morning the royal couple, accompanied by thirty of the finest Elite troops are on their way to the king's hunting preserve. Included are several wagons to bring home the meat for a royal feast.

Prior to leaving, King Nimrod gives orders for three of his runners to go to Ninib to watch for the soldiers who would come to town to take jewelry and herds. He gives them express orders not to tell his city administrator regarding their visit. When the men are found, the runners are to track them to their hideout and assess the strength of their group.

"I have a question of you, my Queen."

"Yes, my King."

"Why is it I have been visiting the same young lady each week, week after week after week? You have been so good at telling me their time to conceive that it has puzzled me somewhat. Are you slipping?"

"She is one of my special projects, my dear. She has proved very, uh, resistant to our normal methods for conceiving. But, good news, she is now with child and you will be able to move on, starting with our return from this trip."

They set up their tents for the evening, and as the men are about to prepare who would be the beaters and so on for the hunt, King Nimrod informs them that he did not want any of the typical hunt preparations for tomorrow.

"Just set up to gather my kills and place them on the wagons after gutting them. Set your usual watch for the Queen's protection and well, just relax." As the King walks away, one of the guards looks perplexed.

"Relax, did the King say? How do I do that? Am I allowed to relax with the King here?"

His fellow guards laugh at him and one interjects, "You best follow the King's orders or you'll be out of a job."

The King and Queen relax and enjoy walking in the cool evening air of the mountains. "This is worth the trip alone, Nimmie. What a beautiful place. It reminds me of home."

"Maybe I should take you back to the home of our childhood and give up on this life of king and queen. Maybe we should buy a few thousand sheep and live the life of a shepherd." Pause.

"Maybe I could keep just a few maids, too." Pause.

"And a few of the Elite." Pause.

"Could you build us a small palace to come home to?" Pause

"And a small temple?" Pause. They both laugh. "No."

The night seems short due to their having to endure the noise of the crickets, hour after hour. As the dawn comes the camp is busy with the sounds, smells and sights of breakfast in the woods and preparation for the hunt.

King Nimrod instructs his guards to stop at the edge of the preserve, which causes a bit of confusion and angst among the men.

"But your grace, we cannot come to your defense, should the need arise. Not that you need our help, of course, but if anything should happen to you, what would we tell General Jared? Or worse, what would we tell General Zag?" Several guards groan at that prospect.

"I'll be fine," guaranteed Nimrod. "The Queen will be fine. We'll both be fine." The guards mumble among themselves, but how do you argue with the King?

Nimrod and Semiramis enter the preserve with Nimrod carrying the package, his bow and a full quiver of arrows and one spear. Semiramis carries an extra bow and a second quiver of arrows on her back. They look like Tarzan and Jane gone hunting their favorite pet animals.

Once inside the preserve and out of view of the guards, Nimrod takes off his clothing, unwraps the package and dons the skins of Adam.

"Feel any different?" quizzes Semiramis.

"A little scratchy, but no, no difference."

"What'll we do next?"

"Let's walk in this direction. I saw some movement in the bushes."

They walk towards the movement the King mentioned and as they near the brush, out steps a male and female lion with two cubs. The male roars a defiant roar and the female's ears flatten, her teeth bared with an almost hissing sound emanating from her mouth.

"Ah, Nimmie, are you sure? These animals might not have gotten the message about the skins."

As Nimrod approaches with Semiramis now behind him, the lions stop their noises and sniff the air. In a moment, the lions change from aggressive and protecting their young, to literally kneeling with their heads between their front paws. The cubs, too, assume the same position as their mom and dad.

With four arrows they are all dead.

"The young ones are extremely tender to eat."

"Nimmie, that is amazing! Let's do it some more."

So, they spend the next several hours walking through the preserve finding unsuspecting victims to execute. The skins of Adam give the animals the anticipation that those wearing the skins would be friendly. Those who survive the day's events would know better, and the animosity of the animal kingdom toward man would grow by leaps and bounds. After hours of "hunting" the toll of the dead is thus; lions, gazelles, bears, mountain goats, Arabian Oryx, fallow deer, leopards and fox, all dead, killed by those intrepid hunters, Nimmie and Semi.

They finally tire of hunting, aka-slaughtering defenseless animals, and return to camp, giving instructions as to where the guards can find the animals they have killed. Nimrod returned with his hunting attire neatly folded and repackaged, and he once again is dressed in his regular royal clothing. Both quivers of arrows are spent, and all that is left of the weapons is Nimrod's spear.

The guards spend the next several hours dragging, gathering, gutting and loading the animals into the wagons. The wagons, once loaded, leave for Babel, while the royal couple and their entourage spend the evening relaxing.

The next morning they all travel to Babel, with Semiramis regaling in the King's exploits of the previous day. While you and I may have a difficult time telling the stories of killing helpless, indefensible animals, Semiramis raises her story-telling to an art form. But the truth and the whole, bent, distorted truth shall make you free. But then again, perhaps Semiramis knows how much her husband needs this boost to his damaged ego, especially after his crushing blow at the lips of his dying mommy, and the weeks and months of recuperation it took to bring Nimmie back from the threshold of suicidal depression.

I mean, what's a few lies, a few tall hunting tales, if it saves a life? Who cares what means to the end it takes, as long as the end justifies the means, especially for a special person -- someone above the ordinary peons such as you and me -- and their special gift for the world? You know -- a special athlete, politician, actor or actress or a televangelist: an apple, an apple, an onion.

Nuradad and Shahmanesor have slowly but steadily been building their little empire out of the sun with malcontents and deserters of the several cities overtaken by the Babylon machine. News of Kish and Berosus' deaths travel to their camp and yet no one has the complete story. Most of what they know is supposition and hearsay. Nonetheless, a major competitor has bitten the dust, and so they have benefited by their demise. Boo-hoo. Boo-hoo.

While their empire grows into the tens of thousands, the need for ways to sustain all those people grows too. Then, there is the task of training such a large group for warfare when there is no warfare. Gee, and how do you form a cohesive, mean, lean fighting machine out of scum, quitters, whiners and sexual deviates that couldn't make it in the real world?

Stealing food on the hoof is okay, but wouldn't do for tens of thousands of men, plus a few, good women. Normally these are not the types who would want to grow their own crops and watch their herds increase, for nothing. Stealing some jewelry and animals, destroying an occasional canal, or enticing a young boy to go hunting for arrows at night around the palace with a candle isn't real warfare; not even for this bunch of misfits. The gruesome blood oaths now being administered could not keep everyone happy by just hanging around the mountains.

It is in such a lull of activity that two runners for Nimrod are captured, following a group of jewelry and animal thieves from Ninib – Aericas and Earron. Blood lust runs very high by the time the captured men reach the robber camp. Without an out-and-out war, killing two of Nimrod's runners is a very close second. But not just killing, the absolute pleasure in torturing them put goose bumps on their boiling blood lust. This is far more fulfilling than broken canals that are repaired within hours of being broken.

The two men are stretched between two posts by means of ropes tied to their wrists and ankles. On each end of the four ropes is a wooden turn screw, keeping the ropes taunt. Each day one of their guards select one of the four turn screws to tighten and turn, thus causing the joints of that limb to separate just a little. I say "just a little", but the pain it causes now that each of the four ropes of each man is taunt produces sweat to appear all over their bodies, forcing their bowels to evacuate. Tears fall incessantly and blood drips from all the pores of their skin. The one thing the torturers could not do is make these two men cry out "uncle" in pain.

They are asked questions regarding all sorts of silly things, questions to which the answers are absolutely meaningless. It is their torturers justification to peel another fingernail off, or toenail off for not answering. The giddy attitude of the torturers is, at first, shared by the thousands of men watching on. These two Christian men, men of ideals, have behavior that is in stark contrast to the losers watching them. The tolerance for pain these two men have is probably something neither you nor I can ever hope to achieve. We whine and cry because our hair is messed up, hold the wedding, boo-hoo. I don't look right. Who really cares?

Their tolerance for pain was bred almost as a condition of life, of tolerance taught by a Christian father whose word was his bond. Tolerance was their badge of honor and would not be broken in this life. And that tolerance extended to those around them, recognizing that not all would have their ability. Recognizing that others had their own peculiar gifts, and that they need not walk around as though they were God's gift to man.

So, it isn't much fun after a few days. The thousands of men who gather around at torturing time in the early morning, grow weary of the peeling and the tightening. Why? Because, the two men would not even give the thousands of onlookers the satisfaction of a scream, or of a cry, begging them to "please stop", or just an audible moan. I mean for crying out loud, give us something to enjoy, damn it!

With their feet and hands bleeding, blood beginning to appear at their lips and through their skin, onlookers are reduced to a trickle and then, to just a sparse few.

Begrudgingly, the thousands know that these two men are better soldiers, runners, men than themselves. Respect. Respect to a degree that the thousands would have cheered their deaths, as the limbs finally disconnect and pop from their bodies. Would have cheered, had not their leaders, their task masters, been ever present to remind each man that they could be next, if so much as a cough emanates from their lips.

The intended lesson of these two men's deaths, is: this is what happens to a devoted follower of Nimrod. Unintended lesson is these are the kind of men that they would someday have to face on the field of battle, a very unsettling thought for cowards.

A guard hacks the ropes holding the remains of each man and lets the pieces fall to the ground, where the burial detail carefully places the men on a wagon. There is no loud, boisterous laughing, no drinking celebration as the wagon makes its way to the graveyard. Instead, silence, respect and honor greet the passing of the wagon.

It is at this time that Bouhous (Zaggai) stands as the two men's bodies approached.

"Sit down," whispers Lenka. "Someone will see you and report you." Bouhous stands, not knowing why he honors the two dead men by standing as their bodies pass by. This little brood has grown to four sons who watch their father and stand next to him, holding his hand.

"Good men," said Bouhous.

No one would report Bouhous. He lives in his own little world and no one wants into that disturbed place. His temper towards all but his family is enough to know about him. There is no need to find ways to annoy him, regardless of edicts from leaders or task masters.

"Daddy, I have to pee," whispered the little one. So the family walks to their home with their little dancing son.

Lenka had a reputation, before Bouhous, as an easy girl for the men to pal around with. What caused her to become this fiercely loyal wife to a half-wit is a puzzlement to all. And Bouhous is a real nut job. He would walk down a street as normal as you and me, when suddenly he would have a fit of screaming and cursing. Lenka is the only human who could calm her husband. Actually, their sons are growing into that role as well.

Should anyone try to physically calm Bouhous, aside from his family, he, or they, would be violently attacked and beaten. If others did not intervene and restrain him, he would beat them to death. Then, when the fit subsided, Bouhous would continue on his way as though nothing had happened.

At times Bouhous would grab a neighbor's pet cat or dog and pet it. Lenka and the boys knew better than to have their own pets. If a fit came upon Bouhous, then he would tear the pet limb from limb, oblivious to the screams of the animal being dismembered.

No one yelled at Bouhous, no one confronted him regarding his actions. Lenka would slip the destroyed pet's family what little money she may have had, coupled with sincere, sorrowful sadness. The neighbors have come to accept these frightful happenings, out of respect for her and the boys, out of fear of Bouhous, and because there is absolutely no other recourse.

The army loves the brutal man who would be led into battle chained to another to keep Bouhous from wandering away or from killing his own comrades. The man with Bouhous is there to simply resupply Bouhous with spears, his favorite weapon, and the various weapons he requires. Bouhous has absolutely no regard for his own life, none. Zero. Zip. Nada.

So, it is with some trepidation that you find you are assigned to fight with him. This particular handler has been with him when Bouhous has been surrounded by ten armed men, and without flinching, killed each and every one of them, most with his unusual spear: it had a point on both ends. He would thrust it into an opponent in front of him, pull the spear out, and kill an opponent behind him. As his handler you learned to dance around him, like his little peeing son.

Lenka ran away from home when she was twelve. Father had wanted her to marry an old friend, and I mean old. Lenka did not want to marry, let alone the old man friend. The night before the proposed wedding, Lenka took one of her father's horses and fled for the mountains. Two of her oldest brothers helped in the escape and gave her directions to what was Nuradad's hideout. Unable to fight like a man, she did what she could to show her worth and it was thus that she earned the reputation as easy. For her it was nothing. It wasn't like she only had ten coins and each guy took one. She had more coins than she could possibly use, and so why not share. That is, until Bouhous came into her life.

Maybe it was Bouhous's vulnerability that drew her to him. In any case they grew to be a couple, and at the age of fifteen she married her choice of a mate. Four children later she was more in love than ever. Yes, it was a brutal experience, especially with no family, no real friends, as there were precious few of the men who were married. Any who were, seemed to use this occasion to distance themselves from their wives and children. You know men!

With the ziggurat completed, a ceremony is planned and the town elders are going all out with their preparations. While nowhere near as extensive as the original celebration for Nimrod being crowned King, it is impressive, none the less.

King Nimrod is asked to address the throng of well-wishers who have gathered. It was a wise move by many towns to send a delegation to "ooh and ah" over the Tower of Babel. It comes under the heading of keeping your friends close and your enemies closer.

Toward dark, the crowds have congregated at the base of the Tower, where they sit and are served food by wandering servants. Riplakish calls those thousands present to order, and then proceeds to give all present a boringly informative history of Babel, of King Nimrod and Queen Semiramis, the building of the Palace and the number of wives, and now concubines, the canals and the newly constructed bridge to East Babel and, of course, the Tower of Babel.

According to Riplakish, it is the tallest building on earth. Certainly it is the tallest ziggurat, prayer tower, so that anyone could go there and feel closer to God. He also tells them about the United Council of Cities that meets in the Tower, whose purpose is to create peace in the world. And harmony and … The man could talk and talk. Finally, with the accomplishment introductions done, he introduces the main speaker, King Nimrod, to a thunderous ovation. No one is sure the ovation is due to Nimrod's popularity or to being thankful Riplakish is finally done speaking.

King Nimrod rises and then strides royally to the pulpit where he thanks Riplakish for his kind, but lengthy, introduction. Riplakish blushes when the audience laughs slightly. Nimrod takes a moment to pause and look over the assembled guests, during which time whatever conversations or movement of chairs cease.

He looks directly into the eyes of the closest as well as those most distant. "Ladies and Gentlemen, I am honored to have the opportunity to say a few words regarding the strides, the improvements, the military advancements Babel has made. I do not desire to make you feel uncomfortable by mentioning our military achievements, and yet without them, much of what you see, perhaps all of it, would not have been possible. God did not intervene when we were being pummeled constantly by some of the very cities you represent, or by the bandits, the cowards that hide in our nearby mountains.

God did not build our hundreds of miles of canals or build the bridge that unites the two halves of our beautiful city. The men you see before you," he motions to the elders seated behind him and has them stand as he starts the round of fully intense applause for them, "they did it. They supported me, they supplied our troops, our engineers and architects. They deserve much of the praise, the accolades, the cheers, and yet they are among the most humble men I know, except perhaps Riplakish." A full round of laughter and applause. Riplakish blushes, as he is not paying attention and is not sure what was just said about him.

"I jest, of course: he is among the hardest working of them all. And not just the elders of Babylon, but the average businessman, like Berakhiak, owner of the brick factory. Every brick you see in the ziggurat he has fashioned." Nimrod pauses and it is obvious he is emotional. "And a dear friend who is no longer with us, Puli-ilu: just a common worker at the brick factory. Due to a childhood accident Puli was brain-damaged and yet hired by Berakhiak to make bricks. He was later killed by a drunken group of, and I am sad to say, military men, drunken military men, the same type of drunk that killed a ten-year-old boy simply collecting arrows. True, it was not murder but a horrible accident, yet both dead due to alcohol blurring the senses.

I bring this up so you may know we do not see ourselves as better than others, better than you. We are striving for excellence. We want you to join us in our quest. We want you to follow our dream, no matter how hopeless you think you have it. It is our quest with our United Council of Cities to have peace in our lifetime, no matter how hard, how impossible you think that dream may be." He is stopped by another thunderous applause. "And yes, sometimes war is necessary to achieve peace.

Right now there are thousands of bandits, cowards amassing in the mountains to our north, looking for the opportunity to destroy all we have achieved. Do you think that is right?" He pauses and there are a few scattered, "No's!" "Well, do you?" Much more forceful group of "No's!" "Should we, should you, allow these lazy, cowards to destroy your city, your way of life?" Even stronger "No's!"

"Do you think God will intervene on your behalf?" Strong "No's!" Is it His job to do so?" Mild No's!"

"Well, I think it's mine. I think it is my job to rid the world of cowards like them. Will you join me?" Strong "Yes's.!" "Will you join me?" Everyone stands and shouts, "Yes, yes, yes!" The cheering goes on for several minutes.

King Nimrod motions for all to be seated. "Then join us. Join our unilateral army to rid the earth of these parasites, and any other scourges of civilized people. Join our Council of Cities, send your delegates as soon as you can to participate in planning for peace." A modest applause follows.

"It has been said that if we do not study history and understand it, then we are doomed to repeat the failures our past leaders have made."

"Will you join us?" Enthusiastic "Yes's.!"

"All you here tonight can be part of your cities as well. Progress can be made when there is peace in the land. You and I can bring that peace we desire, that we deserve. Our strength added to yours," he points to a particular person, "and yours," points to another, "and yours," points to yet another person, "will do what God has not thought to do. We, with our puny bodies and puny minds can bring to pass that which God has not, perhaps cannot, do.

He created the world then destroyed it – all but eight people -- and still people hate and kill. God's creation. God's children. And we have the opportunity to do what even God cannot. We can choose to unite together and rid ourselves of murderers, thieves and rapists." Cheers from the audience.

"Join us to no longer be bound down by foolish traditions like waiting for God to do what we can do for ourselves. Why do we yoke ourselves with such foolish things as what the prophets have told us? No man can know of things yet to come! And if they do, what good has it done us – you and me?

These are but foolish traditions that are meant to bind us down, to keep us from thinking for ourselves. Look at what we've created here in Babel without God, without prophets, without sacrificing the very best that we created ourselves! We cannot know of things we cannot see.

Now, there's talk of a Christ who is to come, somewhere, somehow, who will forgive you of your sins. Can you know of this as a surety?" Pause. "Can you?" Mutterings of "No." This is ridiculous. This is the work of a frenzied mind, a mind trying to lead you into a belief of things which cannot be.

You know, and I know," he points to his hands and biceps, "each man fares according to his efforts. Therefore, we prosper according to our own genius. Berakhiak fares well due to his great ability to make bricks, not because someone will someday forgive him of his sins. What sins? Helping the poor like Puli-ilu?

Sarsous fares well because he knows how to make Jerk meat for our army and Omer fares well by making the best tents, the best awnings, the best of anything of cloth. And Omar's blind: did God help him? Did he?" Chorus of "No's!" "He did it on his own.

And as to the military, we conquer and bring peace to the land according to our strength, and therefore, it is not a crime. We do not need to be forgiven for looking out for our own people. General Jared and General Zag are men of peace. Once again, I implore you to join us, and you and I will make the earth a place where all men and all women are free to wander, to work as they may. Will you join us, my brothers and sisters?" Enthusiastic yells are heard of "Yes, yes, yes" and then, "Nimrod, Nimrod, Nimrod."

Those who do not agree with the King in bashing God are in a very small minority. They are also very quiet. The elders all join in by raising their hands above their heads and forming a chain, chanting and cheering their King.

Later that same evening in the Temple, Nimrod and Semiramis are front and center in a ceremony aimed at drawing their military leaders closer to them. The temple is full of only the most loyal, most cut-throat of all the army, including Zag. But not Jared.

As the ceremony closes, Semiramis stands and offers her comments in favor of supporting Nimrod as the only leader they will ever need. "He reigns supreme. I would die for him. Will you?" The answer comes back, "Yes, my Queen." "Will you die for him?" she repeats louder and stronger. "Yes, my Queen," comes roaring back the answer. Zag comes forward and kneels before King Nimrod and Queen Semiramis, All the men kneel before them as well.

"I die, you, my Lord, my King, my God."

In mighty unison the men repeat, "I die, you, my Lord, my King, my God."

THE END

Characters

CHAPTER ONE

Tabansi – Ham's runner
Cush – son of Ham
Ham – son of Noah
Noah - the prophet
Semiramis – future wife of Nimrod
Nimrod – son of Cush
Japeth – son of Noah
Shem – son of Noah
Zag – slow-speaking friend of Nimrod
Jared – friend of Nimrod
Lugal – son of Ham
Naiama – wife of Noah
Logan – servant/friend of Lugal
Fenchristo – friend of Nimrod
Rayas - brother of Fenchristo

CHAPTER TWO

Mariana – wife of Tabansi
Ava – eldest daughter of Tabansi
Mia – Ava's twin sister
Kadenram – trader with large flat wagon
Jasher – older brother of Nimrod
Aericas – Tabansi's eldest son
Earron – Tabansi's second son
Parahayker – Tabansi's third son
Urtylgur – soldier, night of truths

Redgaru – soldier, horse stolen from
Berosus – son of Kish the bandit
Kish – head bandit
Tyjeffiry – soldier in Babel
Cyrus – soldier in Babel
Taydalor – brick worker
Kiwayneid – garrison commander
Omar – blind tentmaker
Sarsous – jerk meat maker

CHAPTER THREE

Puli-ilu – retarded man
Jessem – Puli-ilu's 10 year old brother
Terah – elder of Babel, father of Abraham
Riplakish – chief elder of Babel
Nukhush – younger sister to Semiramis
Fransigas – Semiramis's aunt in Anat
Zamama – wife of Jared
Shamshi – wife of Zag
Gechina – wife of Fenchristo
Catalin – wife of Rayas
Khufu – pharaoh of Egypt
Babryaniifi – pharaoh's envoy to Babel

CHAPTER FOUR

Tashshigura-mash – head priest of Babel's temple
Thoth – minister or religion in Babel
Molach – Nimrod's temple name
Priest of Baal – Nimrod's temple name
Nuradad – captain under general Zag
Shawnesor – cheater cousin of Nuradad
Chiamaka – slave released by Nimrod
Mahonri – brother of Jared
Entressia – Shamshi's aunt
Jacobar – Shamshi's uncle
Nazibugas – drunk garrison commander
Abasi – stern yet fair garrison commander

Lufian – Jared's five year old son
Tonya – sister of Lufian's friend
William – Lufian's friend
Berakhiak – owner of brick factory
Paz – Lufian's friend
Zaggai – son of Zag

CHAPTER FIVE

Gyurka – old man neighbor hit by Zaggai
Tiflumany – oldest daughter of Zag
Lenka – Zaggai's wife
Bouhous – Zaggai's name with robbers
Captain Bittor – captain to Jared
Captain Lionel – captain to Jared
Zarek – captain to Jared
Dalziel – Nimrod's spy at Kish's
Captain Bomani - spy of Kish
Dertelli – spy and aide to Chiamaka

CHAPTER SIX

Etan – Babel city elder
Yakov – Babel city elder
Erik – captain, child killed
Ronnre – leader of 400 from Calneh
Tammuz – slow witted son of Nimrod
Elka – wife of Cush
Canaan – son of Ham and Mariann
Hadeon – elder in Calneh
Tupac – grandson of Hadeon
Hanza – dog in Tukulti

CHAPTER SEVEN

Captain Enoka – captain to Zag
Captain Leksi – with general Zag
Captain Wit – with general Zag
Captain Varian – with general Zag
Captain Ruka – with general Zag
Toko – leader of four at square
Antandra – stubborn wife of Nimrod
Zorian – delegate from Nur
Enoch – delegate from Nur

CHAPTER EIGHT

Amathjuli – wife of Nimrod, future wife of Terah
Adolf – womanizer
Casamantha – 6 year old daughter of Rayas
Abeni – 18 year old daughter of Rayas
Ohanzee – soldier

CHAPTER NINE

Pani – guard at Nimrod's palace
Rudra – Pani's partner at palace
Nodin – oldest son of Bouhous/Zaggai
Fadeyka – captain to Nuradad
Standa – captain to Nuradad
Cliwt – one of giant leaders
Rablry – one of giant leaders
Virgin – one of giant leaders
Ghiwdht – one of giant leaders
Qahos – one of giant leaders
Alorus – Nimrod's temple name
Merjuri – young giant stone cutter

CHAPTER TEN

Gisella – 12 year old daughter of Jared
Rashidi – Nimrod's physician
Taneli – friend of Gisella
Sophia – oldest daughter of Jared
Angus – son of brother of Jared
Tynicole – wife of brother of Jared

CHAPTER ELEVEN

Mydelini – young daughter of Zag
Father- Lenka's dad
Mother – Lenka's mom
Abram – son of Terah
Lauren – daughter of Jared
Gilgah – older son of Jared
Jacom – oldest son of Jared

CHAPTER TWELVE

Alairi – youngest son of Zaggai/Bouhous
Atti – Nimrod's hot-headed son
Orihah – son of Jared
Ammon – high priest to Nimrod's temple
Wamichellta – minister of religion to Nimrod
Nahor – son of Terah
Haran – son of Terah
Sarah – wife of Abram
Isaac – son of Abram
Esau – twin son of Isaac
Jacob – twin son of Isaac
Evanovich – administer in Resen
Savanahela – his wife
Nathaniel – guard in desert
Willy – guard in desert
Ben-Jacob – son of Bouhous/Zaggai
Ben-Daw – son of Bouhous/Zaggai
Zadok – Resen leader
Dr. Yutaka – doctor to Nimrod

CHAPTER THIRTEEN

Korneli – elder of Babel, son of Riplakish
Nardia – wife of Korneli
Amiri – elder of Babel
Ukisher – elder of Babel
Vanida – three year old daughter of Jared
Omparkesh – old man, memory gone on palace grounds

CHAPTER FOURTEEN

Tarsuinn – recruit for youth army
Sakda – Tarsuinn's dog
Lamech – Noah's guard
Sopheap – unfaithful wife to Nimrod
Zikomo – Sopheap's male friend
Thaddeus – and Elite guard with Nimrod
Samrang – retarded baby of Sopheap's

Printed in the United States
By Bookmasters